Miranda Glover has written two previous novels; *Masterpiece*, a contemporary art story, which was shortlisted for the Pendleton May first novel award, and *Soulmates*, about nature, nurture and the shared life of twins. She also edits a women's magazine and teaches creative writing. Miranda lives in Oxfordshire with her husband, a photographer, and their two children.

Also by Miranda Glover

MASTERPIECE
SOULMATES

and published by Bantam Books

MEANWHILE STREET

Miranda Glover

TRANSWORLD PUBLISHERS
61–63 Uxbridge Road, London W5 5SA
A Random House Group Company
www.rbooks.co.uk

MEANWHILE STREET
A BANTAM BOOK: 9780553817652

First publication in Great Britain
Bantam edition published 2009

A CIP catalogue record for this book
is available from the British Library.

Addresses for Random House Group Ltd companies outside the UK
can be found at: www.randomhouse.co.uk
The Random House Group Ltd Reg. No. 954009

The Random House Group Limited supports The Forest Stewardship Council (FSC), the leading international forest certification organisation. All our titles that are printed on Greenpeace approved FSC certified paper carry the FSC logo. Our paper procurement policy can be found at
www.rbooks.co.uk/environment

Typeset in 11½/14pt Goudy by
Kestrel Data, Exeter, Devon.
Printed in the UK by
CPI Cox & Wyman, Reading, RG1 8EX.

2 4 6 8 10 9 7 5 3 1

Dedicated to the memory of my late father,
David Leitch, who knew these stories before I wrote
them down, and in celebration of his grandson, Fen,
my own golden-haired boy.

Acknowledgements

Brave, committed and insightful friends and family have been critical to my writing of this book. Thank all of you who made me stick to my word counts, concentrate harder than I ever have before and who read and commented on *Meanwhile Street* as it evolved. You mean the world to me. Thanks also to Charlie Viney, Francesca Liversidge and all the team at Transworld for your unswerving support. And finally, thank you to all those people who have the kind of lives I have written about in this book. You make London what it is; a challenging, yet ultimately inspiring place to be.

Part One

1

Maggie shifted the sash and positioned herself at the open window, her weight balanced against the first-floor sill. A premature end, she thought sadly as her kingfisher eyes swept Meanwhile Street. Above the terraces the sky was a faint blue, dotted with puffball clouds that reminded her of Ireland, of home. April had been parched and now the natural world was upside down. Daffodils coming up with daisies, blossom falling early. News reports blamed global warming. With that and the terrorists whatever would become of the next generation? Maggie had wanted children but she and Gerry had always been too busy looking after other people's lives to create a family of their own. They'd been in service for two generations. The Fisks were art dealers and it had been a colourful existence, yet fundamentally a barren one. These days she often wondered if it had been for the best.

A speeding bicycle distracted her from her commonplace reminiscing. It shot round the corner and headed down the west London street, zigzagging slightly as it passed densely parked cars. Maggie's eyes followed the skinny youth crouched over the bike's frame, like a character escaped from the pages of a comic book. She knew him well, young Connor Ryan, a child who'd mutated overnight into this strange being, a gangling teenager with a nervous energy and a tightening frown. Presently he skidded to a halt further down the road, outside number fourteen, the basement flat he shared with his dad, Joe.

'Hello there, Connor,' she called across to him. 'Early to be up and about, dear.' The boy didn't respond; seemed lost to his own preoccupations. Maggie watched as he swung his leg over, glanced furtively back the way he'd come, then slung the bike across his shoulders and vanished down the steps, squeaking metal gate left ajar behind him.

What'll he be doing up with the sparrow? And not so much as a good morning, either, Maggie tut-tutted into her tea. She used to have an influence over Connor but recently it had waned. Maybe he'd found himself a girlfriend on the Beethoven Estate, she pondered, or taken a paper round, even. She knew that was unlikely – his lot weren't known for their endurance. There hadn't been much in the way of work coming from their household for years. Recently she knew that Connor had been hanging around with her neighbour Janice's daughter Shelly, rather than going to school. She thought about the girl now. Shelly was wayward, a bad influence; a teenage mum with a two-year-old, still living at home. Connor was fifteen now. Soon time to leave school, no doubt without a qualification to his name.

Like Maggie, Connor's lot were Irish, but she was Limerick-born, the Ryans were from Dublin, quite a different breed. She'd hardly had a thing to do with Joe since Connor's mum Lorraine had gone, a long while ago, back to an aunt in Cork – or so Joe had confided in Gerry down the Ship. Maggie wasn't sure she believed the story; in fact it was hard to believe anything Joe Ryan told you. There'd been rumours that Lorraine had been going with a black man and that they'd moved to one of the estates round Stockwell, south of the river. It still wouldn't surprise Maggie, all these years on, to bump into her down the bingo, or in the post-office queue, with a couple of coffee-coloured kids spinning around her knees. Not that Maggie got out that often any more. Chance sightings – or opportunity for any local gossip – became less likely with the mounting hours she spent marooned up here, at her open window.

Either way, after Lorraine had left Maggie had taken care of Connor now and then. He'd been a good boy with a sloping grin and a sideways look that made you feel affection whether you wanted to or not. As a child he'd had shining golden hair you couldn't believe was real, and eyes cut like emeralds, imported direct from Donegal, she used to tease him – you never saw eyes that colour on an English child. But now Connor's hair was shaved short, dulled to mid-brown. And his eyes lacked the gleam of their infancy.

Connor had been a talker, too. Nineteen to the dozen. He could spin words the Irish way, used language like a ladder to laughter or – when necessary – as a route to escape. Now it was hard to get a word out of him. Connor still sat on Maggie's top step once in a while, elbows on knees, fists firmly shut under chin, mouth closed like a barrier, watching the world go by. But he seemed to have lost the knack for smiling. Or he'd stand below her window, hopping from one leg to the other as he called up, 'Need anything from the Harrow Road, Maggie?' She often felt something was unsettling the boy. He never came out and said what it was, but Maggie made it clear she was there for him, if the time ever felt right to fill her in. Recently there'd been an atmosphere. She couldn't put her finger on it, but there'd been movements in the street. Local kids were up to something. It was hard to pin it down to details but Connor seemed to be touching faintly around it, circling the situation like the pale stain left by the rim of a wet glass.

Maggie took another look up and down the quiet street. A local estate agent's car pulled up and a man, young enough to know nothing, got out, his shiny grey suit glinting in the early sunshine. He glanced up but instead of greeting Maggie he looked away again quickly and pulled a mobile from his trouser pocket, hit a number and began gabbling. Maggie grimaced; to him she knew she was just a nosy old lady with no interest in a mortgage. If only people bothered they might discover she had more to offer than they let themselves believe. Maggie was cultured and well travelled. She'd seen Vienna, Paris and had even caught a glimpse of the Polish pope in Rome. She had paintings on her walls with valuable signatures on them that this boy would be too ignorant to recognize. From the commission he could make on just one of them, he'd no longer have a need for that cheap suit. Property prices were tumbling, the market was on its knees. He couldn't make the kind of money she had on her walls from his estate-agenting, not a chance.

A van now pulled up and an older, oily-looking man with shaved short hair and pale jeans hopped out. He took a green For Sale sign out of the back of the van and, following the mobile-speaking agent's sharp gestures, positioned it on the railings of a house four doors to the right of Maggie's maisonette. Without exchanging a word, the two men then returned to their own vehicles. Maggie watched as they drove off. Go-getting mercenaries, she mused. Over the past decade they'd inflated properties on streets like this so no one with any sense could afford to buy here any more. Even so, new money had not rid them of the underlying problems. Meanwhile Street was too cosy with the Beethoven Estate for that; people floated between the two, mixed like whisky and water until the boundaries clouded. You saw a lot from a first-floor window. Maggie's knowledge of the area would put the local community police to shame. She sometimes thought she should offer her services. She'd soon bring their crime figures down.

She continued to watch the street. The identical terraces stood in silence, facing one another stoically. They shared matching black iron railings, keeping each house separate from the next; the lives inside tucked up in their own compartments for now. Behind the gates each property had six front steps leading up to a front door at raised ground-floor level, while a second set led down to a basement door. A handful of houses remained unmodified – like the one that had just gone up for sale – but most were separated internally into two or three flats, made clear by the number of external bell pushes. Maggie didn't need to look any more, she knew the floor plans of these houses better than those local estate agents themselves, all the way up one side and back down the other. You could tell each one's status by the colour of its front door; black for council, red for WCT (*Wellbeing Charitable Trust*), any other for privately owned; indeed, over half the houses were held in the WCT, which had taken it over from the Church Commission in the sixties. These had become a first rescue point for newly arrived immigrant families. Hence the impossibility of upgrading the area. Not enough of the property was in private ownership for that. Maggie's own door was red.

Early in the morning, the houses always seemed hooded, as Connor had just been, their front-bay curtains closed, their secrets lying dormant inside, along with the slumbering residents. And regardless of their status, at this time of day they all looked alike, other than for those with For Sale or To Let signs hanging from their railings. It was amazing how quiet it was here; just fifteen minutes by bus from Marble Arch. Not that she'd made it that far for a while, she thought, as she drank the dregs of her tea. A cat with a black coat gleaming like liquorice slipped round the gate of number sixteen, darted across the street and leapt up and along the brick wall that separated the steps of numbers nineteen and twenty-one. Now it sat directly beneath her, watching too.

Maggie's thoughts fluttered to Gerry as she got down from her stool and headed for the kitchenette, reached for his cup hanging on the dresser; the same as hers but blue. Over a year already, since he'd gone. Her three surviving sisters in Ireland wrote cards on the anniversary, but here in Meanwhile Street people were too preoccupied to give

Gerry much thought any more. A year was a long time in other people's lives, in their memory banks. She placed his cup next to her own, added tea bags and clicked the kettle on. She wouldn't confess it to anyone other than God, but Maggie always made Gerry a cup of a morning, added sugar and milk, as she'd done for the last forty-three years. Then she'd place it on the side table, next to his armchair, position herself back at the window and share in a chat.

'Connor's heading for a fall, Gerry,' she muttered presently. 'Someone needs to have a word with Joe, or find Lorraine, get her to take some interest.' She took a noisy sip of her tea. 'I know you don't think I should help them out, but they're like family to me, Gerry, the children in the street. You know how much time I spent with Connor when he was small.'

She didn't feel his presence; sometimes it was as if he was still there. But not today. She sat quietly for a while, pondering the predicament alone. Eventually, when her cup was empty, she went back into the kitchenette. Gerry's tea was now lukewarm. She poured it down the sink then washed the two cups together, placed them on the drainer to drip dry. Habits were hard to break when you were her age; seventy-six – or was it seventy-seven? – this birthday. Sometimes she wondered what she was still doing here. Why she hadn't gone back to Limerick? But as her careworker Azi had recently remarked, if Maggie went who would be left to watch over the street? The comment had made her cheeks prickle with heat. She knew it was true; who else would there be to pass the story of the day between its busy inhabitants? No one else had the full picture, the Technicolor, so to speak. There'd been countless times when she'd made a difference, when someone had locked themselves out and she'd had a spare key, or a delivery man had not known which house was awaiting a new fridge or settee.

More than that, she'd always been there for the street's children. Over the past twenty years she'd watched the first lot, like Connor and Shelly, grow from babes in arms to wild young things; she'd seen a host of others come up behind them, too. There'd been many a time when she'd helped a struggling mum out with a few hours' babysitting here and there. And teenagers like Connor hadn't stopped needing her, either. Their needs had simply changed. Now they wanted her for a chat about this and that, a row with their families or their lack of finances, or just as a place to escape to for a minute, away from the city's strains. In return they helped her out, brought her shopping, put out the bins. She didn't mind giving them the odd bit of pocket money. It was a relationship, with give and take on both sides. She held the keys to seven doors, she'd told Azi with glowing pride – well that says it all, Azi had replied. The trust of Meanwhile Street sits in your palm. Then she'd taken Maggie's cushioned hand between her cool ebony fingers and given it a gentle squeeze.

There was no one to talk to about Gerry, though, not really; at least not about her continuing grief. Nobody was close enough to really care, apart from Father Patrick, who visited her on the first Wednesday of the month at four; but even he seemed increasingly preoccupied with other affairs, like the new fund-raising initiative for St Bride's. She wondered sometimes about the nuns at number seventy-two. Perhaps they'd be more attentive; but they were only wee young things, pasty-faced Catholic girls in royal blue habits, girls who'd had the confidence knocked out of them with the back of an Irish father's hand, well before they'd taken their vows. If Maggie were honest, she thought they'd be better off removing their veils and making real lives for themselves as teachers or nurses, with husbands and children of their own. Instead they wasted their efforts picking drunks up off rubbish-strewn floors, helping teenage girls with their illegitimate newborns – trying to save lost people from themselves. And that was something Maggie knew about, something only age could teach you, that no one but God could save you; that mere mortals could never truly mend their ways.

She placed herself back at the window and waited for some distractions; for people to start making their way to work and school. Communication had changed since she'd come here, and so had the nationalities of her neighbours. Now many didn't speak English at all, communicated with her only in smiles or the flicker of an eye, the gestures of their hands; to comment on the weather, the latest news from Baghdad, or Kandahar. Some, like Janice's Shelly, said it was 'disgusting' the way they arrived with their lives stored in laundry bags on their backs, hordes of flea-bitten children in overwashed cotton trailing behind. They swiped these London homes straight from under the noses of good old-fashioned working-class English families like theirs, whose own needs slipped another notch down the rehousing list with each new delivery from the immigration office.

Although Maggie felt a degree of sympathy for Shelly

and her little one, Demi, she also felt that the best place for a single mum like her was at home with her own mother, as Shelly was with her mum Janice, for support. And she couldn't blame these foreign people for taking what they were offered, either. Most had come persecuted and traumatized, and Meanwhile Street was a safe haven which could help them get back on their feet. She and Gerry both knew how it felt to be without a life raft. She didn't judge anyone for finding themselves in a capsizing boat and fighting not to drown. When they'd arrived from Dublin in the fifties they'd had less than nothing, less than nothing at all. Thank Jesus for the generosity of the Fisks. Without them, who knew where she and Gerry would have been? The street now contained a true world community and that was something to be proud of.

It had been the late 1980s when they'd moved into Meanwhile Street. Recently Maggie had counted no less than sixteen nationalities living behind its doors. Back then the area had mainly contained a mix of Irish, like her and Gerry, and Afro-Caribbean, like the King and Gladys, in the basement beneath her, alongside working-class white English families like Janice and Shelly, who'd got their houses off the council. Most go-getting council tenants had since sold out and moved to the suburbs, their houses snapped up by middle-class professional families who could just about afford the inflated prices here but not over the Harrow Road in Notting Hill, where they secretly dreamed of living one day. These were people like Immy and Gordon opposite, a nice couple with a wee one called Milo and a Czech nanny called Katya, an alabaster beauty with calculating aquamarine eyes. Others were earnest young doctors at the hospital in Paddington just a mile up the road; or creative types, photographers or TV people, from the BBC or film companies. One such was Billy the documentary maker who, she mused, was usually up and out first. He lived above Connor and Joe, at number fourteen.

She watched his door and sure enough Billy soon emerged, already talking on his mobile phone, bleached hair standing on end. He was dressed in the same white T-shirt, grey army fatigues and trainers she'd seen him wearing yesterday. He looked as if he'd slept in them, she thought. He worked too hard; one day he'd keel over, have a heart attack if he didn't watch out. Smoked red Marlboro, too, just like Gerry had. There was one in the side of his mouth right now, perched on his bottom lip. It had been the death of poor Gerry. She'd warned Billy of the fact. Out of his back pocket Maggie could see his wallet hanging precariously. He pointed his keys like a gun at the old white Jag parked up. It bleeped as he triggered the heavy doors to unlock. At the sound, the black cat jumped from the wall and vanished up the street. Billy continued to talk as he dropped the Marlboro, mobile under chin, opening the driver's door to get in.

'Mind your wallet, dear,' Maggie called down as he slipped into his seat. Billy looked up for a moment, confused, spoke again into the phone, then hung up.

'What's that, Maggie?' he called up to her with a likeable grin. Billy had one of those sandpaper voices that carried well, the kind only made that way from years of inhaling smoke.

'Your wallet, dear, it was falling from your pocket.'

Billy raised his lean body from the seat, felt underneath and pulled the wallet out, shook it at Maggie, then started the engine. A moment later the car glided off up the street like a grand old sofa on coasters. As it turned the corner it rose and tilted slightly and you could still see Billy's elbow, resting indolently on the ledge of his open window. Meanwhile Maggie shifted her own arm position slightly, resettled on her stool and glanced the way of the vanished cat.

It was often quiet here, but never for long. Moments later, Dren, her Kosovan neighbour, appeared. He was late this morning, had usually left already to plaster walls with his brothers before the light arrived.

'Morning, Maggie.' A shy smile accompanied his soft words.

'Morning, Dren dear. Late today?'

He nodded and raised a hand as he headed left, towards Reeling Road. He and his brothers had all come to London with their young families at the same time. They lived in various streets around Kilburn Lane and had recently made enough between them to invest in an old blue van with a spluttering exhaust. Maggie was pleased for them. They were hard workers, a decent lot. Most nights Dren would arrive home late, narrow shoulders slung low over his slight frame, curly hair spattered with paint, plaster dust in the fine creases of his brow, charcoal circles beneath his eyes.

When he'd first arrived with his wife Ada and their children, he'd looked haunted; now he just seemed tired. Maggie remembered Dren looking too young to have three children, a mere boy with his girl on his arm, their olive-skinned infants before them. They could have come from an earlier era, one she could just about recall, immigrants from the Second World War maybe, not the 1990s and from Southern Europe. Dren had been wearing an old grey suit, its pockets sagging, its knees bagging above a pair of dusty leather shoes. It was less than ten years ago, but in that time it felt as if Dren had bypassed middle age and become prematurely old, in his now paint-pocked jeans, Shoe Express trainers and nylon bomber jackets.

Ada had a gold front tooth; still wore black, lace-up boots with hard heels and peacock-coloured shawls. When they'd first arrived her children would cling to the folds of her embroidered skirts. Now the older ones spoke fluent English with west London accents, walked themselves home from school. She'd borne three more since they'd arrived, and they had no more of Kosovo in them than Shelly or Janice.

Ada's lack of language skills meant she relied on her older kids to ask Maggie for favours and Maggie was always happy to oblige – generally to watch the smaller ones for a moment while Ada popped up to the grocery shop for bread or milk for the baby. She'd position the buggy beneath Maggie's window with an engaging smile, gold tooth glinting; right where the old lady could see the infant's white head of curls above a protruding pale forehead, feet kicking happily at the London air. The blonde baby was the opposite of her dark-haired siblings and mother, but the spit of Dren.

She watched now as his slight frame disappeared around the corner by Ali's grocers. Beyond the language barriers there seemed to be less time for chatter these days. People were always in a hurry to get somewhere else – apart from the children, of course, who hung out in the street endlessly now the days were getting longer and lighter.

It was at that moment that she heard it: a short sharp yelp, followed by a muffled groan, then a silence so complete it felt deeper than the one that had preceded it. It was the kind of silence you get when the birds all stop singing at once and the air goes still, that moment just before a summer storm. It seemed close by but impossible to place. Maggie glanced up and down the road, but only the blossom stirred in the breeze. Then she looked at her watch: still only 6.46 a.m. Strange. It was a human cry that had no good in it. She listened to the blankness for a few moments more, then stopped trying. She'd soon know what was awry. Before long the rest of Meanwhile Street would be up and about, preparing for what, until now, had seemed like a regular Wednesday morning in the middle of May.

2

Gordon woke with a start. Was sure he'd heard a cry – no, more of a squeal. Maybe the sound had come from his dreams, for now all he could hear were his wife and child's sleepy breathing. It was as if the umbilical cord were still connected between Immy and Milo, he marvelled, even though there was already a third heart beating inside his wife. Gordon lifted one of Immy's leaden arms off his chest gently and replaced it on the duvet. Next he shifted Milo's slightly damp left leg off his right thigh and slid quietly from the bed.

Easing the blind to the left, he glanced out of the first-floor window. Opposite, Maggie was already cocking an eager eye up and down Meanwhile Street, even though it was only, he glanced back to the alarm clock, 6.47 a.m. She was in her dressing gown done up with a lace bow under her neck. Her hair was in its net. Even so, despite her age and state of undress, Gordon suddenly caught a glimpse of her past beauty. Her eyes were still bright, the cheekbones defined and the pale skin unusually taut for a woman approaching her eighties. She must have been lovely when she was young.

Like himself, Gordon mused, Maggie must have hopped straight out of her eiderdown to her regular vantage point, keen to fathom what that sound might have meant. Try as either of them might, however, first straining their heads left, then right, Meanwhile Street retained its guarded early morning air. Whatever had made these two inhabitants take note was now keeping itself to itself, behind one of the street's firmly closed doors. Gordon noticed that the blossom was already falling, the pavements sprinkled with it, white petals blown off by last night's winds. It reminded him of first seeing their house, a year ago already. The cherry blossom had definitely enhanced its charm. Unfortunately by the time they'd moved in last November the trees were spindly and bare, and the street had taken on a duller, more desolate air – especially after dark.

Maggie had been there the first time they'd come here. She'd watched a touch suspiciously, he'd felt, as he and Immy had loitered on the pavement, waiting for the eager South African estate agent to show them round. They were living in the expensive end of Maida Vale back then, nearer Little Venice and the smart delis, but with Milo's arrival they'd wanted more space. If they could have afforded it, they would have gone all the way up to the quieter local suburb of Queen's Park, with its large leafy gardens and café on the park, but here, in the hinterland between the two districts, the 'cheap seats' as Immy called it, she'd urged that they could buy a whole house, with enough space for an au pair, and tons of room for Milo to hare about in, too. The markets had slipped so much, money wasn't what it used to be. Gordon hadn't been sure to begin with, but in the end he had given in. The area was a bit rough for his liking, edged on its third side by the infamous Beethoven Estate, an ironically named area of low bass tones and regularly heightened tempers. It was one of Westminster's wastegrounds for its urban misfits: drunks, junkies and those dependent on welfare. The people, in fact, Gordon wrote about for the newspaper.

The characters who filled his stories often came from those very estates, or others like them, dotted not just all over London, but across the country, too: New Labour's ever-increasing underclass. Just recently he'd reported on the gang-stabbing of a young lawyer, walking home alone from the Tube to his fiancée. Two fifteen-year-olds were now in custody, their lives and those of their respectable families shattered. It wasn't until these kids woke up in the cells that they seemed even vaguely aware of the magnitude of their crime, the moral dimension, or indeed the punishment that was about to befall them. Two miles up the road, in Hampstead, family houses were still selling for millions, despite the downturn. Gordon knew that London had become a place of social extremes. Nevertheless, he understood Immy's rationale. After all, Meanwhile Street was still in Central London. From here he could ride his scooter round town, saunter down to the flea market, even go by foot into the West End, at a stretch. It was a place, like its name, he had joked, where they could hang out meanwhile, if not for ever.

As they were heading off after that first visit, Maggie's husband Gerry had appeared at the window and lit a cigarette. He watched them for a moment, then tipped the ash from his fag out into the waiting ashtray on the sill. Immy had smiled up at him. 'G'day to you, dear,' he'd called down, his tone as thick as Guinness. Gordon had remained silent, looked the other way. As they'd driven back to their flat he'd confessed that the old couple made him feel surveyed, that anonymity was half the reason he enjoyed living in the city. Immy had laughed at him, argued that an active community was one of the benefits of moving into a less flash area, an area devoid of the new breed of London Eurocrats who left for work at six a.m., returned at midnight. Here there were 'real' people, old-style Londoners who looked out for each other, were properly local, knew your name and cared about what happened to you. Immy could be persuasive. Gordon was persuaded.

The Sunday morning after they'd moved in, an ambulance had pulled up silently outside Gerry and Maggie's house as Gordon had walked back from Ali's shop on the corner with the newspapers. It stayed for more than an hour. He and Immy had tried hard not to notice, but every few minutes one or the other of them had taken another glance out of the sitting-room window. Eventually it left again, without a patient, and they had breathed a sigh of relief.

'One of them must've had a turn,' Immy mused. 'I'll pop over later. Introduce ourselves and see if they need any shopping.'

But by mid-afternoon, however, the ambulance had been replaced by a blacked-out transit van. Two muscular henchmen had then mounted Maggie's front steps, thickset as a pair of Rottweilers let off their leashes. Moments later they'd heaved a body out in a black rubber bag, zipper done up. Maggie had stood aside in the doorway to let them pass as curtains up and down the street had twitched in sympathy. Six months ago, already. Gordon looked back over at her now. Poor old bird. Maggie was craning her head this way and that, evidently still trying to source that sudden noise. She glanced directly across the street and in at Gordon's window. And then she beamed.

Gordon dropped the blind. Since his initial mistrust, he'd grown fond of Maggie, but still he didn't want her to see him stark-bollock-naked before seven in the morning – or ever, in fact. The day before, Immy had told him casually that Maggie had offered to take care of Milo for them if ever they needed an extra pair of hands, what with the new baby imminent – 'You can have a key to my house, I'm happy to look after a spare for yours,' she'd urged. Immy had declined, after all they had Katya, their Czech au pair, but Gordon could tell she was touched by Maggie's offer. He'd been less impressed – particularly by the suggestion that they give Maggie a key. He knew that some of the established families from the street had a key to Maggie's. Janice and Shelly were always in and out of her front door, but he wouldn't have felt easy with his own key hanging off someone else's hook. Immy had shrugged indifferently, but in her eyes he saw that she wasn't certain she agreed. Gordon felt affection for her open nature – she came from a small village in North Yorkshire where doors were rarely locked – and he knew she liked any sense of that small-time community she could find in London. Maggie's offer symbolized connectivity, a community, to Immy. He understood its appeal for her. It wasn't Maggie but the others he wasn't so sure about;

Shelly particularly. She was mates with their West Indian neighbour's two daughters, Ranika and Teshari, lumpish girls in their late teens. There was no sign of a father, and their full origins were unclear; Gordon wondered if he had been Indonesian, or perhaps Sri Lankan, as there was an indefinably Asian twist to their looks. The three girls had gone to the local comprehensive together and there was really no harm in them. It was Shelly's wider gang that made him uneasy.

One of them, an anorexic-looking white girl with crooked teeth, had managed to get a flat from the housing trust at the far end of the street. She must have played the system to get it, or been in a sink lodging of some sort, a halfway house, or young offenders' institute. Gordon hadn't said anything to Immy because he didn't want to make her anxious, but he was sure they were doing drugs in that flat – probably crack. He didn't want to sound racist either, as if he was stereotyping, it was something he was acutely conscious of avoiding in his work, but recently Shelly had got a new black boyfriend called Marlon. Young and slick, he and his younger brother roamed the area like wild dogs in their flash white jeep, the kind of car it was unlikely they could have come by honestly. Gordon wouldn't trust Marlon with a penny, let alone a link in a chain to his own front door.

He put on some pants and went to take a pee, then returned to watch Immy and Milo as an increasingly familiar knot of anxiety tightened in his chest. On the one hand it was astounding to him that having sex with Immy – however great, which it generally was – could produce this wry, curious little boy, and a second child on its way, too. On the other hand, since Milo's birth his own mortality felt more palpable. Gordon's work took him into the darker side of society, to places where life was precarious, where community failed and political solutions floundered. The fragility of the human condition was brought home to him every day. His recent campaign to increase drug-awareness through London's secondary schools had gained attention from the government. He'd been shortlisted for a social commentator prize at the national journalism awards. Ironically, these achievements only increased his concerns. Part of him hankered for the past, when he had been less needed, less responsible, less successful – less conscious. Now the stakes felt higher. There was more to lose and further to fall. He'd tried to explain these feelings to Immy last night. 'You're having a classic mid-life crisis,' she'd soothed, resting his hand on her hot, tight belly. 'You'll get through it – we'll get through it.'

He looked down at his wife and son asleep in their bed now and shrugged off his disquiet, then glanced once again at the clock: 6.56 a.m. He peered once more around the blind, more distractedly this time. To his surprise a drama, which clearly had its inception at the door of number twenty-one, was unfolding, indeed heading across the street towards their own front gate. For a moment all Gordon could do was stare in morbid fascination, then his mind fast-threaded the scene into a running narrative. Shelly was stumbling across the street in a black T-shirt, *Paradise Beach* written across it in fluorescent pink, a pair of black, baggy men's boxers beneath. Her long brown hair was tumbling chaotically around her pixie face, her pale feet were bare and a gash in her cheek was gushing blood on to Demi, her toddler, who was screeching in her arms. Gordon glanced up to clock Maggie's reaction, but the old lady had already disappeared. No one else was to be seen in the street. He took the stairs two at a time and opened the front door.

Ranika was already out on the steps next door with Shelly. Demi had been taken inside the house, still wailing, and Ranika's mum was consoling her. Shelly's blood was dripping all over the steps, spatters had reached their own threshold and were being absorbed by the blossom, staining it red. For a moment Gordon contemplated contamination, HIV. Stepped back.

'Shall I call for an ambulance?' he asked.

Ranika nodded.

'It was Marlon,' she murmured. 'The fucker pistol-whipped her.'

By the time Shelly had been mopped up and carted off by the ambulance, Maggie was firmly ensconced on the pavement outside the gate on a kitchen chair that Ranika's mum had brought out for her, along with a fresh cup of tea in her own floral mug. One of the other old ladies from the street, Betty, and her white rough-haired terrier had appeared to hear the story and Earl, the West Indian postman, was standing there too, hand on top of his post trolley, shaking his head in theatrical dismay. Ranika was down on her hands and knees, legging-clad rump in the air, scrubbing the steps clean of Shelly's blood with a stiff-bristled brush and a bucket of cold bleachy water.

Gordon watched her for a moment, impressed by her ardour, musing that the ability to clean must have been hard-wired into her system; then he heard Milo stir and went back upstairs to fetch him from Immy's sleeping arms. He carried the child down to watch the aftermath with him; it was social documentary, right on their own front step. As Maggie continued to roll the story out a police car pulled up. Two officers got out and one approached her.

'Sorry, love,' he said, without preamble. 'But there's been a serious incident, we're going to need to cordon off the street.'

'What'll you be doin' that for, officer?' Maggie retorted, her incredulity rising with her voice. 'We all know Shelly and she'll be at the hospital by now. Best you call her mum, Janice. She works nights, at the supermarket, the big one off Ladbroke Grove, be coming off her shift any minute.'

The policeman ignored her.

'Come on now, could you all move back into your houses. We have an armed suspect somewhere out here. Oh, and apparently a baby to find, too.'

'Don't worry about the baby,' said Ranika with a chew on her gum. 'She's inside with my mum.'

As the policeman ushered them all off Gordon glanced up and noticed that there were already police cars stationed at either end of Meanwhile Street. They were loitering behind cordons of fluorescent orange tape. An armed officer was checking in and out of each basement stairwell in turn, presumably looking for Marlon, the absent villain of the affair. His jeep was still outside Shelly's house. Evidently he hadn't used it for his getaway.

'Nee naw, nee naw,' said Milo enthusiastically as Gordon

closed the front door. Marlon must have escaped on foot; could be hiding in anyone's garden, although Gordon was pretty certain he wasn't the kind of guy who'd hang around long enough to catch his breath, let alone lie in wait for the police. Even so, he found himself standing at an angle behind the dining-room curtains and peering down into their own back garden, a patioed area the size of a postage stamp, just to be on the safe side. Certain that the coast was clear, he headed down the second flight of stairs and into the basement kitchen with Milo on his hip, to heat up a bottle of milk for him and make himself a cup of coffee.

After all the drama, he felt parched and slightly wired, too. Perversely, it was a feeling he found he quite liked. As he drank his coffee, he thought about Immy. So much for a real London community. Frankly, he thought, with the new baby coming, she for one could do without this kind of reality.

'Nee naw, nee naw.'

Milo had seized his bottle from Gordon and was energetically pushing it along the floor like a car. Spatters of milk spread over the newly laid granite tiles, reminding Gordon of the mess Shelly's gash had made on the steps out front. Best check it had been cleared up before he went to work, and not give Immy the details, either.

He scooped Milo back up and nestled his face into his child's neck. Milo shrieked, then shoved his bottle in his mouth and began to suck on it frantically, his body relaxing more with each glug. Moments later the milk was all gone and his eyes were glazing over. Best to keep this early morning story between him and the delectable, oblivious Milo, Gordon decided, as he sat on the sofa with his heavy son on his chest and zapped on *Charlie and Lola*. The drama would only freak Immy out. He glanced at his watch. Ten to eight. Soon time to wake up Katya, hand Milo over and get himself ready for work.

3

At 8.31 Clare appeared from the doorway of number twenty-eight and put her briefcase down on the porch to fumble in her handbag, checking for keys.

'Morning, dear,' Maggie called out insistently.

She'd been back at her sill for more than half an hour now and so far had only managed to inform two inhabitants of the early morning commotion. The street was no longer cordoned off and the only signs left of Shelly's earlier drama were Ranika's bucket and brush, propped up drying inside her gate, and a policeman stationed outside Janice's front door, watching over Marlon's white jeep.

'He'll have to come back for it at some point, and we'll be here waiting for him,' the policeman had confided in her. He regretted the opener, for Maggie hadn't left him alone since. Encouraged by his apparent confidence in her, the old woman had already made him two cups of tea, accompanied by shortbread biscuits. And she hadn't stopped her gassing since.

'Everything all right, Maggie?' Clare enquired, nodding towards Janice's flat as she straightened back up, smoothed the skirt of her new Karen Millen suit down over her skinny legs. Then she picked up her briefcase, ready to go.

'Marlon hit Shelly, blood everywhere – she's been taken to the hospital,' Maggie began, cantering through the story, keen to stop Clare in her tracks.

Clare made a face that almost looked like sympathy.

'Fill me in later, Maggie, I've got a meeting,' she called up, then she gave a cursory wave and set off up the road for the Tube, heels clacking.

Clare didn't have time for neighbourhood gossip this morning, and once Maggie started you couldn't stop her. The incident was inevitable, if depressing. Shelly and her own son, Max, had been friends when they were younger, and she felt sorry for Janice. Shelly had become wild when her dad had died, what, more than four years ago, and she'd fallen in with a bad crowd. She'd been close to her dad, shared his sly, shark eyes, and, from all accounts, his bad attitude. Marlon was from the Beethoven, his lot were rough too, a dysfunctional family of many mixed-up parts. Shelly was just as unpleasant in her own way; trampled all over Janice, used her as a free babysitting service for Demi, a roof over their heads when it suited her, not when it didn't. But Clare didn't have time to think about them now. It was a new day in her new life and she was on the move.

She even felt new, with her honey-highlighted hair and expensive grey suit – optimistic, even. It was only her second month at the Lottery and she liked to arrive early at the West End HQ. It was a good opportunity for her – and for Max, too – money coming in, regular paid holidays she could take outside term-time. At thirty-eight she wasn't getting any younger. There was no longer time to lose. She'd figured out that her boss, David Sanders, hid a hard centre beneath his blanket of gentle encouragement. She wouldn't get caught out, not this time. She'd stay on her toes; keep him happy. As his PA she got to see every policy document that crossed his desk and had already noticed a couple of opportunities for self-promotion. She needed money; she needed this to work. She thought briefly about JJ's last visit from Guadeloupe: it had seemed to hold such promise, and yet, as ever, had failed to deliver – particularly for Max. After he left on Sunday, Max had refused to come down from his room all day and Clare was sure she could hear his muffled sobs beneath the incessant replaying of his dad's latest CD.

It wasn't fair, it wasn't right. JJ had promised Max a trip over to Guadeloupe this summer to meet his grandmother, not to mention the countless cousins of whom he'd only ever heard in lyric form, but she was already worried that JJ would let their son down. Something, inevitably, would come up and then she'd be left trying to explain. She feared for Max's future without the regular input of a father, even if the father was as unreliable as JJ. And it seemed to her more important now than ever, now he was fifteen, adolescent and ridden with teenage angst. There were things she couldn't teach him any more, and things he was thinking about that she could no longer second-guess. She didn't like leaving for work before Max went to school – and she worried about him catching the bus to Kensington, especially since the bombs. But he'd got into the specialist music academy there, for playing his sax. He'd taken after his dad in that respect, whether she liked it or not.

The schools around North Westminster were underwhelming. At least she had saved him from that. Their area was the borough's dumping ground for its drug dealers and users, its entire immigrant quota and general clutch of underachievers, those with special physical or psychological needs, or, like her and Max, single-parent families, reliant on tax credits and council accommodation to make ends meet. Max had been brought up with this often colourful, sometimes tense backdrop; it was his playground. Clare was all too aware that he already knew how to get by in it better than she ever would.

The lights changed and Clare scurried across the Harrow Road with the rest of the crowd, all heads bent towards the canal bridge that arched over the Great Western Road. As she left W9 for W11 her mind switched from Max left behind to her day stretching ahead. She had her first meeting on behalf of David Sanders, with a man called Paul Carter at Hackney Council, for him to present their case for funding their 'diversity in schools programme'. She'd felt flattered that David trusted her to go alone, even though she realized he'd asked her to shield him from Hackney's inevitable disappointment at the amount of cash on the table. It also felt like a test. Her phone calls, and particularly last rash of emails with Paul Carter, had been welcoming – flirty, even – and when he'd suggested they held the meeting at five she couldn't help but wonder if it might be followed by an after-work drink, something she'd never had before, something that sounded grown-up, professional, and slightly illicit. She hadn't had a boyfriend for a while, had given them up after her last screw-up, felt the intrusion had been too disturbing for Max.

There were these two Somali guys who'd appeared in Meanwhile Street last summer, who were living in the basement flat beneath them. One of them, Zahir, had the whitest eyes and teeth she'd ever seen, the most alluring smile and incredibly fine, slender hands. He was tall and gauche – or so she'd thought. He'd flirted with her from the start and she'd gone out with him a couple of times, then they'd got high on grass at the Notting Hill Carnival and the next thing she knew they were having explosive sex in his basement while Max slept on oblivious in their maisonette above. The intensity of it freaked her out, it had felt a bit too passionate, too intimate, even – if sex could be such a thing. She hadn't done it for a while, and his thorough, almost ravenous exploration of her body had left her feeling unexpectedly exposed.

Afterwards she had felt the need to retreat. By contrast, Zahir's appetite for her seemed to quicken. Clare was used to being on her own, in charge of her and Max's destiny, but now each time she came home he seemed to be there, waiting for her, hovering at the bottom of his steps with some kind of suggestion for the evening. It made her claustrophobic and she'd quickly backed off. She decided she didn't trust him either; wondered what they were up to down there with their countless computers, their big black dog which they left barking all day in the garden. She'd seen photographs of severely mutilated African bodies on one of the screens and they had made her stomach lurch. She'd asked him what they did a couple of times and he'd shrugged a little, talked of the European Court of Human Rights, of campaigning for his fellow countrymen, for Somali asylum seekers to have a better status.

As time passed, Clare began to wonder if Zahir's explanation hadn't just been a foil, if he and his mate weren't actually plotting something or other. They barely left the flat and the other guy, Jaka, didn't seem to speak at all, as far as she could tell. He just seemed to watch. Wouldn't surprise her if they were terrorists, she'd finally decided, and she wasn't going to start getting involved with all that. London was full of it, or 'Londinistan' as Max had called it the other day, chuckling beneath his hoodie. He'd thought himself smart for making a political joke; the problem was it just wasn't funny, all this shit going down and the constant raids around their area. After 7/7 there'd been a load of arrests, all within a square half-mile of Meanwhile Street. It had freaked Clare out.

The thing with Zahir had been a huge mistake and it had taken months to loosen the ties. Now they hardly spoke but he was still sulking, she could tell, and that made her feel ill at ease. If his passion was anything to go by, he could well hide a temper beneath his controlled exterior. But maybe, just maybe, along with the job, she told herself now, it was time to get back out there, to have a go with this guy Paul, to forget about Zahir, and JJ, too – time to start trusting again.

As she headed past the bus station and under the Westway overpass Clare realized a crowd was growing outside the Tube. In the ticket hall the cordons were going across – yet another security alert. She cursed silently and fished in her pocket for her mobile, dodged traffic to get to the bus stop on the other side of the Great Western Road. As she joined the fast-lengthening queue she gave Max a wake-up call.

'Heya, Ma, whassup?' he asked distractedly.

Max's street language was becoming increasingly new order, heavily influenced by his friends, and it often left her behind. It was hardly a surprise. After all, he'd grown up with the best of the rest, the first-generation kids from the world's latest trouble spots, all now more Londoners than, well, even than Maggie, who still had Ireland circulating in her blood, even after half a century in west London. Max and his mates might have had the world's war zones bubbling under their lids but the brew always came out the same: pure, twenty-first-century London; sharp, streetwise, energized.

'Don't forget your key,' she said. 'And watch yourself outside. Something's happened at Shelly's. There's a police car there. Oh and I've got that meeting, I'll be late.'

Clare enjoyed giving Max that information about her work, it sounded, well, as if she was becoming important. It mattered now that Max could respect her for who she was, away from him, as a role model for his own future. He was old enough to recognize the significance, to be proud of her. Before she'd always had to take whatever work was available, jobs to fit in around picking him up and dropping him off, reliant on endless favours from friends, just to pay the rent. This was a chance for something more.

She'd spent most of her twenties trying to 'get into the music business', which actually meant going to a lot of clubs and raves, producing CDs to promote emerging indie bands who never got further than the circuit. JJ was a regular DJ at Subterranea, a club under the Westway, at Portobello Green. She remembered the day they met as clearly as if it were yesterday – it was hard to accept it was already sixteen years ago. JJ had been on the decks from 10 p.m. – she'd booked him as a warm-up for the bigger names coming later. He'd enticed her with his loose smile and leading eyes, his gleaming conker-brown skin and gym-honed physique. From the start she should have been warned off by his all-too-easy laugh. She knew it hinted at a deep, volatile energy, something she wouldn't be able to control, but she'd found it blinding. Before long he'd come to stay 'for a bit', just while he got himself 'sorted' with his own place. He'd spent the last few years travelling around, playing at a club in Ibiza in the summer, back home in the Caribbean for the winter, had started to mix his own CDs which sold well on the circuit, had quite a reputation now.

Max's conception was fast and unexpected and JJ couldn't hack it, he wasn't ready to grow up, take on a kid. He moved out before the baby arrived and once Max was born Clare had to stop working. Since then she felt she and Max had just hobbled along, with JJ intermittently in and out of their lives, year in year out – until now. Suddenly something had shifted in her. She'd entered a new stage. She was a decade older and wiser; even had a job on the fringes of the Establishment. It was all over with him, really over, she knew as she got on the bus, for her as well as for Max.

* * *

Back inside number twenty-eight Max texted Casey, 'Ready?' as he made himself toast and gulped orange juice straight from the carton. Then he shoved his feet into lace-loosened Nikes under his frayed grey school trousers that were already too short again, and grabbed his black rucksack, bulging with school books. He took a quick glance at himself in the kitchen mirror. He had Malteser-brown eyes, dusky skin and soft cheeks that could blush – and often did. He smoothed a hand over his almost black hair that had none of his dad's curls, all of his mum's fine wispiness, and blinked. Then he headed on out, sax case in hand, slamming the door behind him with a backwards kick of his left foot.

'Morning Maggie,' he called as he saw the old lady, settled in her usual place, opposite.

'OK, Max,' she replied. 'Casey was just out looking for you.'

As she spoke, a slightly built West Indian boy with a tick shaved into the left side of his number one appeared from a door two down. A puckish smile lit his tidy face as he saw his friend and Casey waved cheerfully at Maggie as they fell into step. Max had got so tall they looked comic together, this little West Indian boy and his towering friend. They took the opposite direction to Clare ten minutes before, towards the bus stop on Reeling Road, glancing with vague interest at the policeman outside Shelly's as they passed him by.

Max and Casey kept themselves away from that lot; they did crack and stuff and neither wanted to know more. Con Ryan had started hanging out with them recently, and they knew he was being used for traffic. He'd always been a bit of a geek, a misfit, and needed the attention. Casey and Max knew that Shelly's lot meant trouble for him. They were using him as their carrier, they were both certain of it. Con denied it but it was clear he was in way out of his depth. He was only fifteen, like them, was supposed to be at the same school as Casey, but never went any more. His family seemed to turn a blind eye. Con didn't have a mum, and his dad Joe and his cousins were a fat bunch who sat around all day on brown velvet sofas. You could just about see them as you passed by the basement window, lounging in their slobby tracksuits watching Sky Extra; empty cans of Special Brew strewn across the floor, fag butts outside in the basement well, along with Con's bike. When he was sober, Joe was nice enough, but he seemed to spend most of his time down the bookies or in the Ship, sinking pints of Guinness while Con hung around on his bike outside.

'Did you get a text from Michael?' Casey enquired as they stood together waiting for their buses.

Max couldn't disguise a smirk.

'Sick,' he said. 'Gladys's grounded him till Friday. Won't be at youth club tonight.'

'You goin'?' Casey asked, grinning.

'You?'

'After football.'

Casey was fanatical about soccer, at ten had already signed as a Chelsea schoolboy. He attended the comprehensive on the Finchley Road where the rarity of a good left foot had proved a life-affirming skill off – as well as on – the pitch; it gained you respect. He had the reputation for having the tricksiest feet in the borough. Max kind of liked the music academy he went to in Kensington. He nodded as his bus pulled up. He got on and turned to see Casey lean back against the window ledge of Ali's and pull his iPod from his bag.

'Later,' Max said, holding up his hand as the door swung shut.

He flashed his Oyster card as the driver nodded him on. There was only standing room and he edged his way towards the back where he could lean against the rail. He'd become accustomed to the journey, hardly noticed its monotony or his fellow passengers any more.

As the bus jolted past the countless discount shops, Asian grocers and Arabic Internet cafés that lined the Harrow Road he let his mind wander back to his favourite waking subject: Casey's cousin, Sammy. After last night he was pretty sure he'd finally lost out to Michael, with his cool Florida drawl and endless supply of gizmos, sent over from New York by his mum. When Michael had arrived in Meanwhile Street three years earlier, the plan was for him to stay for six months, maybe a year, while 'Mom gets herself fixed up with a new job and us a new apartment in Brooklyn'. Michael's dad was never mentioned and Max had the feeling he might have landed himself in the nick for some kind of fraud. Clare had told Max it sounded like Michael's mum had taken a 'geographical'. She said it often happened in the States, when something went wrong. You just packed up your bags and headed for a new state – to start over. Meanwhile Michael was staying in London with his Aunty Gladys and her dad, the legendary King Jacks, who was now well into his seventies but still mixing those Jamaican decks on Powis Terrace each August bank holiday. He may have got old, but he was still one of the highlights of the Notting Hill Carnival.

Michael had benefited from his great-uncle when he first arrived in Meanwhile Street, for no one would mess with a kid related to King Jacks. But for all the parcels that arrived from his mother, no airline ticket for Michael's return trip was ever enclosed. There was now even mention that she might be on her way across the Atlantic, to try and make a go of it in London too. She was working for a homeopathic company, Michael had boasted, some kind of place where you held parties at home to sell product on commission. She thought it might take off in London. For his part, Max was pleased he'd never gone back. Michael was so much part of their scene Max couldn't imagine how he could ever leave again, not now, especially since they had set up the band. Michael had a thick, bluesy voice, even at fifteen, and with King Jacks' contacts who knew what the future might hold for them – if they stuck at it. Max considered Michael a brother – more important, he guessed, in the end, than Sammy, but still he couldn't help but feel a stirring of jealousy when he thought about last night.

Max retraced the evening now as the bus jerked on down towards Queensway. They'd all mooched down to the local park to watch Casey play football. Afterwards they'd been larking about. Sammy was with her mates from North Westminster College, but none of them were anywhere near as fit as her, with her teased long hair, pretty round face, her long, cow eyelashes, and that diamond glinting in her belly button. *Sugar babe* was written in white sparkly swirls across her pale pink crop top. When she laughed she displayed a row of perfect gleaming white teeth, and between them he caught occasional glimpses of a glistening pink tongue. The image made Max feel slightly uncomfortable. He shuffled up on the bus and swapped his weight from one foot to the other, then back again, to try and shift her from his mind. Sammy was Casey's cousin, lived one block down on Seasonal Street, had hung out with them since primary. She'd always just been this little kid, until recently, when everything had started to change.

Last night Sammy and Michael had been wrestling each other in the bushes, apparently, for a last piece of gum, she shrieking a lot and him chuckling in his naturally deep, honeyed way. When they finally reappeared Casey had muttered, 'Next time get a room.' Everyone but Sammy had sniggered but she'd faked indignation and after too long a pause to score a point back, had retorted, 'Shut up, loser.' Then she'd sidled a touch awkwardly over to Max. He'd tried hard not to notice, kept his hoodie up, bent over his console. She'd sat herself down close to him on the bench, crossing her bare legs at the knees. He'd forced his attention on getting to the next level of his game. She'd leaned in closer and asked him his score in soothing, almost apologetic tones. Her switch of attention made him uneasy and he was relieved when Michael said it was time to go.

When they'd got back to Meanwhile Street it had already been dusk, after ten. They passed Shelly and that lot outside their new mate's flat at the end. They always gathered there in the evening now, and recently a few new, older guys had started hanging around with them too. They wore black and white bandannas round their necks, symbols of their new 'gang'. As usual the girls had been sitting on the front wall, smoking, pushing prams backwards and forwards with a foot, dummies stuck in their kids' grimacing mouths. One of them was Shelly's girl, Demi, he thought.

A black Lexus with smoked windows had pulled up and Max had spotted Con standing behind the wall, between two of the girls. He'd jumped over and approached the car as the window slid halfway down and something was passed into his waiting hands. Then he'd got on his bike, vanished off towards the park. The car window had slid shut again and the car had pulled away from the kerb, cruised off, slowly. Max and his lot pretended not to notice, carried on walking. It was always coming and going, that car with its blacked-out windows and deep bass tones thumping like a slow heartbeat. Sometimes it pulled up outside Maggie's, to talk to Shelly. Max didn't like it and he didn't like Con being involved with it, either.

Just then they had made out Michael's Aunty Gladys halfway down the street, loitering at the top of her basement steps, thick hands on her hills of hips, passing the time with Maggie above.

'You're in shit,' Casey had murmured, shoving Michael into the road.

'Bothered?'

Michael dodged off then, back on to the pavement.

'Whatever,' Sammy had added, sashaying her hips with a touch more exaggeration than before.

Max had remained silent, head hung low. He was hating the way they had started to flirt.

Now Gladys had spotted them.

'You get yourself here, Michael,' she'd hollered, her Southern twang ricocheting up the street to meet them. Sammy had turned back so she could look at Michael and she stuck out her tongue and giggled. In turn he shot her a wide grin, his beautiful face shining mischievously under the lamplight, then dodged past her and galloped on ahead. They all watched from a distance as Gladys frog-marched her nephew down into the basement, green check housecoat flapping, twisting her rear to make it down the narrow steps.

The bus was taking too long this morning, Max suddenly realized, breaking with his reflections and looking out at the London traffic. It was snarling up past Porchester Baths and on towards Bayswater Road. He was going to be late for school. As it finally pulled over he made a snap decision and jumped off, pulled up his hood and trotted off towards Hyde Park, rucksack slung over his shoulder. It would be quicker to go across the park and pick up another bus on the south side. Max knew how to work this city. Its countless routes, its twists and turns circulated with the blood in his veins.

4

Back in Meanwhile Street life was rising like fish surfacing to snap at a mayfly. One by one people appeared from out of their front doors, glanced at the policeman standing by Marlon's jeep, then got their heads down and set off for their jobs and schools. Gordon had roused Katya and handed Milo over. She was hard to get up in the mornings and it wound him up, especially now Immy was so close to her due date. Katya didn't do anything in a hurry, but Milo loved her and she was reliable. She'd been with them for seven months already, and it had worked out just about fine. Katya didn't hang around them when it was her time off, either, kept her private life to herself. At the weekend she was rarely seen for dust. Gordon and Immy didn't enquire and she didn't offer details. Probably best left that way.

Katya was a pretty girl and a couple of times recently when she'd tipped up in the kitchen in a barely-thigh-covering T-shirt to put the kettle on, Gordon had had to remind himself that he was happily married. She had that wandering look about her, a look that was best left unexamined and a way of holding your gaze, her lips just slightly parted, that was unsettling. Immy was aware of such undercurrents, kept a mental note of them, but was thrilled that Milo loved her so much. This was true and essentially, Gordon knew, all that really mattered. She made their lives work. The details, Gordon supposed, were secondary. It would still be amazing, however, just once in a while to find her up, dressed and ready for the day before he had to galvanize her. But Gordon disliked confrontation and Immy had said that he shouldn't get involved, it was her business, the au pair, one thing he didn't need to worry himself about. Gordon gave Milo a final squeeze, put on his jacket and then headed out into the street.

Maggie was at her window and spotted him as he crossed over to have a quick chat with the policeman. She didn't understand it, how the younger generations dressed. You'd think at a newspaper they'd expect suits, but when she'd said this to Gordon once he'd thrown his head back and laughed. 'Only on the City or news desks, the guys who do the press conferences,' he'd replied. He always wore the same thing, a loose white linen shirt, a casual jacket and jeans – she supposed it must be the media look. She wondered how anyone in the office knew who was the boss. Gordon always looked neat and tidy, however, with his dark hair cropped nice and short – and he was clean-shaven, too. With his small black portfolio case slung over his shoulder, he carried a gentle air of authority that suggested he was knowledgeable about the world.

Gordon stood with his hands on his hips, head craned slightly forward, chatting quietly to the police officer, too quietly for her to listen in.

'Tell me if it makes it to the paper, the story, won't you now?' she called down.

She didn't usually get his broadsheet, a bit too lefty and intellectual for her, although she'd never tell Gordon that; but she might just have to if it featured Meanwhile Street, wouldn't do to miss news printed about her own doorstep. Gordon looked confused for just a moment and then he laughed.

'Will do, Maggie, of course,' he said, before turning to fake-dodge the Kosovan kids who were hanging around by the railings in their green school sweatshirts. Then he headed off to catch the District line.

While they waited for Ada to get the baby dressed, the children were watching the policeman outside Janice's. One at a time they dared each other to run up to him and pull a face, then run away again. His mouth was set in a professionally even line, hands behind his back, and he tried to ignore them, focused on Marlon's jeep, as if any moment now it might take off by remote control. He didn't like dealing with neighbourhood disturbances; the nosiness of neighbours, their snivelling little brats. It rarely led to an arrest.

'They don't mean any harm, officer,' Maggie cajoled and he looked up and offered her a tepid smile, annoyed that she could read his mind.

The old woman's banter was wearing thin and he'd still got two hours to go. He, like everyone else, doubted they'd be seeing Marlon again. It was a waste of the Met's time. Nobody round here gave a damn about police presence any more. If the little shits wanted to commit a crime, they'd go ahead and do it, whether an officer was in the vicinity or not. The more petty crimes there were, the less chance the police had of dealing with them and the more chance the kids had of getting away with them. Even in a case like this, of aggravated assault, the girl was unlikely to press charges. There'd been no witnesses and she'd be smart enough to know her accusations were unlikely to get past the first round. Nationally, less than one in ten of violent crimes reported the previous year had ended in a conviction; often the charade of maintaining order felt like a waste of everyone's time and money. Most worryingly, the kids on the street seemed as aware of the fact as the police were themselves.

A black cab pulled up and the officer watched as a late-middle-aged woman got out slowly and leant back in to pay the driver. She had a couple of orange supermarket plastic bags at her feet and was wearing a store uniform. It must be the victim's mum, Janice, he thought, correctly. She had a small face, meanly creased by the years, beneath a head of furious, dark grey wiry hair. She was as thin as a wafer and as she looked up towards Maggie he could see that her face was surprisingly suntanned, if angry.

'The little bugger,' she began without preamble. 'He's gone way too far this time, way too far, fancy trip to Mexico or not.'

'What a shame, dear; a terrible shame,' responded Maggie, warming to her task of consolation. 'And after all his generosity.'

The previous day Janice and Shelly had got back from a package holiday to the Mermaid Hotel at Cancun, just the two of them, with Demi, of course; courtesy of Marlon. He'd even paid for their new passports and a case full of summer clothes for Demi to take with her. Before they left for the airport Janice told Maggie she'd wondered if he was about to propose to Shelly, whether this trip might not have been a sweetener, 'for her old mum'. Marlon had said he was doing it to say thank you to Janice for putting up with him – and the baby – even though, he said, it wasn't certain it was even his. He'd winked at this comment and roared with volatile laughter that had just too much force in it to leave Janice feeling comfortable. Marlon's pupils were always pin-sharp and active, tiny, jiggling dots inside earth-brown eyes, surrounded by the whitest of whites. Once or twice he'd burst a blood vessel in the corner of an eye and the contrast of the tendrils of red against the whiteness was startling; macabre.

It had taken Janice a while to get used to Shelly going out with a black man at all – but he wasn't 'foreign' like the Iraqis and Kosovans were, the Moroccans or the Poles even. No, Marlon was born and bred a west Londoner and his parents were, too. They were almost as London as London itself, even though the family was complicated, with countless half-brothers and cousins whose names she could never remember, however often they were mentioned. She'd been beginning to get used to him, or so she had thought.

'How's Shelly doing, the poor girl?' Maggie now sighed.

'Sixteen stitches, it'll leave a scar,' Janice replied dejectedly before leaning down to pick up her plastic bags. 'They're keeping her in for her own security, until they find him, so I'll be taking her things over in a while, says she won't press charges, though, so they're wasting their time.' She nodded towards the officer and scowled. 'Hanging around on my doorstep, upsetting the street.'

'Well you be sure to send her my love when you go back down there.'

Janice nodded before disappearing off down the stairwell to her front door with her groceries, pointedly ignoring the policeman as he stood aside to let her pass.

Once inside she dropped her shopping, leant back against the wall, shut her eyes. She was worn out, had done a double shift, seven p.m. to eight a.m. – and now all this. Then she looked around her. The lounge was turned upside down. Looked more like they'd been raided than that Shelly and Marlon had had a set-to. The settee was upturned, the dresser drawers emptied out, letters and papers scattered across the floor. The DVD player was hanging from a wire between the floor and the TV set. Janice's ornaments had been swiped off the mantelpiece on to the hearth. A head had broken off one of her blue china cats and its decapitated body had rolled across the carpet, where it now rested between a copy of yesterday's *Express* and an empty pack of B&H.

She knelt down and picked up Shelly's last school photograph, its frame cracked, the glass shattered. The photo had been taken when Shelly was thirteen. Her dark hair was tied up in neat pigtails and a bright, hopeful smile lit her young, fresh face. Marlon must have stood on it deliberately, she thought with mounting disgust. Janice traced the impression of her daughter's untainted left cheek with her index finger under the shards; snagged it. A droplet of blood oozed out. She put it in her mouth and sucked. How could so much have altered, in so short a time? And now, to make matters worse, Shelly would be scarred for life.

It had all begun to disintegrate with Eddie's death, four years ago. There were no two ways about it, he had been a rock for Shelly, if not, to be honest, for her. Over the years Janice had simply learned to manage her marriage, generally by keeping quiet and out of his way when one of his tempers overtook him. By contrast, Shelly had always known how to calm her dad and had always remained exempt from his outbursts. It had crossed her mind more than once that Shelly had learned her behaviour from her dad, that he was where she got her feisty nature. Janice had never been one for tantrums; in general she kept her furies on the inside.

Since he'd died, Shelly's behaviour had become more extreme, her own rages more regular. She'd become more addictive in nature, as well – and not just to cigarettes and destructive relationships. Janice was well aware that her daughter dabbled in drugs, often provided by Marlon and his friends. Eddie had had a habit of his own, but it hadn't been drugs or even alcohol, really. He'd been addicted to the betting shop on the corner of Reeling Road. And when things hadn't gone his way, a few pints would go down and it was she who'd feel the force of his fist. Eddie had never touched Shelly, not once, of that Janice was certain. There'd never been weapons in their home before and when Eddie had hit her he'd never left a scar. Never anything like this incident between Shelly and Marlon. A gun? What was Marlon thinking of? It made Janice's skin go clammy. What if he'd actually shot one of them?

Janice got up off her knees, placed the broken picture on the empty mantelpiece, took a crumpled tissue from the pocket of her uniform and blew her nose. She stepped over the mess and headed into the hall, glancing into her daughter's room. The bedclothes had been pulled back and the faded pink floral sheet Shelly had had since childhood was soaked with blood. Drips were smeared across the laminate wood floor that she and Marlon had laid, only a month before. Shelly must have held something up to her face to stop the bleeding from there, Janice decided, because it stopped, abruptly. On the door frame she saw more smeared marks; bloody fingerprints. There were more along the barrier of Demi's cot. She felt nausea rising, darted into the bathroom, threw up bile.

She thought she'd understood why Shelly might be unwilling to press charges against Marlon. When she'd seen her, grey-faced and bandaged at the hospital earlier, it had sounded rational.

'It won't cause nothing but aggro if we get the police involved,' Shelly had reasoned. 'Marlon didn't mean nothing, reacted to something I'd said; he'd taken the gun off Stevie for his own protection. He was planning on getting rid of it today, any more trouble and he'll be back inside. It's the last thing I want. Dem'll be upset.'

Shelly had been ranting, yet despite her recent shock had seemed defiant rather than afraid. Her dark eyes had that set look about them that reminded Janice of 'steady Eddie' as he'd been known to his mates. Nothing would change her mind if she'd decided, Janice knew that much, and as she'd sat at Shelly's hospital bedside less than an hour ago, she'd thought she agreed with her. But now she was sitting in this mess she wasn't so sure that she could let it be. Marlon had done all this, if Shelly was to be believed, simply out of rage. He'd gone completely mental. Maybe, she pondered as she wiped her mouth and flushed the toilet, the real reason for Shelly's response was fear, of what else he was capable of, or maybe of what his mates might do next. The police would offer her protection; they'd said so, but it wouldn't protect her from his friends, even if they got Marlon behind bars. Janice had turned a blind eye to the comings and goings of his gang, had tried hard not to notice the dealings that took place between them all on the street, but she wasn't born yesterday. She thought about Mexico, about Marlon's friends, and once again she retched.

When Janice had put the place back together she headed outside with three bin liners full of the recently broken parts of their lives – including Shelly's bedclothes, they were too bloodied to bleach clean. She'd go back to the hospital this afternoon, but first of all she needed to sleep. She was on shift again, at eight. The policeman was still outside her gate. But now he was accompanied by a community officer. She actively ignored them as she put the rubbish into the black bins, but they spotted Janice and called down to ask if they could 'come inside' for a few moments to catch up. It didn't seem she had much option but to agree. They were already making their way down the basement steps and it wouldn't do to have a set-to in the street. She nodded her head resignedly and let them in behind her.

They sat in the cleaned-up lounge, the two coppers on the settee, with Janice perched forward in her armchair, small hands clasped together, in a subtle show of defiance. The community officer introduced himself with a slimy smile. She wasn't going to be got around that easily. She recognized him from his daily patrols of the area, but immediately forgot his name.

'Your daughter insists she won't press charges,' he began with an optimistic expression. 'But we would advise, strongly, that you try to persuade her otherwise. This is a serious incident and one we can't ignore, whether she chooses to make a statement or not.'

Janice remained tight-lipped.

'We understand this is a frightening situation, Janice.'

'Mrs Warwick if you don't mind.'

'Sorry, of course, Mrs Warwick; but it's to your advantage to try and help us. We're here to protect you.'

Janice couldn't help but let a 'Pah!' escape from her lips.

Both officers sat more upright and when the community officer spoke again, his tone had shifted to the edge of terse.

'Was there anything particular you'd noticed that had occurred over the past week or two, anything out of the ordinary that might have triggered Marlon's aggressive reaction?'

Janice opened her mouth to speak, then closed it again. She was about to say there couldn't have been, because she and Shelly had been on holiday, but something stopped her. Less is more, she told herself and shook her head, dazedly. The less they know about us, in every way, the better. It was something Eddie used to say and maybe, at least on this count, he was right.

She thought about their trip to Mexico again, about Marlon's friends, the ones who'd come to the hotel on their last night, plied them with tequila, made them feel special. Her innards quivered. What had Marlon and Shelly rowed about this morning? And what, she wondered, with a stab of fear, had he been looking for?

'Talk to Shelly about it again, Mrs Warwick,' went on the officer. 'We'd like you both to think very carefully, about yourselves – and about Demi, too. It's for your own security. We need to find Marlon. But we can't keep an officer out here all day. We'll have to wait for someone to call with a sighting. The station's on short staff and we've got other emergencies that need attending to.'

All of a sudden she didn't know if she felt fearful or relieved – after all, with them gone Marlon could come back.

'So you'll be off now then, will you?' she blurted.

'Unless you can think of any reason for us to stay,' the officer replied carefully. 'You only have to say. If you're worried or have any information you want to share, any information you might have been thinking of keeping to yourself, please tell us now.'

Janice looked down at her hands, fiddled with her wedding ring, thought about Eddie. Marlon would never have been allowed in the house if he'd still been alive, let alone managed to take such a hold. Eddie would've killed him with his bare hands for less than this.

'No officer, there's nothing. It was nothing more than a domestic. You know how these teenagers can fight. If I think of anything once you're gone, I'll call.'

The two policemen got up. The first one handed her a card.

'Use this number,' he said. 'It goes directly through to the drugs team.'

The words stung but Janice had a face that knew how not to react. She showed the officers out, double-locked the front door, keyed the phone number from the card into her mobile, then went into her bedroom at the back of the flat.

Janice slid her feet out of her shoes, took off her uniform and hung it on a hanger on the outside of her wardrobe door. She'd be back in it later. Underneath she was wearing a flesh-coloured slip and even paler tights. She rolled them down over her knees, then sat on the bed to take them off. She had a bunion coming on her left foot and it hurt. Too much standing up in cheap shoes; she'd need to go to Shoe Right on the Harrow Road; buy some cushioned lace-ups. She cursed at a ladder in the left ankle and threw the limp tights at the bin under her dressing table. They flopped in, but one foot remained hanging over the side. She left it where it fell and put a grey towelling dressing gown over the top of her slip, locked the window and the door, turned out the light and got into bed, phone clutched to her chest, closed her eyes and fell almost immediately into a jumpy, half-wakeful sleep.

At some point during the next hour her phone rang and she answered it, half-consciously. It was Marlon. He sounded strung-out, different.

'Where did Shelly put Demi's case?' he demanded. 'I need it, Janice, I need it today.'

'What?'

'From the fucking holiday, you stupid cunt. If I don't get hold of it by lunchtime, believe you me, Shelly's little fucking accident is going to be the least of her problems.'

Before she had a chance to respond, he hung up.

5

At 9.45 a.m. Katya said goodbye to Immy, who was standing in the front doorway in her rose-patterned dressing gown and soft pink suede slipper-boots, belly protruding like a watermelon before her. Maggie surveyed them from the window.

'How ya feeling, dear?' she called.

'Good thanks, Maggie, very good,' Immy said, patting her belly unselfconsciously. 'Only two weeks to go now.'

Milo waved up at Maggie as Katya turned his buggy in the direction of Lizzie B's, the nursery at the end of the street.

'Hello young Milo, going to the drop-in?' Maggie called.

'Maggie, Maggie,' Milo replied, craning his neck up to look at her, way above him, a mere speck near the sky.

Katya gave the old woman a cursory nod and busied herself with Milo's straps. She could do without a chat with that inquisitive old crow. She was always up there, watching. She was sure she'd even seen her curtain twitch as Katya had slunk home in the middle of the night – not always alone. Maggie had opinions, of that Katya was certain, and she wasn't interested in hearing them. The Czech Republic was full of old women like her, women who remembered too much about the past and now had nothing better to do than mind other people's business. It was one of the things she had come to London to escape.

'Be back by twelve, won't you?' Immy said, shifting her attention from Maggie back to Katya and the child. 'I want to get Milo off to sleep before I go for my swim at two.'

'Of course,' agreed Katya calmly, then turned towards the nursery again.

She went to Lizzie B's most mornings, unless she had something more pressing to attend to, in which case she'd walk up the street in the direction of the nursery so Immy would think that was where they were going, then quickly turn the corner and buy Milo a packet of Chewits from Ali's before hopping on the number six into town. Otherwise it was convenient and sociable to go to the nursery. Once they were inside Milo hardly gave her a backward glance, was too busy playing with the cars, or sand, or water trays and paint to need her attention. It almost felt like time off. It was where she had met her only London friend, a Polish au pair called Melina who lived further up Meanwhile Street. Over the past few months each had become the main introduction for the other to a language that neither clearly understood. There was ample opportunity for misunderstanding but it hardly mattered. They rubbed along together, somehow. They'd chat over Nescafé while the little ones played, then usually hang out together for the rest of the day. She'd arranged to meet Melina there this morning.

Katya slowed as she passed the house two doors up, glanced back to be certain Immy had gone inside, then looked down into the basement window. Monitors glowed dimly on three desks set against the walls. Sitting at one and looking up at her now was her new acquaintance, a Somali guy called Zahir. She'd met him by the front railings the other day. The weather had been so hot in this city. Everyone had been outside. She'd sat on her front steps and chatted to him while Milo had napped. It was the most important thing that had happened to her in seven months. She'd thought of little else since.

As they had hung out in the sharp midday sunshine, Zahir had introduced himself, told Katya he'd been in London for just under a year, and asked her if Milo was her child.

'No, I am just au pair,' Katya had affirmed. 'Not ready for kids of my own now. Maybe another day.'

Then she told him about Immy and Gordon, how kind they were, how they gave her time off when it was due; arranged her English classes, which, admittedly, she rarely bothered to attend.

'Where do you come from?'

'Prague,' she'd replied. 'A long way from London.'

'It feels that way?'

'Sometimes,' she'd confessed with a quick smile. 'It's one of my sisters' birthdays today.'

'You have many?'

Katya hesitated. Personal questions, very quick. She had glanced up at him. Zahir had smiled encouragingly back. He was beautiful to look at and she had wanted the conversation to go on, not to falter. She needed a reason to stay here, looking at him. He seemed carved from black stone, tall and lean with a bright smile and very long fine hands which he was holding loosely together in front of him. There was a thick gold ring on the index finger of his right hand and it shone like precious treasure against his dark skin. She felt the urge to touch it. He wore a long white cotton kaftan shirt over faded jeans, slip-on red leather mules. She sensed an energy in him that was appealing, sexual. She instinctively picked up on that scent. It had something to do with the way she was made. She decided to take the plunge.

'Two sisters,' she said, 'and my mother, who is teacher. My father, he is dead.'

'I'm sorry. When did your father die?'

'In prison when I was small. He was political activist. Trade-union man. Put away for his opinions. He die of heart attack. This is what they say.'

'Before communism fell?'

She nodded. No one had mentioned that to her here, not even Gordon.

'How old were you?'

'It was 1987. I was . . . four,' she said. 'He die for democracy.' She couldn't avoid the irony that crept into her voice. 'My mother, she is never over my father's death.'

Zahir had looked down at his hands, then up at her again. His face was full of compassion.

'It is impossible to get over these deaths,' he said presently, gently. 'But we must never give up on making things better for our mother countries.'

Katya didn't quite understand his meaning, but guessed Zahir was talking about Somalia. The civil war there, she knew, had been atrocious, the suffering beyond anything. She didn't know what to say next but didn't need to try too hard, because Zahir was already asking another question.

'Your mother, what does she teach?'

'She is economic at the university, very high, works very hard. My sisters and me, we raise ourselves. You know, it is like we owe our father everything, we have to show by our ways that we are thanking him, all the time. We must not forget the cost of our freedom. There is little time for play.'

'Is that why you came to London? To play?'

Katya returned what was clearly a flirtatious smile.

'I finish my law degree. I come here to live for a while in the present, to forget my history.'

Zahir laughed at that, his white teeth gleaming. 'Our histories chase us,' he said.

'I just want to feel easy,' she smiled back. 'And you, what is your story?'

'I fled the civil war. Now I campaign for those who cannot get out. I respect anyone who has died in the name of democracy.'

Milo had begun to stir. Katya got up from the steps to lift him out of the buggy. It was time for lunch. She felt thrown a little off balance by this man. She'd been raised on her father's political heroics and had come away from Prague to escape from his legacy – for a while at least. His reputation had made expectations of her family too high. Clearly Zahir was politicized. She wanted to play in London, it was true, but she wasn't sure she wanted to play with someone who cared too much about putting the world to rights. Her father's political ardour had left her with a moral act she couldn't – or simply didn't want to – follow. She'd just finished her studies, had come to London to be anonymous and to relax a little. Despite this rationale, she was attracted to Zahir and knew she would want to see him again.

'I must take Milo home for lunch,' she had said casually. 'See you around.'

'Come check your emails sometime,' he'd replied.

Today, when he saw Katya, Zahir beamed and leapt up from his chair. Moments later he had opened the door and appeared at the bottom of the steps.

'Hello,' she said, then she giggled, leaning a hand on the railings and fluttering her eyelashes. Katya was beautiful, in a cool way, with her Slavic-hewn face and perfect, opalescent skin, and she knew it.

'Heh, Katya, you come later, use the Net?' he tempted.

She shrugged, tipping her head to one side.

'I will see. I go now to nursery with Milo – home for lunch.'

She waved a little wave and shoved the buggy off along the street, aware he was watching her slender hips sway, just a little. Maggie was watching her, too, with a frown on her face. She threw the old lady a stone-cold glare.

'Nee naw, nee naw,' urged Milo, pointing eagerly over the road.

Katya had already registered the police car parked up outside Maggie's. An officer was sitting in it.

'Yes, Milo, nee naw, nee naw,' she replied disinterestedly, her mind fixed on possible plans for later in the day.

They entered the nursery foyer and signed in, glancing quickly up the list. Melina and three-year-old Helene were already inside. A young woman approached Katya wearing a half-veil and a long smock dress over jeans and trainers. She was visibly pregnant. She had a bright face and a beautiful creamy complexion, a generous smile. This was Aishah, the Moroccan key worker who ran the morning sessions.

'What happened in your street this morning?' she asked Katya as she helped wrestle Milo's coat from him. Katya hung it and his mini rucksack up on a red peg and looked curiously back at her.

'Why you ask?' she enquired. 'Nothing happen, I think.'

'When I got to work the end of Meanwhile Street was cordoned off.'

'Cordoned, what is cordoned?'

'It doesn't matter, 'spect it was nothing.' She grinned, then bent down to speak to Milo at his level.

'We're making biscuits this morning, you want to help me?'

'Nee naw, police car,' said Milo and followed her inside.

The nursery was cleverly laid out in a series of small interconnecting rooms and a central, circular area so the kids could roam free while being observed. The play session lasted an hour, before they were given fruit on plastic plates while the adults tidied up. Then there was always group singing, which Katya loathed, before home time. Milo knew his way around and immediately rushed off in search of a police car. Katya followed and found Melina in one of the side rooms, sitting on the floor with Helene surrounded by plastic animals. Helene had a zebra in her mouth and Melina was trying to persuade her to take it out.

'She is stupid like her mama,' Katya remarked.

'That's unkind,' replied Melina, but smiled nonetheless. 'Helene is not a bad kid compared to her brother.'

Katya sat herself down next to Melina at an angle so she could observe Milo while they chatted. He banged his cheek with the ambulance he was now clutching, then lay down on his side and started saying 'nee naw nee naw' all over again. Strange, thought Katya distractedly, but probably harmless – unlike Troy to whom Melina had just referred. Helene's older brother was a whirlwind of dangerous intelligence, the kind of child who sought out peril with relish. He was five, and thankfully for Melina, at school all day. He had white-blond hair and the bluest, sky-deep eyes; a devil cloaked in the garb of an angel. When challenged about his bad behaviour he would respond with a steely, dispassionate stare, quickly followed by a defiant smile. Melina didn't feel it was her job to try and change his conduct, simply to contain it, and to survive her time with him, particularly as, in his parents' eyes, he could do no wrong.

'What he did now?' Katya enquired expectantly. With Troy there was always something diabolic afoot.

'Last night he take lid off Calpol bottle, drink all the pink medicine. I take him to A and E,' Melina said.

'What is this?' asked Katya.

'Emergency unit at hospital. They make him sick with tube to get it out. Then he scream all night. I hate him.'

'My God, he be junkie at twelve,' Katya retorted.

'Don't say it!' Melina gasped.

She was slight with colourless skin, straight shoulder-length brown hair, thin lips and a smattering of very dark freckles on her nose. Her eyes were an indeterminate colour; sometimes they appeared pale brown, at other times hazel. Her normal expression was a slight frown but when she laughed, as she did now, her features loosened and suddenly she could become deer-like, and very pretty.

'Where was Lulu?' Katya enquired.

'Oh I don't know,' Melina sighed. 'I take him in taxi.'

Melina's working days generally merged into the evenings. Often the parents didn't come home when they promised and their mobiles were usually switched off when Melina tried to call. Katya thought it was disgusting and often urged her to find a new, kinder family, one like hers. They lived in a big, rambling house like Immy and Gordon's, but unlike their modern decor, Tim and Lulu's house was shabby and dusty, full of old furniture that needed reupholstering, cracked oil paintings, old musty books. None of the cutlery matched and the china was chipped. The kitchen was unfitted and its centrepiece was a big old cooker they called an Aga, which never heated anything properly. Melina might not have had much at home in Krakow, but everything in their apartment was pristine – and matching. These people lived like their house was a museum.

And she was slightly afraid of Tim, too. He worked in advertising, was glib and overconfident. He often came to stand behind her at the kitchen sink, on the pretext of reaching for a mug from the rack above her head, so that his body had to press against her back; or he would lean around her to retrieve a plate from a shelf so that his arm had to rest momentarily about her waist. She had a feeling he thought it came with the territory, this flirtation with her, but for Melina his attentions were a mild threat. She often worried what she would do if he decided to go too far. Katya would know. Even so, Melina felt she had only just settled in London and didn't have the confidence to move on.

'They really not good to you,' Katya told her. She said this almost every time they met.

'I know, I know,' Melina shrugged. 'Tim think it is funny.'

Troy's father often shrieked with delight at the tales of his son's misdemeanours, as if his insubordination would prove a worthy life skill. In fact, Troy was the image of Tim, who too had something spoilt about him, a small, skinny man with thinning grey hair and the same rebellious grin as his son. He had a temper. He didn't get angry with her or the children, but Melina often heard him flying off the handle with Lulu from their bedroom on the top floor of the house, his wife whimpering pathetically like a scolded spaniel. She partly felt Lulu deserved it; she was spoilt too, didn't work and didn't care for her kids; was self-obsessed and silly. Even so, Melina felt sorry for her, worried that if she weren't around, Tim might go a step too far and really hurt his wife.

Melina didn't want a future like that. She was determined to make something of her life, but she knew poverty and wasn't going back to it. At least at Tim and Lulu's there was always food in the fridge, her own bathroom and a double bed. At home there was almost nothing. Her mum, who worked at the local hospital, was alone in Krakow now; her dad had left years before. No one knew where he was – it had been a relief, his disappearance. But her mother was ill at the moment; had caught an infection on one of the wards and been forced to take a month off work, with no pay. Melina wasn't going back there to a life of bedpans and sickness; nothing would make her. She was happier to stay here for now, even with Lulu and Tim, sending money home.

'You look so tired,' announced Katya languidly.

'Too much the kids,' Melina replied, rolling her eyes. 'After lunch I must go shopping.' With this she brightened, almost glistened. 'You want come? I go to buy my mama birthday present, me some clothes.' She hardly spent a thing, although today she intended to treat herself.

'No, I have to stay home with Milo, Immy go swim after lunch. Maybe I come to see you after school, we have tea with kids?'

While they were making plans Helene had toddled off and was busy arranging a couple of rag dolls in their buggies, putting covers over them both. The two au pairs watched idly, playing with their mobile phones. Then Katya's bleeped and Melina looked over her shoulder. Katya subtly pulled it away so Melina couldn't read the message.

'Is from that guy Zahir, the one in the street,' she

confided, unable to contain herself any longer. 'He want me go drink tea at his flat.'

Melina smiled knowingly. Katya was enviably beautiful, in a dangerous kind of a way. Men were always after her. There was a touch of damage about her, the reasons for which Melina was yet to work out, but she seemed to thrive on pushing boundaries, on taking risks. Katya had a taste for Arabic men, whom she would get to buy them drinks in cheap West End nightclubs. Melina had met her at Lizzie B's after her first week in London. Recently she'd stopped going out on the town with her; Katya had left Melina in the lurch once too often, swinging off delightedly with some slim-hipped, dark-faced suitor at dawn. Melina would be left to find her solitary way home on a night bus. There was never an apology or explanation the next day. Melina knew she should probably steer clear of her, but she needed a friend and for now Katya was all she had.

'He is beautiful and sensitive,' Katya was saying, but Melina was only half listening. Her attention had been diverted by a toddler approaching Helene, who was now happily at play with a pram and some dolls. As Melina watched, the new arrival clonked Helene squarely over the head with a doll. At once Helene let out an outraged wail.

'Stop it, Demi,' called a voice.

Katya's neighbour Ranika appeared, bustling towards the two infants.

'Sorry,' she mouthed at Melina with a friendly grin and picked the child up. Demi kicked her legs and started to scream.

Melina tried to calm Helene while offering a pram to Demi, whose tears stopped as soon as they had started. She began to push it around frenziedly, rocking the dolly from side to side. Helene watched morosely, shuddering through a veil of tears and mucus. Melina took a tissue from her sleeve and wiped the child's face.

'Ranika lives next to me,' Katya murmured, glancing sideways at Melina with a quick smirk. 'The other side to Zahir.' Then she turned her attention to Ranika. 'This is not your baby, no – is girl other side of street?'

Ranika laughed. 'Yes, Demi's Shelly's daughter, over the road,' she said. 'She's in a bit of a mess, I'm just helpin' her out.'

'She not bring Demi here?'

'It's not her scene to be honest, but Aishah's a friend of mine, and she's going to look after Demi this morning, while we go and get Shelly sorted out.'

Aishah came up to them. 'Right, Ranika. I'll hang on to Demi until I hear from you,' she smiled.

'I'll try and be back by 11.45,' said Ranika, looking at her watch. 'Shouldn't take me long to get to the hospital.'

Katya looked enquiringly at the two of them.

'Her boyfriend hit her – uhmmm – with his gun,' said Ranika quickly. 'Split her cheek open, the fucker.'

It took a lot to shock Katya, but her jaw dropped.

'I can drop Demi home if you want,' she offered impulsively. 'It will give you extra fifteen minutes.'

'Brilliant,' Ranika replied without a moment's hesitation. 'See you at around twelve then,' and with that she was off, leaving them all with Shelly's little girl in their care. Demi and Helene had started to play together, more equably now, the row apparently forgotten.

Melina didn't like the way the child was being passed from hand to hand, and it also surprised her that Katya had been so willing to offer to help. Personally she would rather not get involved with people who talked so easily about carrying weapons. It scared her. Meanwhile Aishah took a quick look around, went over to the drop-in's entry door and clicked the lock down, then glanced out of the window.

'Let me know if you want to leave and I'll let you out,' she announced, then lifted the veil from her head.

Melina looked shocked and Aishah laughed.

'It's all right, there are no men around. I've locked the doors.'

Melina couldn't help but stare. In six months she'd never before seen Aishah's head unveiled. She looked a lot younger. Her long sleek brown hair was tied back in a neat plait. Melina felt unexpectedly sad, as if Aishah had let out a very special secret without being aware of its value. Aishah caught her looking and laughed. Melina laughed too and the moment of melancholy passed.

'Why do you wear it?' she asked, feeling emboldened.

Aishah paused for a moment, played with the veil between her hands. 'Don't know really. My mum never did, but when I got to around seventeen, my friend and I thought we'd put it on. It wasn't religious or nothing. Made us feel we were displaying our culture. Being raised here, we felt as if we'd lost our sense of it. Then I met my husband and he liked it. Now it would feel odd to take it off.'

'Like you are naked?' asked Melina.

Aishah paused again and looked quizzically into the middle distance.

'No, not really,' she replied finally. 'More like I'd vanished.'

'Vanished?'

'Like a puff of smoke! Gone!' Aishah said wistfully. She paused for a moment then laughed self-deprecatingly, and turned as Demi started crying again.

'I want my nana,' the little girl snivelled as Aishah picked her up.

'Come on, everyone. Time for some singing,' she called out. 'We need to try and keep this one occupied today.'

6

You wouldn't notice St Matthew's Church unless you knew it was there, slightly sunken into the corner of Reeling and Halfpenny streets. It was a post-war construction, a fifties block containing flats around the church itself, for the old people and 'nutters' – as the local kids would say – to inhabit. The spire was obscured by an enormous plane tree that needed cutting back. There was a bus stop outside, where double-deckers frequently waited with their engines idling while their drivers switched shifts.

Mark Scoles, the resident vicar, heard about Shelly and Marlon's fight from the two police officers who'd just been to see Janice. They paid Mark – as he was simply known by all – a visit at 11 a.m., just as he'd finished prayers with his morning congregation. On weekday mornings St Matthew's was akin to a grown-up nursery, a place for the over eighties to be entertained, to be kept occupied – a place to forget. Mark was painfully aware that most of them were only here for the singing and the snacks. He wasn't sure where God came on the list, if at all. Sometimes he felt his church was simply a combined residential and day-care unit; a drop-in centre with prayers thrown in for free.

He invited the police officers to take a pew, then expertly guided this morning's motley crew into the adjoining hall for their tea and biscuits. When he reappeared they explained the reason for their visit, enquiring whether any of the congregation had mentioned Marlon's attack on Shelly.

'Just off our patch, really,' he told them apologetically. 'Most of this lot come from the flats. Might have more luck at youth club tonight; the kids will know what's going on. I'll see what I can find out. But first I'll pay Janice a visit. She used to come with Shelly but she's been off my radar since Eddie died. I'll let you know if anything significant comes of it, confidences excepted, of course.'

Once he'd managed to clear the remaining tea-sinkers from the hall, Mark locked the church and made his way to Meanwhile Street. It was a perfect late May morning. Small puffy clouds scurried across a pale blue sky, and the cherry blossom was swirling and falling along Meanwhile Street – hard to imagine such extreme violence happening in such a peaceful spot. But Mark wasn't naive. He'd been around the area for a decade and little surprised him any more. He'd had such high hopes. For a brief moment he wondered if it were time to move on, to find a quieter way. But then he thought about the people here, their need of him. He felt it was his duty to help them. He inhaled deeply and continued to make his way up the tranquil street. Nothing stirred, not a sound, until he arrived at Janice's front gate.

'Morning, Reverend,' Maggie piped up from her window

above. Mark stopped and raised a hand above his eyes to shade them from the sun.

'How are you keeping, Maggie?' he asked jovially. Maggie was a local character, although, with her Catholic spirit, one who'd never grace his pews.

'I've been better,' Maggie began confidingly. 'What with all this trouble this morning I'm feeling a bit shaken up.'

'Terrible, yes, terrible,' agreed Mark. 'In fact if you'll excuse me, I was about to pay Janice a visit.'

'She's been home a while,' Maggie informed him. 'And the police have just given up waiting for Marlon to return.' She nodded towards his car. 'I told them I'd call if he showed up. No point in them hanging about with me here to keep a neighbourhood watch. You just knock hard, now. If she doesn't come straight away, knock again. She may have taken to her bed.'

Mark descended into the basement. His initial knock met with silence, so he followed Maggie's advice and banged again on the black door, a little harder. Still nothing inside stirred. He tried once more, was about to leave a card when he sensed a presence, glanced in through the nets and spotted Janice peering out as if through a shroud. Moments later he heard her unlocking the door.

'Mark,' she said, apprehensively.

The vicar looked in at Janice, standing there in her towelling dressing gown, grey hair tightly permed like a scouring pad, face as hollow and ageing as an old boat left in a dry dock. He was shocked by the change in her appearance since Eddie had died. Then she'd been middle-aged and now, as if with the flick of a switch, she'd become old. Janice's arms were tightly folded across her chest and she certainly wasn't moving aside to let him across the threshold.

'Heard about Shelly this morning. I thought you might need someone to talk to,' he offered. 'It must all have been very upsetting – with Demi and everything.'

'Everything?'

'Well the hospital, the disturbance in the flat.'

Janice eyed Mark and wondered how far she could or should trust him. After Marlon's call she had lain awake and fretted. She felt hazy and her bones ached from being on her feet all night. At least her next shift was mainly on the checkout and she'd be sitting down. They needed someone to talk to, that was for sure, her and Shelly.

'You better come in,' she said. 'Don't want the whole street listening in.'

Maggie heard the door click shut and sat back on her stool with a deep sigh. She would have enjoyed hearing a bit more of their conversation, wondered what it was Janice was about to confess to the vicar. She liked Mark, but in her view he was still a bit young to be sharing in your spiritual needs – Protestant, too. When she was a girl it had been considered a sin even to cross the threshold of their churches. She remembered him arriving, fresh-faced and eager; the year New Labour had got into power. He reminded her of Tony Blair; was about the same age and had the same high hopes for social change. But neither had counted on the mounting effects of those terrorists – or the drugs.

It was coming up for eleven thirty; always the quietest point in the day. Generally, it was the one hour when you could be sure nothing would occur. People were by now settled into their morning tasks, and although their stomachs might be starting to growl, it wasn't quite time for lunch. By ten to twelve some would be on their way back again, mums with their toddlers, local workers for their lunch breaks – if they were local enough to get home in the middle of the day – and the shift workers from the hospitals to their beds for some daytime slumber. But for now Meanwhile Street was tranquil, pretty, unencumbered.

Loneliness took a swirl inside Maggie as the breeze lifted the blossom up momentarily from the pavements, then let it fall again. Azi would be showing up at around a quarter to, she consoled herself, with lunch. Maggie was peckish today, what with all the commotion. She'd already been up for hours. Usually, truth be told, she didn't have much of an appetite; could survive on a bowl of soup alone. It was something to do with the permanent ache under her ribcage that spread outwards and through her like an irregular pulse. She should go to the doctor's, she knew, but something was stopping her. She wasn't sure she needed to hear what they might say. Just felt the need to let it all be. But she liked Azi coming all the same, it gave her a routine. And today, after filling her in, she might even be up to a bowl of that creamed rice for dessert.

Maggie sat watching and the street remained silent. She was heading for a light reverie when a movement from the end of the road caught her attention. She sat back a little and picked up her vanity mirror, then angled it to see the end of the street without peering out too far. A couple of hooded youths were loitering at the corner. One of them jogged up the street slowly, reaching into the pocket of his bagging black pants as he moved. He pulled out a remote, pointed it at Marlon's car and flicked the locks up. Without a moment's pause he was in the jeep and had taken off. It wasn't Marlon, but his younger brother Stevie. He'd chosen the right moment; there'd been no one around to witness his approach – or his speeding departure, either. Best she call that officer.

Maggie felt in her pocket for his card and was about to get herself down off her stool to reach for the phone when she became aware of a clunking sound. The top of young Connor Ryan's head now appeared from his basement well. The boy was bending down, dragging something heavy up the steps. She watched with rising curiosity as he stopped at the top and crossed to her side of the street, pulling a navy blue case behind him, like a disobedient dog. The wheels rattled up on to and along the pavement awkwardly as he headed towards her. Maggie sat watching quietly until Connor was standing directly beneath her window. He didn't look himself; was jittery, and if she wasn't mistaken, he had a purpling bruise about his left eye. The poor wee beggar, she thought with a pang. Someone must have hit him.

'Are you all right there, young Connor?' she called down kindly. 'You look as if you've seen a ghost.'

Connor looked up at Maggie woefully.

'I was hoping I could ask a favour, Maggie,' he said.

Connor looked wasted, small and dirty, she thought,

just as he used to when he was younger. In those days she'd pick him up and give his face a good lick and polish with a cloth, then sit him on her knee with a drink and a rich tea biscuit while she told him tales passed on from her own mother. In some respects, Connor was the closest she'd ever got to having her own child; when she was a nanny she was always respectfully sidelined, kept in her rightful place, but with Connor it was different. For one he had Irish blood, and for two, any love he got was critical because it was rare. Maggie nodded and threw him her keys. Connor caught them in a single hand.

'Come right on up, dear,' she said. 'And I'll fix you a glass of squash.'

Ten minutes later and Connor was sitting on the settee with Maggie next to him, holding a drink and a biscuit. He wasn't interested in them, just sat looking miserably at his grubby hands. The sofa was a bit too low for Maggie these days and her legs were stretched out wide before her, the tops of her pop socks showing just beneath her knees, her pale blue housecoat slightly too short to cover them up. By contrast Connor sat forward with his blue-nylon-covered legs crossed at his ankles, and his knobbly elbows, poking out from a faded, nondescript grey T-shirt, on his knees. His hair smelt musty as an old junk shop, his clothes of stale sweat and dead smoke.

'Now then, dear,' Maggie said, 'what's troubling you?'

Connor glanced up at her sideways, as he used to when he was small, but his green eyes were dull, his mouth set in a grimace.

'I can't take any more, Maggie,' he croaked.

His voice was hoarse, either from shouting or crying.

Maggie knew what he was talking about: that it was to do with Joe. For once she didn't offer him advice, knew too well you couldn't come between a father and a son. The trouble Connor was talking about ran down the years, through the generations, like a curse. It wasn't something you could solve in a day.

'He gets so pissed and then he whacks me,' he mumbled, 'even if I'm sleeping. I don't know what I'm supposed to have done.'

Self-pity made Connor's body tremble. Maggie put a consoling arm around his shoulder and patted gently. The trembling increased and Connor emitted an immense snort as a series of shudders overtook him. His shoulders heaved with the effort of it and tears poured down his cowed face. He was like a river whose banks had broken, she thought, all that tension released, flooding out. She let him be and minutes passed.

'There, there, Connor,' she consoled, as he eventually began to calm. 'Don't cry now, child. The air will clear.'

Connor's head jerked up and he looked at Maggie, square on. His mood had shifted, from fragile to combative. He wiped an arm across his face and then across the front of his T-shirt.

'I've cleared out and I ain't goin' back.'

'How about your mum? Maybe it's time to get in touch with her?'

Connor looked confused, wiped his face again, directly with his T-shirt this time, then looked down, between his knees.

'I've got no mum. The cow fucked off before I could run fast enough to chase after her.'

Maggie felt pained, patted his back again.

'Anyway, how am I supposed to get in touch with her now? I don't know where she is,' he added unhappily.

'Your mum was only a bit older than you when she had you, Connor dear. She couldn't cope with your dad. But things might be different now. She'll be older, wiser. Maybe she needs you to give her a little encouragement. Someone must know where she's got to. A mother never forgets her child. She loved you, you know. She used to sit on those steps with you on her knee and sing you nursery rhymes. Until it all got too much, she never left your side.'

Although Connor's face still held its steady frown, he seemed to be settling down, absorbing her words.

'Your mum wasn't a bad sort, Connor,' she went on. 'She would buy you sweets and take you to church. She tried her best but in the end she just couldn't cope with the drinking.'

Connor seemed to bristle at this, sat up a bit straighter and took a sip of his orange squash.

'What was there to stop her taking me with her, then?' he asked. 'She left me with him and look where that's got me.'

'Connor, maybe you should start going back to school. You can stay put here for a bit with me if you like. I've got the back room. There's a divan.'

He shook his head. 'There's nuffink for me at school. I'm already excluded and I'm leavin' next month anyway. They've all given up on me. Best I just disappear.' With that, Connor got up. 'Can I leave my stuff here, Maggie? Just for now.' He rubbed his eyes on his forearm and snorted revoltingly. 'Just till I get myself fixed up with somewhere else to go?'

'Just wait a few more minutes, dear,' Maggie said. 'Remember how you used to play chess with Gerry? You were so good at that. You'd sit here at the table with him for hours, playing and chatting. Shall we have a game now? It'll calm you down.'

Despite himself, Connor grinned at her and for a moment they were back there, before he was old enough to understand the reality of his lot. But before she could respond his thoughts had shifted and the grin had retreated.

'I've got to go, Maggie,' he said earnestly. 'I have stuff to sort out. Maybe I'll come back and we could play later?'

There was something Connor wasn't telling Maggie; she could sense it. He was even more guarded than usual. The thing with teenagers was that they couldn't find a way to communicate even when they had something they desperately needed to say – particularly then, in fact. But she also knew better than to push when the time was wrong for confessions. She'd try again later, when he was calm.

'Why don't you just lie back there and close your eyes, young Connor Ryan,' she soothed. 'I think you could do with forty winks.'

But she knew it was too late. Connor was already half-way out of the door.

'Thanks, Maggie,' he said, turning to her dully, all his emotions now cleaned out. He looked younger again, she thought; and for a moment absolved. 'But there's stuff I need to do, people I have to see. I'll check in with you later.'

Maggie nodded sadly and watched as Connor hesitated. She thought she glimpsed a moment's conscience cloud his green eyes. Then he moved forward and pecked her lightly on the cheek, turned and went. By the time she got back to the window there was no sign of him, or of anybody else. Azi was late. In Meanwhile Street the trees continued to rustle and the pavements were empty but for their fallen petals.

Mother of Jesus, she thought suddenly. Marlon's jeep. I forgot to phone the police.

7

At 11.45 the toddler session ended at Lizzie B's. Aishah had firmly replaced her veil and the carers and kids were making their way out of the drop-in in clusters. It was very noisy. Everyone was keen to get their toddlers home with enough time for lunch and a nap before going to collect their older siblings from school at three – apart from Melina, of course, who was determined to go directly to the stores, whether Helene was tired or not. She couldn't wait until the weekend because no doubt Lulu would leave her with both of the kids, and there was no way Melina would take Troy to a shopping mall. Life was too short. In the past half-hour Demi had rejected Helene as a playmate in favour of Milo, and right now the two of them were busy wrestling one another on the floor while Melina buttoned up Helene's navy wool coat, and Katya retrieved their two buggies. Ranika had not left one for Demi.

'She'll just have to walk,' Katya reasoned. 'It's only one block.'

Other women were also busy strapping in their over-tired infants and one by one were shoving them out of the swing doors. Aishah stood waving each one off, until only Katya and Melina remained inside. Melina plonked Helene into her seat and gave her a sippy cup of juice.

'If you want meet me at school, quarter past three. I pick up Troy then; yes?'

Katya agreed as she grabbed hold of Milo, lifted him up. Demi continued to writhe on the floor, giggling with her booted feet in the air.

'And I will tell you all about my cup of tea with Zahir,' she added, glancing down at Demi. 'But first I must take Demi h—'

Katya's words were interrupted by a loud grunting sound, then a yelp. Both girls turned as Aishah tumbled across the floor and landed on her bottom next to Demi. Two young black men shoved their way past her. Before either of the au pairs could grasp what was occurring Marlon had grabbed Demi. In one swift move he had tucked her like a roll of carpet under his arm and hauled her out of the nursery, Stevie following behind. The whole event took less than thirty seconds. Melina helped a shaken Aishah back on to her feet and she went to peer out of the doors again, just as Marlon's jeep raced off up the street, tyres squealing.

'The idiot,' Aishah said. 'That is not how you're supposed to pick up your kid from school.'

'Who was it?' asked Katya.

'Marlon of course, and his brother. They often pick Demi up, but something's wrong. I'd better call the police.'

Immy was hovering on her front doorstep when Katya and Milo entered Meanwhile Street, her head craned up towards Maggie's window on the other side of the road, where both the old lady and Azi could be seen leaning out. Ranika was standing below the window with another police officer. As soon as Immy saw her son she ran down the steps, out of the front gate and up the street, pregnant belly forgotten, and grabbed the rather dozy and now bemused Milo from his buggy. She held him up close to her, his short legs curling about her waist, above her bump.

'Poor, poor you,' she murmured. 'The policeman just told me what happened.'

'Is OK,' Katya replied nonchalantly. 'They did not want Milo, it was Demi, Shelly's one. It must end in their tears, not yours.'

Immy attempted to smile through the blur of her tears. Katya combined an impermeable outer shell with a pragmatism that was foreign to Immy. She felt the need to be close to Milo after this. 'I'll feed Milo, then put him down,' she said impulsively, 'and I won't go swimming. I have a hospital appointment this afternoon, so can you take over again from me at two thirty instead?'

'Of course,' replied Katya smoothly. She was pleased. It would give her more time to see Zahir. 'Then I take Milo to tea at Melina's.'

As she skipped down the basement steps she could see Zahir sitting at the window poring over his computer. She tapped on the glass. When he saw Katya he leapt up and opened the door. Then they stood grinning at one another.

'We go to Baghdad Café?' he suggested. 'They make the best mint tea.'

Katya nodded. The café looked great. It had only opened the month before, down at the other end of Reeling Road. It was an Arabic hang-out, more like those you usually passed on the Edgware Road, not the kind of place a white Eastern European girl would go alone. But she liked the idea of being seen there with Zahir. It was exotic, filled with frenetic Middle Eastern music, heated debate, delicious-looking hummus, halloumi and buckwheat salads, flat breads and freshly squeezed juices. Narghiles lined the pavement tables outside. There was a back room full of computers, too, cheap Internet access. She wondered if Zahir would offer to pay.

'Come, one minute,' he added, beckoning her inside. 'I need to turn off the computers.'

Katya followed Zahir into the spotless white hallway, devoid of personal objects other than a couple of large brown suitcases leaning against the wall. At the end of the corridor the door into what she imagined was the kitchen was shut. Behind it she could hear the dog barking. Zahir shouted something foreign towards it, then turned left into the front room. He began talking to someone and she imagined his flatmate Jaka was there. She'd half hoped they would stay inside, in private. She followed Zahir into the room and was surprised to see, instead of Jaka, a familiar-looking young white boy sitting at one of the computer terminals, back to the window.

He lived further down the street with his dad; had the appearance of a street urchin from Prague in his old grey T-shirt and blue nylon tracksuit bottoms. There was a purple bruise around his left eye. He looked as surprised to see Katya come in as she was to see him there. They exchanged a brief, questioning glance but no words. At the same time Zahir hit the screen saver on his monitor and whatever he was working on flashed to an empty blue.

'Come back later, if you want,' he said to Connor, who now got up and slipped past them both without a word.

'You friends?' Katya enquired casually as the boy let himself out.

'Something like that,' Zahir replied neutrally.

Katya felt butterflies stir in her stomach. He was very commanding, very handsome.

'You ready?' he asked.

'I guess,' said Katya but she stayed where she was, blocking the door to the hallway, with one arm resting on each post. Zahir laughed and she laughed too as he approached her.

'I can't get past,' he said in mock complaint.

'First you must give me a kiss,' she replied. 'And then maybe I let you go.'

8

Marlon was sitting in the jeep's driving seat, drumming his fingers manically on the steering wheel. A sheen of sweat glistened on his brow and his eyes looked shot. Stevie sat beside him, eating a sub and drinking Lucozade Sport. They'd been holed up in a friend's lock-up in Hendon for the past hour, with Demi strapped into her car seat in the back. Marlon had shoved her dummy in her mouth and she'd gone off to sleep without a murmur. Being with him was normal to her, even if their exit from the nursery had been rougher than usual. It didn't ever take her long to settle when she was with him. Next, he had texted Shelly: 'I've got Demi. Get the case by 2nite. Mickey's in the hood.'

Then the two of them had sat there wondering what to do next. The rest of their crew had chosen this moment to vanish. Your gang knew when you were in too deep. Mickey was scary, ran one of the biggest rackets in north London: cocaine and smack. He'd recently done a stint inside and had come out harder and, if it were possible, scarier. He was renowned for his happy use of violence. It was rumoured he'd personally done three murders; ordered a handful more. He was an old schoolmate of Marlon's dad, who was currently doing time for aggravated assault, although Marlon had never mentioned that to Shelly. Just told her he was back in Jamaica for a while.

It was beginning to sink in that they hadn't thought this through properly. They didn't know what Shelly was playing at. After Stevie had picked up the jeep, their decision to kidnap Demi had been reached in a flash of inspiration – they could use her as a bargaining tool. Everything else had happened too fast. Shelly had been determined this morning not to give Marlon Demi's suitcase; she'd said it had gone missing from the flat, that her mum must have put it away, or lent it to someone. They'd have to wait for Janice to come back from work to find out where it was. And that was when he'd hit her with the butt of his gun. Now the boss was after him and if he didn't find the fucking stash then he had told Marlon he wouldn't be seeing his twentieth birthday.

'What we gonna do next?' Stevie asked his older brother, trying to sound casual. Marlon shrugged, cut some more coke.

'Might help us figure it out,' he snorted another line, breathed it in deeply, hoped to lose his anxiety, but it didn't work. He had sweat on his brow. Nerves and drugs. Bad combination. Made your pulse race too fast.

'Maybe Shelly wasn't lying, maybe her mum really has lent the case to someone,' he said.

'Maybe she never understood it, why you sent them to Mexico,' replied Stevie. 'Maybe Shelly never said nuffink to the old girl.'

'There was no sign of the pigs when you got the jeep,'

said Marlon. He sat up straighter, turned to Stevie. He'd come up with it, a solution. 'We'll go back now, with this,' he nodded towards his crotch. The handle of a pistol was poking out of the waistband of his jeans. 'I'll tell her I'll hurt Dem if she won't tell me.'

Stevie nodded enthusiastically.

'Let's do it,' he said.

With the coke taking effect Marlon and Stevie suddenly felt invincible, their energies rising again with the drug racing merrily through their veins, dancing behind their temples. They each had another line so the high would stay with them for the trip, then left the lock-up and began to drive back west. Within twenty minutes they were turning back into Meanwhile Street, 50 Cent pumping from the stereo in time with their heartbeats. Demi dreamed on, oblivious; her head on one side, dummy now fallen from her mouth into her lap.

The music blocked all other sounds from the city, so it wasn't until they were slowing into Meanwhile Street that Marlon and Stevie became aware of a helicopter circling directly above them. It was followed by police cars coming at them from all directions. There wasn't even time for a chase. It was all over in seconds. But Marlon was wired and with all that charlie in his bloodstream he felt a new rush of adrenalin. It suddenly seemed a good idea to try and run for it. Forcing the jeep into a handbrake turn, he flung open the door, then dived on to the street. Stevie crouched down on the floor of the car and hid his head in his hands. Marlon hit the tarmac running and the next thing there was an officer pointing a gun at his face and he was pulling his own pistol from the front of his jeans. Before he had a chance to release the catch he felt a massive punch, then searing pain in his right shoulder which knocked him to the ground. Blood spread quickly around him in a pool. From the force of the hit Marlon knew he'd been shot, but that he was still very much alive.

He passed out to the squawk of his daughter waking up.

With the helicopter thrumming relentlessly overhead for the previous hour, Immy was anxious. She'd paced the house in time with it, trying to follow its movements from the windows, but whichever way she gazed she couldn't quite see where it was hovering. The sound made the baby kick uneasily in her belly. This in turn made her pulse rise, just a touch. Her body ballooned beneath her skin. She felt slightly out of control with it, recalled this stage with Milo: how the baby suddenly seemed to take over, how you became the vessel, it the dominating life force inside you. It was a curious, existential feeling. After months of nurturing it inside, suddenly the baby seemed to become alien, something that needed to be expelled. She reminded herself she must write it down; it would make good copy for an article. Like Gordon, Immy was a journalist, but she was a feature writer for glossy women's magazines like *Red*, *Woman and Home* and *Easy Living*. Her subjects were love and real life and making a go of things; the kinds of features that reappeared, reshaped and repackaged, year in year out. It was not quite what she'd anticipated for herself, having hoped for something higher; but now, with this new maternal stage in her life, she could see its benefits. The main one was that she could work from home.

She popped her head around Milo's door for the sixth time since she'd put him down only half an hour earlier. She felt anxious after this morning's drama – she needed to be certain he was safe. Reassuringly, he was still sleeping peacefully in his cot; one leg thrown sideways at an angle. His mouth was slightly open and a silver line of dribble ran from it on to the sheet, leaving a small round damp spot next to his pillow. In his hand he clutched a toy ambulance. He looked so like Gordon that it brought tears to Immy's eyes; God, she felt emotional today. She wiped them away. It must be the baby; she was brimming over. She closed the door quietly, then glanced at her watch. It was two o'clock now – she calculated she'd let him have another half an hour, then wake him in time for Katya to take over.

The sound of a helicopter was definitely rising. Immy heaved herself up the stairs and stood looking out of the bathroom window at the pale blue sky, punctuated by billowing white clouds. One helicopter was moving above her, over towards the front of the house. The sudden sound of a gunshot raised her anxiety to panic. She left her vantage point, moved to her bedroom and peered out at the front. Police cars were blocking either end of the road and Marlon's white jeep was stationary at an angle, just below their window. The driver's door was wide open and a young black guy lay in the road, bleeding from a wound in his shoulder. Armed police officers stood around him guns drawn. A baby was in the car and she was screaming. Inside Immy's stomach something cramped.

*   *   *

A few minutes later, Katya left Zahir's flat and made her way up the steps to his front gate. She'd heard a helicopter and some kind of commotion going on when they were in his bedroom at the back of the house, but at the time she and Zahir had been too wrapped up in each other to take a look outside. They'd never made it to the café. Once he'd started kissing her, they couldn't stop. She was amazed they even made it to his bedroom, he nearly fucked her there and then, on the corridor floor. Her clothes were strewn across the flat and she had carpet burns down her back. Katya thought she was quite experienced but she'd never encountered such a sexual force as this; Zahir was strong and powerful and she felt ravaged by him – in the best possible way. She was annoyed by all this commotion, it detracted from her high. She wanted to hang on to it for as long as possible – until the next time.

An ambulance was creeping off up the street in silence, blue lights flashing. Five police cars and two more ambulances were littered at different angles along the kerbs like Milo's toy cars left abandoned after play. Katya glanced over at Janice and Shelly's house with mounting interest. Of course the commotion was related to their earlier scare; so it wasn't over yet – or was it? Janice was standing at the top of her steps with Demi in her arms and Mark Scoles was next to her. Evidently, one way or another, Marlon had brought the child home; but by the look of things not without a fight. That family all needed to be locked up, Katya thought. Maggie had come down from her perch for the second time in the day and was standing at her own front gate too, walking stick to hand, talking to a police officer. She caught Katya's eye.

'It's OK, dear, everything's all right now,' she called across the street to her cheerfully. 'The police have arrested Marlon and Stevie, it's all over, nothing for you and Immy to worry about.'

Katya nodded and turned to go up her own front steps. Why did Maggie think she'd be so interested, she wondered spitefully – although, of course, she was naturally curious. She would have liked to go back and inform Zahir of the commotion, but there wasn't time, she'd promised Immy she'd be home at two thirty and it was, she glanced at her mobile, two twenty-eight right now.

As she turned her key in the lock and pushed the door open she heard the distinct sound of someone wailing. Initially she thought it must be Milo, waking up from his nap, but then she listened again. It was a curious sound, deep, guttural. When she heard it a third time, she realized the sound wasn't coming from Milo's room at all, but from his mother's.

Katya pushed open Immy's bedroom door and found her kneeling forward on the floor, her arms under her head. She was groaning pitifully, her blonde hair hiding her face.

'Oh my God,' said Katya.

'It's OK,' Immy panted. 'The baby's coming, but Gordon's called an ambulance, they're all on their way.'

She grimaced as another contraction took hold of her.

'What can I do?' Katya implored helplessly.

Immy looked up, her face radiant. Amazingly, she

smiled. 'Just get Milo,' she panted. 'Try to keep him away from me. He's witnessed enough drama for one day.'

Katya picked Milo up out of his cot, headed downstairs and opened the front door just as one of the ambulances that had been in the street all along pulled up at the kerb next to their own house. Two female paramedics in green uniforms got out. She stood to one side and directed them up the stairs as Milo shrieked 'Nee naw, nee naw' with delight. He was still clutching the toy ambulance he'd pinched from Lizzie B's. Katya couldn't quite keep up with it all, one minute kidnappings, the next amazing sex, now more police everywhere, a baby arriving and then, to top it all, Milo to appease. So much for escape from reality. It was all kicking off here. Even so, the recent moment with Zahir made her calm. She kept thinking back to it, every other second. She could still feel the sensation of him, inside her. Because of it she felt strong, as if she could handle anything.

Katya took Milo down to the kitchen and turned on the TV so he wouldn't hear his mother's cries. Presently Immy was helped from the house and Katya rang Gordon to tell him to go directly to the hospital. She glanced out of the sitting-room window, with Milo on her hip. Two policemen were once more stationed outside Janice's house and now the street was well and truly cordoned off, crawling with a forensics team clad from head to toe in white suits and matching plimsolls, like spacemen searching for moon dust. Katya couldn't believe she'd missed it all. She and Zahir had been too engrossed to notice a thing beyond his bedroom walls. She thought about it again and felt a renewed flicker of sexual energy. By the time they'd finished and she'd had a shower it was all over. Marlon and Stevie had already been taken away.

She couldn't help but smile to herself as she thought about it. She couldn't wait to tell Zahir what they'd missed. No doubt he was still sleeping. And for now there was no point hanging around here. Katya needed to get going with Milo if she was to keep her appointment with Melina. She had so much to tell her, and Milo would be better off playing with Helene than pacing around the house waiting for his baby brother or sister to arrive home.

'Nee naw, nee naw,' repeated Milo as she strapped him into his buggy and set off up the street, past the space-men, in the direction of St Matthew's Primary School. Milo watched the men with his mouth wide open. Katya leant forward and popped a Chuppa Chup lolly inside.

If you didn't look closely you'd miss the entrance to St Matthew's, tucked as it was up a small cobbled mews, like the awkward crook of an elbow lodged between the long arm of the Harrow Road and the fisted knuckle of Malvern Park. But you couldn't miss the noise of the children from inside its high grey brick walls: a tropical cacophony, high notes scored over the low boom of traffic from the flyover two blocks away. This melting pot was releasing its contents of London kids through the high Victorian school gates, smallest first; every child carrying a unique mix of its parents' continents, dreams and disappointments in its eyes.

After a day in their high-windowed, airless class-rooms the boys kicked and shoved as they fled from their incarceration, nylon ties skewed, sometimes chewed, faded royal blue sweatshirts trailing in their wake, along with fleeting memories of lessons just past. The girls were less forceful, took their time, held hands and giggled in their blue-checked frocks, then looked around wide-eyed and expectant for their parents and carers.

Melina felt a slight dampness down her back, under her arms, on her brow as she stood waiting for Troy to appear. She was overdressed for this sudden change in the weather from sharp and cool to warm and humid: a red-and-purple-striped polyester tank top over a white T-shirt, faded hipster jeans. She peered over heads, looking out for Troy. She'd rushed to get here on time; strode through the underpass then up along the canal from Queensway, shoving the screeching Helene in the heavily laden buggy ahead of her. Moments earlier she'd not only smelt but tasted something fecund in the early summer air, a depth of salty moisture with the faint hint of metal or blood in it. A stream of police cars, then an ambulance, shot past her as she waited to cross the Harrow Road. Someone must be dying, she contemplated, but felt unmoved. The sirens produced a regular backdrop to all other sounds in London, like the birdsong back home in the countryside outside Krakow – white noise, which once you'd got used to you almost didn't notice any more.

Now she rocked the buggy harder, trying to appease the squealing toddler strapped inside as she chewed constantly yet without satisfaction on her stale gum. She daren't let go of the buggy or it would tip backwards. Earlier she'd gleefully attached countless plastic bags to its handles. Melina had spent the early afternoon at

Whiteleys, the classy local mall, a gleaming white edifice adorned with spouting fountains and shiny escalators to guide her into the gaping jaws of the high street's most enticing fashion stores. She'd been trying to find a present for her mother's fortieth birthday, something a bit special, and had done well. For thirty pounds she'd secured three bagfuls of designer rip-offs, mostly from H&M, some for her mum, some for herself. As a result of her trawl, however, three-year-old Helene had missed her lunchtime sleep and was overtired. Her earlier squealing was now rising to a brain-bleaching caterwaul. Melina felt at once guilty and irritated.

Earlier she'd bought the child a Happy Meal from McDonald's, but an hour on the cardboard box of delights seemed only to have hyped her up. Her crimson face was now sticky with ketchup and tears. She was still clutching the plastic Bratz doll she'd got at the bottom of the box, tucked tantalizingly in a plastic wrapper under the shiny golden nuggets she'd sucked on then discarded once they'd turned grey and sweaty. Melina reminded herself she'd have to coax the doll off Helene and clean out the crumbs before Lulu got home. Luckily the child wasn't yet speaking properly. Lulu wouldn't be pleased to know that her au pair had dragged her daughter around the shops; but what more could Lulu expect, for eighty-five quid a week? Melina was in a catch-22, but so were Lulu and Tim in their own way. She knew it wouldn't be easy for them to replace her. Helene and Troy had both grown familiar with Melina, she'd stuck it out for six months now and they were all settled into a certain routine – and to be honest, Lulu couldn't really cope with the kids, which was ironic since Melina was only twenty, and Lulu was the same age as her own mother.

'Lulu is at yoga,' she told Katya as she saw her approaching, with Milo kicking his feet restlessly, lollipop dribbling glucose down his chin.

Katya rolled her eyes. Neither needed to translate that yoga was a euphemism for countless Lulu sins, from shopping to long lunches to hair appointments, and, they even wondered, to an afternoon lover somewhere in the foreign depths of her white middle-class version of their city.

'There's been more guns in the street, the men who take Demi,' she told Melina now, 'and Immy gone to hospital to have baby.'

'Crazy this city,' Melina said, swivelling her eyes skyward.

At that moment Troy appeared, lurched himself at the buggy and slammed his school bag into Helene's face. As she screamed louder Melina grabbed his arm and wheeled the buggy round in the direction of home. Katya followed behind with Milo, struggling now to get out of his pushchair to join Troy, his older, tantalizing accomplice.

The police at the end of Meanwhile Street pulled the fluorescent orange cordon to one side to let the girls in. The forensics team was in the middle of the road under Maggie's window, and a Westminster Council pickup truck was lifting Marlon's white jeep into the air. Various neighbours were watching, mainly women and kids making their way home from school. Maggie was back at her window as the girls headed down Meanwhile Street.

Troy had run on ahead and was hanging off his front gate, watching the pickup truck. Maggie was calling out questions to him about school, which he failed to respond to in any meaningful way. The two Iraqi children now appeared from Ali's on scooters and screeched down the road towards them, faces beaming. They were wearing their own bright green school sweatshirts, crown-shaped emblems emblazoned on the front. Their school was further down the league than Troy's, a community-funded establishment without the Church of England to support it. The Kosovan kids went there too. They stopped by Troy and watched the pickup truck and the forensics team.

'Hello girls,' Maggie called to Katya and Melina. 'Any news from Imogen yet?'

Katya shook her head.

The Iraqi kids said something to Troy and nudged him in the back.

'What is it?' Melina enquired.

'They want to know which war you come from,' Troy said triumphantly.

'Which war? What do they mean? I come from Krakow.'

'Everyone here comes from a war,' the older Iraqi child, Mohammed, replied. 'You know, we came from Baghdad, after the first Gulf War.' He nodded across the street to the house next to Maggie's, where the Kosovan kids were also hanging off their railings, watching the police clean-up operation from the other side. 'Gyoza comes from the Bosnian war. Which war do you come from?'

Melina laughed uneasily.

'I guess the cold war,' she answered, and looked up at Maggie who was still smiling down at them.

'Bang bang you're dead,' shrieked Troy, making a pistol with his fingers and sending signals up at Maggie. Then he turned the fake gun on himself, opened his mouth and pretended to shoot into that.

'Bang bang,' repeated Milo.

Troy laughed maniacally, turned and shot at Milo.

'That's enough, Troy, come.'

The Iraqi kids scooted off giggling as Melina chivvied Troy through the front gate before her, then turned and pulled Helene's buggy in behind them. Katya followed with Milo, who was now kicking determinedly in an effort to get out. Helene, finally, had fallen asleep. Melina hoped Lulu might come home to take over. It was too late really for Helene's daytime nap, she'd be fractious all evening.

'I saw Lulu head off with a suitcase in her hand, just before all this drama,' Maggie called, as if reading her mind. 'Has she gone away again?'

Melina didn't respond, just turned her back and put the key in the lock. 'Sometimes that old lady is too nosy,' she murmured to Katya as the door opened. She spotted a predictable note propped up on the stairwell, her name printed on it in bold black Lulu capitals.

'Noisy – yes. Silly old cow,' Katya replied and they both giggled. Melina understood that Katya had misunderstood her, nevertheless that was also funny in its own way.

Melina shoved the buggies to one side of the hallway and went to grab the note.

'Mel, had to go to see my sister – she is not well. SORRY! Will try my best to get back tomorrow. Tim will be home late, too. Fish fingers in freezer for kids. Thanks a zillion. Lx'

Katya read it over Melina's shoulder.

'Fuckeen bitch,' she said.

9

Max bunked off Maths and got an early bus home. He'd had jazz at lunchtime and had some new music to learn, wanted to practise before he went back out. Clare had texted to say she wouldn't be home before seven, so he knew he'd have some free time without her nagging him about homework. He missed the rush and got back in forty-five minutes flat. It was five thirty when he entered Meanwhile Street. The police let him through the cordon and Maggie watched him approach. He was a good-looking boy, with thick lustrous dark hair, big dark eyes, dusky cheeks and shapely lips. He must have been nearly six foot already and was still growing. He didn't quite fill his frame yet, and walked in a slightly gangling way. But that would change. He would be handsome. You wouldn't believe he and Connor were the same age, she thought. By comparison with his scrawny appearance, Max looked like a god.

'Your mum's not home yet,' she called across to him before Max had even got to his front door. 'Did you see what happened?'

Max shook his head, leant against his front railings and

looked up at Maggie with a grin that confirmed her view that he was a good-looking boy. It lit up his face and made him look open and generous. Clare should be proud of herself. As he stood there, she told the tale for the third time.

'Do you want me to make your tea?' she added kindly once she was done.

When he was younger, Maggie used to child-mind Max sometimes, if Clare worked late, and Max knew the old lady still felt a responsibility for him – indeed for all the kids in the street, especially Con. She was their real neighbourhood watch, their municipal nan. Max found it a bit embarrassing nowadays. Hadn't she realized he was old enough to look after himself? Even so, he would hate to hurt her feelings.

'I've got homework to do, Maggie. Thanks, anyway,' he called up politely. 'Let me know if you want anything.'

Actually, Max was a bit worried for her, with all this shit going down. Some of the older kids at the other end of the street had been going round to Maggie's rather too often recently, seemingly getting in her groceries. They were part of a gang, called themselves 'The Crew', thought they were in some kind of rap video. He'd seen them showing off their blades and had heard rumour that at least one of them carried a gun, not that he'd ever seen it, hoped he never would. They called the area their 'hood', their 'end'. Max didn't trust them, worried they might be taking stuff from Maggie.

He knew Shelly too well to trust her intentions as honourable. She'd been there for ever, just like him – they'd practically grown up together. But she'd gone well wild in her teens and now he was almost scared of her. Max felt Maggie continuing to watch and he half turned to offer her a reassuring wave before slipping into his dark hall. It was always gloomy, even in the middle of the day, and he switched on the light. One wall was painted sunflower yellow, the other violet; his mum hadn't been able to decide which she preferred, so had tried out both – three years ago now. She'd never got round to choosing or finishing the job off. They'd sanded the floors themselves, so they were all uneven and if you weren't careful you'd get a splinter. Covering the half-painted walls were two hangings of Hindu gods whose names he didn't know. They'd found them at Portobello market. Above him was a glass chandelier with only two of its eight bulbs working. He picked up the post from the mat – all direct mail but for one bill from the council – then moved through to the newly decorated sitting room.

Clare had gone to Ikea up Wembley as soon as she'd got her first pay cheque. Gauzy pale purple drapes now hung in the bay window, and the two small sofas were covered in new stripy red and orange throws. 'I thought they'd cheer the place up,' she'd enthused. Max wasn't sure they didn't just miss the mark. Clare had also bought a desk, so both of them could study at home; it sat in an alcove one side of the fireplace, already stacked high with papers. He added the post to it now. The TV sat on the other side, with an ugly gas fire between, surrounded by the only quality item in the room: an original Victorian marble fireplace that had always been there. Clare had just hung a large gilt mirror above it. They'd haggled for it at Camden Lock last weekend, then carried it home between them on a crowded bus. It made the room appear bigger. Max looked up close and squeezed a whitehead on his chin, then he turned and went into the kitchen, opened the fridge and got some juice. He drank it straight from the carton as he put some bread in the toaster. Four pieces of toast and Marmite later he went up to his room to work on his latest tune.

An hour later he'd finished playing, changed out of his uniform and was ready to go out again. When he left the house, Maggie had gone, but her window was still open. The breeze pulled the net outwards, like a puff of smoke. He texted Casey and moments later heard his friend come up the front steps to fetch him. The forensics had finished their work and the police had removed the cordons, their work for the day complete. All that was left to mark the earlier dramas were two yellow signs, one at each end of the road.

Aggravated attack, 6.45 a.m.

Firearm incident, 2.30 p.m.

All info contact police . . .

You saw them everywhere in London these days, not just in the dark spots where you knew crimes took place, but halfway up Oxford Street, outside brightly lit cinemas or restaurants, in front of police stations or at Sloane Square tube, at the gates to Buckingham Palace or halfway up the Strand. When they first started to appear around the city the signs seemed to act as warnings of a silent danger, just out of reach, such as assaults and robberies. In recent months they seemed to have got more sinister. The first time Max saw a yellow sign that said MURDER it had freaked him out – FIREARMS incident, too. But it was funny what you could get used to. Now he hardly even bothered to read them. But this was different. This was on his patch and it involved people he knew.

'Wonder where Shelly is,' he said as he and Casey left the information behind them and headed up Reeling Road. He didn't want to bump into her tonight. Sometimes she showed up at the church, high and jittery. He hoped she was still at the hospital.

'My mum says it's better for all of us if they clear out, her and Janice, better for the street,' said Casey pensively. They darted across the road before the lights, descended the steps, pushed the church doors open then disappeared inside. They both thought youth club was a bit minging but it was still somewhere to go. Mark was a good guy, not like your normal vicar, youngish, more of a community worker, and he didn't wear his dog collar outside services. He also didn't care if you were religious or not, or where you came from, or, to be honest, even what religion your family practised. Everyone knew he just wanted to get the punters in. He once told Max and Mohammed that if he'd been born in Delhi no doubt he'd be Hindu, if in Iraq then, like Mohammed, he'd be a Muslim. As it was, he'd made it into the world in Norfolk, so here he was doing God's work in the Christian Church. He'd been a governor at their primary school and had taken the sports lessons with them, often offering the boys games of football in the park after school. If they thought about it, just as Maggie was their surrogate nan, Mark was a bit of a collective father figure for them all – not that Max or Casey would ever tell anyone they felt that way.

The pews had been cleared away for the club, but

things hadn't really got going yet. Kids were loitering around the edges of the church in small groups, all-male or all-female, heads down, the girls texting or whispering, the boys shoving at one another, larking about. Mark had given Max, Casey and Michael permanent use of an old storeroom behind the altar to make their music in; they had it all set up with instruments. They wanted to make a CD and were trying to get funding for studio time, laptops and software. Mark had offered to help the kids plan a concert sometime in the winter. It was now May, which gave them six months to practise. They were trying to come up with a name; had thought of 'The Meanwhile Street Crew', or 'MSC', but hadn't quite made up their minds. And they needed lyrics. No one had come up with many of those either – they'd started to download some from the Net to tinker with, but hadn't got much further. Because Michael was grounded there was no point in practising tonight anyway. They'd just hang. It cost £1.50 to come to club, but it wasn't bad – for that you got pizza, coke and TV, plus table football and snooker. Max and Casey now casually perused the crowd, around twenty in all, every face known. Sammy called out to them; she was with a couple of her mates, Solange and Tyra, huddled together like hens clucking in a corner. Casey and Max acknowledged them with half-formed shrugs and headed for the pool table. Max was sure they were being talked about, tried to ignore them. Mark was around, moved casually between the groups for brief chats, careful not to impose.

* * *

It had gone seven thirty when Clare came out of the Tube station to a text from Max informing her of his movements. She walked round the cordon and up Meanwhile Street, past a yellow police sign, assuming that it was simply calling for witnesses to the attack on Shelley this morning. She was too tired now to bother to cross the street to read it. She came through her front gate and immediately sensed a presence, glanced down at Zahir's flat expecting to see him, and was surprised instead to see Connor Ryan hanging around in the basement well.

'You all right there, Con?' she asked curiously.

He looked wan and, if she wasn't mistaken, he had a bruise around his left eye.

'Just waiting for Zahir,' he replied.

Clare paused for thought. It was strange: Connor involved with Zahir. Superficially Zahir was a compelling character. After Connor, next it could be Max. She could imagine that Zahir would like that; it would be a way to get back at Clare for rejecting him. But now wasn't the time to ask questions, to warn Connor off, or even to ask about that bruise. She didn't have the reserves.

'Come up if you want anything, love,' she added feebly and Connor nodded, looked away, as she turned and let herself inside.

Clare kicked off her shoes, slumped down on the sofa, hit the on button with the TV's remote, then groaned as she thought back to her afternoon. At four o'clock she'd switched off her PC and tidied her already tidy desk. Two copies of the funding documents were printed out and sealed in clear plastic folders before her, ready for presentation. She had slid them inside her briefcase and snapped it shut. Before she left the office she'd slipped into the Ladies and touched up her make-up, brushed her hair and, after a moment's hesitation, sprayed a touch of DKNY on to her pulse points. It was ridiculous to feel nervous and she chastised herself as she took the lift down; really she was no more than a messenger, the post girl. She caught the Tube to Liverpool Street then a bus along the Whitechapel Road, arriving at Hackney Council offices off Victoria Park ten minutes early. She'd waited outside, phoning Max to pass the time. He didn't reply so she'd left a short message. At the reception she asked for Paul Carter. The young white girl behind the desk had eyed her uninterestedly and dialled his extension.

'Voicemail's on,' she said. 'D'you say you had a meeting?'

Clare nodded.

The girl looked nonplussed, dialled another line.

'There's a Clare Mitchell here,' she said. 'Says she's got a meeting with Paul.'

As the receptionist listened to the response she glanced back up, surveying Clare with a marked lack of interest. She was no more than twenty-one, thought Clare, increasingly self-consciously.

'Yeah, right, OK,' the girl said slowly, then clicked the extension dead with a quick flick of her long inscribed fingernail. 'Secretary's on her way down,' she added and nodded towards a row of three colour-drained chairs. They looked as though you might catch something from them, like a public-loo seat. Nevertheless, it felt like an order, so Clare pulled her skirt down over the backs of her knees and sat right on the edge of one, crossing her legs at the ankles. She smiled weakly at the receptionist, who stared blankly through her and took an excessively jaw-stretching chew on her gum. Clare looked away, embarrassed to have seen it, and put her briefcase on her knees, tapped it nervously. She couldn't work out what it was about this whole scene that was making her feel so insecure. Was it the anticipation of meeting Paul Carter, or was it this charade of being a professional 'out on the block'? Suddenly she was missing the comfort zone of Meanwhile Street, of Max banging around clumsily in his room above the kitchen, pretending to do his homework, of Maggie's prying eyes. She had thought she needed this other world and a professional identity to escape to, but right now all she wanted to do was return to the security of home.

Presently a large African woman in a peacock-patterned lapa appeared and threw Clare a pitying smile.

'I'm so sorry to keep you, Ms Mitchell,' she said, holding out a hand. 'Paul had to leave urgently, his nine-year-old daughter's broken her arm and his wife needed him to rush to the hospital.'

Clare thought of her recent hopes for an evening spent in the possible company of this man, a man she hadn't even met, a married man, in fact, with a primary-school-aged child. She felt slightly sick.

'He asked that I should take the documents from you,' the woman continued, settling herself down comfortably on the chair next to Clare's, 'and that I apologize for not getting in touch before you arrived. He only got the call from the Whitechapel Hospital half an hour ago, and under the circumstances, I'm sure you understand, he had to leave right away.'

Clare nodded too vigorously and fumbled with her briefcase, handing over the plastic folders.

'Ask him to call me when he's had a chance to look at them,' she said, standing up, 'and wish him and Mrs Carter all the best.'

She left hurriedly, relieved to be back outside, breathing in the city's air, took a deep slug of pollution then began her long journey back across town.

She leaned forward on the sofa and switched channels on the TV, just in time to catch the London news broadcast that followed. Meanwhile Street appeared on the screen, in the mid-afternoon sunshine. The cherry blossoms were fluttering in the breeze and beneath them was Marlon's white jeep, being lifted on to the back of a Westminster Council pickup truck. The tale of Stevie and Marlon's antics unfolded. It wasn't a good night for Max to be out, she thought suddenly, and rifled in her bag for her phone, sent him a text, demanding that he was home by nine.

10

Melina cooked fish fingers and baked beans for the children while Katya watched the television with them in the den that adjoined the kitchen. As she prepared the food, Melina considered the day's dramas. She knew who all the people involved were, but had never spoken to any of them. Even so, the idea of such violence made her uneasy. She thought about the evening ahead, on her own again with Troy and Helene, and all of a sudden she wanted to cry, wanted to go home and see her mum. Then Katya came into the kitchen.

'Gordon called. Immy is still in labour. Why not I stay here, we feed and bath kids, then drink some of Tim's vodka?' she suggested.

Melina's mood picked up a beat.

Once the kids were fed, bathed and Milo was dressed in a pair of Troy's Pokemon pyjamas, they put them all back in front of the television and switched on a pirate of *Shrek the Third*. Then the girls returned to the kitchen. Soon they each had a large glass of vodka on ice in their hands. Melina retrieved her shopping and tried on all her purchases, one after another. The final one was a very pretty soft silk shift dress, the colour of caramel. Katya took her make-up from her bag and painted Melina's face. She made her look older, smarter, and definitely more available. Despite Melina's protests, Katya then galloped up to Lulu and Tim's room, rifled around in Lulu's wardrobe and selected a pair of very high sandy-coloured shoes. She brought them down to the kitchen and got Melina to put them on.

'You look like model,' Katya grinned, pouring them both another vodka.

Melina took a large gulp. Katya was definitely succeeding in cheering her up. Maybe she liked her more than she had so far allowed herself to. She lifted her glass up and chinked it with Katya's.

'Bottoms up!' she said, knocking the rest of the vodka back in one.

It was now seven thirty. The girls sat together at the kitchen table. The alcohol loosened Katya's tongue and as they drank she told Melina about her lunchtime exploits with Zahir. First she mentioned that when she had arrived Connor had been there. Melina knew the boy because he was friends with Clare's son Max. Clare in turn was friendly with Immy. A couple of times Connor had been round to the house with them.

'I feel sorry for this boy,' Katya said. 'He has not mother, is usually alone with that drunk father and all those strange aunts and uncles. You can see them when you walk past. It is dirty and disgusting. He is still only child.'

'Do you think Zahir tries to help him?'

Katya giggled suggestively. 'Don't know but he help me. He really is big boy,' she said.

Melina was shocked but at the same time the vodka had taken its effect, and she found herself giggling so hard that she had to leave her chair and double up to try and contain her hysterics. Tears streamed down her face, blurring her recently applied mascara.

Katya watched her for a moment with a sly grin, then picked up her mobile as it bleeped.

Baby girl born 6.46 p.m. Caesar but both well. Home by 9.15 for Immy's bag then back to hospital! G

'Immy and Gordon have daughter,' she announced.

The girls poured more vodka and raised their glasses to the new baby.

When Katya looked at her watch again it was already ten to nine.

'I must go and put Milo to bed,' she said regretfully.

A black cab had entered Meanwhile Street and pulled up outside Janice's. Shelly got out. She was wearing skinny jeans and a black leather jacket over a white T-shirt and she carried a small holdall. The left half of her face was patched with white gauze that stood out like a beacon against her tanned skin and long dark hair, which was tied back. She surveyed the street quickly then ducked down the steps to her own front door, let herself in. She could hear Janice murmuring to Demi, and approached her bedroom to find her mother in her supermarket uniform leaning over her granddaughter's cot. When she heard Shelly she turned and put her finger to her lips. Shelly nodded and left the room, went into the lounge and lit a B&H, sat on the sofa and turned the TV up. Presently Janice appeared, and leant against the door frame looking down at her daughter.

'You back then?'

Shelly nodded and took a drag.

'I've got to go, supposed to be at work half an hour ago.'

Shelly didn't answer, blew smoke into the air.

Janice watched her silently for a moment, wondering where all the innocence had gone.

'He could've killed Demi, you know that, don't you?'

Shelly looked blankly up at Janice. 'Where's the case, Mum? Where's Demi's case? If he could of had it, none of this would of happened.'

Janice let out a cynical laugh, came into the room and picked up the pack of B&H from the table, took one out and lit it.

'So that's what this is really all about. I wondered when you'd get to it. He already rang and asked me. He was going mental.'

'What have you done with it, Mum? You could get us all killed.'

Shelly's voice was rising with each syllable. Janice recognized the change coming over her daughter, had heard the tone many times before, not only from Shelly, but from Eddie too. Shelly was on the brink of losing it. Janice sat down on the arm of the same chair she'd been seated in this morning, when first she spoke to the police officers, then to Mark; then to both again, later in the day, after Marlon got shot. Mark had advised Janice to handle Shelly carefully tonight. Said they should both try and step back from the situation, just for a moment.

She had been cynical about his advice at the time, but now it returned to her and made some sense. She had not told Mark about Marlon's demand for Demi's suitcase, or that she had since worked out why he might be looking for it. She had wanted to, but something had stopped her – Eddie's adage that less was more, perhaps. Beneath the surface, however, rage was bubbling up inside her. If Shelly hadn't got involved with Marlon in the first place none of this would be happening.

'The case was empty, I leant it to Connor. I didn't know he wanted it back,' she said finally, calmly, looking Shelly in the eye. The words inflamed her daughter like a match to fuel.

'You know that's not true,' Shelly shrieked. 'Oh man, what the fuck are we going to do?'

Janice drew heavily on her cigarette. Her mouth tightened like a dried walnut.

'I wish we'd never went to Mexico,' she muttered bitterly.

They hadn't discussed this, not before, not at the time, not after, but they'd have to now, they had no choice. They'd all pretended it was normal, their holiday, a treat, a time outside things, like other people could afford to have. Janice had needed to believe it, had wanted to believe it; and she'd nearly succeeded in convincing herself it had been what it had seemed, at face value. Meeting Marlon's two foreign 'friends' at the bar had been the turning point, the moment when she'd really understood what they were all there for, but even then she had said nothing to Shelly, had not wanted to acknowledge the truth; it was too frightening. They were big dark-haired Latin men in their thirties who only spoke broken English. They wore jeans, black shirts and heavy gold jewellery. They'd bought her and Shelly drinks, Demi an ice cream on the terrace outside their hotel, then they said they wanted 'to check the quality of your accommodation'. One of them had laughed at the statement, a laugh with no humour in it. Shelly had caught her mother's eye as she'd passed them her key to their room. She did not seem surprised by the request, more defiant in the face of Janice's evident confusion. Once they'd gone into the hotel, Shelly had looked away from her mum, and taken another sip of her cocktail.

Janice found she couldn't speak, distracted herself by fussing with Demi. She was trembling, hadn't wanted to understand what was happening. It had been the moment, she'd known, that they'd got themselves into something very, very bad. Half an hour had passed. Neither of them spoke and the men never came back. Eventually they went back to their room. It was locked. Janice had the other key. They let themselves in. Nothing seemed to have been disturbed and the men had gone. The next day they had left for the airport. Nothing unusual happened after that, and they'd arrived home without a hitch. Janice had tried to put the incident out of her mind, decided to believe it was all her own imaginings, that they hadn't been up to anything after all.

They'd only been back an hour when Connor had appeared, looking for Shelly. 'She's sleeping off the jet lag with Demi,' Janice said. She was putting Demi's holiday clothes in the washing machine. Connor stood in the doorway to the kitchen watching her. He was in a bit of a mess and his left eye was red and puffy.

'What's been going on?' she asked. 'Looks like someone's had a go at you.'

'Had a run-in with my dad,' he told her. 'I'm off out of there. Came to tell Shell.'

It had seemed to make sense to lend him Demi's empty case, to pack his stuff in. It was sitting there, by the front door. She sort of wanted to get rid of it, of anything that reminded her of the holiday. Felt easier without reminders lying about. It wasn't until Marlon's call this morning that it had dawned on her that the case might not have been quite as empty as she'd thought, after all. It had been heavy, for sure, but she'd assumed that that was the way it was made. Or had she?

'Marlon organized it all, before we left. The cases, they were specially designed,' Shelly said heavily now. Her hands were shaking. She took another drag on her cigarette. 'Mine was the main one and he's got that, yours was clean.'

'Well thank you for leaving me out of it,' Janice snapped.

'But Demi's had certain things inside the lining . . . things he needs. Now he's in custody God knows who'll be sent round to get it off us. We're all in shit, Mum, deep shit.'

Janice didn't really need to hear it; she'd worked it out already. Since Marlon's call this morning, she'd pieced it all together. When she'd been clearing up, she'd noticed that Shelly's case had gone. Marlon had taken that one.

Demi's was smaller, must have been used for the overflow.
'It's not too late,' Janice replied waspishly. 'We can get it back from Connor.'

'Why the fuck did you give it to him?'

'He came over yesterday, looking for you. Seemed upset, Joe had 'it him. Said he was leaving. I lent him the case so he could pack his stuff in it.'

Shelly got up. Her temper was rising again.

'How could you be so fucking stupid?' she shouted. 'Why d'you think it was so fucking heavy? When Marlon came for it he went fucking mental.'

She grabbed her bag and made for the door.

'I've got to find Con, now. Before one of Marlon's friends does.'

Janice got up too and grabbed her daughter firmly by the wrist.

'Not now, my girl, I'm off to work and you can't leave Demi on her own, not tonight, not after all that's gone on. It's not safe.'

Shelly hesitated, then sat back down and got her mobile phone out of her bag, started texting frantically. Then she dropped it on the sofa, lit another cigarette and took a long drag. She blew smoke out from the uninjured side of her jaw as Janice wearily put on her coat and made her way to the front door.

'You're in no fit state to do anything but sleep. Lock yourselves in, don't answer the door or the phone and when I get back in the morning we'll go round your Aunty Betty's,' she ordered.

* * *

Max spotted Con slouching against the church hall's wall looking jumpy and dishevelled, the bruise purpling around his left eye.

'Shoot some pool?' he said encouragingly, but Con just shrugged and remained where he was, watching, scratching every now and then at his neck, his arm. Max felt a pang of guilt. Connor seemed out of sorts, on edge – and although he didn't particularly like the guy they had a history, shared a past. It was a bond, whether he liked it or not. No choice. They'd all been at St Matthew's together, he, Casey and Con, Shelly and her lot too, in fact, but they'd been three years older. Con had always smelt of stale chip fat, never washed his hair, always had nits. He only had one school sweatshirt and as the year went on it would become progressively grubbier and more threadbare. He used to chew his sleeves. He'd never had the confidence to do much, could have been good at sport but always hung back. He'd had a wicked sense of humour and a random way with words which was rare, could always turn a quiet phrase to throw a teacher off course. Now their threesome had split and Casey and Max hardly saw Con any more, apart from at youth club. Casey and Max tried to stick together through thick and thin but it was harder even for them, now their bus journeys to school took them in opposite directions across town.

Max thought for a moment of going over to talk to him but then Mark approached Connor, so instead he turned to shoot another ball.

Connor was slouching against the stacked chairs, looking at the floor. Mark got the sense he was feeling under pressure from someone or something – no doubt to do with Shelly's lot. He decided to see what he could find out, and casually asked him how it was going.

'Alrigh',' Connor replied, kicking at one scuffed trainer with the other.

'Looks like you had a disagreement with a brick wall,' said Mark. 'Does it need seeing to?'

''snuffink.'

Connor continued to look down at his feet, drummed his fingers against the chairs. He couldn't quite keep still. Seemed on edge. Mark stood quietly next to him for a while, watching the other kids. He thought Con might wander off, but when he didn't, he tried again.

'Hear you're not so crazy about school at the moment.'

'Not worth it, leave next month. I uhmm . . .'

Connor faltered, stopped short and glanced momentarily at Mark.

'Go on.'

'I've left home,' he concluded, flatly.

Now Mark understood the origins of the bruise. He felt a twinge of anger and a thud of disillusionment. Joe was pathetic and limited and he drank. It had always been the case. But in all the years he'd watched this family, Mark had never known him to hit Connor. Even so, it came as no surprise. Mark tried to disguise a sigh. He didn't know how to take kids like Connor through the eye of the storm and pull them out the other side, as well-adjusted adults who would not make the same mistakes their parents had made. He was no longer convinced it was possible, not even with God by his side. When he began here, he had believed his church could make a difference. But he was no longer sure.

'How about we sit down tomorrow and run through some options?' he tried, nevertheless. 'Tonight you can sleep at the vicarage if you like.'

'Can't,' Connor retorted quickly, glancing towards the church entrance. 'Got stuff to sort out.'

'If you're in any kind of trouble, Connor, I will try to help you,' Mark said carefully. 'We can talk about it. Before it gets out of hand.'

Connor's face visibly softened and he looked down at his old trainers again. Mark felt the urge to pat the boy's shoulder reassuringly but knew you had to be very careful about physical contact with these youths; such innocent gestures could be misconstrued. He was clear about the boundaries, never overstepped the mark.

'Your God can't help me, and nor can my dad's,' Connor mumbled. 'Catholic or Prod, makes no difference. Out there the evil's stronger.'

Mark understood his cynicism, how could he blame Connor for it? God had done nothing to help him. Lorraine's lip service to religion hadn't stopped her leaving him, and his father showed no commitment to his Catholicism other than through his curses.

'What about your mum?' he asked. 'Could you stay with her for a while?'

'Don't even know where she is,' Con replied. 'Fat lot of use she's been.'

'OK,' Mark replied gently. 'Wait here, let me get something from my office. I won't be a tick.'

As he headed up the stairs, Mark thought about Lorraine. She'd been a regular at the church just after Mark took over: a Northern Irish Protestant with a pretty yet untrusting face, a sharp tongue and an even sharper eye for an opportunity. She'd bring the child along to the church with her on a wrist leash, still sucking on a dummy, a couple of years after it was strictly appropriate. Connor had been the most charming of children, with his mother's golden hair that gleamed like syrup, and her appealing looks. He remembered Lorraine's smile, the same as Connor's, the kind of smile that carries the pain of disappointment in it. Lorraine had not had it easy. She'd once confided in Mark that she'd married Joe when she was a rebellious teenager with an overwhelming desire to kick out. He'd been a few years older than her, had the gift of the gab and a bit of money to treat her right. At the time he'd had a job as a scaffolder – was raking it in.

They both came from Kilburn and his Catholicism had been part of the appeal. It had had the desired effect of alienating her from her parents, which in turn had made her feel independent. There were five of them in Lorraine's family, Mark recalled, all holed up in a high-rise off Kilburn High Road. Lorraine had needed an out. But she'd only been seventeen at the time and when Connor came along she was still a month short of her eighteenth birthday. By the time Mark met her Lorraine was twenty and suffering the consequences of her adolescent whims. Joe's drinking was already out of control and he hadn't worked for more than a year. They were living in the basement council flat on Meanwhile Street and a couple of Joe's cousins had recently moved in. Lorraine had complained to Mark that they spent their days gambling in the betting shop off the corner of Reeling Road, and their nights watching the TV. When he came home Joe was often restless and a bit handy with his fists. Mark had felt sorry for Lorraine back then, had wanted to help her and Connor to get away from Joe. But Lorraine soon found a different, more self-interested distraction.

In his congregation was a man called Sherman Brown, a gentle West Indian with a ravine-deep laugh and shimmering eyes that flickered with the promise of escape. He'd been an irregular attendant at the church since he was a small boy, had been raised on it from the late fifties, when he had first arrived on the Beethoven Estate from Jamaica with his parents and two brothers. Sherman was a simple fellow, worked in the sorting office off Malvern Park. Lorraine fell for his ease of nature, for the opportunity. It surprised and somewhat dismayed Mark that when she finally left Joe for Sherman, she didn't take Connor too. It was as if she needed to begin afresh, that Connor was part of Joe, part of her past. Mark had tried to persuade her to go back for her child but he sensed growing repulsion for Connor in Lorraine, for all he represented about herself. He had become a symbol of her misery and her shame. She couldn't carry him into her future and survive. So she'd left him with Joe and vanished to south London on the arm of her new suitor. Neither had been seen in the church since, but rumour told of a continuing involvement with an assemblage of infants now draining their underwhelming resources. Maybe she kept having them to block out the memory of her firstborn.

* * *

Mark picked out the housing files and made his way back into the church. He looked around. To his dismay, Connor had vanished.

'Gone,' mouthed Max, pointing at the doors.

Mark frowned deeply, approached the pool table and put the file down on the wooden edge.

'What did he say?'

Max shot another ball as Mark watched thoughtfully.

'Nuffink,' he said, 'but I reckon he's in shit.'

'What do you mean?'

'It's Shelly's lot,' Max replied, then moved around the table to take his next shot. He wasn't going to say anything else.

Mark understood and didn't push him. Instead he stood back against the wall, where he'd been with Connor moments earlier, and monitored the kids as he tried to think what to do. He'd endeavoured to keep an eye on Joe and Connor after Lorraine had gone, and to give his father his dues, Joe had tried hard to care for the kid, with the help of various 'cousins' who came and went – generally people who needed a roof for a while. And of course there'd always been Maggie, ever eager to take a hold. Connor had made it to school at St Matthew's most days, and Mark had always encouraged him to join in after-school clubs, football down the park and so on. He was naturally lithe, quick on his feet, but had no confidence about him, would hang back, wait to be picked for the team and always played in defence, would never come forward on the attack. He had the ability but none of the esteem. Occasionally Mark would spot Joe with Connor in Malvern Park. Connor would be playing on the slide, the swings, Joe sitting on a bench with his friends, a can of Special Brew in a brown paper bag by his thigh.

Now Connor was losing his lustre; often looked haunted and watchful. Inevitably he'd become a teenager who was harder to love than his infant self had been. He'd lost his golden hair to a number one at the barber's shop and his rather soft physique had given way to a sinewy, malnourished teenage frame, a scrawny body that had a touch of the feral about it. Mark assumed Connor had had his hair cut off in the name of self-protection and maybe finally to get rid of the nits. Throughout his childhood Connor had itched. He also had his mother's way with words; was quick-witted when he needed to be. If challenged he could always find a phrase or two to divert attention away from himself. The thing about Connor, Mark knew, was that he wasn't the failure; it was the system that had failed him.

Mark wanted to do something about that now, before it was too late. He pondered what the options were as he stood there, observing the other teenagers. They were all socializing, not getting up to tricks but learning the skills of adult life: the interaction, coping with the first waves of attraction for the opposite sex. Connor, on the other hand, was back out there roaming about in the dusk, no doubt alone. Mark wondered about care. At fifteen it was hard to persuade a child that it could be a good thing. It was on the cusp of being too late. He wondered about the church, whether once he was sixteen, a temporary solution might be to let him come and stay at the vicarage, which comprised a series of rooms behind the church building: a kitchenette, a study, a sitting room and two small bedrooms. Connor would then be old enough, legally, free to make his own choices, whether to stay or go. Perhaps he could help out with the soup kitchens, the various church events. The hall needed painting, too. It might get him focused, keep him off the streets. He'd think about it overnight, Mark decided, then make some enquiries for the immediate future in the morning.

He tried to focus on the rest of the kids now, moved forward to talk to a group. The boys were starting to mess about, to get a bit more rowdy without his attention on them, and the girls were shrieking more loudly. He watched as Solange sidled up to Max with a sideways grin and asked if they could have a chat outside. Max shrugged to cover his embarrassment, glanced at Mark, gauchely. Mark grinned back as Max casually followed her through the swing doors and out on to the darkening street.

'Sammy asked me to talk to you,' Solange murmured to him conspiratorially as, moments later, they sat on the high wall by the out-of-order phone box, the known local score shop for smackheads after hours.

Max looked at his Nikes and tried to hide his excitement. Solange paused to survey a chip in the paint on one of her fake fingernails. Max glanced up at her. He failed to conceal the look of hope spreading over his face.

'She kind of fancies . . . Michael,' she carried on, staring straight into his give-away eyes. 'Will you find out if he wants to go out with her?'

Max looked back down at his Nikes. He felt he might fall forward with the humiliation of it. His mobile bleeped, a text from his mum.

'I love you, miss you, be home by nine!' it read and for

once he was pleased, not irritated, by her show of affection. Solange was eyeing him curiously.

'Got to go,' he told her as he put the phone back in his pocket. 'Tell her I'll see him at the weekend.' His voice shifted an octave up, then back down, uncontrollably. He pushed himself down to the ground with his hands, then began jogging off towards home. He couldn't handle any more of this teenage love stuff, it made him feel unstable.

'Wait up, Max,' he heard Solange call, but didn't look back. To his confusion, there wasn't a picture of Sammy, but of his dad crowding his head, his dad as he was about to leave last Sunday morning, standing at the foot of the front steps in his baggy jeans and white linen shirt, gold tooth gleaming as he threw Max a final shiny smile and a false promise of a summer holiday together. He didn't believe it would happen. JJ had always lied. And now Solange's words had to go and make it all feel worse.

As he turned the corner a gust of spring breeze lifted the blossom from the pavement and scattered it into the air. Night was falling. Shelly's mates were hanging out on the steps of number seven, like last night. But Shelly wasn't there; must still be in the hospital, he thought, with a moment's relief. Nevertheless, there was an atmosphere. They were all huddled a bit tighter than normal and there seemed to be none of the usual party mood brought on by early evening Class As. Then he noticed Con behind the wall, sitting hunched on the steps, his hoodie up, smoking a rollie – probably a spliff. Max raised a hand to him and Connor nodded back.

'Hiya Max,' one of the girls called out pointedly as he passed.

He heard another one titter, another say something, then they all guffawed and he increased his pace, crossed to his side of the street to avoid further interaction.

Maggie was at her window, hairnet back in place. Everything at this end of the street, at least, seemed to have returned to normal, what with Marlon's white jeep and the policeman gone from outside Shelly's house. Relief spread upwards from his belly as he noted the porch light on at home, and as he let himself in he heard the sound of Clare in the kitchen, making a cup of tea.

'Hi babe,' she called into the hall. 'D'you have a good day?'

Max cocked his head around the door. 'Yeah, all right I guess.'

Clare had changed out of her suit into a pair of jogging pants and a new white T-shirt she'd bought on the weekend up Kilburn High Road. Her damp hair was piled up on top of her head in an emerald and pink paisley silk scarf he'd bought her when they went to The Big Chill last year. It was the first time she'd taken him with her to a music festival and it had been an awakening. He would be a musician. He knew it now. Clare glanced at Max as she stirred her tea with her right hand, then leaned over to sling her left arm round her boy's shoulder.

'D'ya fancy a takeout from the Cyprus?' she said. 'I can't be assed to cook. We could eat it in front of *Celebrity*.'

Max turned to give his mum a hug. She'd taken a shower, smelt of apple shampoo and baby lotion, felt warm, reassuringly homely and clean. He didn't like it, he realized, that she got dressed up in that suit each morning and went off to work. It made him feel a gap inside – as if he was really on his own now. And he didn't like the stuff that was going on outside in the street, either. He wasn't sure how he was going to carry on avoiding it. They'd all get sucked in. It was what happened. Connor had already crossed to the other side. He wished he could think of a way to stop it, to bring Con back, even though he didn't even really like him that much any more. His failure made Max feel uneasy. It wasn't far from where he was to where Con had gone. Even Maggie supported it in her own way, he thought. He used to think his dad would be his escape route, his way out, but that was no more than a pipe dream. He hugged his mum tighter. She was smaller than him now, her head was against his shoulder.

'What's that for?' she laughed girlishly, dropping the teaspoon and turning to hug him back. Max didn't answer, just held on and shut his eyes. She rocked him to and fro like she used to when he was small, and for once he didn't mind, just stood there and let her stroke his hair.

'We'll be all right,' he heard her say, as if she knew what it was that was pulling at him, making him sad, but how could she? It was everything, and nothing, all at the same time.

'Come on,' she added, pulling away and pinching his cheek teasingly. 'Let's go get that takeout, don't know about you but I'm starving.'

While Max and Clare were getting ready to go out, Shelly scuttled up from the basement steps opposite and watched the street. Her temper was sparking, burning through her.

To extinguish it she'd need to get hold of Connor Ryan. Now she knew he had the case, all her attention had turned from her mother to him, the little tosser. If he hadn't borrowed it Marlon and Stevie wouldn't be in this shit, and nor would she. He'd pay for it; she'd make sure of it. But she had to find him first. She'd texted round but no one seemed to know where he was, or if they did, they weren't saying. Shelly waited and watched, felt jittery, in need of a fix, had had a line to keep her going but was in need of more, and she had none left. Normally Marlon supplied her. Her cheek was aching, from the cut, the stitches and the tension spreading through it from her temples. Without Marlon she was nothing; had no one, was totally alone. Her mum was wrong about one thing: he'd never have hurt Demi. He loved the kid; was always showing her off to his mates, bought her a gold slave bracelet and a pair of baby-pink All Stars. Whatever they'd done today, it was all just because of the suitcase; it was her mum's fault, stupid cow, if anyone's, for giving it away, and Connor's for accepting it.

Without the case Marlon and Stevie had been desperate and then they'd gone and blown it: aggravated assault, firearms, kidnap. They'd be inside for years. Shelly couldn't bear the idea of being without Marlon. No one else took care of her in quite the way he did. And if she was honest, she was shit-scared, too. She knew it wouldn't be long before someone came looking for her, looking for the case; someone who wouldn't stop at damaging the side of her face. She needed to get to Connor before they did. She needed to now – and she needed another hit, too. In fact she needed that even more than she needed to get to Connor. She went back down to the flat and looked in on Demi. The child was out of it. She wouldn't wake up now. Slept heavy, like her mum. Shelly went into the kitchen and dug around in Janice's various store-cupboard tins, found thirty quid wrapped in cellophane, took it and made for the door. Next thing she was up and off along the street.

The girls were hanging outside the house on the corner, at least six of them. As Shelly sidled up they all stared at her in silence, dragged on their cigarettes. She pulled herself up on the wall next to Lena, in her usual place at the end of the line, lit up herself, and waited.

'Mickey's been round,' said Lena eventually. 'Said he had a message to give directly to you. Call him.'

Shelly's hand went involuntarily up to her face and touched the gauze covering the wound. Mickey was Marlon's 'boss'. Shelly had never met him face on, and never wanted to. She always hung back when he was about. She had only ever been introduced two ranks down the line, to his minders, and that was the way she wanted it to stay. He was a big scary Jamaican in his fifties, who always wore a black suit. He was an old mate of Marlon's dad's who ran the biggest drug racket out of the Beethoven. He'd done time for murder, wasn't afraid of violence. Apparently enjoyed getting blood on his hands. She shivered.

'Marlon's really fucked up this time,' Lena added with a mean little smile. 'Won't be seeing him around for a while.'

The other girls tittered but no one spoke. Shelly wanted to scratch Lena's ugly little eyes out but she needed a fix more.

'Can you help me out, I need it bad,' she mumbled.

Lena surveyed her steadily, then turned and whispered something to the girl sitting next to her. She pushed herself down off the wall and beckoned Shelly to follow her inside. Once the transaction had been completed they reappeared. Shelly's mood lifted slightly as the drug took effect.

'It's Con,' she blurted to Lena. 'He's got something they want. He's going to fucking ruin it for all of us. Tell him, if you see him, that he needs to get the case to me, before they get to him.'

'He's only a kid, you shouldn't of got him mixed,' said one of the other girls piously.

'I didn't, it was my mum,' Shelly said, then faltered, sensing movement. She turned to its source. Connor was crouching by the stairwell. Aware he'd been caught out, he stood up and eyed her defiantly, then smirked nervously at the girl who'd just defended him. A silence had descended over the group, a sense of anticipation. Shelly's anger reignited. Con twisted to get round the gate but she stepped in front of him. His smile gone, his green eyes caught hers and flashed hopefully, then clouded.

'Where the fuck is it?' she snarled. Connor shrugged, then smirked again. 'What?'

'Don't fucking laugh unless you want a fucking eye poked out,' Shelly spat. 'Where the fuck is my suitcase?'

Some of the other girls had moved to stand either side of Shelly. Connor stood up straighter and fiddled with his hood nervously. Muttered something.

'Speak up you little fuck,' Shelly shrieked. 'Where is it?'

Connor shrugged. 'Dunno,' he said. 'Lost it.'

He tried pushing past her, but Shelly wasn't about to let him go, not until she'd got what she wanted. She gave him a little shove. Connor's hands went up and he fell back against the wall. He pulled himself back on to his feet but Shelly pushed him again as the girls drew in around him like a net. One of them pressed something into Shelly's hand, something heavy and cold to her touch. Shelly flicked it so the blade flashed under the lamplight.

Connor saw it and his eyes widened with alarm.

'Don't think I won't use it, you little cunt,' she spat.

He stepped forward again and this time dodged left, towards the one gap between the girls, but it was no good, one of the others now pushed him back and another one shoved him. He stumbled, then fell off the pavement into the road. Before he had a chance to pull himself up again the girls' feet had begun to fly. The one who had been defending Connor hesitated for a moment, then she, too, moved forward to join in.

Back at Melina's, Katya had one last vodka, then she carried Milo down the steps in her arms. It wouldn't be long before Gordon was back and she needed to get him home, into his own cot. He was already fast asleep. She met Clare and Max coming back from the Cyprus with a plastic bag of food and a large bottle of Diet Coke. They exchanged greetings and began to walk together down the street.

'Earlier I came by your house,' Katya mentioned cheerily, emboldened by the vodka. 'To see Zahir.'

Clare stopped in her tracks. 'What did you want with

him?' she asked, cocking her head to one side. Katya was pretty. It was easy to guess what Zahir's intentions were, but did Katya have any idea what she was getting into?

Katya smirked, and glanced briefly towards Max, who was observing the pavement, pretending not to listen. 'He is just friend,' she said casually.

Clare shook her head wearily. 'He's not the sort of friend you want or need, Katya,' she stated. 'Have you seen all the stuff he stores on those computers? Photographs of unspeakable atrocities, mutilated bodies, I've never seen anything so grotesque. Wouldn't trust someone who spends his days looking at stuff like that. You don't know what he might be about to do.'

Katya shifted Milo's weight slightly and stared back defiantly. 'He is human rights activist,' she replied coolly. 'He campaign for asylum seekers like himself, who want to get away from such terrible crimes against themselves. Why you don't like?'

'I wouldn't put your trust in him, that's all,' Clare replied carefully. She hesitated, then added, 'There's something going on down there, with all those computers, the dog; wouldn't be surprised to see him on a wanted list. There are terrorist cells all around this area, you only had to witness the police activities after the 7/7 bombs to know that. There's something fundamentalist about him.'

Katya felt her principles stir; it was pure, blatant racism, prejudice, that was all. She had left Prague to escape from such moral misjudgements. Maybe the woman was jealous. She wasn't so young any more, maybe lonely. Probably wished she were as pretty as Katya knew she was herself.

'Just because he is Arab does not mean he is terrorist,'

she replied, shifting Milo's position on her shoulder again. 'All people can be good, or bad, wherever they come from, whatever religion they practise.'

Clare snorted with derision. 'Whatever,' she said. 'Your life, not mine.'

While they were talking Max had moved on ahead, his attention distracted. Something was happening next to the house on the corner where Shelly and her mates hung out.

'Mum, look,' he urged.

There was a gang of kids in the road, shouting and kicking at someone or something on the ground.

'We must go, see,' Katya declared. 'Stop them.'

Clare glanced at Max whose hands were deep in his tracky bottoms, head hung low. Instinctively she would have turned straight into her front gate, but now she felt the need to regain the moral high ground.

'Stay here,' she ordered her son and began to stride towards the gang. Katya trotted behind her, carrying Milo who was still asleep and getting heavier by the moment. Ignoring his mother's orders, Max skulked up the street behind them. As they got closer, the shrieks got louder, nastier. Meanwhile a minicab came around the corner and had to pull up short on the other side of the fight. One of the doors opened and Gordon got out.

At first he didn't notice Katya and Milo, was too busy trying to see what was causing the blockade. There were at least seven girls standing in a circle and they were kicking and punching at someone in the road. Gordon felt his pulse rise and a tightening in his throat, just like he used to on the playing fields at school when someone shouted 'Fight!' He would have liked to turn on his heel as he always did back then. Instead, however, he stepped forward tentatively to get a better look.

Katya and Clare had seen him and stopped short on the other side of the gang. Both were secretly relieved by Gordon's arrival: surely he'd sort it out. But to their surprise, he didn't now intervene. Instead, once he'd glanced into the circle, Gordon stepped back and pulled his mobile from his pocket, began dialling. The minicab driver, evidently having made his own snap decision not to get involved, or to wait for his money, loudly reversed his car and pulled away.

Max had a sick feeling in his belly. There was only one person he could imagine could be in the gutter: the one person who was missing from the crowd when he'd seen them earlier on. He moved forward but Clare tugged at his arm, pulled him back again. One hysterical voice was shrieking above all the others, a voice they knew all too well. It was no great surprise it belonged to Shelly Warwick. The other girls were following their leader's example, swearing and laying into the person on the ground repeatedly with their feet, their fists and their voices. The sound of feet kicking into something soft made Max retch. He could see him now – Connor was lying on his side in the foetal position, arms up, covering his face, not even attempting to defend himself from their onslaught. Shelly was directly above him, feet kicking hardest.

'Stop it, all of you, stop!' Katya suddenly screamed angrily. She moved forward urgently, despite still cradling Milo. The child woke up and looked around, bewildered.

With the sound of Katya's voice, Gordon dropped his phone into his pocket and strode around the gang towards her.

'What the hell are you doing out here?' he demanded, wrenching his son from her arms.

Katya was about to respond but Shelly was now looking wildly up at them both, sweat on her brow, the wounded warrior with her bandaged face. She stepped back from her victim and the others followed suit. Connor was left shuddering on the ground with everyone staring down at him. Shelly turned and spat defiantly on to his face, then eyed Gordon challengingly.

'Fuck off!' she shrieked. 'Fuck you all.' Turning on her heel, she flounced off down Meanwhile Street, leaving them all staring in silence after her.

Slowly Connor pulled himself up on to his feet. Clare put a hand on his arm but he shrugged her off. Dark red blood dripped from his nostrils. Without stopping to wipe it away he too spat into the gutter and began to limp off, his walk quickly becoming a lopsided run. Within a moment he'd vanished into Reeling Road. The other girls were taking repossession of the buggies earlier left discarded by Lena's gate, and they too began to swagger off together, giggling, at their own leisurely pace. None of them seemed in a hurry to escape the scene, or in the least bit concerned by the state in which they'd left Connor, or by the man with the phone, or the threat of the police turning up.

'You deesgusting whores,' Katya hissed towards their backs.

Clare stood behind her with Gordon. Max stayed

slightly apart, looking mournfully after Connor. Gordon had handed Milo over to Katya again and was back on the phone. 'He's just left the scene, headed up Reeling Road,' he was saying. 'Yes, yes, I see. Right. Good, good.'

Lena turned back towards him. 'The pigs won't do nothing,' she sneered. 'He deserved a mashin' for the shit he's got Shelly into.'

Gordon ignored her. 'Right, as soon as you can. Good. Thanks. Bye.' He hung up.

Everyone stared at him. Gordon looked at the ground uneasily. His face was ashen and he seemed to have shrunk into himself.

'I should've gone after him, Mum,' Max mumbled disconsolately.

'It's not our business,' said Clare, reaching to hold his arm.

Max shrugged her off. 'Well then whose is it?'

'Someone should have gone,' Gordon agreed, looking between them.

'You hardly dived in, you pompous prick,' Clare blurted, putting an arm around Max. This time he let her. She could feel him trembling.

Gordon opened his mouth, then shut it again. Turned away from them and watched the end of the street, as if expecting the police to show up, or Connor to come back. Nothing stirred.

'Dunno what you're waiting for,' Clare called. 'Too late now.' She spoke gently to Max. 'Come on, love, time to go home.'

She was right. Gordon knew it. There was no sign of the police arriving, and no one left to report on the attack, in any case. It was as if nothing had happened. Lamps were sending a soft glow over the fading light. Even the trees were still. The calming breeze had died, the air was thick and flat and the street was extremely quiet. Drip by drip, rain began to fall; big, fat sploshes of it, landing on the pavements and quickly forming puddles in the cracks, mottling the blossom lying there. Max and Clare followed Katya, Gordon and Milo home silently.

The sounds of the city seemed to re-enter their senses, sirens, car engines, motorbikes, a raised voice, the deep beat of music from an open car window. Lights were on in most of the front rooms but most people still had their curtains open, the day having faded so subtly that they'd yet to notice it was gone. Some rooms were kitchens, others living rooms, bedsits or bedrooms, with embossed or striped wallpapers, or magnolia paint on the walls. Inside different lives played out: people were slouched on sofas watching TV, or drinking glasses of wine or beer, or mugs of tea; others were tapping away at computers, or cooking late dinner. Some were lying on or in their beds, talking on phones. One young man appeared naked for a moment, then pulled his curtains closed. Max nudged Clare and she almost giggled, would have done if her thoughts hadn't been with Connor. Katya, Milo and Gordon went up their steps and entered their house without saying goodnight.

'He'll be OK. Someone'll clean him up – his dad maybe,' Clare said without conviction, her arm still round her son as they headed through their own front gate.

'Yeah, right,' mumbled Max.

'He didn't seem badly hurt,' she continued feebly.

'Maybe it'll teach him to keep away from those girls in future.'

'I don't think that's the kind of lesson he needs,' mumbled Max.

As Clare followed him up their steps, the cooling take-away still in her hands, she glanced fleetingly down at the basement. The lights were on. Connor was sitting at Zahir's desk, face tilted up towards Zahir, who was standing before him with his back to the window. He had a cloth in his hand. Connor's face was highlighted by an office Anglepoise lamp.

'Maxi, love, look!' she exclaimed.

Max paused and glanced down into the basement window. Zahir was now wiping the boy's face gently with the cloth.

'He must have gone round the block and re-entered the street from the other direction,' Clare gabbled excitedly. 'While we were all standing down there, wondering what to do. He'll be all right, you see.'

Max looked confused, shrugged. He had avoided Zahir ever since his mum had implied she thought he might be a terrorist. Before that he had quite liked the guy, he had always been friendly to Max, ready to chat. There weren't many older guys around you could talk to like that. Even so, he thought it was odd that Connor should be down there.

'It's weird, him with Zahir,' he muttered, turning his back to Clare and putting his key in the lock.

Clare agreed with Max about that, but at least someone was taking care of Connor – even if Zahir was a trainee fundamentalist. For tonight, in her heart, even that would do. It meant they could rest easy. Oddly, she suddenly felt the urge to spit down into the basement, just as Shelly and Connor had spat into the street; then was repulsed by her own impulse. It was getting to her, the atmosphere, debasing her. Zahir's growing relationship with Connor was peculiar, insidious, weird, as Max said. The same applied to Zahir's relationship with Katya. What was there for Zahir to gain from any of it? He was a parasite, another symbol of everything that had gone wrong in this city, another person who was here without roots.

What were she and Max supposed to have done when the girls attacked Connor? She couldn't have had Max running off after Connor, could she? She couldn't be the one to mop it all up. It would have just involved them further, and on the other side of Connor was a well of trouble, deep water with Class A drugs swirling around in it. She wasn't prepared to go there, wouldn't allow Max to touch upon it, either. She'd do her damnedest to protect him. After all, it wasn't her fault that Connor had got into all that stuff; it was her responsibility, surely, to see that Max did not. Life was precarious enough. Even so, as she shut the door behind them, prickles of shame crept up Clare's back, making her damp beneath her clothes.

Gordon paced around the sitting room next door, trying to piece his emotions together, but his brain felt disconnected, his pulse was racing and sweat trickled from his neck down his back. He'd shifted from high elation to bitter humiliation in the turn of a corner. He'd been delighted by his daughter's birth, then knocked off balance by witnessing that fight. And he felt scalded by

Clare's personal reprimand, too. How could anyone think of him as a pompous prick? Yet, in some ways, he knew she was right; he'd judged them all for their inaction, but had done nothing himself. Gordon retraced the moment he got out of the cab. He'd seen Connor lying in the road. He hadn't known what else he could have done; the girls were laying into their victim, and he'd spotted a knife in Shelley's hand. It wouldn't have been safe for Gordon to try and stop them. Physically he was in the minority – they would probably have hurt him. And yet maybe they wouldn't have done? Maybe a show of masculine strength and authority would have deterred them from dealing further blows. Maybe he should have waded in, helped Connor up from the ground, refused to let him leave without someone's support. Maybe he should have chased after him up Reeling Road and urged him to come home and stay with them for the night; or taken him to A&E to get checked over. God knows how many breaks and bruises they'd inflicted.

Gordon knew about the dangers of taking the initiative, he'd written a series of articles about it. There'd been that poor guy recently, got stabbed in the neck on a bus for trying to stop a scuffle, another one who tried to stop a burglar and got stabbed through the heart on his own threshold. Gordon had followed the protocol, the official police line, and called 999 for assistance, rather than trying to take control of the situation himself. Shelly for one was armed and clearly out of control. Theoretically he was justified in his response. Nevertheless, Gordon's conscience was dragging at his guts, telling him he should have gone with a deeper instinct, to stop those girls, to protect that vulnerable boy. And yet at the time the instinct simply hadn't been there. It seemed to have been deadened, extracted, and he didn't know when or why. Why, when it came to dealing with violence first-hand, had he found himself so incapable of intervention?

He thought back to the morning, to Milo and Immy sleeping so gently, so soundly, and to his sense of disaffection, of restlessness. The past twenty-four hours had done one thing, at least – shaken him awake. Now he had to come to terms with the shift in perspective. He felt strangely energized. Then he thought about Immy, lying in hospital with their newborn daughter, and all the possibilities that that threw open. He realized he should feel intense gratitude for his lot and stop hankering for something more complicated, more selfish. He should throw all his efforts into making life for himself and his family healthier, safer.

They couldn't stay here in Meanwhile Street for much longer. They needed to take advantage of their privileged background, go somewhere that would give them the space and balance to enjoy the children's childhood: a safe haven. And then he needed to think about his role in society as a whole, to look more broadly at his work, its impact – or lack of it. He wasn't a doer, he knew that, he was a thinker; but maybe his thinking could have a greater effect than it currently did through his column inches? He might not be someone who could wade in and stop the rot from the inside out, but he wondered, in any case, to what extent his pontificating for the paper reached out and touched the lives of people like Connor Ryan. He'd always convinced himself that his opinions were read by the policy-makers, that therein lay his influence. But deep down he had a feeling they made very little difference. Maybe it was time to get off the paper, to get involved in an organization that had a proactive role in changing the way kids like Connor lived? His mind was jumping from theme to theme, from issue to issue; he needed to make sure that whatever he did counted for more.

Katya entered the room looking sheepish, with Immy's packed hospital bag in her hand. She'd had a quick check through it: tiny white Babygros and nappies that looked too small for a human baby, white cotton nighties, a present wrapped in Shrek paper for Milo's first visit. Everything had been considered, well in advance. 'I'm sorry,' she blurted as she held it towards him. 'I was just walking home from Melina's – we give the kids tea and bath together. Then I saw fight, it was necessary to see if someone hurt.'

Gordon surveyed her standing there looking sad and apologetic, and he couldn't feel angry. Of them all, her instinct had been the correct one. She'd gone forward, had put herself on the line for the sake of a boy she hardly knew. The problem was, in so doing, she'd also put Milo's safety at risk. It had been a day that Gordon would never like to see repeated. But he couldn't blame Katya for that, not directly. They'd chosen to live here, and it seemed this kind of incident came with the territory. He took the bag from her.

'We've got a beautiful daughter,' he said, feeling his mood rise back up a touch. Katya smiled, clearly relieved at the change of topic. 'I need to get back to the hospital.'

Gordon walked out into damp air. The rain was falling

more heavily now. It sprayed his face, cooled his temples, made him conscious of the sweat lying on the surface of his skin, of his heightened state. He was still running on adrenalin from the day, the birth, then Connor's attack. He glanced quickly up at Maggie's window. He wouldn't have minded seeing her, telling her his news, and also warning her of Shelly's recent actions, just in case the police did come by. However, like many other inhabitants in Meanwhile Street, she had now drawn her curtains. He decided to leave her alone. It was gone ten and everything was quiet. He pulled his collar up and walked hurriedly towards the Harrow Road to hail a cab. As he stood on the pavement he kept his eyes peeled, just in case he spotted Connor Ryan.

Maggie was sitting alone in her lounge, as always of an evening, surrounded by her wild-animal ornaments, brass knick-knacks, bells, boxes and little souvenir ashtrays, her photographs of Gerry and her sisters. One of them, Irene, had sent her a postcard today. She was settled into a convalescent home just outside Limerick after a recent hip operation. Maggie held the card in her hand. On the front was a photograph of a vase full of pretty pink roses. She glanced down at it every now and then as she watched the late news, waiting for a repeat of the earlier report on Meanwhile Street's drama. Sure enough, here it was again, Marlon's car being lifted into the air. If you looked closely, as she did now, there she was at the edge of the screen, just for a split second, talking to Janice and that girl Katya, who was caught on film too, leaving that African man's flat. No doubt she was up to no good.

Maggie wasn't one bit surprised. It made her heart flutter with excitement above that nagging pain, seeing yourself as plain as day on the other side of it, the telly. It was almost like being famous. She was chuffed. She had just appeared, all over the city, in other people's houses. If only Gerry had been here to see.

With the report over, Maggie heaved herself up and switched off the TV, on the set and at the mains. She moved to the kitchenette and boiled a pan of milk. It was time for her nightly cup of Horlicks before she took herself off to bed. She had half expected Connor to tip back up but she knew what teenagers were like; often they didn't do what they said, didn't know what it was that they meant to do next, even. Connor was probably off somewhere with a mate, crashing on their lounge floor, Maggie forgotten for now. She worried for him but she couldn't change this time for him, could only be there, if he needed a refuge. She'd felt flattered he'd trusted her enough to come by earlier, and was certain he'd be back soon enough. She perched in her dressing gown at the open window with her warm drink and made a last check. She felt a sharp pain under her ribs and her breath became short. It had started to rain.

Dren wandered up the street, hair full of builder's dust. He was later than normal, and she wondered if he'd been down the pub with his brothers for a couple of pints after work. He looked up at her and she caught his bright smile in the lamplight.

'Goodnight, Maggie,' he said gently as he turned in and mounted the steps to his front door. Maggie raised a hand silently and watched as Ada opened the door to him and stepped out on to the threshold. Dren took his wife in his arms and held her close, then pulled away and gave her a quick kiss on the end of her nose. Ada laughed like a schoolgirl as they disappeared inside. Then she heard their door click shut behind them.

The pain had subsided, left behind it just that irregular dull, pulsating ache that she was almost getting used to. Last month when she'd seen the doctor he'd mentioned heart disease. Maggie tried to brush the thought to one side as she finished her Horlicks and reflected on the day, on Shelly's face, Marlon and Stevie's violence, on Immy being taken off to hospital. It hadn't been your regular Wednesday; not at all. And now Maggie was too tired to sit here any longer. She took her cup and placed it on the draining board, then descended to her bedroom, slowly. It was getting harder by the week for her to get down there unaided, and the pain was becoming insufferable. She'd have to do something about it soon. She knew she would. In the hallway sat Connor's blue case. She glanced at it for a moment, then dragged it after her into her bedroom. For some reason unknown to herself, she shoved it underneath her bed and pulled her eiderdown over so that it couldn't be seen. Then she heaved herself on to and finally into her bed, took a look at the time. It was late for her, already 10.45, and she switched off the light.

11

Melina slipped off Lulu's shoes, then one at a time she carried the sleeping children up the two flights of stairs to their beds. She felt tipsy. It had been fun, chatting to Katya – like sisters, even. It was so quiet in the house that when she returned to the kitchen to clear up their glasses she was taken aback to find Tim sitting at the table. He looked tired, had deep bags under his eyes, his stripy shirtsleeves rolled up to his elbows, collar open a couple of extra buttons, displaying a few dark wiry hairs on his chest. When he saw Melina he did a double take, then he smiled approvingly. In front of him on the table he was cradling a full glass of vodka.

'I wondered why the bottle was out waiting for me,' he said, teasingly. 'Are you going to a party?'

Melina blushed deeply and wiped a finger underneath her mascaraed eyes, suddenly conscious that her tears of laughter must have caused them to smudge. When she looked back at Tim he was still observing her. He gestured down at Lulu's shoes on the floor.

'I went shopping, then Katya came and persuaded me to try on my new dress. She said I needed high shoes so

I borrowed Lulu's for one minute, just to see how it look,' she mumbled apologetically.

Tim roared with too-loud laughter. 'Put them on again, Melina, I'd like to see the full effect.'

Melina looked down at the shoes, discarded like toys on the kitchen floor. She shook her head emphatically. She felt childish, like Helene when she put on her Snow White dress and clip-clop heels, then trotted around the kitchen.

'Don't be so timid,' Tim urged. 'I'd love to see how they look. The dress is really very pretty.'

Melina knew she should refuse to do as he told her, that she should make an excuse and go to her bedroom, lock the door behind her. But Tim was in charge and she was too embarrassed to disobey. So she did as he ordered, slipped the shoes back on to her feet and faced him. Immediately she stood taller but she was shaking, too. She tried to smile her fear away but her tongue was dry in her mouth and she felt giddy in the heels. She needed to lie down. But Tim was standing up too now, between her and the kitchen door. He was grinning wryly at her performance. He stepped forward and took a stray hair from her face and put it behind her ear. She trembled. His breath was too close to her. It was sickly and sweet and a vein was pulsating in his temple. She took a step back and stumbled. Tim grabbed her wrist, helped her stay upright.

'And I didn't realize you had a taste for vodka,' he told her, moving closer still as his grip tightened. 'If I had, I definitely would have offered you some before.'

Tim was not a big man but he was strong. He was so

close now that he had become nothing but a blur of flesh and sweat. His breathing was thick and damp against her face and it was becoming more sour as it mixed with hers. He had one arm round her waist, and his other hand was still clenching her wrist.

'Please . . .' She tried to protest but as her mouth opened he forced his lips on to hers and thrust his tongue deep between her teeth. Nausea rose in her mouth. She tried to twist her head away and his teeth clashed with her bottom lip. She tasted blood as he shoved her violently up against the wall, winding her. She tried to squirm away from him but his hold was too firm. His breath was coming fast, it was rasping and his face was now buried in her neck, his mouth sucking at her flesh. His free hand had shoved its way up under her dress and she felt his burning fingers rip her flimsy underwear to one side. Then he forced them violently inside her. He was very strong, too strong for her to stop him. She felt her legs give way but it made no difference – she was shaking uncontrollably and he had her pinned to the wall. Now he had removed his fingers and was undoing his trouser zip. She tried to wriggle free of him but it was no good. Her dress was up around her waist and he was thrusting himself inside her. She groaned as she felt her body lose its strength to resist.

Melina had no idea how much time passed, but when she finally regained her senses Tim had gone and she was lying at the foot of the kitchen stairs in her ripped dress. There was sick all over her face and down her chest. She slowly pulled herself upright. She was shuddering and freezing cold. She must have been there, lying like that, for some time. She could hear Tim moving around upstairs, his bedroom door closing, then silence. Finally, feebly, she pulled herself to her feet and headed up to her own room very slowly, very quietly. Shakily, she peeled off the ripped, stained dress that had filled her with such delight, only hours before. The irony stung along with the taste of sick in the back of her throat. Her body ached, all the way down her legs, inside her, where Tim had so recently trespassed. She headed into the shower room and turned the hot water on, then crouched in the tray and put her arms around her knees. Later she locked her bedroom door, climbed into her bed and hid in the dark.

At midnight Connor left Zahir's house. He appeared from the basement as quietly as a city fox, looked this way and that, then across at Maggie's darkened window. He paused, as if considering his options, then began to walk towards number fourteen, hands deep inside his pockets, head slouched forward inside his hoodie. The rain was sloshing down now in bucketfuls. He walked like a puppet cut from its strings, legs wonky, shoulders hunched at different angles. You could tell at a glance that every limb hurt. He slowed as he approached his front gate, paused and looked down into the well. The lights were on in the lounge and you could just see the stretched-out legs and socked feet of three men: his dad, and Connor's two uncles. The TV in the corner broadcast the late news to an audience who'd passed out from booze. They'd all be there now, sunk into their settees, until morning.

Connor watched and still he hesitated. Then he put one hand on the gatepost, as if to pull it open, but a movement down the street caught his eye and he glanced up. A gang of three chunky-looking geezers were hanging around by Ali's. Their dark frames huddled together in the shadows, away from the street lamp. Connor sensed menace. Then headlights flashed on a black Lexus outside Shelly's and his stomach hit the back of his throat. She was standing on the pavement, looking into the window, then up and towards him, pointing. He knew that car and who it belonged to. Mickey was about and there was only one person he was looking for. Connor knew he should leg it but felt frozen, for the moment, to the spot. His body hurt and his brain was fried. He needed sleep. The car's lamps had already alerted the men to his presence.

'Oi,' someone was calling to him, 'Connor, wait up. We need to talk to you.'

They started to move rapidly in his direction.

It took Connor no more than a split second to make a decision. He may have been slight, his entire being might have been in pain, but fear made him nimble. He turned on his heel and ran away from the men and the car, as fast as he could, through the rain. The men ran too, shouting after him. The car followed. At the end of Meanwhile Street Connor took a sharp right and headed for the darker alleys of the Beethoven Estate, alleys where cars were too wide to roam. The Lexus came to a halt at the corner but, as he ran, Connor was aware of the men's footsteps drawing nearer. He didn't know where he was going; just knew he had to go, had to go now, right away.

'Stop, you little fucker, we need to talk to you!'

The tone had become harder, more angry. They were getting closer all the time. Connor ran on, blindly, fear making him move faster and faster. Now blue flashing lights were following too. Even so, he didn't stop. Didn't trust any of them – anyone. He ran down an alley and found himself in an open courtyard, surrounded by high-rise blocks. Cars could get in there. He looked back. No footsteps followed. At least it seemed he'd lost the men. Perhaps the police had scared them off. But where should he go next? The pigs hadn't gone, they knew their way around, would be here any second. He didn't want to explain nothing to no one. Wasn't sharing any stories.

Right then the police car swung into the courtyard. A girl came out of one of the blocks and he slipped inside before the door swung shut, then stopped for a moment, back against the inside wall. His breath was now so short it made his chest ache. He had a broken rib or two, he was sure, and they dug into his body like knife blades. Every part of him hurt, even the air that he heaved into his lungs tasted sick, and he was in a cold sweat. He looked out on to the courtyard. The girl was talking to three policemen who'd got out of their car, gesticulating towards the entrance of the block where he was hiding. They followed her gaze and then they all headed towards the door.

Connor didn't hesitate, turned and fled up the stairs, two concrete steps at a time. He could see Shelly's case in his mind as he ran. He'd had no idea, when he borrowed it, what he had coming to him. No fucking clue. He turned another corner, up another flight. It was probably still sitting where he'd left it, in Maggie's hall. He saw the old girl, handing him the squash and the biscuits. He remembered his broken promise to play chess with her tonight and he felt bad. He climbed on, another two floors, round and round. Maggie was the only one who'd ever done him any good. He wasn't going to lead no one to her front door. There must have been drugs in the lining. Shelly must have been in on it, but not Janice. Shelly was a cunt. He turned up another flight. He could hear the pigs on the stairs below him. They seemed to be getting closer. No one was as knackered and fucked as he was. Something inside him was hurting so bad he didn't know where it was, or how much further he could go. He looked up. Two, maybe three flights to go and then what? Didn't matter, he wasn't turning round. The footsteps were rising fast. Their approach gave him more energy to move. His chest felt fit to split and the stench of urine poisoned the air, but still he climbed. He'd go and get the case from Maggie tomorrow, empty out his stuff and give it back to Shelly. Get his hands and Maggie's clean of it. But he'd never lead anyone to her. Maggie was all he had. Finally he had made it. Connor came to a halt on the tenth and top floor. But there appeared to be nowhere left to run. The policemen's footsteps were getting closer all the time, but they were landing more slowly now, one after the other, slap, slap, slap, on the cement stairs. He only had a moment to think.

There was graffiti on all the walls. He knew those tags, the marks of another crew in the hood. Fuckers he didn't trust, with scars to show for it. Mickey held them in his palm too. He looked down the corridor, seeing metal-framed windows all along, lit by low-level strip lighting. Most of the bulbs were out, those working throwing only a gloomy light between dark spaces. At the end was a black metal door with padlocks down the side – the way up to the roof. A broken window had swung open near it.

He moved towards it, then painfully heaved himself up to look out. There was a narrow sill and, above it, the roof. He climbed up and then pulled himself out, snagging his hoodie on the broken glass as he clambered up on to the roof. A tangle of wires and cables, and a large generator with the words DANGER DO NOT TOUCH on one side, covered the grey tarmac surface.

He stood up and breathed in. It was windy and pissing down, but it was still surprisingly warm. He held his head back and let the rain fall on to his sweating, bruised face. All about and above him was sky and spray and a hovering helicopter and satellites twinkling like stars through the cloudburst. Down below were more blocks of flats and the tops of the trees in blossom and blue flashing lights, illuminating the branches from beneath like weird pale blue forests out of some narcotic fairy tale. For a split second Connor felt like a giant standing there, exalted and on top of the world, but a moment later he felt precarious, like a fledgling bird, tipped out on the edge, perched and ready to fly away.

He heard a grunt and looked around as the head of one of the policemen appeared above the ledge. The sight almost made Connor want to laugh. He moved back towards the other side of the roof, then stood there, watching, as the man was boosted out and up on to the rooftop by one of his colleagues. He took a moment to pull himself up, then looked around and clocked Connor. He began to move towards the boy cautiously, one hand raised.

'Steady now, calm now,' he said breathlessly.

Connor observed him for a second with total

detachment. The man looked all right, kind even. Strong and fit and serious. About the right age to be his dad. Maybe he was someone's dad. A good dad. One who didn't hit you. Maybe he was someone like Mark, or Zahir, a man you could talk to, who helped you out, a good bloke, one you could trust.

The pain stabbed again through his ribs, his lungs and into the base of his back and Connor flinched, then he turned away from the policeman and walked closer to the edge of the roof. He gazed out across London, this city of lights and noise and people, and chaos and loneliness and confusion, and wondered briefly where his mum was in all of that. He wasn't born yesterday, knew stories of her going back to Ireland were a lie. She was down there somewhere, living out her life without him. Connor glanced back round at the officer and caught his eye, held it. He still had one hand raised and was watching Connor, with clear concern. Despite himself, Connor smiled that smile that everyone talked about, the one that caught you unawares. The officer was drawn in by it and, after hesitating briefly, he smiled back, cautiously. Connor Ryan watched him for a moment before turning to look back over the city. And then he jumped.

Part Two

12

It was one o'clock in the morning and if you hadn't known better, you would have thought Meanwhile Street was experiencing a peaceful, if rain-sodden night. Most of the three-storey houses lay in darkness, and the street lamps shed a soft glow down the shiny wet road. The rain continued to fall relentlessly, tap-tapping on the roofs of cars, muffling all other sounds from the city, and the blossom dropped in clots on to the pavement, making it slippery underfoot. A black cab whirred down the street, its tyres squelching as it pulled up outside number thirty-two. The passenger in the back leant forward and paid the driver, then opened the door to get out. There was the sound of laughter, then Gordon's voice said, 'Yeah, thanks a lot mate, yeah, will do,' and the door clanked shut and the cab pulled away again, wipers clearing the misted screen. He should have got home from the hospital in a matter of minutes, but the roads around the Beethoven had been closed off and a helicopter was hovering over one of the tenement buildings. It had taken fifteen minutes to negotiate their way round.

'Gunboat Alley round here mate, that's what we called it in the old days,' the cabbie had chirped.

If it weren't for the events of the day, Gordon might have smiled. Instead his thoughts turned to Connor and the words stirred him up. He felt gutted by his earlier inaction, a growing sense of shame.

The house lay in silence. Gordon crept into Milo's room and stroked his sleeping son's hair. He suddenly looked enormous, lying there with his legs stretched out and his thumb in his mouth: a child who already had his own experiences of this city pulsing through him. Gordon felt a mixture of sadness and joy as he considered the singular focus on Milo they were losing now their daughter had come along. He felt altered by it, unsure. He left Milo sleeping and flopped on to his bed, where he lay listening to the sound of the rain falling.

Gordon was restless, tried to focus his mind on Kitty Louise. The infant had been born by emergency Caesarean section after a protracted and in the end, quite frightening labour for Immy – and for him. At one point he had truly feared he might lose his wife and or his baby. The experience of watching Immy's belly being sliced open, seeing her insides, the sac with the baby in it, was chilling. Even so, the drama of it had all but been obliterated by the ensuing fight in the street. However hard he tried to fix Kitty's unfurling features in his mind, all Gordon could see was Connor Ryan's bloodied face, his pathetic figure lolloping off towards Reeling Road like a wounded dog, and all he could feel inside was a growing sense of shame.

What if that child had been Milo? How could he call

himself a decent father, a good human being, when he could watch someone else's child being kicked to within an inch of his life? Would he have stood and watched while a bunch of teenagers attempted to break his own child's bones with their feet? Would the threat of a knife have stopped him from intervening then? Of course he knew the answer. Connor Ryan was no stranger, the boy had even been in their house with Clare and Max once or twice. What had made him hesitate and reach for his phone rather than wade in and stop the girls? Personal safety? Perhaps he really was spineless, 'a pompous prick', as Clare had called him. Gordon had always feared confrontation; at school he had always avoided 'bundles' in the playground, been happier in the classroom than on the playing field. Not that he had been a wimp; he'd been a fair sportsman, good at cricket, at tennis, and a long-distance runner. In life he had a reputation for tenacity, determination, and had always thought that, when the circumstances required it he could be brave. But tonight he knew that by failing Connor he had also failed his family – and himself.

As Gordon drifted into a fitful sleep, Billy pulled up in the only available gap in Meanwhile Street, a few spaces down and on the other side of the road from his flat. He'd had a long day, was making a documentary film about street kids in Bangalore, the contrast in their lives to the newly emerging Indian superclass, fuelled by a racing economy. It was supporting a new breed of Bollywood celebrity actors and actresses. His production company had been commissioned by the Discovery channel; it had been a coup. But Billy was feeling the strain; they'd been forced to commit to a small budget and unrealistic production times to win the work, and now they were facing the repercussions. He was living off no more than five hours' sleep a night and it was catching up on him. He'd resorted to a cocktail of illegal substances to keep him going, speed and cocaine being his Class A drugs of choice. Tonight he was high and wired and knackered and buzzing, all at the same time. They were nearly finished and the film looked strong. Nevertheless, in four hours he'd need to be up and back there again. As he crossed the street he noticed a police car parked outside his flat and it made him nervous: he was carrying. He ducked back into the car and left his stash in the glove compartment, under the driver's manual. He locked the Jag for a second time and crossed again, casually. Two police officers, one male, one female, had got out of the patrol car and were peering down the well into Joe Ryan's front window. The curtains were still open and you could see three people sprawled out, sleeping on the sofas.

Billy nodded towards the officers as he mounted his front steps. They were now banging hard on the basement door.

'All right?' he enquired.

'Are you a neighbour?' the female officer asked.

Billy nodded. 'Has something happened? Is the boy all right?'

Billy had lived in Meanwhile Street for six years and had watched Connor grow from cheeky nine-year-old to strung-out teenager. He wouldn't have been surprised if he'd got caught up in something illegal, it was inevitable, for a kid like that. He had no one looking out for him; Joe was always pissed.

The officers didn't speak.

'The problem is,' Billy went on, 'Joe drinks so much you're unlikely to wake him now; he'll be passed out down there till the morning. Does Connor, his boy, need bailing out? He's a good kid really, just hangs around with some bad influences. He's only fifteen.'

The officers looked up at Billy, then they looked at each other. The male officer spoke quietly to his colleague, then into his walkie-talkie. It was dawning on Billy from the look on their faces that something serious was going down. He thought back to his journey home, to the ambulance and police cars gathered round the corner at the Beethoven.

'Has something bad happened to him?'

It was the way they stood, the way they looked. They'd come, not looking for anyone, but to deliver bad news. Billy didn't know where his conviction came from, whether from the grey pallor of the officers' skin, the fact that neither seemed willing to look him in the eye, to answer his question, the way they talked in hushed tones into their walkie-talkies. It was all of that and something more, a general morbidity about them. Billy suddenly felt sick. One of the officers now nodded severely to the other and they ascended the steps to stand on the pavement, looking up at Billy. He came back down to join them on the street.

'He's dead, isn't he?'

No one spoke.

'He's dead?' Billy repeated urgently.

'I'm afraid so,' said the male officer.

There was nothing anyone could do to wake Joe, and in the end they all decided that really there was little point. Billy stood letting the rain soak him and found he was shaking all over. He explained about Connor's mum, Lorraine, how she'd left them all those years before, how no one really knew where she was, although there'd always been rumours that she was living with some guy in south London somewhere. He didn't think Connor knew that, the kid thought she was in Ireland and he probably wouldn't have recognized her if he had seen her. She'd walked out when he was barely four, and on the few occasions Billy had been inside Joe's flat – when there'd been a real emergency, like a power cut because they had failed to put money in the electricity meter or when Joe had been unconscious and Connor hadn't been able to get to school and Billy had taken him instead – there'd been no sign of her, no photographs. But these were just fragments in a life that Billy knew in no greater depth. He was talking too much and too fast. It was partly the shock and partly the drugs. Even so, he found himself agreeing to accompany the police to the hospital morgue to identify Connor's body. He made himself shut up as he sat in the back of the car and they drove him to his miserable destination. He was dying for a fag, for a fix. He drummed his fingers rapidly on his knees, trying to breathe deeply, in and out, trying not to rattle on any more.

Behind them, the rain continued to fall in Meanwhile Street. It was hard, angry rain, and it flooded out of the sky like a deluge. It was unusual for this time of year, such a heavy downpour. April had been unseasonably hot; the world seemed turned upside down, rain when there should have been sun, sun when there should have been rain. Nothing made sense any more, not even the seasons.

They arrived back two hours later. Billy felt mashed. At the morgue, they'd pulled the cover back and Connor had been lying there, but it was a Connor with a story he didn't know, a story that had happened fast, in the past twenty-four hours, since he had last seen him pulling his bike up from the basement, on his way somewhere, looking pale, maybe, but definitely, at least physically, in one piece. The Connor in the morgue had been through more than a single fall. The police said he'd been beaten black and blue before jumping. His skull was smashed by the impact with the ground and his eyes were wonky and puffed with bruising. Strangest of all, his dead mouth seemed set in an almost-smile.

Now Billy was back in Meanwhile Street with only an hour before he needed to be up again, but there was no point trying to sleep, no point even in lying down. His brain raced with disturbing images and his heart was filled with grief. He went to his car, opened the glove compartment and retrieved the stash of white powder waiting for him there. What was the point in making films about fucked neighbourhoods in India, he thought angrily, when everything's so fucked up outside your own front door? He sat in the driver's seat and snorted the cocaine quickly, then leant back and shut his eyes, relieved, let it take effect. He didn't know if he'd ever be able to block out what he'd just seen. Connor's death mask was burnt like a print in his mind, like an indelible scar, a call to arms. He would have to do something about this, he'd have to ask questions, he'd have to find out why.

The rain continued to beat down on the top of his Jag. It sounded like a fast drumbeat, or the noise your heart makes in your ears when you're paralysed with fear, as Connor must have been, he thought, to have jumped off the block. He tried to have a conversation with the child in his mind. In the end, Billy guessed that Connor didn't know why he jumped from that tower, any more than Billy or the police did; they'd told him that Connor had turned and smiled before he made his exit. He seemed still to be smiling in the morgue. Connor was probably high, probably didn't know what he was doing up there, probably didn't understand why he was being chased, or even really what he had been running away from; Billy bet that all Con had known was that he wanted to be free. The expression on his bashed-up face was a grin of fear. Billy's head fell forward. Inside his eyes the images of Connor were turning grey. And then he passed out.

The rain continued to fall as the rest of the inhabitants of Meanwhile Street slept. Maggie dreamt of high days with Gerry out at County Clare, with Connor's case stored safely beneath her, under the bed. Shelly slept restlessly, thinking about Marlon as the ache in her jaw intermittently invaded her slumber. Gordon drowsed uneasily, twisting and turning inside the duvet until he was knotted up in its folds. Katya lay in her single bed below him and she, too, slept fitfully, her body craving rehydration after all the vodka she had drunk with Melina. Clare and Max slept heavily, dreamlessly, with full stomachs after a late evening together on the sofa eating garlicky takeaway food. Dren and Ada made love in their spring-weakened divan bed, silently and without rushing so as not to wake the children, and then they fell asleep in each other's arms and had parallel dreams about life back home, before there had been a war. Joe Ryan's dreams were penetrated by the horses he and his cousin Jim had bet on that day. It felt as if he were actually there, putting on his bets and winning the jackpot. Every now and then he emitted vibrating snores that rattled from his fluid-filled lungs into the damp basement room. Billy slept in his car, his neck developing a crick from its unnatural angle that would cause him pain in the editing suite tomorrow. His psychedelic dreams contained Connor's dead face set upon the body of a street kid from Bangalore. Connor was running away from Billy, who chased him through the Asian city's noisy, dusty, snaking alleyways. Opposite, Tim slept deeply, sated, without conscience and without dreaming, oblivious to the damage he'd just wreaked on one young Eastern European girl's life.

Melina lay a floor below Tim in her room, acutely awake and listening. In the depths of the night she heard the sound of a motor whirring outside. It was four a.m. A van's engine was idling. She heard its doors clunking open. Then she heard Zahir's dog stir and begin to bark in their garden, but her body felt strapped to the mattress by invisible ties and she didn't move to see what had caused the disturbance. After a while the van doors snapped shut and the gears started grinding. Then she heard it driving away as Zahir's dog howled.

With each moment that passed she was becoming

more clear-headed. Melina knew she had to get away. She couldn't go to the police; she could hardly speak English and knew they wouldn't help. She'd been drunk, wearing titillating clothes, Lulu's shoes, make-up; she'd look as if she'd been asking for it. Melina thought about Katya and London and her life there, and she knew she wasn't like her Czech friend. However badly things were going back in Poland for her, it was still her home. Melina needed to be there to make a go of her life. She couldn't do it here on her own. She tried to imagine Katya in her place but knew she would have known how to handle Tim better, would not have let him do it. Maybe Katya would have slept with him out of choice, if she could see a value in it, but if she hadn't wanted to she would have known how to avoid it. Life wasn't like that for Melina. She thought about her mother, alone and ill and yet determined for Melina to make a better life for herself in London, despite the sacrifices she'd made over the years in her daughter's name. And she felt as if she had failed.

It was five a.m. now and getting light. Melina finally managed to get out of bed. She looked from her bedroom window. The dawn chorus was riotous despite the fact that the sky was grey and it was raining lightly. She was still trembling slightly as she got dressed in her skinny jeans and trainers, a T-shirt and sweater, her raincoat. She packed her bags methodically, her mother's presents and her own new clothes, trying to keep her breathing regular as she went from task to task. Inside she felt panicky and her heart beat too quickly. She left her ripped dress on the bed for Lulu to find and to wonder at. At ten to six she dragged her two suitcases down the stairs as quietly as she could and pulled them out on to the street. She looked around her and felt like an outsider with no reason to be here. The air was thick and flaccid and muggy. She left one case inside the gate and began to wheel the other down to Ali's. She'd catch a bus to Victoria from there, then book a coach journey home to Krakow. She had enough money, apart from yesterday's shopping extravaganza she had hardly spent a thing here. She'd sent most of it home.

She pulled the first case through puddles of sludgy blossom. It got stuck in the wheels and halfway she had to stop and pull it out. It was then she noticed a man slumped over the steering wheel of his car – either asleep or maybe even passed out, she wasn't sure. He was familiar to her: he lived just along the road, had a safe smile, always said hello. He was around thirty-five, maniacally busy all the time. Lulu had told her that Tim knew him vaguely, that he was quite a successful director. Melina wondered if she should wake him up as she continued to pull the case up to the corner.

Hassim was just opening Ali's and he bid her good morning.

'You watch my case one moment, I go fetch the other?' she asked.

'Oh no, you're not leaving?'

'My mother is not well, I must go home to Poland,' she lied, then turned and made her way back, slowing momentarily as she passed the man in the car again. Her conscience pricked her. What if this man was ill? She should not leave him there, lying like that, in his car. She looked closer. The locks were up and his wallet was sitting abandoned on the passenger seat, a credit card lying invitingly next to it. She tapped lightly on the window but he didn't respond. She tapped harder but still he didn't move. Melina looked up and down the street. It was a dilemma, what to do. She decided to ask Hassim.

Moments later Melina's bags were stored inside the shop and the two of them were heading back towards the Jag. Hassim banged hard on the window. No response. He opened the door. Still the man didn't move. Melina felt sickness stirring inside her – maybe he was dead? She couldn't handle it, started shaking again. It was too soon after her last shock. This is the Devil's own city, she thought. Hassim took hold of the man's arm and shook it hard. At last he stirred and began to come round, looked up at them.

'Shit. I blacked out,' he grinned sheepishly. 'It was a bad night.'

'You don't want to go leaving your money on the seat like that, someone come and nick it,' said Hassim severely.

Billy glanced at the card sitting there, slipped it inside the wallet quickly, then got out of the car and stretched. He looked dreadful, Melina realized, like he had been partying all night and got no sleep; his eyes were bloodshot. He locked the car and walked with them back up to the corner shop through the drizzle, bought a bottle of chocolate milk from the refrigerated unit and drank it down in one as Melina watched him. With each second that passed he seemed more alert, calmer. She said goodbye to Hassim, then went and stood outside, by the bus stop. Presently the man joined her. Melina was next to her cases, umbrella up, waiting for the bus. He stood under the shop awning and lit a cigarette.

'Thanks for waking me up,' he said. 'I'm Billy.'

Melina glanced at him sideways, smiled wanly.

'Are you leaving?'

She nodded.

'Shame, I've seen you with the kids, you always look like you're doing a great job. Where are you heading now?'

Melina explained, for the second time already this morning.

'Wait there,' he ordered. 'My production house is in Soho. I'll drop you at Victoria on the way.'

Melina tried to say no; how could she get in a strange man's car after what had just happened to her? But Billy was insistent, waved her objections away with a shrug and turned back in the direction of Meanwhile Street with a determined stride. She looked hopefully up the road for the bus. Moments later the Jag pulled over and Billy hopped out. Melina watched helplessly as he put her cases in the boot.

'Come on,' he said. 'Don't want to miss that coach.'

Melina wasn't sure what made her get into the car, maybe it was shock, or simple lack of strength after all that had happened, but the next thing she knew they were heading down Warwick Avenue, then along the canal at Little Venice and on to the Edgware Road, in the direction of Marble Arch. The drizzle had stopped and there was a tiny pocket of pale blue in the sky. Billy saw Melina looking up at it.

'Not quite enough for a Dutchman's trousers,' he said,

and when she looked confused he laughed and then so did she.

'You can't go home,' he said. 'Not until you've mastered English colloquialisms.'

'Colloquialisms? What is?'

'There you go.'

Melina had no idea what he meant but she found herself laughing anyway, and so did Billy. It took them both aback. Really they both knew there was fuck all to laugh about.

'Did you know the kid, Connor Ryan, who lived with his dad beneath me?' he asked her as the traffic lights turned red on Park Lane. He had to share the experience with someone, anyone really, and at least Melina might have known who Con was.

'He is friends with Max who live next door to Katya,' she replied confidently. 'Sometimes he is there with Max, but more now he is with Shelly, the girl who was hit yesterday by boyfriend's gun. But then he is with Zahir at lunchtime, Katya and me, we think is strange.'

'Who is Zahir?' Billy asked her, casually, as the lights changed to green. Connor really had been up to his neck in it. Whatever *it* was. Seemed everyone else in the street was involved too, even the bloody nannies. He'd get to the bottom of it if it killed him too.

'He live under Clare and Max. He is Somali asylum seeker. Katya friends with him.'

'Oh yeah? What kind of friends?'

Melina stared out of the window at the drizzle. Hyde Park looked misty and desolate after all the rain, and the pavements outside the Dorchester Hotel were glistening with an oily sheen of water. Steam rose from a vent in the road. Maybe she had said too much. Still it didn't really matter, she supposed. She wasn't ever going back there.

'You know,' she said.

Some things needed no translation. Billy raised his eyes, tapped on the steering wheel, as they circled a quiet Hyde Park Corner and turned down Buckingham Palace Road.

'What was Connor doing there?'

'No one know. Someone had hit him in the eye. When Katya arrive he leave straight at once. It was a strange day yesterday. Many bad things happen, one and then another.'

More than you know, pondered Billy. It was clear she didn't know what had happened to Connor, hadn't been mixed up in it. Still seemed a bit strange she was leaving so early in the morning, and that the posh couple she lived with hadn't offered to take her to her bus. Mercenary bastards.

'So, tell me about Shelly,' Billy encouraged her now. 'What did her boyfriend do exactly?'

As they drove on, Melina explained, falteringly, about Shelly's attack, the incident at Lizzie B's, the arrests in the street. It was good to talk about anything other than Tim, it pushed his abuse of her just a little beneath the surface, helped her to stay in control. Billy remained silent as she spoke, only interrupting her when her English failed and she needed the language to express exactly what it was that she meant to say.

'No wonder you want to leave,' he murmured once she'd

drawn to a close. 'You make Meanwhile Street sound like a war zone. I've lived here for six years and until last night there's been no trouble, no trouble at all.'

'Are you sure? Trouble happens when you are not looking. Maybe you just didn't see.'

'Maybe you're right.'

Billy had pulled up in a bus lane outside Victoria station.

'It's a shame you have to go.'

He meant it. He liked this girl, she had a subtle sense of humour and she was very pretty when she smiled. He hadn't had time for relationships in the past few years. Since splitting from his wife, Lucy, when he was thirty, he had concentrated on work and had occasional short-term flings. He and Lucy had met at film school, got married at twenty-five, divorced when her film-production work really took off and she'd moved to LA. Divorce had been the adult thing to do, they had drifted apart; even so, it had taken him years to move on. He'd recently discovered that Lucy was about to have a baby with an actor in Hollywood, and he hadn't found that easy. But there was something about Melina that evoked a response in him, stirred something up. He reached inside his wallet and took out a card. 'If you find yourself back in town, give me a call,' he said earnestly.

Melina took the card, thanked Billy and got out of the car. He jumped out too and helped her with her cases. And then they stood for a moment and looked at each other awkwardly, both of them suddenly self-conscious. Melina held out her hand. Billy gave it a gentle squeeze, which felt surprisingly intimate. She pulled her hand away gently but definitely and averted her gaze, turned to go, hesitated and then looked back at him.

'What were you going to tell me about the boy, Connor?' she enquired.

Billy looked at her for a moment and almost began to speak, then it seemed that he thought better of it.

'Oh nothing, it was nothing,' he said. 'Have a safe trip home, OK?'

13

The day began as the night had ended: desolate and damp with thick, angry swirls of charcoal churned into a palette of pale grey and white above the houses, and a fine drizzle spraying the street with grimy rain. The bin men looked glum as they lifted the bags of rubbish from behind the iron railings and tossed them with practised nonchalance into the back of the kerb-crawling lorry. It was the kind of rain which almost didn't merit an umbrella, the kind of rain which sends fine trickles of moisture down your neck, within the kind of damp that makes you sweat. The temperature must have been close to seventy. It was oppressive weather, weather for headaches.

Maggie watched the rubbish clearance and mopped her brow with an old handkerchief of Gerry's that she kept in her dressing-gown pocket. She took a sip of her tea and glanced at the clock. Five to seven. Overnight the cherry trees had all but lost their blossom. It lay saturated in lumps on the pavements, like snow turned to dirty sludge after a sudden thaw. The young trees looked prematurely fatigued, bent over like crooked-backed old ladies. It was the kind of day, thought Maggie, when people who can, stay indoors, out of the weather. After yesterday it would do them all good to have a quieter day, a day to get back on their feet.

Dren was up and out first, giving Maggie a sunbeam smile as he pulled his bomber jacket tight around his chest and took off up the street. She drank her tea gloomily. Yesterday had left her feeling down in the dumps. Perhaps it was delayed shock at the violence, the sight of all that blood, Shelly's and then Marlon's, too. And then Connor hadn't reappeared. She was fretting about him. She needed someone to chat to. She glanced over the road, then remembered. Surely Immy would be home soon and she'd be able to hear the baby's cries. That would make up for yesterday, without a doubt. She watched as people hurried off to work or school through the rain. Presently Max and Casey appeared, fell into step, bulging rucksacks on their backs, both acknowledging Maggie with a smile as they headed for the bus stop on Reeling Road. When Ada's kids finally emerged they were all buttoned up in their macs, heads down behind Ada and the buggy which was covered in a plastic, tent-like structure. When Maggie was a nanny they had no such fancy contraptions, good old-fashioned Silver Cross prams with sprung suspensions, only the best for the Fisk children, but no plastic tents ever went over the top. They were designed to keep the rain out. Ada raised a hand to Maggie, but didn't stop to talk. Clearly it wasn't going to be a day for conversation.

Maggie wasn't too perturbed now; her focus had turned to number thirty-two. She was patient; the time would come for the baby's story to unfold. Meantime, she sat quietly, drinking her tea. When the blue door finally opened and she spied Katya emerging with Milo in his green dinosaur raincoat, matching hat and wellington boots, she waved down expectantly. Katya spotted the old lady and allowed a slip of a smile to grace her lips before turning and calling back inside. Gordon soon appeared and leant against the doorway in an old pair of jeans and a T-shirt, apparently oblivious to the rain.

'We've had a girl,' he called out cheerily, 'Kitty Louise, born at 6.46 last night. Poor Immy, she had an emergency Caesarean, horrible it was, but they're both fine.'

Ten minutes now passed as Gordon filled Maggie in on the gruesome details of Immy's protracted labour, loudly enough for all the street to hear, should they have been listening.

'I'll be making her a pair of booties before the week's out,' Maggie called out delightedly, once he was done. 'I've got some pink wool and some blue. And Kitty – what a lovely old-fashioned name. A boy and a girl, what a perfect pigeon pair.'

Gordon grinned from ear to ear as if his face would split, and continued to chat for some time. Katya stood with Milo on the pavement, increasingly impatient to be off without being observed. She had wanted to have a sneaky look in on Zahir before getting to nursery. Now Gordon was filling Maggie in on Shelly's attack on Connor and it was getting late. Maggie immediately lost her smile, said she'd be having words. Then Clare appeared from her doorway. Gordon made a sharp exit and Katya took off at a smart pace, resigned to not seeing Zahir.

Clare was wearing trousers and a navy raincoat. She

spent time fiddling with her red umbrella, then putting it up in order to avoid Katya, then she pulled the black door closed behind her and hurried out into the street.

'Morning Maggie,' she called, too brightly. 'No trouble this morning, then?'

'No dear, all quiet on the Western Front.'

Clare laughed nervously before glancing briefly into Zahir's basement. There was no sign of life down there; no sign of Connor, either. Hopefully last night's drama had blown over, could be forgotten now.

'I'm off to the dentist,' she called back resignedly.

Mr Wang was a Chinese dentist with the nimblest hands you'd ever seen. He worked in a run-down clinic at the base of one of the tenements on the Beethoven, was the only dentist left in the area who offered NHS appointments. You had to turn a blind eye to the decor, but it was worth it to avoid private fees. As Clare approached it now she noticed people milling around outside the surgery, people who at this time of day would usually be on the move: old and young, black and white, kids and adults. A couple of police officers stood behind a cordon by the entrance. Clare sighed. Not another incident. It was too much, really; always made life more of a hassle for everyone else. She wished they'd stop it, these kids with their drugs and their knives and their guns. They thought they were in some kind of movie or a PS2 game half the time, didn't bet on the repercussions. She'd have to keep finding ways to prevent Max from getting involved. A couple more years and hopefully he'd be off at university, somewhere smaller, less charged than London; Durham, or Bristol, perhaps, to read medicine, or engineering. He was bright and she'd never let up; he wasn't going to slip through the net.

Then she saw the bunch of flowers – just one for now, balanced upright next to the building – fading pink carnations in cellophane, misted by the rain. She recognized the type, straight from Ali's for a couple of quid, knew what they symbolized, stopped in the drizzle to absorb it. Two women were standing in front of her, plastic-wrapped in clear raincoats and matching hats, streaked with rain. Both had empty tartan shopping trolleys parked up beside their own bulky frames. They must have been off to the Kilburn High Road for their weekly groceries, Clare reflected, when they'd come across the incident.

'They say it was a child, a boy called Connor, Connor Ryan, they say he jumped,' confided one to the other.

'Sounds suspicious to me,' her friend replied, 'being chased like that, and all.'

It hit Clare like a punch to the stomach, the news. She felt dizzy and wanted to call out. Instead her legs gave way and everything went black.

The next thing she knew she was being administered oxygen by Mr Wang, right there on the street. As she came round, in her mind's eye she could see Connor, early yesterday evening, looking up at her miserably from Zahir's basement well, then later, pulling himself up off the road, mauled and bruised, and later still, inside Zahir's flat again, with a cloth held to his face. At no point had she pressed the boy to come up and take refuge in her flat. She should have intervened. Now it was too late, not only for Connor, she realized with a start, but for them all.

'You knew him did you, love?' said one of the old ladies.

'Come on, let me take you home,' urged one of the police officers, who had been monitoring the situation.

Clare dismissed them all and took off for Meanwhile Street on her own. She needed to get back inside and lock the door. There was no one here who could help her today, no one at all.

Katya parked Milo's buggy at Lizzie B's, glanced down the list and signed them in. She'd got here before Melina today. She helped Milo off with his coat. There were only six carers and toddlers in the drop-in so far, and Aishah was nowhere to be seen. Katya prepared a consoling cup of Nescafé, added extra sugar – fuck her diet – and slouched on the floor while Milo retrieved a book about new baby sisters. As they turned the pages together she felt her mood dip. Was it going to be a disappointing day after all? Story soon completed, Milo hopped off her knee and crossed the room to play on his own in the sandpit. Katya was left observing. Still there was no sign of Melina, but now Aishah appeared and threw Katya a watery smile. She looked as if she'd been crying. Katya glanced around at the discarded toys, two toddlers playing in the water area with its plastic fountain and buckets, another poised at an easel, two unfamiliar kids and their nanny kneeling before a tray of glittery star shapes, sticking them on to paper with glue.

God alive, she was bored. The atmosphere was as subdued as the weather outside, it made you want to curl up and sleep; preferably with someone else. Even the children seemed half-hearted at their play. She glanced distractedly at her phone. She was still half expecting a text from Zahir but again was disappointed. After yesterday she'd been convinced there would be more. They'd fitted together – or so she'd thought. His dark, glistening body writhing on top of her momentarily entered her thoughts. Now her confidence was plummeting, along with her mood. She contemplated texting him, but instead she texted Melina again.

'Where you?'

Just moments later, she got a reply.

'At Victoria. I go home. Tim came back. Very bad. M'

Katya read the text three times to try to decipher its full meaning. She considered the way she'd left Melina, in that pretty, semi-transparent dress, the glossy make-up, the high-heeled shoes, the vodka on ice, and felt her conscience stir. As Milo innocently continued to build his castles in the sand she clicked 'Call'.

After three rings Melina answered. Behind her you could hear the rumble of the city, sirens, people.

'I am in McDonald's. Victoria station is closed for security alert. I miss my bus.'

'What happened Melina, what did Tim do?'

'He, he . . .' Melina faltered, and even through the background din Katya sensed her emotions in turmoil. She looked around the nursery. You weren't supposed to use the phone in here but no one was paying her any attention.

'Did he hurt you, Melina?' she whispered.

There was a pause.

'Yes. Yes, I think he did.'

'What you mean, think?'

'Maybe it is my fault.'

'Oh my God. He rape you?'

'Uh, I think, yes.'

Now Melina was crying.

'What he do, Melina? Oh my God.'

All she could hear was muffled sobs.

'Don't go. I tell Gordon, we will help. You come and stay. We call the police. Oh my God, the evil pig. We sort it out, Melina. We sort it. You must come back. Please.'

'I want go home, Katya. Can't stay here now. I have to go.'

Katya felt shame and repulsion creeping all over her. She had encouraged her friend to put on all that make-up, the shoes, had left Melina looking like a girl who wanted to party. She knew all too well what Tim was like, knew men like that back home, dirty old professors at her university were always trying to get into her knickers. No wonder Tim had got the wrong impression. But that was no excuse for what he had done. She knew how timid Melina was around men, was certain she had not asked for it. The more Katya considered what had happened the more angry she became. She'd have to take Milo home. Work out what to do about this. She would have to do something. She'd need some help. Maybe Zahir would be back by now. He wasn't someone to stand on the sidelines. He would be unafraid of Tim, fearless in fact. There was something heroic about him – he reminded her of her father. He had never let his friends down; it might have led to his own downfall but he had died a hero. She had an image of Zahir pulling Tim out into the street for a very public humiliation, execution even . . . The depth of her anger sent bile to her tongue. Her mother had worked long days and by the age of fourteen Katya and her sisters had had to look out for themselves. They had all received many offers, with their natural good looks and hunger for excitement. But no one had ever touched any of them unless they'd wanted them to. It was about respect, about honour. Tim was an arrogant bully. She wouldn't let him get away with it. Katya collected Milo and left the nursery. She'd go looking for help.

Once Melina had put the phone down she stopped crying, left McDonald's and headed for a pharmacy on Victoria Street.

'I need pill,' she told the female chemist quietly. 'For not have a baby.'

'Contraception?'

'No,' she mumbled, 'for after you do it, to stop the baby coming.'

'You mean the morning-after pill, for after sexual intercourse has taken place? Within the last twenty-four hours?'

Melina blushed, felt tears welling. The pharmacist asked a few questions with practised discretion. Melina provided monosyllabic answers as a tear sploshed on to the handle of one of her cases. Then the woman's expression shifted from practical to enquiring. She asked Melina if she needed further advice, or perhaps someone to talk to?

'I fine thanks,' she replied. 'Please, only pill.'

The pharmacist gave her two, advised her to take them

two hours apart and warned that, over the coming forty-eight hours, she might feel nauseous. Melina left the shop hurriedly, dragged her cases to a bench and sat down. She tore the first white pill from its plastic wrapper, swallowed it quickly. The station was still shut and there were a lot of people in the street, trying to find alternative ways to work. She watched them vaguely, hurrying or procrastinating, queuing for buses, hailing cabs, drinking takeaway coffees, talking on mobile phones. They were old and young, black, yellow, grey, white and brown-skinned; had long hair, short hair, or veiled heads. They wore an assortment of jeans, suits, dresses, coats, smart shoes, trainers and boots. Even with these distractions, the smell and physical force of Tim kept nudging its way back to the surface of her mind, and she shook. She should have been able to stop him, she should have bitten him, fought him, pushed him away. She should have screamed. Yet with her fear had come an inability to act. She despised herself for her passivity; couldn't help but feel she was partly to blame, in that stupid dress, all that make-up and, of all things, Lulu's shoes.

It had gone eleven and there was no chance she'd catch the bus now. The whole area had been closed off and there was no way to get to the coach station. It was raining but Melina didn't notice it. She'd sit here and wait, and once Victoria was reopened, she'd try to book herself on to a later bus.

Katya hurried back along the street through the drizzle, almost colliding at the corner with Clare, who had her head down, red umbrella pointing ahead of her like a shield. She swerved at the last moment to avoid Katya, ignored her and strode on, mounted her front steps and went into her flat. She looked pale and distressed. She must still be sulking about last night, Katya thought, and her anger mounted. Clare was as culpable as the rest of them, had done nothing to help Connor. She pushed Milo across the street. Maggie was no longer at her window, so she parked Milo at the top of Zahir's steps and nipped down. The dog was barking but ringing the bell gained no response, and when Katya pushed her nose up against the window she saw that the room was completely empty. All the computers and papers, even the furniture had gone. She made her way back up to street level, confused and despondent. Where could he be?

A dark blue Peugeot Estate pulled up outside Melina's house and Katya watched Lulu get out. She looked groomed and well rested with her newly bobbed blonde hair and Burberry raincoat, pale pink lipstick and neat pearl earrings. Katya felt her venom rise as Lulu opened the boot and lifted out a small suitcase, then headed up the steps to her front door. Tim opened it and she saw him kiss her on both cheeks, a strangely formal exchange for a married couple. Then he stood to one side, she crossed the threshold and he closed the door behind his wife. Katya wondered what lies Tim was telling her about their latest au pair's mysterious early morning departure, and what lies Lulu was dealing him, too, about her own whereabouts last night. She also wondered how many times all this had happened before. She hesitated in the street with Milo, who was now kicking to get out of his buggy, and then Katya made a decision.

She moved rapidly down the street, pushed the buggy inside Lulu and Tim's front gate, closed it behind her and mounted the steps, two at a time. Before she could give herself a chance to think further she rang the bell. Moments later Lulu opened the door. Katya noted with satisfaction that worry lines were creasing her mouth downwards, momentarily making her appear older than her forty years. Then she regained her composure.

'I don't suppose you happen to know where Melina is?' she asked, affecting gaiety. 'She seems to have taken off in the middle of the night, no note, nothing.'

'It is why I am here,' Katya stated coldly. She glanced around at Milo, who was eagerly straining at his straps.

'Elen, Elen,' he said.

'Do you want to bring him in?' Lulu encouraged. 'Helene would be glad of some company. We're all at a bit of a loss. Tim hasn't even been able to go to work because I wasn't here.' She avoided looking Katya in the eye. 'I've been at my sister's in Hastings, she isn't well, you see.'

Lulu was talking too fast and Katya missed some details. It didn't matter, she caught the gist. Lulu was anxious, knew her version of the tale was incomplete.

Katya accepted the invitation with a curt nod, took Milo out of his buggy and helped him toddle up the steps. It was still raining, lightly. Once inside, she took off his boots and coat and left them by the door, while Lulu observed her silently from the foot of the stairs. Katya could hear a shower running above them and guessed it was Tim, washing the evidence away with the water. Now Milo ran off down to the basement to find Helene in the den. She could hear the TV playing cartoons. No doubt Helene had been planted there all morning. Katya had never seen Tim pay Helene any attention, it seemed he was only interested in 'the boy'. There was no sight or sound of Troy. Evidently Tim'd managed to get him off to school, which both surprised and vaguely impressed her.

'Come on down,' Lulu implored. 'Tell us what you know. Foolishly, I suppose, I got the feeling that Melina was very happy here, with the kids.'

Katya sat down at the kitchen table and considered her position, glanced around slowly. There was no sign of last night's vodka-drinking session, no sign of Melina's things, nor Lulu's shoes. Lulu filled the silence, chattering on about Melina and the kids, about what they would do without her, what a blessing she had been, as she switched on the kettle and retrieved two cups from the dishwasher, put tea bags in a pot.

'Did she leave anything behind?' Katya asked nonchalantly. Maybe there was evidence.

A shadow passed over Lulu's brow. She began pouring the boiling water into the teapot, of necessity turning her back on Katya. Her shoulders seemed tense.

'Only a dress, some old torn thing, on the bed. I hadn't seen it before. She evidently wanted me to throw it out.'

'Maybe it is message.'

Lulu swung around and looked at Katya with exaggerated curiosity.

'Message, what kind of message?' Her voice was clipped, defensive.

'Can I see?' Katya asked.

Lulu hesitated, but only for a split second. She had

brought herself – themselves – to this point, seemed aware that it was too late to retract.

'I go get it if you like,' Katya suggested, getting up and heading towards the kitchen door before Lulu had a chance to resist.

The dress was lying in a crumpled heap on Melina's bed. It seemed Lulu had picked it up, momentarily, then dropped it again, perhaps in disgust, and left it where it had lain, like a shed skin. The shower was still running in the room above her as Katya picked the garment up and examined it closely for herself. There was a rip across the skirt, sick marks on the front and gluey-type stains across the back. She felt repulsion rise as she rolled the dress up and headed back downstairs with it under her arm. Lulu was now slumped at the table, drinking her tea. When she saw Katya she managed a weak smile.

'This dress, it is not old, is new,' Katya said quietly, holding it up between her hands for Lulu to observe. 'Melina buy it yesterday and try it on, for me to see. She was wearing it when I left with Milo after tea. Then Tim come home.'

Lulu looked down at her cup, then up at Katya again.

'I think you'd better go now.' Her voice was low, but firm.

Katya shook her head slowly.

'Your husband, he rape my friend.'

Lulu sprang from her chair.

'Give me back that dress, then get out of my house.'

Katya stepped back and scrunched the dress up in her hands.

'I go, yes, but I take dress.'

She turned quickly and called to Milo, picked him up and rapidly made her way up the stairs. Lulu followed her to the front door, pulling repeatedly at her arm.

'Get off me or I call police,' Katya hissed, opening the door.

'Give it back, Katya, please,' Lulu implored desperately.

Katya shrugged her off; moved faster, shoving Milo out of the house ahead of her as Helene started wailing in the basement. As she turned to grab the child's coat and boots, there was a creak on the stairs and she turned to see Tim standing above them, wrapped only in a small white towel. He was smiling with affected confidence.

'Morning Katya,' he called down cheerfully. 'Lulu, is everything all right?'

Lulu stood between them, staring first up the stairs at her husband, then back along the hallway at Katya. 'Katya was just going,' she said firmly. Her face was pale, her lips trembling.

Katya grabbed Milo's things. 'I make sure you pay,' she snapped as the door thudded shut behind her. She leant down quickly and put on Milo's coat and boots, then stood against the door and took a deep breath of damp air as he began to toddle down the front steps to the gate. Behind her raised voices ricocheted: Lulu's, then Tim's, blending discordantly with Helene's increasing wails. Katya moved away hurriedly, placed Milo in his buggy, shoved the dress underneath and stuck a lolly, unearthed from her coat pocket, fluffy with crumbs, in his mouth. He sucked greedily as she turned him in the direction of home.

Maggie watched Katya with Milo marching down the

street. Something was wrong. Something had clouded her day. Maggie didn't bother to call down, it was clear she would be ignored. But she didn't take it personally. It wasn't like Katya to step out of her routine, whether Gordon or Immy were home or not. She always got back at 11.50, just in time for Milo's lunch and afternoon nap. Today she was a good half an hour early. Maybe it was to do with the baby coming, she pondered. Maybe it had thrown her off kilter – or maybe she simply needed to get the house ready for Immy's return. Sometimes when she watched Katya she remembered her own nannying days. Katya was pretty yet determined, as she had once been. Watching her made Maggie even more uneasy than she was already. She had been waiting and watching all morning, not for Katya, but for Connor to return.

14

Janice and Shelly appeared up the steps from their flat with Demi on Shelly's hip. They had a couple of carryalls in their hands. Maggie watched as they glanced furtively down the street, then back up at her.

'Can we come in?' Janice called.

'I've been waiting for you,' Maggie stated. 'Use your key and I'll be putting the kettle on.'

Moments later Shelly and Janice were sitting side by side on Maggie's sofa and Demi was on the floor between them, sucking on her dummy and playing with an old shoebox of marbles that Maggie had unearthed from a shelf. The women looked pin-thin, thought Maggie, suffering, no doubt, from stress. It still didn't change matters: Shelly had had no right to attack Connor like that.

'I never thought I'd see the day,' she began, 'that you would hit my Connor.'

'He had it coming, you don't know the half of it,' blurted Shelly.

'It's not over yet, not by any stretch,' added Janice.

'He didn't come back to me last night. He promised but

he never came back. How badly did you hurt him? I've got a good mind to call the police.'

Maggie perched back on her stool and waited for an explanation. Out of habit she cocked a quick eye up and down the street. A police car was pulling up outside the Ryans' house.

'Although it doesn't look as though I need to, they're already round there. You've got some explaining to do, young Shelly Warwick.'

Two female police officers got out of the car and made their way down Joe's steps, and Shelly and Janice, having gone to the window, craned their necks to watch.

The officers had been let inside and the door had already shut behind them.

'Oh fuck,' said Shelly.

Demi sat on the carpet, shaking the box of marbles aggressively so that they scattered in all directions across the carpet.

'No need for that language in my front room,' Maggie admonished, eyes still fixed on the doorway of number fourteen.

'Maybe they know where he is,' murmured Janice. 'Someone must.'

Maggie looked back over her shoulder, curiously.

'He was around here yesterday before your set-to. He left . . .' Something made her hesitate, something in the way the two women were eyeing her now, with mounting interest.

'Left what?' Shelly urged, glancing around, past Demi, as if for a tangible object.

'Left home, I meant to say, Connor left home. I offered

for him to sleep here. Joe hit him, before you got your hands on him. Connor told me about it. He said he couldn't go back there again. The poor wee blighter, he didn't need you adding insult to injury. It's not for me to comment on his dad's behaviour, you never really know what goes on behind other people's doors, but you – I never thought you'd turn on him. Honestly Shelly, what came over you?'

'Did he have anything with him?' Janice urged. 'A suit-case? He borrowed it off me.'

A quiet determination took hold of Maggie. She shook her head dismissively, turned her eyes back on to the street.

'I wouldn't know anything about that,' she murmured. 'Seems he just needed a shoulder to cry on. Connor always ends up coming back to me. I expect I'll be seeing him later on. I'll ask, about the case, if you want me to, after I've assessed his injuries, that is.'

'Probably be too late by then,' Shelly mumbled.

She left the window and went over to Demi, got down on her hands and knees and began to pick up the marbles, put them back in the box.

'Come on, we're off,' she told the child, then glanced back up at Maggie, who didn't notice because she and Janice had kept their eyes on the street and sipped their tea as Joe Ryan suddenly lumbered up the steps and out of the front gate. He crossed the damp street, looking neither left nor right for traffic, and stumbled towards them, disregarding the blossom-clogged puddles, un-aware, it seemed, of the rain which continued to drench the pavements, or of the fact that his greying shirt tails were hanging out above a pair of black trousers, buttons undone to his protruding waist. He was unshaven, face ruddy from the booze, hair lank, scraped back from his scalp, and his eyes seemed sunken way back in his skull. When he got to Maggie's gate he stopped, looked up at her and Janice peering out, with Shelly now behind them, Demi on her hip.

'They got him,' Joe choked. 'He's gone from me, my boy, he's gone.'

He swayed slightly, steadied himself on the gatepost, hung his head low and began to sob, then to howl, a sound so deep and pained you could imagine it splitting open the ground beneath his feet. The police car pulled up beside him and one of the officers got out. She looked up blankly at the women gathered at the window, then came over and put a hand on Joe's shoulder, guided him into the back of the car like a lost child being taken home. She got back into the front seat and the car took off up the street. Seconds later it had gone.

Maggie sat slowly back on her stool and shut her eyes, rocking back and forth. She knew what the shock of loss did to you. Knew instinctively that Connor was dead.

'What are we going to do, Mum?' wailed Shelly. 'If they got Con, next they're going to come for me and Demi.'

Janice moved towards her daughter. 'Let's get up your Aunty Betty's,' she urged. 'Right away.'

'Make sure to leave your key,' Maggie whispered after them as the two women shuffled towards the door. She didn't want them to have access to her home, ever again. She couldn't even bear to look at them; her eyes were still shut and she leant her weight against the sill for support as she heard Shelly drop her keys on the table, then the three of them leave the room, then her house.

Time passed and Maggie remained where she was, trying to get a sense of it. She couldn't bear to open her eyes, to face the reality. Connor had been upset yesterday. She'd never seen him like that before, broken in that way. She'd known it was about Joe but she'd also sensed something else. Now she knew it was to do with the drugs. His father's fist might have bruised him, Shelly's feet have brutalized him, but something else must have broken him, a force that she had a sense of, but could not articulate, or visualize; it was an evil that ran like a deep gash through their community. For the moment she didn't even dare to wonder how, or where or when the moment had actually occurred. It didn't seem important. The details would filter out soon enough. There was no need to go looking for bad news, it arrived ravenous as a wolf at your door, without any need for enticement. She wouldn't have long to wait. The very fact of it was all she could endure as she continued to lean against the sill, up there, marooned, on her own, like an unanchored ship in the midst of a storm. There was no solace even in opening her eyes, in watching. As she sat there trying to fathom it, her prayers ran dry, along with her spirit. Seeing Joe standing there, a hollow man in a hollow body, was all the information she needed to understand that Connor had well and truly fallen. And it was now as if his hollowness had drifted up from the street with the breeze, floated in at her window, and taken up residence inside her too.

'Maggie, are you all right, dear? Maggie? Maggie, it's me, Azi.'

Maggie heard her bell ringing repeatedly, then the voice but she didn't have the strength to respond. It was Azi standing down there below her window, where Connor usually stood, where Joe had stood. Then she heard a key turn in her lock, the sound of feet coming up the stairs, and finally the sense of Azi entering her living room. She could smell her scent, a blend of patchouli oil and carbolic soap, then felt the young woman's hand squeezing her arm.

Tepid drizzle continued to spray Meanwhile Street as Maggie sat with Azi and told her what she'd witnessed. Oblivious, other residents went about their midday chores; moving earnestly up and down steps, in and out of cars, shuffling along the wet pavements, sidestepping the puddles. It was a day for keeping yourself to yourself, a day for keeping your head down. Shifts changed and people came home or left their flats or houses to get to work, to do the shopping or to pick up their children from school. Taxis and scooters appeared intermittently, delivery men with sofas, Parcelforce with brown packages to sign for; people with no knowledge, no sense of the tragedy. If you didn't know the news, you'd have believed it to be nothing more than a dank, ordinary London day.

After feeding him, Katya stayed indoors with Milo. He fell asleep easily and she sat on the sofa and grazed on daytime TV, the lunchtime news. Nothing grabbed her attention. She threw her mobile back and forth between her hands like a pendulum, thinking first of Melina, then of how long she had been waiting for Zahir to call. She tried to conjure up his face, but already it was fading. She hadn't known him well enough or long enough for his features to have embedded themselves, yet she could still get a sense of his sweet, olive scent, the shape of his hands, the feel of his smooth skin moving in time with her own. He had to come back, she thought suddenly, passionately. She was surprised at herself. Normally she expected nothing, which had proved a life-saving philosophy, and one that proffered occasional, unanticipated rewards. But this was different. There was something magnetic about Zahir, and it wasn't just sexual. He held her transfixed. There was a purity to him: a goodness, something rare, something she recognized implicitly, something she had known before, a long time ago. Her father had had the same integrity; she'd been able to count on him. She didn't want to think about it now.

She flicked channels to distract herself. Found a chat show. Tried to refocus. But her mind drifted back to Melina. She'd been right to confront Lulu. But it wasn't enough. She wanted to see Tim suffer. She had to find a way. She'd come here to be free of such responsibility. Prague was a small town; she'd lived there all her life, everyone knew your history and remembered it. London was so much bigger, more anonymous. She'd believed that here she'd be able to explore the bigger picture but avoid the detail. But she couldn't. She had to avenge Melina – and Connor Ryan, too. Who could she turn to? She thought about Gordon. His passivity in the face of last night's fight had disturbed her. She'd thought he'd be braver. What if she told him about Melina? How would he react to that? Say it was nothing to do with them, impossible to prove? He'd probably bury his head in the sand.

Katya fished her mobile from her bag, turned the sound on the TV down with the remote and tried to call Melina. The phone went direct to voicemail. She sat back on the settee and wondered where she should go from here. Suddenly she heard muffled sobs close by, sat up straight, listened a little harder. They were coming from beyond the wall. A while passed, then the crying subsided. It was Clare she could hear crying, the last woman in the street with whom she felt any empathy; the last woman whom she would feel any inclination to console. Nevertheless, the sound of her tears raised Katya's concerns. Surely her neighbour's current distress could have nothing to do with Zahir?

For the past two hours Clare had lain on her sofa and sobbed. Now there was a stinging sensation in the pit of her stomach. She knew what it was: her conscience burning inside her, like acid. She'd have to find a way to justify her lack of intervention on Connor's behalf to Max, to convince him that neither of them were in any way responsible for what had happened to him. It wasn't their business, not at all. She also knew instinctively what Max would say: Clare didn't trust Zahir, so why had she allowed him to take care of Connor? This thought made her start crying again, because she knew she'd never find a good enough answer for that.

It wasn't long, however, before she felt the first stirrings of anger mixed in with her grief. Half an hour later and her emotions had shifted again, now to despair. Recently she'd fabricated a certain superficial stability: her job, her haircut, Max's specialist school had all been part of it. Connor's untimely death was shaking this precarious equilibrium.

If she were honest, she'd never liked the boy. When she'd looked at him she'd always sensed their own vulnerability reflected, like an open wound. His death left her feeling not only weak and helpless, but also ashamed. She knew Maggie had always been fond of him, that she'd found it in her heart to offer him sanctuary, but for Clare, Connor had symbolized the edge of things. He'd always been just a step away from failing; she and Max only a step behind. He'd been a constant, stark reminder of the struggle of it all – and she hadn't needed the daily prod. As a result she hadn't allowed herself to feel anything for him. Connor had always been a lost soul, ever since he was small. The knowledge hadn't made Clare like him any the more. If anything, it had made her like him less. She'd chosen to find his all-enveloping smile manipulative rather than endearing; had never trusted a word he said, or what he was up to.

Once, she recollected, when he could have been no more than eight or nine years old, he'd come to play with Max, and when she was absent for a moment he'd stolen a pound from her purse. She'd known it was Connor, as Max knew the price of such an act would be too high. It was only a pound, but back then every penny had counted, and she'd needed it for the electricity meter later that night. When she'd confronted him, Connor had stared her straight in the eye and denied all knowledge of the money, then he'd smiled his precious smile and she'd sent him packing. Five minutes later she'd watched as he'd sidled back past, brazenly swinging a bag of sweets in his hand. When he'd spotted Clare, he'd blown a big pink bubble of gum out and let it pop. Of course she'd known then, as she knew now, that he had had to take the money because it was the only way he was ever going to get a treat. She also knew no one had ever taught him right from wrong – how could they, when he'd had a mother who'd turned her back and a father who spent his days drunk on the sofa? She knew she should have shown him back then that she understood, she should have shown him compassion. It was too late now.

Clare texted Max to say he must come home directly after school, then she got up to make a cup of tea, wondered if she should go and see Maggie; decided to leave it a while, didn't want to be the harbinger of bad news. You had to know your own limits, she told herself; she would leave that to someone who wasn't so close to the brink. She'd go and see Mark instead, she decided. Maybe he would be able to console her.

Once he'd done with the morning service Mark headed up to his office, sat down and assessed his diary. He was preoccupied with Connor Ryan, with the boy's feverish energy at the youth club last night. Connor was mixed up with Shelly, that much was clear – and therefore with her wider circle. He needed some support outside the home. Mark knew Joe wouldn't want him to interfere, that he held his – albeit lapsed – Catholicism on high, but that didn't alter Mark's position. Joe would scorn the input of a Protestant into his son's affairs, but in Mark's view Joe had relinquished any right to criticize when he'd stopped caring properly for his child.

Mark had often seen the downward spiral before: kids like Connor who one moment were mischievous schoolboys, the next, gangling youths in hoodies, handcuffed in the back of police vans. They were dogged with ASBOs, small-court appearances, fines they couldn't hope to pay, periods in detention centres – until they grew up enough to hit the big time with a spell in the Scrubs. Society was afraid of these boy-men who roamed London's streets; ordinary citizens wouldn't want to approach one, let alone a group of them. As a result these hooded youths became increasingly alienated from society and so more volatile, discovering a certain empowerment in their community's fear of them. They had boundless energy and ideas but no one to help them channel these attributes to positive use; there were too few male role models mentoring them or guiding them towards responsible adult behaviour. Most didn't have dads, were raising themselves – and each other. Connor was different, to a degree, in that he did have his father, but what a poor example he'd proved to be. Beneath the surface Connor was still juvenile, a child who needed guidance, a child whom Mark was determined to help.

He took down his rehousing file and flicked through the possible options. None seemed appropriate for a boy of this age, which could be one of the key problems. Mark was too experienced to think that Connor's school would provide solutions. He needed a home with an adult who championed him, who could help him get over his dreadful childhood. He needed someone in his life who could convince him that he didn't need to go looking for an identity on the street, through the kind of people who would use and abuse him. Such lowlife might make him feel valued and needed for a while, only to chew him up and spit him out when they'd done with him. Mark couldn't imagine Connor going into a children's home, and anyway, by the time such an arrangement could be made, he would be sixteen years old and they'd have missed the chance. In the meantime God only knew what would happen to him.

Mark felt troubled by his lack of solutions, got up from his chair, made his way back down into the dark, now locked church, sat in a front pew and lowered his head, put it in his hands and asked the Lord to guide him. Only two options seemed to make themselves known. The first was to go and find Lorraine, to try and build Connor a bridge, to find a way for him to get back into her life, a way that would work for them both. The second which he had contemplated last night, maybe took his role a step too far. He wondered if he should, indeed if he could, invite Connor to come and stay at the vicarage. It would have to be an informal arrangement but perhaps, in conjunction, the two options might just about become a working plan for the future. Lorraine was not an unkind woman, she'd just been a young one who'd been incapable of coping. Years had now passed. Perhaps she was stronger than she'd been back then.

He'd go looking for Lorraine. It was a starting point and you never knew, maybe he'd bump into Connor along the way, would be able to have a chat with him, get a sense of who or what was frightening the boy. He took off his robes and dog collar, pulled a crew-neck navy jumper over his head and put on his black raincoat, then made for the door, feeling better for having an active plan, but as he opened it he came face to face with Clare Mitchell. He didn't speak, simply stood to one side and let her pass before him into his office. She didn't often grace the steps of St Matthew's, he saw more of Max than his mother. But she looked shaken up. Clearly, something had happened.

Clare slumped down on the simple two-seater sofa in his office and put her head in her hands.

'It's Connor Ryan,' she whispered. 'We didn't help him – to be honest, I never even liked him – but now he's dead and it's all our fault.'

Mark felt his sense of purpose, of intent, being extinguished along with the news. When she'd finished telling him what she knew they sat in silence. It was too late. He was too late. God was too late.

For the first time in his ten years here, Mark found himself weeping, and it was Clare who put her arm around him, Clare who became the comforter, Mark the comforted.

Eventually he regained his composure and Clare got up.

'I'm going to make you a cup of tea,' she said.

15

Max got off the bus at Maida Vale and jogged into the park, entering it on the opposite side to the Rose Gardens. All day he'd been thinking about Solange. Something in the way she'd called after him last night suggested she might like him. She was pretty in a less obvious way than Sammy, he decided, less provocative. She had big brown eyes, pale, creamy skin and a sweet smile. And she was shy, like him. He wondered if she'd be in the Rose Gardens with the others. Clare had sent a text at morning break demanding he come straight home from school, but Max was going to pretend he never got it. His mum was always on his case about something or other, wanted to know his every move, rein him in. Well for once she'd just have to wait. He headed past the tennis courts where he used to dream of one day winning a match against his dad, the café where he and his mates often ended up on dull Sunday afternoons, flicking sugar lumps across the empty tabletops until they got thrown out. It was still raining, but less heavily now; a light spray, just wet enough to make you feel hot and damp under the collar, but not enough to saturate your clothes. He felt short of breath in the muggy air, and slowed down. He didn't want to look sweaty when he met up with Solange.

Finally he reached the Rose Gardens, a series of formal sections with central, circular beds, separated by archways. The first was empty so he headed into the next, spotted the girls on the far side, perched in their green uniforms on the arms of two adjoining benches, under a large yellow golfing umbrella. He hesitated. Shelly was standing in front of them in her black leather jacket, hair tied tightly back from her bandaged face. She looked dangerous. Her hands were positioned aggressively on her skinny hips. Demi was next to her in a buggy. There was no sign of Casey or Michael. Max wondered if he should turn back, hang around outside until one of them tipped up, but it was already too late; Sammy had spotted him.

'Hiya Max, have you heard?' she called urgently.

Max sidled up slowly, conscious of a blush spreading across his cheeks. He felt awkward, knew he'd become lanky, kept his eyes to the path as he sat down on the damp bench, at the far end, away from Shelly.

'Heard what?' he mumbled, looking up at Solange sideways for a moment, then directly back down to his feet.

'About Con,' she said. 'He's dead.'

Max felt hot and cold and heavy and light and sick and empty and confused and clear-minded all at the same time. Images flashed through his mind's eye; images he didn't want to see, images that sent shock waves down his spinal cord, images that contracted his larynx and left him high from lack of oxygen.

'He jumped from one of the tower blocks over the Beethoven,' Solange said, coming to sit down next to him. She patted his shoulder with her arm, left it there. He didn't shrug her off. With the physical sensation of her touch, Max suddenly thought he might cry.

'Did he give you my suitcase, Max?'

Max looked at Shelly through the continuing drizzle that was making everything appear misty, or was that the fluid forming inside his eyes? He despised her, thinking about herself even now, about her loser boyfriend and their fucking stash of gear. He looked back at his feet.

'Well?' she demanded shrilly. 'Did he?'

Max tried to take a deep breath, but his throat was too dry and his tongue stuck to the roof of his mouth. It felt thick and heavy and deadened. There was no saliva and the taste rising from his stomach was bitter. He looked back up at her, more steadily, but still felt dizzy. Had no idea what she was talking about.

'I've got nuffink for you,' he muttered. 'Nuffink.'

Shelly scowled down the wound-free side of her face, turned on her heel and flounced off, pushing Demi ahead of her and out of the Rose Gardens. Max put his head in his hands and shuddered.

'When d'it happen?'

'Around midnight,' said Solange. 'Come see. Casey and Michael are already there.'

Max was shaking uncontrollably, wasn't sure if he could stand up.

'Was he pushed?'

'No one knows, some say it was the pigs, others that it was those guys Shelly hung out with – but she denies it, of course. He was chased up there, but what happened at the top isn't clear. Bet it was those nasty bastards. Shelly doesn't give a fuck, all she's worried about is clearing her name. Seems to think he was hiding something that belonged to Marlon, something that's going to land her in the same shit if she doesn't find it.'

Max got up.

'Michael bought candles,' Sammy said. 'We're going to light them where he landed.'

Max moved away from the girls, stumbled towards the bushes and vomited into a knot of thorns. Solange came over, handed him a bottle of water and when he'd drunk some and spat it out, she gave him a piece of gum to chew. Together they then headed out of the Rose Gardens, took a left out of the park, then on towards the Beethoven.

It was odd weather for this time of year. Late May and it seemed that the rain wouldn't stop falling. The sky was already looking bruised and the street lamps were turning themselves on, two hours early. The water ran down the streets, forming streams in the gutters. Drains were getting blocked and the roads smelt slightly sweet and sickly with the dirty water and the blossom and the rubbish that was sinking into it.

Presently they turned from Reeling Road towards the rising towers of the Beethoven. Max allowed the girls to lead him silently towards the block of flats where Con had died as if through a foreign landscape, one he'd never seen before. People milled around and there was noise from rumbling traffic, double-deckers coming and going, their wheels squealing at the lights, tired faces looking out of fogged-up windows, hands rubbing at them in circles to increase the view, but to Max all the sounds were muted, the colours dulled, as if they'd been boil-washed. The rain had become heavier now and he was wet through, but he couldn't feel the water, only the sensation of its weight, bearing down on him, from the top of his head to the soles of his worn-out trainers. He must have had a slight hole in one, dampness was spreading uncomfortably between his toes.

Despite the rain, ahead of them people were stopping to look at the mounting pile of flowers wrapped in cellophane, laid at the entrance to the block. The police cordons were still in place and Solange and Tyra shuffled forward with Max between them until they'd reached the front. On the other side of the cordon, kneeling down by the assorted bouquets, were Michael and Casey. They were trying to light tea lights inside three jam jars, amidst a growing harvest of floral tributes. Solange talked to a police officer and the cordon was drawn back, the three of them allowed to move forward to join their friends. Max heard the click of a shutter and turned to feel the flash of a camera on his face. He blinked at the woman behind the lens.

'*Paddington News*,' she said. 'Were you friends?'

'Didn't know him,' Max said blankly, then turned and made his way towards Casey and Michael.

Once the tea lights were lit, they loitered around for a few minutes. Tyra rummaged in her school bag and retrieved an opened packet of chewing gum, placed it in front of one of the jam jars.

'What are you doing that for?' Casey asked her.

'I gave him a piece of this yesterday,' she said. 'It's like a link to him.'

* * *

Clare paced around the flat, waiting. She'd now sent Max three texts and he'd replied to none of them. He must have heard and chosen to go with his mates. She felt sidelined. He'd turned to them and not to her. He would blame her, she knew it. She didn't know what she could say. At half past five there was a tapping on the door. She opened it hurriedly, hoping it was him, having forgotten his key, but instead discovered Mark standing on the threshold in his dog collar, looking meek.

'Something happened to Max?' she asked, alarmed.

He held up a hand. 'No, no, Clare, not at all, I just wanted to come by and see that you were OK. I was ummm, well, a bit shaken by the news, as you are aware. I feel bad. I was of no help to you.'

She felt surprisingly moved by his apology, warmed by it. When he had broken down this morning he hadn't been a vicar any more, just another human being with emotional needs. She had felt better for comforting him. She looked at him now in a new way, as a male, a single male. He was in his late forties, she guessed, had thick dark hair, slightly greying, kind eyes and an earnestness about him that she found reassuring. He wasn't someone who would push you past your boundaries.

'Strange as it may sound, you made me feel a whole lot better,' she said. 'Now do you want to come in and have a cup of tea, or even a glass of wine if you like? Might cheer us both up.'

'Oh no, I mustn't, thank you,' Mark protested. 'I'm still on duty, you see. I have to go and see the family. But I wanted to thank you, first. It was . . . kind.'

'Another time maybe, perhaps when you're off duty?'

Clare blushed at her own words. Her words sounded, well, like a proposition. She supposed they were. Mark caught her eye momentarily.

'Yes, yes, I'd like that,' he replied with a slightly embarrassed smile, and then he was gone.

When Clare finally heard Max's key in the door it was after six. She was waiting on the other side. A girl was standing at the foot of the steps, and Clare's anger mounted. So he'd been with a girl, not his mates, after all. Perhaps he didn't . . . Then she saw his face and knew she was wrong, that of course he knew about Connor. Max looked different. Older. Wiser. More tired. As fast as it had risen, Clare's anger evaporated and her sadness returned.

She nodded to the girl below, who she could now see was one of his and Connor's old primary school classmates, Tyra – or was it Solange? She'd never been able to distinguish between them. She was about to close the door on the teenager when she thought twice.

'Do you want to come in, love, have a cup of tea?' she ventured.

Max turned and glanced back at Solange. In turn, Solange glanced back at Clare.

'Not tonight, thanks Mrs Mitchell,' she replied. 'Maybe another day?'

'Of course,' said Clare. 'Another day.'

As she shut the door behind her Max dropped his bag and Clare held his tall, gangly frame to her. He tried to move his arms, but she hugged him closer. He felt he might suffocate with her arms so tight around him and he wriggled, shoved her away, a little too forcefully, perhaps.

Clare recoiled. He was rejecting her when she needed him most – more she suddenly knew, than he would ever need her again. There would always be someone else now, whether it was that one or another girl. He wasn't solely hers any more. After all she'd given of herself, he was going to walk away. Clare's future opened up before her, empty. Max looked at her, she thought, as if he could read her thoughts, and she felt a prickle of shame in her temples.

'Come into the lounge,' she pleaded. 'I'll make us a cup of tea.'

But Max shook his head and stayed in the hall, where he was, arms folded across his chest.

'We should've helped him, Mum.'

'Max, we . . .'

'No, Ma. We should've helped Connor. It was wrong of us, to leave him there.'

Before Clare could say more, Max had turned and opened the front door again. And before she could stop him he'd run off, back up the road. Clare stood on the top step helplessly as he disappeared up the street.

'Max, please, don't. Come back. *Please!*'

It was no good. He wasn't turning to look at her, wasn't listening to her words. Max had to get away from her, from here, from everything that had happened. But as he passed the Ryans' flat he found himself pulling up short, stood, puffing and panting, and put his hands on the front railings. He looked down into the well. Connor's bicycle lay abandoned at the base of the steps. As the lights were on in the front room, he could see dimly through the nicotine-yellowed net curtains across the bay window. A number of figures were standing or sitting around. For once the TV didn't appear to be on, but he could make out bottles in hands and smoke rising from glowing cigarette ends. Two women – nuns – in blue habits stood with their backs to the window. He caught a low, mournful murmur and knew instinctively what it was: the sound of grown men crying. He felt sick, turned and ran away, out of the street.

Moments later, Max climbed over the locked gate at Warlock Park and sat down on a swing in the drizzle and swung back and forth, eyes shut, letting the rain saturate him. His phone kept bleeping but he ignored it. At least two hours must have passed before he finally felt more calm. Then he took a look at his messages – one from Solange saying goodnight, the rest from his mum begging him to come home. He got up off the swing and climbed back out of the park in the dusk, back to Meanwhile Street.

Lulu was leaving her house with her two kids, the younger one in her arms, the blond-haired boy tripping down the steps in front of her in his dressing gown and slippers. The car door was open and he watched as the child jumped straight into the back seat, out of the rain. Lulu was struggling to lift some cases sitting by the front door, and the kid in her arms was crying. He hesitated, thought for a moment, then called out, 'Do you need a hand?'

Lulu looked suspiciously at Max, then recognized him.

'Thank you Max, yes please.'

His long legs took the steps two at a time and grabbed the first case. He followed the woman and child to the car, put the case in the boot, then headed straight back up for the next one. The activity shook him out of his daze. There were four cases in all, as well as a large plastic bag stuffed with toys and books. Lulu secured the kids in their booster seats then stood up and turned to watch Max, wrapped her arms around her raincoat. She looked tired – sad, he thought. God, everyone must know about Connor. Bad news travelled fast.

'You going on holiday?' he mumbled.

She laughed as if at a private irony.

'No, no, Max. We're leaving Meanwhile Street tonight. It wasn't ever going to be a place to stay for ever. We're well and truly off.'

She was pretty, he thought, if too old for him to even consider such a thing. His cheeks felt hot.

'We definitely won't be back,' she added with a defeated smile, then got into her car. The kid had stopped crying, was watching him vacantly from her car seat while her brother sat next to her, pale as a ghoul. He spied Max looking at him and stuck his tongue out. Lulu switched the wipers on and indicated to pull away. Max held up a hand in farewell. Things changed, people moved on, he thought; most times without you even knowing they had.

Clare was lying on the sofa with a crumpled paper hanky clutched in her hand, watching *EastEnders*. She glanced up when she heard Max come in. She looked all puffed up, as if she was suffering from flu. Grief was an ailment all of its own, he thought. Leaves you sick.

'You all right now, love?' she asked weakly, blowing her nose.

Max nodded his head briefly. He at once despised

her tears and felt sorry for her, didn't want her weakness around him, not now. But that made him feel guilty, too.

'You're soaked,' she said, as her tears returned.

'Stop it Mum,' he found himself scolding, then got up as she began to apologize, turned and bolted to his room, locking the door behind him. He peeled off his damp clothes, got into some clean boxers and a black T-shirt, lay down in the dark, earphones on, and listened to his dad's tracks on his iPod, the sound turned up high.

'It hasn't got any hair, Daddy,' Milo stated, staring inquisitively at his newborn baby sister.

Immy was sprawled like a deflated hovercraft on the hospital bed with Kitty Louise swaddled in next to her, eyes tightly shut, fingers clenched under her chin. Katya hung back and watched. Kitty had that ancient look of all the other newborns she'd ever seen, an other-worldliness, an ageless and timeless quality that only lasted a matter of hours after birth, that would be contaminated by human touch, by breathing the air, absorbing the sounds of the ward, the taste of her mother's milk. When she was studying she'd worked part-time at the maternity unit in Prague, as a cleaner, had seen a thousand babies arrive. She'd put that on her CV. It was probably what got her the job with Immy and Gordon, although all she'd ever done back there was clean the wards, had never even picked one of the babies up. Naturally, it had been against the rules. Immy looked shipwrecked with a catheter hanging ominously from the side of the bed, a drip attached to her arm and a pair of white surgical stockings stretched tight over her bulbous thighs and down over her puffed ankles.

Childbirth was definitely not for Katya, at least not yet – although maybe with Zahir, she mused absently, with a pang: where was he?

Immy's breasts were billowing and swollen beneath her revealing cotton nightdress. Katya struggled not to shudder. By contrast, Gordon's pride in his wife and daughter was lion-like. He lifted and held his new daughter to his chest, a coat-hanger-wide smile stretching across his face. The incident with Connor was forgotten, at least for now. It was fair enough, she thought, he wasn't key to their lives, just some kid in the street who'd got a beating. Even so, Katya knew Gordon had let him down, and she knew Gordon knew it too. Once the euphoria of his newborn was past, his conscience, again, would start to prick. She wondered what, if anything, he would do about that.

Basically this lot were good, decent people, Katya decided. They deserved this happiness – unlike Lulu and Tim. She wondered what had happened after she left. Their future together was in the balance. They didn't deserve contentment, not after the way Tim had abused Melina. In her own, less obvious way, Lulu had, too. She'd treated Katya's Polish friend like a second-class citizen, a girl from the east, someone to take advantage of. Both Tim and Lulu had some realities to confront and she still felt justified in highlighting the fact to them. In fact, she felt they had more to come. It wasn't over yet. She watched distractedly as dull-eyed nurses drifted along the corridor with drug trolleys and clipboards and more tentative visitors appeared in their side ward, bearing garish bouquets. They searched vainly for vases, settled for plastic hospital jugs, then huddled around the other hospital beds, their damp bags, coats and umbrellas sticking out from curtains pulled for privacy.

The bustle made Milo restless. He climbed down off Immy's bed and began rummaging inside her overnight case for a promised gift. It was a toy patrol car with a remote control to move it forward or into reverse, lights that flashed red and blue on command, and a searing noise like a police siren. He crawled around on the floor with it, squealing and making car sounds in time with the vehicle. Meanwhile Immy heaved one of her breasts out with an apologetic smile and attempted to latch the tiny baby on. Kitty's mouth was quivering but remained limp. Perhaps she was still trying to hold on to her other-wordliness; didn't want to be here at all, to make the transition. Maybe she knew something no one else knew.

'I go fetch you some things from the shop?' Katya asked hurriedly.

'A *Standard* would be great,' said Gordon, 'and get yourself a coffee or whatever.' He gave Katya a fiver and winked.

'I take Milo, for the adventure in the lift,' she grinned and knelt down to retrieve the toddler from the floor.

When they reached the foyer Katya dragged Milo straight outside to check for texts. Before they'd come to the hospital she'd taken yet another look down into Zahir's flat. It was gloomy. He hadn't come back. She couldn't understand it. He'd made no mention of this sudden departure. Under the glass awning disease-ravaged men shuffled around in slippers, smoking, and newly arrived visitors purchased gaudy bouquets from a bulging flower stall. Those leaving looked drained from their encounter with the sick as they waited in the cab queue. Katya looked at her screen. Nothing. Goddamit, where was he? She felt deflated. Miserable. Why Zahir's silence? She didn't deserve to be treated like this. London and everything in it was a dive. She took Milo by the arm and guided him back inside. Bought the *Standard* for Gordon, then headed for the cafeteria.

Some might have called her easy, but Katya never slept with a man unless she thought there might be something more to it. She'd genuinely liked Zahir. Really liked him. And the sex – she'd never experienced anything quite so . . . intimate. She'd loved it, that feeling of being taken over completely, of losing all control. It was good for her. She wanted to experience it again. With him. Nevertheless, as she ordered coffee, Clare's warning about terrorists nudged at her, uneasily. She watched Milo crawling around on the floor with his toy car. She supposed on paper Zahir sounded suspect. An asylum seeker who had escaped a brutal civil war; had entered London on a temporary visa, had too many computers, spent endless hours on the Internet with his silent friend. They were private people with a big black dog; had rarely left the flat since they arrived, until yesterday evening, that was. She thought about their packed cases in the hall, the lack of personal effects around the flat. It was dawning on her that they'd been poised to go. Why hadn't he told her? Perhaps Clare was right: Zahir was a bad person – but if so, how come he had been so loving?

Katya tried to push the thought away, looked vacantly at the front page of the *Standard*. There'd been a foiled bomb plot today, of all days, at four key London railway stations – including Victoria. That must be what Melina had been caught up in. A terror cell was being sought. Maybe Zahir had been involved. Katya tried to convince herself of the absurdity of her premise. Maybe it was the combination of Melina's rape and the attack on Connor that was making her think like this, so wildly. Of course Zahir wasn't a terrorist; Clare was simply mad . . . or was she? What if Katya discovered that Zahir was indeed a member of an al-Qaeda cell? What if he did intend to kill and maim people in the name of his religion? How would she feel if she'd done nothing to prevent him? She thought again about Connor, about Shelly's sickening attack on the young boy, and wished she'd given Milo to Gordon, then waded in and stopped them with her bare fists. Her father would have expected her to. Just as he'd expect her to do something about Zahir, now, too. She was deeply disappointed in Gordon. Maybe she'd have to leave, go and work for someone she could genuinely respect.

These thoughts led her back to Melina. She picked up the phone and called her. Melina answered immediately.

'I try to be in touch,' she said. 'I miss the bus; no more today.'

Selfishly, Katya felt relieved.

'Come and stay,' she urged. 'I'll ask Gordon. He won't mind.'

Melina declined, determinedly, said she felt she couldn't intrude because of the new baby, said she'd try to find an alternative. Katya was disappointed. She wanted to help Melina, but she also needed her. She felt sad and isolated and let down, on all fronts. And she needed to talk to her, above all else, about Zahir. She finished her coffee, picked up Milo and made her way back up to the ward. Milo was losing his sense of humour and Immy looked tired. Katya suggested taking him home. Immy glanced between Katya and Gordon.

'I'm really tired, love,' she said. 'Why don't you all go?'

Gordon looked unsure.

'Get some sleep,' she urged. 'Milo needs you at home.'

Gordon hesitated then leant over and kissed Immy on the lips, stroked his daughter's furry cheek with his index finger. 'I hate to leave you here,' he murmured.

Safer than Meanwhile Street, thought Katya grimly. No one had told Immy about Connor yet. Best left unspoken, Gordon had said, before they got here; after all, Immy had seen enough yesterday, and it had led to this.

While they waited for a lift, Milo pressed all the buttons so that when one finally arrived it took them to the top floor of the hospital, rather than down to the exit. Gordon leant against the back wall and started to read the *Standard* as they travelled slowly in the wrong direction. Something caught his eye and his concentration deepened. Then he handed Katya the paper, bent down and picked Milo up, held him close to his body. The lift was finally making its way back down, stopping at each floor to load and offload passengers. It was filling up and Katya was separated from them as she read the report Gordon had pointed out to her. It appeared at the bottom of page seven: a single paragraph with a small photograph, evidently taken at school, of a good-looking young boy with a mane of golden hair. At first sight he looked only vaguely familiar. But then she realized who it was and what the story was about.

The lift came to a halt at the ground floor and the doors slid open. Katya felt Gordon's hand on her back, guiding her out, and found her feet moving automatically, one in front of the other. Neither spoke as they headed out into the drizzly street. The earlier queue had evaporated and Gordon hailed a taxi, directed the driver home. Milo had fallen asleep on his father's chest. He held the child to him and put a seat belt around them both, protectively. Then he looked out at the rain.

'It's all my fault,' he said grimly. 'I should never have let him go.'

16

Azi was worried about Maggie and cancelled all other appointments, stayed with her for most of the afternoon. The rain continued to splash against the windows and the flat felt maudlin. Maggie was silent, her hands were cold, her skin had taken on a grey pallor with the shock and her breath was rasping. When Azi suggested a trip to the doctor, Maggie refused. Azi told her she would arrange a call-out for her tomorrow, if it didn't improve. Maggie had no appetite, but eventually Azi coaxed her into drinking a cup of sweet tea. Then, at four, two nuns appeared on her doorstep. They'd been sent by Father Patrick, who was down with Joe. With visitors, some colour returned to Maggie's cheeks and she managed to get out of her chair to find a tin of soft rich tea biscuits. She listened intently as the nuns told her what they knew, the police version of Connor's end; then the word on the street that someone had threatened him, chased him over the edge. At last a few tears crept down the creases in her face. Every so often she patted them away with Gerry's handkerchief, a slight sheen remaining.

At five Azi left Maggie with the nuns. Maggie wasn't

sure if she wanted the company or not, but she did know that she didn't want to be alone, not yet, so she let the young girls stay on and the kettle remained hot. She had a picture of Connor, taken when he was a small boy, and she clutched it in her hand. She wasn't sure she believed the story about him jumping off that tower block, thought it more likely that someone had pushed him, or, more likely still, frightened him into leaping. He'd always been afraid of heights. She remembered as a child that Connor didn't even like looking out of her first-floor window at the street, it made him feel 'too dizzy'. She was certain they'd never find out what had happened, you never did. Connor was dead. That was all there was to it.

Maggie's mind couldn't help but drift back downstairs to her cold, dark bedroom, to the suitcase hidden under her divan – and to Shelly's fixation with finding it. She dreaded what she'd discover under the lid; was sure it would hold a clue, but knew it was one investigation she'd be undertaking alone. The nuns used the lengthening silence to close their eyes and recite their prayers. Then she told them she needed to lie down; that they should go now. The girls helped her down to her bedroom and said they'd fetch her in a couple of hours, as agreed, for prayers at St Bride's. Maggie watched around her net curtains as they made off through the deluge. She'd never seen rain like it, not in late May. It was oppressive, threatening – as if God's wrath was being spent, in the name of Connor Ryan.

Maggie wanted to open the case but was too tired to drag it from under her bed. Instead she lay down, set the alarm for seven and closed her eyes. Within moments she was sleeping the sleep of the dead. When she stirred the heaviness in her bones alerted her to the proximity of grief. Nothing but the shock of a bereavement made you feel like this. She'd experienced it several times before in her long life, first with her mother, then her father, and then with her older brother, Kieran, who'd gone far too young. Most recently of course with Gerry. With Connor, however, the weight of her sorrow went even deeper, not just to the very core of her, but somehow through her, too. Her spirit felt diminished. She wondered why that should be – perhaps because his death was so untimely, or perhaps because it felt as if he'd left the door ajar for her to follow him through. Maggie wondered if he'd come to see her because he knew that he was going to die. She wondered if he'd planned the visit in advance, even, if he had known it would be the last time she saw him. There'd been pathos in his visit, it was as if he'd been grieving in advance, for himself. She should have sensed the depth of his fear, should have prevented him from leaving her house, been more forceful, demanded that he stay. One of the problems for kids like Connor was that no one ever told them, categorically, what to do. There were always options: to stay or to go, to learn or to disregard, to eat or to starve, to sleep or to roam. The boundaries weren't there. Instead of providing them with freedom, however, this lack of authority invariably led to misfortune. The lucky ones managed to bypass tragedy – but others, like Connor, became the victims.

Maggie sat on the bed and pulled the counterpane up. She heaved and huffed and puffed, heaved some more until the blue suitcase was sitting there before her bulging knees. Then she pushed the heavy lid back. The case was packed haphazardly, clothes rolled up or squashed in, a few personal effects chucked on top. The first was a photograph in a distinctly greasy glass frame, a school picture of Connor, aged no more than four or five, sitting proudly in his bright blue school sweatshirt, his syrupy hair glistening, his eyes shining with the innocent expectations of infancy, his grin so broad you wouldn't believe the trouble to come if you looked at it. There was a milk tooth missing: the first one, front left, bottom. So he must have been at least five or six. Maggie swallowed hard, took her hanky from her pocket and rubbed at the frame until the greasy film had left his face, then she propped it up on her bedside table and observed it for a while before looking back into the case.

There was a large, very heavy textbook, with the words *SQL for Dummies* written across it in a mock-graffiti style. She opened it curiously: it was a book explaining Internet code. She didn't know that Connor had such interests, that he was in the process of learning something new. Maybe he wasn't, maybe it had simply been an aspiration. She put the book down heavily on her bed, had another feel within the clothes' folds. A second photograph came to light, this time of Connor as a baby, sitting on Lorraine's lap, on a wall somewhere familiar, somewhere she couldn't quite place. Maybe it was round the corner, at Warlock Park, or the wall outside St Matthew's. Both Lorraine and Connor were smiling in the picture, but around Lorraine's eyes were the telltale dark circles that suggested unhappiness. It must have been taken when things were progressing towards their worst. Six months later and she'd be gone.

Maggie put the photograph down and sat back for a moment to contemplate. What was it she was looking for? There appeared to be nothing else of any value in the case; just a bundle of socks, some pants and tracksuit bottoms, a couple of T-shirts, a pair of rancid trainers and some cheap toiletries. The case had felt so heavy. It didn't add up. Maggie heaved herself down off the bed and tipped everything out on to the floor, then tried to flip the case on to its side – and struggled. Finally she felt around the lining. It was thickly padded. She shifted her position and pulled her bedside drawer open, took out a pair of gold nail scissors. Then she turned and made a deep cut. The small but sharp blades easily broke through the nylon lining, but met with a resistant layer of plastic underneath it. She pushed harder and the scissors sank into something soft, like plasticine. When she pulled them out a few white specks were stuck to the metal. She made a longer, more superficial cut along the lining, working into it around the four edges of the case until she'd loosened the entire piece of fabric. Then she gave it a tug and it came away readily.

It was only then she realized the lining was held in place by a tiny zip running around the entire case. Hidden underneath were three cellophane-wrapped bags of white powder. It wasn't difficult to guess what they were, even for someone of Maggie's age. The poor boy, he'd had no idea what he'd got himself into. No wonder everyone had been looking for him. And no wonder he'd been afraid.

Maggie worked her way around the base of the case, and inside the lining on the near side she discovered three more bags. Six bags of something. Quite what, she wasn't sure. Whatever it was, she knew what it signified. And she also knew it was none of Connor Ryan's business, that it had arrived here by default, that Shelly and Janice had infected the boy with their business, business brought to their front door by Marlon. No wonder tensions had been heightened.

Maggie sat back on her bed and shut her eyes. Dear God, she prayed. Help me. She met with a stern silence, so next she tried talking to Gerry, but gained no response there, either. Maggie wondered if she should call the police, or Shelly and Janice; get them to take their dirty drugs away; to deal with the aftermath themselves. She wondered who would be held responsible, and what trouble she'd be getting them into. She didn't care for Shelly but she didn't want to get her any deeper into this, either. There was Demi to think of. Look what had happened to Connor after Lorraine left. Demi needed her mother. Shelly should learn a lesson, but judging by the amount of illegal substances sitting here, an official lesson would be long-term. Janice might be implicated, too. Maggie thought about the effect of them both going to jail, on Demi, first and foremost, and then, to a lesser degree, on herself. She couldn't afford to allow that to happen – could she? Also, if the drugs were discovered, it would be concluded that Connor had been a degenerate who deserved what had come to him. She hated to think of him going to his grave with a black mark hanging over him. The problem was, there was just too much of the stuff for her to ignore or readily dispose of. How could she get rid of it without anyone knowing?

It was already a quarter past seven. Her priorities shifted and she became fixed on the impending vigil at St Bride's. She'd have to revisit this little problem later; it was, by comparison, of secondary significance. She shoved the clothes back in on top of the packages, squeezed the case almost shut and pushed it back under her bed, pulled the counterpane back down, heaved herself up and brushed her fine silver hair with a soft-bristled brush that had once belonged to her mother. Then she put on her tweed coat and sat down to wait. She felt wrung out, exhausted – and dishevelled, too. It would normally have taken her twice as long to prepare to leave her front door, but she knew tonight that no one would care, that no one would be looking her way.

On the dot of seven thirty she was ready and waiting when the nuns knocked. Maggie stood heavily and reached for her stick. There was a minicab waiting outside and the nuns helped her into the back of it. Then they were all off in the direction of St Bride's, off to see Joe, off to pray for Connor.

Billy's Jag swung into Meanwhile Street as Maggie's minicab trundled out. He spied the old lady bunched up inside, a creepy-looking nun on either side of her, guessed where they were heading. All day he'd struggled to get the documentary finished, but after last night his usual pursuit of perfection seemed unimportant, fine details inconsequential. He'd cut corners. Usually they'd all go out now, to celebrate the final edit. But tonight wasn't usual. A kid called Connor Ryan had changed all that. Billy didn't explain to the crew; couldn't get the words out; guessed it was shock, left as soon as he could, headed back through the rain, wipers steadily clearing the screen, back and forth, back and forth. He wanted to check in with Joe; see if there was anything he could do, not that he could think what that might be. But now he'd spotted Maggie going off to the church he guessed that Joe would be there too; and when he knocked on the basement door he wasn't surprised to be met by silence. Billy felt deflated, morose and excluded, but didn't want to join them, either, couldn't hack churches at the best of times, particularly Catholic ones; the incense made him want to gag and he was an outsider, wasn't family, or even a friend. His presence wouldn't be understood.

He loitered in the basement well and stamped his damp feet, stared emptily at Connor's bike, lying there in a puddle. Leaves clogged the drain; it needed sweeping. He made a mental note to do it for them – for Joe, the hapless git – in the morning. Connor's broken face flashed through his mind yet again as he made his slow ascent and opened his own front door. He was dying for a fix, but tasted a new flavour, a bitter revulsion for what his body craved. All day he'd thought about it and a map had grown inside his mind. It was no ordinary map but a spidery, black and white illustration showing dark blots of countries, dissected by circuitous lines and broken arrows, airport symbols and stick people with guns, then streets with tiny dots of more people on them, people skulking in dark corners, people doing deals. Billy was one of those people, and he knew that Connor, somehow, had become a victim of his, Billy's, needs. It was a net, and they'd all been ensnared.

Until now Billy'd been able to convince himself that his drug-taking was a controlled affair and that, morally, he had a right to put whatever he wanted into his own bloodstream, that it was nobody else's business, whether it was legal or not. Overnight, Connor had changed all that. Billy didn't know the detail, or even understand the bigger picture, but one thing he did understand was that the child had been sucked in. He'd seen him recently, hanging out on the corner with those girls, jailbait in their high-heeled shoes and short skirts, eyes glazed from too many Class A's. There was no way, any more, that he could score another line, drop another pill. It would make a mockery of Connor's tragedy. Billy had never been one for abstinence, he was addictive, craved adrenalin rushes, was a workaholic, a drugaholic; a fast-lane junky. It was all available, all around him. But Connor was dead and it was over now.

He lay down on his bed in the dark, tapped his fingers on his chest then shut his eyes, recognizing a fatigue that had been building for months. Connor had sledgehammered it home, his wrecked state. It was time to sleep, to clean up – and it was time for something else, too. Time to make a difference. As he drifted, Billy wondered what he meant by that, how he could alert kids like Connor to the dangers of the city, whether he could do it through his work, whether there was any point; then he felt his phone vibrate in his pocket, and saw a number he didn't know. He picked up.

'Hi, Billy, it is me, Melina.'

Billy took a moment to connect. A lifetime had passed since his daybreak trip to Victoria station.

'Hi,' he replied. 'Are you back in Krakow?'

He heard the girl sigh.

'Melina, what's up?' He put a hand behind his neck, rubbed the tension out. In a minute he'd have to smoke a cigarette.

'My bus, it was cancelled. Bomb scare.'

'Where are you?'

'Victoria. I don't know what to do.'

So that was it. She was stranded. Billy glanced at the clock. Seven forty-five. He suppressed a yawn. Despite it all, as he listened to her voice he felt his anxiety ease. Knew what he needed to do next.

'I'm on my way,' he said.

'You sure is OK?' Melina's tone had lifted.

'Well you can't carry all those cases on the bus, can you?' he replied, as he felt a childish grin spreading across his face. Billy couldn't fucking believe it, the change that was coming over him. Elation was springing up through the funeral pyre of his misery. He was startled; it had never happened this way before.

'Wait where I dropped you this morning,' he reassured her. 'Don't move. I'll be there in half an hour.'

Billy made for the bathroom, splashed cold water over his face, spiked his hair up, sprayed a touch of Paul Smith on his neck; then headed back out into the rain. He glanced momentarily down the well at Connor's bike, at the Ryans' dark, silent front room, and shivered. Then he got into the car.

After the earlier chaos London was now running

smoothly again, and soon he was pulling in at Victoria. He spied Melina leaning against the wall with her bags piled on top of one another, and for a moment he hesitated, wondered if he should drive on past. She suddenly looked foreign, insignificant; just one of thousands of young Eastern Europeans who'd made their way to London to seek a better life. You couldn't escape them, they were everywhere; in the streets, the bars, the restaurants, serving you in the supermarkets, cleaning your flat, cutting your hair.

Melina's skin looked sallow under the lamplight, her features pinched, her hair lank from the rain. She wore cheap clothes that pastiched style, a fashion raincoat that was too thin to keep her dry. If he hadn't known her as Melina, Billy knew he wouldn't have noticed her at all. That was the point. She was one of the new kids on the immigration block, an insignificance to a London old-timer like Billy. She was standing precariously on the bottom rung of the city's ladder, while he'd already spent a decade clawing his way up. It took a while to get the hang of London's complex game, to create your own unique strategy for playing it; a while more to get an opportunity, to get experience, to get noticed. Finally, Billy was becoming successful. This last documentary was good; good enough perhaps to get him discussed in the right, almost impenetrable circles. Maybe he didn't have time for Melina right now – maybe her woes would simply become his burden?

His attention switched briefly back to Connor, to the boy's crushed body, his smashed-up face. How long would it take for that image to blur? He already knew it would never completely evaporate; that on some level he'd have to live with it, always. All he could hope for was a fade; a reduction in the intensity of the frame. Only an hour ago, he reminded himself, he'd been contemplating a drug-free future, a future within which he could make a difference. Well, here was his chance. Melina was alone, vulnerable and in need of his support. He felt a moment's doubt – did he really want to get involved? Could he? Should he? But then she glanced up and spotted his car, and as her face relaxed into a sweet, sweet smile his doubts evaporated. Yes he could, and he would. He pulled up at the kerb and switched on his hazards, leapt out and went round to greet her.

'Hop in, out of the rain,' he urged as he opened the boot, grabbed her bags and put them inside.

'There was bomb scare; they close the station. My bus cancel,' she explained, looking sideways at Billy as he drove her off through the rain, then she turned and watched the city as they passed it by.

Melina hadn't known if she should call him, but he'd felt like her safest bet. She was beginning to feel very sick; was sure it was the second pill that had done it. Her stomach was cramping, over and over. She could have booked into a cheap hostel, but with all her cash on her, as well as her pain, she felt vulnerable. Tim's abuse was beginning to feel distant, like something that had happened to another version of herself, in another place and at another time. Since it had happened, she'd been plunged into this impersonal London hubbub, observing the crowds surging this way and that. One moment they seemed like an amorphous, unified mass, the next like thousands of bubbling atoms bursting out in all directions, talking on phones, eating fast food, drinking coffee, listening to music on their headphones; self-immersed and intent. When Victoria had finally reopened she'd shuffled slowly round to the bus station and was informed she'd have to come back in the morning. Melina didn't feel anything as she absorbed this latest information, no great care or anxiety. As time ticked past she only knew one thing, that she wanted to lie in a bath, then curl up and go to sleep. She could still feel Tim on her skin; inside her. There had to be a way to get him out she thought in panic.

'Home.'

Billy's voice cut through her reflections. Melina glanced over at him, startled. A good twenty minutes must have passed. They'd arrived in Meanwhile Street and he'd parked outside his flat. She glanced briefly towards Tim and Lulu's dark house and felt even more sick. Lamplight shone on to an empty parking space in front of their railings. Neither of their cars was there.

'You were miles away.'

She looked back at him, confused, and Billy laughed.

'Doesn't matter.'

'Today is very long very strange day,' she apologized.

'Sure has been. You hungry?'

She shook her head. 'No, I feel really not well. I need bath, please.'

Soon Melina was submerged, allowing the water to soften and soothe her skin. She couldn't believe Tim had raped her; it would always be with her now, an internal, invisible wound. All day she'd wondered how she could rebuild from here, but even in her confusion and sickness, in Billy's presence she knew something miraculous was happening: she had found something pure and positive and precious. This man who was almost a stranger was instinctively familiar. When he'd greeted her at the station it was as if she already knew him, knew all the possibilities that awaited them – and most importantly, knew that he wouldn't let her down.

Melina tried to balance these thoughts with caution; was aware she was naive, vulnerable, and that today was definitely not the day to meet a new friend, let alone to fall in love. Perhaps her emotions were nothing more than a reaction to Tim? She'd had boyfriends back in Poland, but had never felt convinced by her feelings for any of them. She'd wondered if she were incapable of loving; if her father's effect on her had been to make her untrusting of men, if her mother's reluctance to involve herself with any man since he'd left them might have rubbed off on her, if she might live her life out alone. But now she'd met Billy. She could hear him moving around in the flat and it felt reassuring. He was humming under his breath as he entered the kitchen, opened and shut a drawer, stirred a teaspoon in a cup.

She pulled herself upright in the bath and stood calf-deep in the water, took a bar of soap between her hands and turned it over and over to produce a thick, sudsy lather. Then she began to wash her skin, starting with her face, then her neck, her arms, before working her way down, over her stomach, between her thighs, down her legs, to her shins, her ankles, her feet, between each toe, until she'd cleansed every part of her. Then she lay back down in the water and rinsed the suds away. Finally she got out, dried herself and got dressed again, catching her features in Billy's bathroom mirror. Her dull eyes were sunken into a sallow skin, her lips looked pale; she tried a smile but it didn't look convincing. She was weak-looking, imploded, a pathetic, violated child with no real prospects ahead of her. Billy was a successful adult, a film-maker, a director, no less; someone who could take his pick of women, someone who didn't need to waste his time on her. After this morning, he was evidently feeling charitable. She needed to rein in these new emotions. She took a few long, deep breaths, turned and left the bathroom.

Billy was in the sitting room, lit by one side lamp, smoking a cigarette. The room was painted wine red and simply furnished, with shelves of neatly stacked hardback books, mainly on photography and film. A large Andy Warhol print of Marilyn Monroe hung on the wall above the fireplace, and a series of black and white film stills in silver frames were hung in even spaces along the walls. The floorboards were stripped, the wood stained dark. Billy lounged on a long brown leather sofa, his feet stretched out before him in thick grey wool socks. Opposite was a deep-seated green armchair and above it a large flat viewing screen. He gestured towards the chair and Melina sat down in it, hunched her legs up as her back sank comfortably into its soft cushions.

'Tea?'

'In a moment,' she said.

'Already made it.' He gestured towards a cup on the coffee table next to her. Melina picked it up and took a sip. It was hot and sweet.

'I so tired,' she said apologetically. In fact she felt her body uncoiling, after the tension that had twisted inside her like a spring all day, but the sickness remained, just beneath the surface.

Billy observed her curiously, kindly. Her melancholy made him ache; she was utterly compelling, movingly sad, like a woman in an early Picasso painting. What had made her so sorrowful? When he'd seen her last week she'd been with that other au pair, Katya. They'd been giggling conspiratorially at something one or the other had said. There'd been an ease to their step, a light-heartedness. Something significant must have happened to so alter Melina's mood. Maybe she knew about Connor after all? Billy sat up, swung his legs round, stubbed out the cigarette, leant forward with his elbows on his knees.

Melina felt his eyes absorbing her. 'What you think?' she enquired.

'I just wondered,' he said. 'If you'd heard about Connor Ryan, if that was what is making you sad?'

Melina creased her eyebrows and looked at Billy expectantly.

'Connor?' she said.

It was too late to retract. 'The boy, Connor, I mentioned him this morning, on the way to the station.'

'Ah, yes, Max's friend,' Melina replied vaguely. 'His mother, Clare, is friend with Katya's family.'

'He died.' Billy leant over to the side table and picked up a packet of Marlboro, took another one out and lit it. He felt foolish, overwhelmed. 'He died, last night; jumped, from a tower block.'

'Oh my God,' Melina exclaimed. 'Is terrible, really.

Why he do this? Was because of drugs? Everyone in this street does the drugs. He was mixed with them, the ones at the end. I see him there in the evenings, on the wall with those girls and the babies.'

Billy was silent for a few minutes. 'I feel responsible,' he eventually said haltingly. 'The boy lived right beneath me and I did nothing to help him. He was just a kid, with a fucked-up family. It was going to happen. I should have stopped it.'

Melina looked at Billy, confused. He felt responsible? How? Why? It was not his fault. It was this place, it didn't know how to protect its people. That was all.

Billy sat for a few moments smoking, and Melina sat watching.

'Billy,' she tried finally. 'Is not your fault. Is the father, the school, the police, the kids with the drugs, but is not you. You are hard-working man who leave early, come home late.'

Billy looked up at Melina, held up a hand to stop her in her tracks. 'Yeah, and I do the drugs too,' he blurted. 'You see, Melina, I am responsible. Do you get it? I do the drugs. He was just a kid, but the drugs must have got to him. The bullyboys with their big cars, they need boys like Connor to traffic the stuff round the city. And I buy it on the street, so I'm as responsible as the next person who does it. I'm gutted, Melina, totally gutted.'

Silence stretched between them. Immediately he had spoken, he regretted his words. He didn't want to scare her away.

'I've got to stop. I can't do any more,' he said eventually.

'Please, Billy, don't be too unkind to yourself. You are a good man.'

So maybe she'd give him a chance. Billy felt relieved, smiled at Melina but shook his head. 'I've been preoccupied, selfish, satisfying my desires, ignoring their impact. It's over. It's time to make a change. I can't do it any more. Not after what I saw last night. It's over.'

'You saw?'

Billy nodded grimly, then lay back along the sofa while Melina found herself sinking deeper into the chair. Her eyes drifted shut. She was going to have to sleep, despite this shocking news. She didn't have a choice. She kept drifting in and out of consciousness. Then Billy was getting up. She opened her eyes. He was standing next to her chair, by the window.

'Joe's back,' he said. 'I better go down.'

'You want I come?'

'No, stay here, rest. I've made up my bedroom for you. I can take the sofa.'

Melina listened as he let himself out of the flat, then heard muffled voices, people heading down the steps into the basement, the door being opened, then shutting again. Then she fell asleep.

Inside Joe's flat the air was thick with misery. The flat stank of rotten food, stale cigarette smoke and body odour. There were piles of stuff everywhere: free local newspapers and takeaway food trays, direct-mail flyers and phone directories still in their cellophane wrappers, dirty clothes and encrusted towels. Objects tumbled from overstuffed cupboards and covered every available surface. The stench seemed to ooze from everything, like stale sweat from open pores. Billy thought he might retch. Couldn't hang about down there for long.

Joe had his two hefty cousins with him. They'd been at the morgue, then the church, and finally down the Ship for a swift Guinness. Billy offered his condolences.

'Thank you for going to see him, last night, mate, with the police,' Joe replied sheepishly.

Billy nodded soberly. It must have been hard for him, Billy recognized, to refer to his final failing of Connor, his failure to wake up when his son was already dead. It reflected the entire history of his relationship with him; he was never there, had never managed it. Not even when it was too late to have an impact.

'It was the least I could do,' he said, turning his face away.

'Can I get you a nightcap, son?' Joe responded, looking around for a bottle.

One of the other men lifted a plastic bag from his deep jacket pocket and Billy saw a screw top poking out of it. He held his hand up.

'Not for me, thank you. I'll be heading back up. But let me know if there's anything I can do to help with the arrangements, you know. You might need me to fetch and carry with my car.'

Joe nodded and slumped down on the sofa. His pitted gut was hanging out of his trousers; his face was pale and sweating and his breathing was thick and heavy. He wasn't going to be a long-termer himself, Billy thought gloomily. Then he felt a moment's anger stir. The man was a fucking mess; look at him, lying there like a sorry piece of shite inside his own squalor. He couldn't be more than forty, only a few years older than Billy himself. The anger didn't last, switched in a second to pity. Joe was incapable of helping himself, let alone his son. Billy tried to imagine him five stone lighter, with clean hair and clothes, in a clean flat; sober. Joe could have been someone else, he realized, someone completely different. But then so could we all. His own shame was close to the surface. What had made them all fail themselves and each other like this?

Billy could find no excuse for his own behaviour. He'd been born into privilege, had gained a great education, from an early age had been taught how to be one of life's players and was busy succeeding. Despite it all, he'd spent the past decade shoving the white stuff up his nose. By contrast, Joe's pathetic, impoverished history ran through his veins like a polluted river. From the start he hadn't stood a chance. How could his miserable lot not have infected Connor?

There was a time when it had seemed Connor had had potential, that he was different, when he'd looked like a little prince: a little prince who'd been born into the wrong caste, with all that golden hair and those extraordinary, chlorophyll eyes. Even Joe had been aware of it, half-cut or not. He'd taken pride in his child's aura, had bragged about his extraordinary beauty – even though it had evidently come up through Lorraine's side. You could almost imagine a fairy godmother waving a magic wand and suddenly Connor would have been trimmed and tidied, dressed up in a pair of grey shorts and a blazer, attending a prep school. Smart in class, deft on the rugby fields, striding towards Oxbridge without a backward glance to his history, he would have been a shining example; a boy with a bright future.

Billy captured a few frames of Connor in his mind; they replayed like a short film. A boy of nine or ten appeared, turning the corner into Meanwhile Street on a metal scooter, zooming home from school on his own, head down, face deep in concentration, right foot pushing the past out from under him, trouser leg flapping in the jet stream. The boy had glanced up at Billy as he'd dodged him and he'd grinned, a grin as quick and sharp and exhilarating as a hit of cocaine. Billy remembered thinking back then that the boy had star quality; that one day he could be in films, or on the stage. How had they all let him slip through the net?

Melina was sitting where he'd left her. She'd clearly drifted off into sleep but was now feigning wakefulness.

'Melina?'

Billy crouched down in front of her – it was strange – she'd just done it again, clocked out. She was beautiful, pale and ephemeral. He wanted to stroke her face.

'Go to bed,' he said. 'It's getting late.'

'Yes, I have bus to catch, at eleven.'

Billy frowned, felt mild panic.

'You're going, tomorrow?'

'I have open ticket; for bus, yes.'

'Do you want to go home? You can stay, you know, that is, if you want to,' he was gabbling, couldn't stop. 'I finished my film today. I'm off work, at least for a week or two. We could hang out; you know, get over all this stuff that's been going on, together.'

'I don't know what I want,' she said feebly. 'All I know is I had to leave that house, get away from that man.'

Billy searched her face; read the anguish and understood it. His chest tightened. 'You're going to be safe here. You don't need to leave, I'll never hurt you, never make you go anywhere you don't want to go.'

She didn't know where it came from, but Melina found herself smiling up at Billy. He didn't know where it came from, either, but he found himself grinning back.

'Let's see how you feel in the morning, if you want to stay or go,' he suggested. 'It'll be up to you.'

He showed her to his room, left her at the door. Melina shut it behind her with a light click and Billy returned to the sofa where he lay for a few minutes, absorbing his latest shock, thinking about Melina and Tim. He wasn't going to let her down the way they'd all failed Connor.

Eventually he got up and crept into the hall, listened at his bedroom door for a moment. He could hear her breathing deeply, called her name a couple of times but Melina didn't respond. Then he let himself out of the flat and headed off up the street.

17

Katya put Milo straight to bed. When she came back downstairs she found Gordon drinking a beer in the sitting room.

'I've called the police, told them I saw the fight, and they've asked me to go in and make a formal statement in the morning,' he told her.

It's as if he's only one who saw it, Katya thought huffily. He seems to think he's the only important one. She didn't reply, but sat down and watched sullenly as he paced the sitting room, drinking from the bottle, frowning and sighing occasionally. She wondered if he was beginning to feel bad, hoped so. He had every reason to. He should have stopped the girls, any brave man would. He could write all he liked, hide behind his newspaper desk and his comfortable salary, but when it came down to it, what did he actually do to change society? Nothing.

Katya often glanced through his liberal paper. It was intellectual, didn't get read by the people who lived on the harsh streets. It wasn't easy out there. Gordon and Immy had privileges, nice clothes and food and holidays and girls like her to clear up after them, for little money. How would Gordon react if she told him about Melina? Probably phone the police again – and what a lot of good that would do. Katya knew that her father would have been round there, that he would have made Tim pay for his actions; humiliated him privately and publicly.

Before long Gordon had finished the beer and went down to the kitchen in the basement to fetch a second one from the fridge. He came back upstairs with it, sat down on the sofa opposite her.

'It's hopeless,' he said. 'Hopeless.'

'Connor, he was at Zahir's yesterday lunchtime,' she blurted. 'Now he has gone, and the computers, too. I don't understand. What is their friendship?'

Gordon looked incredulous. 'Why would Connor have been there? And you, too. I had no idea you knew those men?'

Katya stared at the floor. 'Zahir, he is my friend,' she mumbled. 'Is very strange. Maybe Clare was right about him. Maybe he is terrorist after all.'

'Terrorist? Well, I think that's highly unlikely. He's challenging the European Court of Human Rights on asylum for himself and his people. I've talked to him about it many times. I was planning a piece for the newspaper.'

'I think he is good man, too,' Katya replied, smiling. She was unable to hide her relief.

Gordon noted it, sighed. Jesus.

'Maybe you should go and talk to Clare. Find out if she knows what's been happening in there over the past twenty-four hours, see if she knows where Zahir's gone,' he replied. 'If you're still suspicious after that we ought to call the police. But Katya, I don't have much truck with this terrorism paranoia.'

Maybe it was just the shock of hearing that Connor had died that had affected her reasoning. Even so, Katya knew she would do anything to find out where Zahir was, even go and see that stupid woman. She got up, pulled her phone from her bag and checked for texts, in the final hope that he might have called her. There was a message, but it was not from Zahir, but Melina.

I stay at Billy's. 14 Meanwhile St.

She reread it with curiosity. Gordon was sitting back on the sofa with his eyes closed.

'I go now to Clare,' she said, then went into the hall and put on her red macintosh.

'I'll wait up,' Gordon called, woozily.

It was still raining. Katya stood on the threshold and looked left along the street towards Billy Crouch's house. The lights were on in the front window, but not in the basement flat's bay, where Connor had lived with his dad. What was Melina doing with Billy Crouch? Katya had met the guy in the street a few times, he seemed friendly, if a bit frantic. She had had no idea Melina even knew him. She felt a stirring of jealousy, couldn't help it. He was an interesting guy. She hadn't thought Melina could grab the attention of someone like that. She considered going there, but then thought again. It was getting late. She needed to go and see Clare, straight away. She glanced across the road at Maggie's house. The lights were on in Gladys's basement, and a soft glow warmed the curtains in Maggie's bedroom on the ground floor too, but the windows above in Maggie's first floor were in darkness.

The old lady must have gone to bed early. Katya felt a deep pang of sorrow for her as she flicked the latch on their iron gate and passed through, allowing it to clang shut behind her. Then she turned right and made her way to the next house along.

Maggie sat down heavily on her bed. It had all but finished her off, the church. She was bleary-eyed from crying and her body ached so you would have thought it had been stuck through with pins, like a voodoo doll. She didn't have the energy to do any more than get herself into bed. There'd be no brushing of teeth, taking of heart pills, or netting of hair tonight. She pulled her stockings off, unbuttoned her dress and pulled it over her head, then dug around under the pillow for her nightdress. Connor's photograph followed her every move. His eyes seemed to have changed expression. They carried a sadness beneath their twinkling surface that she hadn't noticed this morning. She swung her swollen legs round, slithered them down under the sheet and pulled the blankets up over her. The dampness outside seemed to have entered the bedroom with her, and Maggie shivered. She wouldn't be doing anything with the case tonight. No one knew that Connor had brought it to her, that was certain. She recalled looking up and down the street while he'd dragged it towards her front steps yesterday morning. There'd been no one around, apart from that prowling black cat. She still had time to work it all out, before the funeral, time to plan.

She reflected on the evening as she lay in the dark. All sorts of people had crawled out of the city's shadowy spaces to enter St Bride's, a vast gothic church on the edge of Kensal Rise, to mourn for Connor Ryan, some of them no doubt attracted by the report of the death on the day's early evening news, which had caused them to feel they were in the media spotlight. There was nothing like a bit of attention to get backsides onto the pews. Of course Joe was at the front with all his shabby excuses for cousins in their bagging trousers and moth-eaten jackets. They'd sat beneath the glittering altar, bent double, inconsolable. A photograph of Connor had been propped up underneath the candles, the same school photograph that Maggie had found in his suitcase.

As people arrived they moved forward, made the sign of the cross, then patted Joe's shoulder gently before retreating to lower their own heads. The nuns from Our Sisters of Mercy sat together in front of Maggie like a line of turtle doves in their matching blue habits; heads tilted forward, silent and still. There were a number of old-timers from the area who always appeared and kept the numbers up, as well as a gaggle of awkward-limbed, wary-eyed kids who must have known Connor from school. They sat bunched uneasily together towards the back, as if waiting outside the headmaster's office for detention. One of the girls snivelled noisily. Maggie imagined it to be her first experience of death. Later Dren showed up, still in his plaster-dusted clothes. He looked handsome but downcast, stood meekly at the back before kneeling to pray. After a few minutes, he left again. Only Lorraine was conspicuous by her absence; but then Maggie hadn't expected her to change the habit of a lifetime.

Maggie had conversed with God and Gerry, crying

a baptism of tears into her crumpled tissues. She was devastated by Connor's death. If only she could get through this week, she thought desperately, get herself over to that funeral and give him a right proper sending-off, then really she would have had enough of this mortal coil, would be eager to throw it off. Her chest pained her, she wasn't well and she had no interest in seeing the doctor tomorrow. What was the point any more, if she couldn't even protect the people she loved, even those who lived on the street around her? One thing, however, was for certain: she wasn't going to let the boy go to a pauper's grave. If it were left to Joe, Connor would end up in some low-ranking plot at the back of Kensal Rise Cemetery, disposed of with no one but the locum priest in attendance. Maggie rolled over in bed. She took Connor's picture from the table, held it close to her heart over the eiderdown and shut her eyes.

Across the street, Clare had fallen asleep in front of the television. She hadn't had the energy to get up and turn it off; hadn't been able to see the point of making the effort. Eventually Max had come down from his room and found her there.

'Mum, Mum, wake up.'

'What's the time?' she mumbled, pulling herself upright, and looked across at her son.

'Ten o'clock,' said Max. 'I think Zahir's back. The lights are on and the dog's barking. Do you think we should call the police?'

'The police, why? We don't want them round here.'

'They need to question Zahir about Con. If he's a

terrorist and Con was involved with him, perhaps there's something bigger at stake, a plot. The computers, they've all gone, disappeared in the middle of the night just after Con died. I've been trying to work it all out. I don't reckon that fight with Shelly had anything to do with Con's death. I think he was running away from Special Branch, or MI5 – I reckon he was in on some kind of plot with Zahir, I reckon he was part of a cell. Maybe they're about to blow something up – or maybe they were responsible for the bomb scares in London today – maybe it's been blocked but the police haven't caught the suspects yet. I saw it on the news, said people should report anything suspicious. Well, I think it's suspicious that they cleared out in the middle of last night and I think it's a weird coincidence that, at the same time, Con leaves Zahir's and gets chased off by some men who no one can identify. Why did he jump? What was he afraid of? Must have been bloody scared of something. Must have thought he would be off to Guantánamo Bay. No wonder they've cleared out.'

'Max, wow, hold on, what are you talking about? Will you calm down, slow down.' Clare put her hand in front of her eyes as if to shield them from her son's onslaught.

Max ignored her. 'I've spent the last hour online, Mum, checking the latest news reports,' he went on doggedly. 'I bet it's them, I bet they're the ones, man. You said it yourself, not to trust him, not to trust Jaka. Now it's time to deal with it. We can't keep turning our backs.'

'Don't you think, if the police were aware of some terror cell in Meanwhile Street, that they'd have been round here by now, checking up on it? Do you really think they'd just leave them to get on with it? You're talking at sixes and sevens, love.'

'Well if you won't do anything about it, I'll just have to,' Max retorted, stomping out of the lounge and back up the stairs.

Clare followed him but Max had already reached his bedroom, shut the door in her face and locked it. As she stood outside it she could hear him on the phone. She went downstairs and glanced out of the bay window, craned her neck down into the well. Light glowed from the front windows for a moment, then went out. Moments later she heard the front door open, then close again. Two hooded men ascended from the basement steps, a dog on a leash before them. Sure enough, it was Zahir, followed closely by Jaka. They moved off, shoulder to shoulder, heads bent forward to protect their faces from the rain, the big black dog slouching ahead of them like a mild threat. With the dog gone, there was a good chance the men wouldn't come back either, she reasoned. She was relieved. It was simpler all round, that way. She didn't like Max's obsession with this, wondered if the anger he was now directing towards Zahir might really have more to do with his fury at JJ for letting his son down than his distress at Connor's death. Her guilt stirred.

Ten minutes later there was a knock at their front door and Clare called up to Max, 'Happy, now?' But when she opened up it wasn't the police but Katya, standing before her in a red mac. Clare moved to one side and gestured for her to come inside. Katya took a single step in, pulled her hood back then stopped. Clare looked her over. She was so pretty, this girl, had perfect, pale skin, not a blemish or a line. She was so young, yet somehow sure of herself. Katya didn't smile, just stared back at Clare. There was something insolent about her disregard for Clare's age and authority, her wisdom. Clare wondered what she could possibly want with them, at this time of night. Max had appeared, was standing halfway down the stairs and observing her too. Katya's face was free of make-up and she was damp and dishevelled, but even so she was enviably beautiful. Clare wondered how it must feel to be so naturally attractive. Max had sat down on the stairs quickly, tongue-tied. Clare watched with mounting annoyance as Katya shot him a quicksilver smile, as if to say, I know.

'I come to talk about the boy,' she murmured.

'Better come in,' said Clare abruptly. 'It's been an upset for everyone.'

Katya sat and waited in the front room as Clare disappeared into the kitchen, then came back and handed her a cup of tea.

'If you want to know about Zahir, I'm afraid I can't tell you anything more than that I just saw him and Jaka leave with the dog. They seem to have cleared out.'

Clare watched Katya, could see her words had upset the girl and felt a further moment's guilt, but then it passed. Secretly, she was beginning to reverse her views about Zahir being involved with terrorism. As Max had been talking about it tonight, the whole idea had suddenly sounded far-fetched. Even so, she had no idea how Zahir had become friends with Connor and she still didn't want him about. He reminded her of her own fragility, her own failings.

'He helped Con last night, after the fight, cleaned his face up,' she said. 'But I don't know why or what happened next. Maybe he had something to do with it, we just don't know.'

If Katya wasn't mistaken she saw a slip of a smile pass Clare's lips. Was she almost enjoying the idea of Zahir's possible link to Connor's death? Katya looked at her with contempt. Clare was wrong about Zahir and it was all to do with her own issues. Where men were concerned, Clare had obviously been rejected. She was lonely and embittered, had a look of disappointment about her, a look that said the world owed her a living. Katya understood well that you had to fight for what you wanted, whether it was workers' rights, human rights, or the simple right to be loved. Clare had shut herself down, and surveyed the world around her with unjustifiable judgement. At that moment Katya hated her, felt tainted by her. No doubt Zahir had simply been helping Connor, which didn't surprise her.

Max had been leaning against the door frame. He came and sat down opposite her. 'I wonder if someone came to see Zahir when Con was there late last night and frightened him,' he began slowly, glancing at his mum. She's infected her son with her poison, too, thought Katya.

'Perhaps,' Max continued, 'Con overheard something he shouldn't have. I think he left the flat and they chased after him. That's when the police spotted the commotion and got involved. I think by the time he was at the top of that tower block Connor knew he had a lot of explaining to do, and he was too afraid to do it. I think he jumped because it seemed the best of two bad options.'

It was time to go. There were no answers here, just pure fantasy. Katya had no idea what Con had done – or why – but was convinced it had nothing to do with Zahir. 'Why would Zahir want to hurt Connor? What was his worth to a man like Zahir? I don't believe it,' she stated firmly. 'Gordon is writing story about Zahir's fight for his people. They are asylum seekers from brutal, brutal civil war. We must all respect and help these people, not make them feel they have no worth. You persecute them. It's disgusting.'

Katya's sudden outburst left her hot with anger. She got up. Clare stayed where she was, on the sofa. Katya hurried to the front door, her heart thumping with rage. When she opened it, two policemen were standing on the threshold.

'Excuse me,' she said, and slipped past them, out into the wet night, as they now made their way into the flat.

A man was stalking up the street and Katya hesitated inside Clare's gate to let him pass. He glanced at Katya from under his hood and paused. It was only then she realized it was Billy Crouch.

'Hi,' she said, her mood brightening. 'You have Melina staying?'

Billy nodded.

'She text me.'

'She's kind of upset, not feeling great. She's gone to bed. I was just, er . . .' He hesitated.

Katya looked at him inquisitively, wondered how much he knew, what Melina had told him; imagined not very much. But Billy was looking back at her now as if there was something else he wanted to say. He was standing under the lamplight, which illuminated his narrow, lined face, pale blue eyes, straight nose, thin, pale lips, sharply defined cheekbones. She observed him in pieces, then blinked and took in the whole effect again. He was attractive but she guessed that hard living had prematurely aged him.

Billy rubbed his hands together and stamped his feet. 'Bit cold with all this rain. Doesn't seem to want to stop,' he said.

Why was he filling time? Katya let her glance wander to Tim and Lulu's house. The only light on was in their bedroom on the top floor. Lulu's car wasn't outside. Billy followed her gaze.

'I was just heading there, actually,' he said.

So he knew.

Billy dug his hand in his pocket, retrieved a crumpled cigarette pack and offered one to Katya. She refused it. He pulled one out and lit it deftly, took an angry drag.

'The bastard can't just get away with it.'

'Perhaps you should come into my house first,' Katya suggested. 'I have evidence.'

Billy raised his eyebrows.

'We need to be very clever. Police no good, do nothing,' she added.

He took another drag of the cigarette, threw it into the gutter. 'Lead the way,' he said.

Gordon was waiting in the sitting room for Katya to return, drinking his third beer. He knew Billy from the street but also by reputation – there was someone who was digging into the difficult arenas, putting himself on the line. But what was he doing here, now, with their Czech au pair? Was there any man under fifty in this street that she didn't have a connection to? It sure had been a strange day. Gordon was beginning to realize that there was a lot about Katya that he didn't know – or maybe just hadn't bothered to find out – another example of his complacency, his general attitude of less is more to the real issues that surrounded him. Suddenly he wondered about her history, her upbringing in Prague. She must have been born, he calculated quickly, during the final throes of communist rule, would have been what, three, when the regime had finally toppled? The velvet revolution, that's what they'd called it: there had been no violence when Havel took over. And now here she was, a beautiful young woman in twenty-first-century London, caught up in a more brutal urban chaos, one that seemed to affect them all, despite their individual political leanings, their aspirations or their pasts. He would make it up to her.

Billy took Gordon's hand and shook it firmly.

'Hi, mate, how are you?' he asked.

'Better before all this happened,' Gordon said. 'Beer?'

Billy shrugged. 'If you're having one.'

Gordon went down to the kitchen and fetched two more bottles. He was beginning to feel a bit sozzled. When he came back Katya had disappeared and Billy was sitting on one of their leather sofas.

'Your last documentary was great,' said Gordon.

It had focused on child labour in China, kids as young as seven working for high street chains from which he and Immy often bought clothes for their own child. The film had been discussed on prime-time news; politicians had debated the issues it raised in Parliament.

Billy took a swig of his beer. 'Cheers; but to be honest, after all this I wonder why I'm bothering to look outside London for stories.'

Gordon surveyed Billy's expression. The guy seemed really upset. Maybe here was someone he could really talk to about Connor. Drink made him bold. 'I feel responsible,' he said.

Billy's eyes creased.

'There was a scuffle in the street,' Gordon expanded. 'Shelly, who lives over the road from us, you know her? She was kicking the shit out of Connor and I didn't stop her. She had a bunch of girls with her and they were all high and I thought I spotted a blade, so I stepped back and called the police and then Connor ran off before they came, and I didn't follow him. I'm gutted. Ashamed of myself.'

'Ah, right, Connor, yeah,' replied Billy, evasively. 'I think we've all had our parts to play.'

Gordon was confused. 'Sorry, wasn't that what you were talking about?'

Billy hesitated, looked around for Katya but she hadn't returned. 'Partly. Yeah. In fact, I identified Connor for the police last night. Joe was drunk, they couldn't wake him up.'

'Shit,' said Gordon.

Billy looked down at his bottle. 'It's fucking tragic,' he said.

The men sat in silence, nursing their beers, then Katya reappeared with a flimsy piece of caramel-coloured fabric dangling limply between her fingers. Billy took it from her, shook it out and looked carefully at the garment. It was a silky shift dress, ripped and stained. He continued to examine it closely as Gordon watched. Katya sat down on the sofa and looked at Gordon. And then, instead of returning to the topic of Connor, she began to talk about her Polish friend, Melina.

To her deep annoyance Gordon seemed to take the story with a degree of scepticism. A wry expression settled over his face as she recounted the events of the previous evening. Once she had relayed the tale, as far, at least, as she knew it, he confirmed her suspicions.

'Are you certain it was a clear-cut case of rape? I don't mean to disbelieve Melina, but Tim's an all right guy, and it sounds as if she might have simply got out of her depth, what with the vodka, the dressing up. Maybe she didn't know how far to go, or when to say stop.'

Katya glared at him. 'My friend is not liar,' she retorted. 'And this is not hypothetic story from your newspaper. He is rapist and she is victim. We must help her.'

Gordon shrugged. 'OK, so let's say you're right. Even so, almost impossible to prove. Very, very few cases, even ones that go to trial, are ever proven. Last year only five per cent of reported rapes even made it into the courts. The statistics are shocking. Especially when the case involves two people who live under the same roof. The fact that Melina was drunk will also be a hurdle. I feel sorry for her, don't get me wrong, but I'm simply telling you the way it is.'

Billy had remained silent during this exchange, but now he added to the debate. 'She's got integrity, Gordon, and even though I get where you're coming from, I agree with Katya. I don't know what it is, sorrow, stunned disbelief, innocence, that makes me believe Melina. She was running away back to Krakow this morning, but her bus was cancelled and I brought her back. We should help her, if we can.'

'Does she want you to?' asked Gordon. 'Many women don't want the additional stress and humiliation of a legal battle after something like this, would rather just put it behind them.'

They sat in silence. They all understood that it was a fragile situation, made more difficult because, as Gordon rightly assumed, Melina had already made it clear she didn't want to report Tim. In the end, surely, that had to be her call? It was her right not to alert the authorities to her own abuse, wasn't it? But something which none of them could ignore shifted their inclinations towards action. And it wasn't about Melina at all. It was about Connor Ryan. No one had got involved with him and now he was dead. All three of them felt a degree of accountability and through it a responsibility not to let Melina down – even Gordon – but quite how to help was hard to define. As the night got later they spun the issue round and round but came to no conclusions. After a couple more beers Billy said he ought to go home and check she was sleeping soundly.

It had gone midnight. Gordon and Katya stood at the door together and watched as he turned left out of their gate. Most of the houses were in darkness. The only sounds to enter the street came from cars driving down the Harrow Road, the noise of their engines softened and distorted by the continuing drizzle. Even the rain seemed tired of itself, falling resignedly, having nothing left to soak. Everything was already drenched: the roads, the pavements, the gutters, the roofs of parked cars gleaming under the lamplight, even the black cat who strolled up the middle of the road.

Letting himself inside, Billy tiptoed to his bedroom door and pushed it ajar. Melina was lying on her front, her lovely dark hair tumbling loosely around her dreaming features. He felt immense tenderness for her, then a sharp stab of anger at what Tim had done. He pulled the door to, went into the living room and made himself a bed up on the sofa. Despite everything, he fell asleep quickly with a profound sense of belonging. Somehow it would all be all right, he realized. So long as she stayed.

18

The police went into Zahir's flat early the next morning, before Maggie had even made it up to her window. A middle-aged man with a belt of keys clanking around his lager-bloated waistline lumbered down the steps and let them in. The sound woke Max and he was immediately alert. He perched behind the nets like a private investigator and watched. Ten minutes later they came back out. He had pushed his window sash up so he could listen in, undetected. This was his story, he had brought it to their attention. He needed to keep abreast of developments.

'The bastards were three months behind with the rent,' he heard the fat man wheeze as he locked up.

'Well there's no sign of anything illegal goin' on down there,' said one of the officers. 'Let us know if you hear of anything suspicious.'

'Bloody foreigners trying to get legal status here,' grumbled the landlord loudly. 'Pain in the ass. Best they don't come back.'

Then they all went away.

Max lay back on his bed, disgruntled. He was certain their complacency would come back to haunt them when Zahir and Jaka were done for some terrorist plot or another. Then they'd realize. He'd done right to bring his suspicions to their attention. Someone had to take responsibility round here. After all, this was his home. Unlike so many of these people, Max wasn't just passing through. He had nowhere else to go. Suspected terrorists like Zahir were his very real problem. Everyone needed to be more alert, more watchful. You never knew what might happen next. Who would have thought it, that Con would be slouched against the wall at youth club one minute, dead in the morgue the next? It was too random. He couldn't get his head around it, it made him feel out of sorts and angry all at once.

'So what happened?' Clare asked him the next morning as she poured them both a cup of tea.

'They were lame.'

Clare checked the kitchen clock. Had to leave for work in five.

'Maybe there is nothing to prove, Max. Maybe I was too judgemental,' she said sheepishly. 'Maybe Zahir is just a strange guy, not a terrorist after all. Perhaps he's just been damaged by what happened to him in Somalia.'

'Pah!' said Max.

'And next time you think of bringing the police into a local affair, perhaps you should think twice, Max. We don't want them hanging about outside our house. People will think we're up to something. Perhaps you should be concentrating on your schoolwork, not your conspiracy theories.'

Last night Clare had not been able to sleep. She knew she'd planted this idea in Max's head and she knew what teenagers were like. Once they had hold of something, it could run away with them. Katya's visit had made her think again. Maybe she had got it wrong after all, maybe she'd blamed Zahir for her own emotional shortcomings. It was hard to look herself in the face and admit it. She'd seen photographs on his computer that had turned her stomach, but maybe had been too quick to judge the reason for them being there. He had said they were evidence of the heinous slaughter of his Somali people. Perhaps that was true.

'Talking of school,' she added, pouring herself a second cup of tea, 'aren't you going to be late?'

Max shrugged, refused to answer. He couldn't work his mum out. Yesterday she was all devastated and struck down by Connor's death, but today she'd woken up, had a shower and come down here calm as you like, as if nothing had happened at all, as if it was an ordinary day. He chomped on his Marmite on toast, looked out of the kitchen window at the overgrown back gardens below and to either side of them. People didn't bother much with cultivation around here. Most didn't have ownership, so why bother? If the council or WCT weren't going to send someone to service it, it wasn't going to happen. A family of foxes lived in the undergrowth to the left. He'd seen them late at night, heard them too, barking slyly in response to the howls of Zahir's black dog. There were probably rats down there as well. In contrast with the rest, Gordon and Immy's back garden next door was a haven of Buddhist peace with its decked terrace, pond, fig tree and rare exotic plants, wire above the high fencing to keep undesirables out – that went for people as well as vermin. It stood out like a garden of paradise within a sea of junk – and junkies. In the current climate, that connection made Max laugh out loud.

Clare came and stood next to her son and asked what was funny. He was so much taller than her now. She'd never get used to it. He shrugged, crunched his toast.

'Max,' she tried carefully now as she put on her raincoat and checked her hair in the mirror.

He didn't answer, took another bite.

'Listen love, I know it's all been a big shock, but we can't feel responsible for Con – for anyone else really. We just have to make sure we're OK, make a go of it, you know, get out there, get on with it. I am as sad as you about Connor. But we can't turn the clock back.'

Max sniggered cynically. Clare ignored him, adjusted her collar, leant forward to pull a rogue lash from the corner of her eye, then felt in her handbag, retrieved a pearlescent lipstick and touched up her thin mouth. She had a long, narrow, horsy face that seemed to stretch even longer and thinner when she was feeling down, like now, and very fine hair that was often wispy around her ears. She pushed stray pale strands back behind them on both sides now. At the corners of her grey eyes she could see new creases, age lines. Life only went in one direction. She turned back to her son and eyed him earnestly. He stared back, his face set for challenge.

'Max,' she began, her tone hardening in line with his expression. 'We need to keep a grip, we need to get on with it. I have to go to work and you have to go to school.'

'Can't,' Max mumbled. 'Not today. I'm sick.'

He smirked. Clare knew that kind of smirk, it was one

only teenagers know how to perfect. It came not from humour but from emotional confusion, and was intended to try the patience of the receiving party – generally a teacher or parent – as it was trying her now. There was no point arguing with it.

'Well stay home, don't get mixed in anything and I'll call you,' she said, moving forward to peck him on the cheek. Then she left the house.

Max didn't know what to do next. A rock at the pit of him kept him rooted to the house. He couldn't move far or fast; needed to stay home, in Meanwhile Street. He wasn't sure what it was he was waiting and watching for, but he got a kitchen chair and positioned himself at the threshold with the front door ajar, to wait and watch anyway. If the last few days had taught him anything, it was that stuff happened when you stopped concentrating, in the moments when you thought nothing was going on, when you were preoccupied with your own deal. That was when the shit kicked off; that was when people got up to stuff, when they got hurt. Today he wanted to be aware of it, as and when it happened. He didn't want any more surprises. Con, for one, he decided, wouldn't be dead if they'd all been a bit more on the case.

The rain hadn't quite stopped, but if it hadn't been raining before you might not have noticed it now. It was little more than a certain degree of moisture in the air, but if you stood outside for more than a minute you became aware that your hair and skin were becoming slightly damp. The drops were minute, almost like steam. It was muggy today, oppressive, and the sky was a forgettable blank grey. Every so often a plane appeared from between the blustery folds then vanished again, carrying its load out of here, off to somewhere better, some place where the skies were clearer. Max watched them with longing. He knew where he'd go, if he could. He toyed with his mobile, wondered if he should text his dad; check in, remind him of his promise. He began tapping letters, then deleted them. He wasn't robust enough for the disappointment of rejection today, or even worse, one of those familiar, lingering, pain-inducing silences that would stretch around him and then tighten. He wouldn't do it to himself, not now.

'Max, are you all right there, dear?'

He glanced over the road and for once felt reassured to see Maggie settling at her window, held up a hand in response, shrugged.

'Terrible, isn't it?' she called down. 'I'm not sure I can even bear to watch the street today, knowing that Connor won't be passing me by.'

Max felt the rock in his stomach get heavier. Maggie attempted a smile, but then she took out a hanky and he saw her wiping her eyes. She sounded very croaky, not well at all. He felt sorry for her – sorrier, he realized, than he did for himself.

'Can I fetch you something, Maggie?' he offered shakily. 'Any chores you need done?'

'Connor always did my chores,' she sniffed. 'It's beyond me, Max, beyond me.'

Max felt helpless and embarrassed by the conversation, didn't know what he was supposed to say next, guessed maybe he should go inside after all. But then the door opened at number thirty-two and Katya appeared with Milo on her hip. She manoeuvred his red buggy down the front steps and strapped the little boy in. He was dressed in his dinosaur macintosh and wellies again, clutching a toy police car in his hand.

'Hello, dear,' Maggie called.

Katya looked up at the old lady. She appeared forlorn up there, definitely not herself.

'How's the baby?'

'Good,' smiled Katya kindly. She thought for a moment, then added, 'Maggie, are you all right?'

Maggie's expression shifted readily back to despair. Yesterday she couldn't have talked about Connor, not at all, but today she felt compelled to discuss him with anyone who was prepared to listen.

'Well, you know, dear, I don't think I'll ever get over it.' Her voice was unusually hoarse. 'Connor, he was like flesh and blood to me – family, almost. I cared for him when he was smaller, he always came back to me, he trusted me. And now, well, I can't say I can see a future for myself, everything's topsy turvy.' She pointed up at the sky and coughed throatily. 'The seasons, the time for dying. I can't make any sense of it any more.'

Katya, Milo and Max all now watched her helplessly, their necks craned.

When Maggie woke this morning her face had already been wet and since then she couldn't seem to find a way to dry it. Every new moment brought a new thought, and with it more tears. They streamed down her face incessantly. She had no way of stopping them. It was just like the rain.

‘Shall I make you a cup of tea?’ Katya offered.

Maggie shook her head. ‘Not now dear, Azi will be coming, but perhaps later, when you have a moment.’

Katya nodded, said goodbye and headed on up the street with Milo. She paused outside Max’s gate and smiled. He grinned back, his embarrassment triggered once again by her beauty. She really was something else. Katya glanced down into the basement. Max followed her gaze.

‘Police came,’ he informed her. ‘Didn’t find nothing, it was clean.’

Katya’s brow unfurled in a second and her face relaxed, making her look even fitter. ‘Did Zahir come back?’

So she’d been having a thing with him, thought Max; just like his mum had last year. Jeez. Why didn’t women learn? Any guy who looked as cool as that had to spell trouble. He shook his head and Katya smiled back bravely, but it was no disguise for her sadness. He watched as she made her way off up the road. Everybody was so fucking miserable round here, he thought suddenly. No wonder Con topped himself. Just then, his phone beeped. It was a text from Solange.

Comin over 2 cheer you up.

In spite of himself, Max’s spirits took an unexpected leap.

Katya took Milo to Lizzie B’s and bumped into Ranika in the foyer. She was holding Demi by the hand. Thin, dark lips gave definition to the child’s otherwise sallow face. Mucus leaked from her nostrils and her hollow eyes didn’t respond to Katya’s smile.

'Surprised to see you here,' Katya commented, turning her attention to Ranika.

'Problem with kids, you got to carry on doing stuff, whatever. Like riding a bike, innit? Have to get back on.'

Katya looked confused and Ranika laughed heartily. She was a loud, abrasive person with an immense rear. Why were so many British girls so fat? In Prague they took care of their figures, would not be seen dead in public like that. It was disgusting. Ranika bent down to unzip Demi's glistening pink puffa coat. It had the word Bratz written across the back of it in jarring silver letters. Katya instinctively distrusted everything about Ranika.

'Shelly's having a check-up, said I'd take Demi,' Ranika said over her shoulder. ''Snot her fault, any of this. D'you hear about Con Ryan?'

Katya nodded.

'Terrible, innit. Shelly says people will point the finger at her, but it weren't nuffink to do with her, Con went off after their little scuffle, didn't see him later, didn't have nuffink to do with any of it. Between you and me, she's not coming back. She and Janice going to stay at her aunty's, see if they can get a transfer and you know, I think it's the best thing they can do. There ain't nuffink but bad vibes round here.'

Katya didn't understand half her words, but the gist was clear enough.

'Running away,' she murmured, perfect blue eyes fixed coldly on Ranika. She wasn't about to humour her.

Ranika opened her mouth to speak, then seemed to think better of it. Katya preoccupied herself now with Milo's raincoat and soon the two girls were making their separate ways into the nursery. Ranika immediately entered into a whispering debate with Aishah, while Katya took Milo off into the second play area to fetch the entire emergency brigade. Soon he was playing happily so she made a Nescafé, sat down on the carpet and texted Melina. Melina immediately replied, 'I come lunchtime with Billy'. Katya felt her mood rise slightly. At least that meant she hadn't run away to Poland this morning, as threatened. She still had a friend here, even if Zahir had left her. Katya had lain awake in bed last night trying to work out how to avenge Melina's rape. The injustice of it thumped inside her head like a hammer. Unchallenged, Tim could, no doubt would, do it again. She needed to know what Melina wanted them to do about it. Billy would be behind her, even if Gordon wasn't.

Maggie was still at her window as Katya came back past. She looked haggard, older. It was shocking, how bad news could hit you. Katya was surprised by her feelings of compassion towards someone for whom, only a few days before, she had felt nothing but contempt.

'Do you want to come in now, dear, for a cup of tea? I have a biscuit for wee Milo there, and something for you to give to Immy, too, for Kitty Louise.'

Katya hesitated. She'd planned to give Milo early lunch before Melina arrived.

'Can you make him cheese sandwich?' she enquired.

Maggie managed a weak smile. 'Of course I will, dear, and take the crusts off for him, too.'

Katya crossed over the road and caught the keys Maggie threw for her from the first-floor window. She'd never been inside Maggie's maisonette before. It reminded her of houses back in Prague, with its 1950s embossed flock wallpaper, hard-wearing, cheap nylon carpets, hefty lace-covered dark-wood dressers and shelves crammed with a thousand trinkets: commemoration cups and saucers, hand-painted thimbles, multicoloured glass cats, miniature porcelain figurines. On the walls was a strange mix of modern drawings and paintings in plain wooden and silver frames, many of which seemed out of place inside this otherwise gaudy treasure house. Milo sat down happily on the settee, in precisely the spot taken by Connor only forty-eight hours earlier, and Maggie switched on her old television. It spluttered into life just as *Tom and Jerry* hit the screen. Milo settled in for the duration, thumb in mouth.

'He tired after nursery,' Katya explained, still keenly observing the pictures on the walls.

'Let him have a moment's quiet time before I make a sandwich,' Maggie said. 'I worked for Austrian art dealers down in Cork Street for over thirty years,' she added, following Katya's eyes around her walls. 'Gerry and I came to London in the fifties with not a penny in our pockets and if it hadn't been for the Fisks, in poverty we would surely have remained. Gerry became their driver and I looked after the children, then the grandchildren, too. When we finally retired from service, Mr Fisk senior arranged for this maisonette. He sat on a funding committee with the WCT and we were slipped in through the back door. They'd give us works as a bonus, mainly by Austrian artists. See this,' she pointed eagerly at a yellowing sketch above Milo's head. Katya leant forward and looked more closely. It was an ink sketch of a pretty young woman. 'That'll be me by a certain artist called Oskar Kokoschka, a very fine gentleman who would come and stay with the Fisks from Vienna. He and I got on like a house on fire.'

Katya raised her eyebrows. 'The house, it was on fire?'

Maggie laughed and Katya was pleased. Any distraction for the old lady from her current misery had to be a positive thing.

'No dear, it means we were friends, we got on famously. He would draw me and sometimes he gave me the pictures. Look, it's signed, to me.' She tapped her finger on the bottom left corner of the drawing. Written faintly in pencil was, 'For Maggie, with fondest regards, Oskar'.

'Nice,' said Katya.

She had vaguely heard of the artist, or at least thought she might have done. Maggie had a history, away from here, of course, a past, when she was young. Katya felt her affection grow. She looked at Maggie: she seemed very frail, and when she spoke her lungs sounded full of fluid.

'Maggie, you must sit, how are you feeling?'

Maggie sat down heavily on the chair and shut her eyes for a moment. Her face had shifted to black, as if a storm cloud had suddenly passed the window and drawn all the light out of her in its wake.

'I'm broken, Katya, sorely broken. I'll never be over Connor Ryan, not in all my days.'

'Maggie, you'll recover, you will see. Once there is funeral it will be different. Sad, but different.'

Maggie attempted a smile, but Katya's kindness only made her tears return. She knew she'd never recover. It had been selfish of her to confess her unhappiness to

Katya, she hadn't meant to, but there was something about this young girl that she suddenly recognized, had an affinity with: her beauty and her determination. It was why those artists drew Maggie – they'd said in another world she could have been their muse. It was hard to imagine it now, sitting here inside the weight of her years, her skin mottled and worn, stretched and sagging. She had once been somebody else. Somebody with a purpose and a future. She looked down at Milo for comfort, but he only made her think of Connor and her tears flowed even faster.

Katya put a hand out and patted Maggie gently on the shoulder. 'Come,' she ordered the old lady. 'I will make tea. I begin to understand the English. It always makes the world better.'

'And I'll make that cheese sandwich for Milo,' Maggie resolved, holding her by the arm and pulling herself back up.

As they headed for the kitchenette she knew, suddenly, instinctively that Katya was the one she could, indeed would, trust. She wondered how to approach the issue as she shakily spread two pieces of white bread with Stork margarine, then placed two Dairylea cheese triangles between them. Katya watched as Maggie cut off the crusts and sliced the sandwich to make four neat squares. Next she reached inside the cupboard and pulled out a bottle of Robinson's orange squash, previously kept there for Connor's visits, and poured some for Milo. Finally, she took an apple, cored it and made little boat shapes, which she put in a small bowl. She placed everything on a tray, then Katya put a card table in front of Milo, and gave him his lunch. He sat happily, eating and drinking, eyes still fixed firmly on the TV screen.

The two women sat down and drank their tea. Maggie held the young girl's blue eyes with her own age-paled version of the same. Katya gazed back and in Maggie's face, suddenly, certainly, she saw her own impression, more than fifty years ahead of her; like a momentary glimpse into a future, a future where she, too, would be seventy-eight years old, sitting in an armchair, talking to some young woman or other about trust and honesty and integrity and holding the world together. Maybe that woman would be her granddaughter, maybe not, either way she felt certain it would happen. It was what she had disliked about Maggie, she suddenly knew, from the start – her knowingness of Katya, her likeness – but it was what she now understood that she might learn to love her for, too. It was instinctive, this feeling, and as she watched Maggie she knew the old lady was seeing not Katya's future but her own past, the moment when she too was no more than twenty-three years old, embarking on a future that was impoverished and unclear. And Katya knew that when Maggie was that young person she had held a strong belief in doing what was right, a clear sense of her social responsibilities, along with a determination to succeed. She understood that Maggie would no more have stood by and watched Connor being beaten to a pulp than she would have refused to help Melina avenge Tim's abuse of her.

Eventually Maggie cleared her throat. When she spoke her tone was conspiratorial. 'There are a couple of tasks I need to do and I need someone to help me. Someone I can trust.'

Katya knew she should feel suspicious. Instead she found herself nodding.

'You will help me?' Maggie asked.

'What is you need, Maggie, I will help you.'

Katya was surprised by her conviction, but she wasn't going to let this sad old lady down. Other people might not stand up to the test, but she would.

'Good girl,' Maggie said with a watery smile. 'If you give me a hand, we can pop down to my bedroom and I'll explain everything.'

Milo was slumped back on the sofa now and his eyes were beginning to flicker. In a few moments Katya knew he'd be asleep. She took the remnants of his lunch away, retrieved a bottle of milk from her bag and put the teat into his mouth. Milo began to suck on it greedily. Then she helped Maggie up from the settee and together they made their way slowly down the stairs.

A deep chill seemed lodged inside the dark room, which was dominated by a large iron bedstead covered in a blush-pink eiderdown. Beside it was a picture of Connor. Katya recognized him, not from life, but from the photograph she'd seen only yesterday, in the newspaper. This image marked another regression, from pre-adolescent to a boy of about five years old. He'd been even more striking back then, a golden child with bright green eyes. Despite the mugginess outside, Katya shivered. Above the bed was another remarkable artwork, framed in gold, this time much larger and looser. It was a watercolour of a woman in a yellow dress, sitting in a wicker chair, shading her eyes from the sun. Maggie sat down heavily on the bed and followed Katya's eyes, first to Connor, then to the wall where the painting hung.

'That's by Oskar Kokoschka, too,' she said. 'I was a little older, it was the summer holidays and the children were back from boarding school when he painted me. We were staying at the country house of friends of the Fisks in Kent. There's an oil painting of it somewhere, this was what they called a preliminary sketch.'

'Maggie, you were beautiful,' Katya said.

Maggie looked wistful.

'Oh yes, dear, that I was. Just as you are today, Gerry used to say I was as pretty as a picture. In fact, the painting is the first thing,' she went on earnestly. 'I want you to take it down to the West End, to the gallery in Cork Street. I need you to do it for me, straight away. Today. Ask them to buy it from me. Right away. For cash. I've written a letter to Mr Fisk junior. He'll do it for me, I know. I cared for him, as a child. He's always said if I ever need the money, Oskar's pictures are worth selling. Will you do it for me, Katya? Please say you will.'

Katya looked at her curiously. Maggie sounded desperate, needy.

'Why you sell it? Why you need the money?'

It worried her that maybe someone was coercing or blackmailing Maggie. Maybe it had something to do with Connor's tragedy?

'For the funeral, dear. For Connor's funeral. I won't have him going to a pauper's grave. He needs a fine sending-off. If we leave it up to Joe, he'll be in with the vagrants at the back of the cemetery. I want him up front. I want only the best for him.'

Her voice was wobbling with emotion. Katya felt guilty for upsetting her again. She put out her hand and touched Maggie's arm.

'It's OK, Maggie, don't cry. I'll do it,' she said. 'You give me address. I sure Gordon will drive me there. But first I must check on Milo.'

Maggie reached her own hand out into the air, as if to stop Katya in her tracks.

'That's not all, dear,' she added firmly. 'There's something else, something a bit more . . . involved.'

Katya had reached the door, stopped. There was an edge to Maggie's tone that sounded ominous. Whatever she had to say, Katya was suddenly uncertain that she wanted to hear it. 'OK. First I check Milo, then come back,' she agreed uneasily and nipped up the stairs to find the child fast asleep on the settee, the bottle's teat sliding from his mouth. A stream of milk had leaked down his chin and saturated his collar. She removed the bottle, wiped his mouth and clothes with a cloth, found a tartan blanket on the back of the armchair and placed it over him. Then she came back downstairs. Maggie was leaning forward on her bed, her legs wide apart, tugging a case out from beneath, pushing it forward, between her knees. Her breath was short. Katya knelt down on the floor. 'Wait, Maggie, I do it.'

Once she'd pulled the case clear of the bedstead, Maggie lifted the lid. Katya listened as the old lady falteringly explained what had occurred: how she'd watched Connor coming up the road, how he'd come in and cried, asked her to look after his stuff, then gone away again – and how Shelly and Janice had visited later and mentioned their missing case. She told Katya that she hadn't trusted their intentions, had remained silent about it, in an effort to protect Connor – or so she'd thought at the time – from them. Now she described how she'd opened the case up and found something quite unexpected inside. With this, she slid her hand inside the ripped lining and lifted out the first plastic-wrapped package of white powder. Katya eyed it suspiciously. Didn't touch. Shit, she thought, shit. Already in too deep. Knowledge was ownership.

'There are six of them,' Maggie said.

Katya waited – and watched.

'I want you to get rid of them for me, Katya, without anyone knowing. I can't do it myself.'

Maggie's face was set as hard as flint.

'Me?'

Maggie nodded.

Katya sat back on her haunches to reflect on the recent moment upstairs when she'd thought she'd seen something of herself in Maggie. She'd never touched, let alone used drugs. She knew junkies in Prague, they revolted her, they were for losers, scum. But she didn't want Maggie to be saddled with this, either. It wasn't fair. It wasn't right. And most importantly, it wasn't her fault.

'Why you want me to do?' she asked weakly.

'I trust you, dear,' said Maggie. 'It's an instinct. I won't have Connor's memory tarnished because of this. I tell you, I'm certain he didn't know what was in there. He was duped. Someone knew, though, that he had this case, and they wanted what was in it – Shelly for one. But whoever chased him, they evidently knew too. The thing is, I'm sure he had no idea. He would never have left it with me. Not in a million years.'

'Put it back under the bed,' Katya urged her. 'Let me think. I come back to you. For now, let me just take the picture. Oh, and I must have address in Cork Street. How much you think it worth?'

'Oh I don't know today, dear,' Maggie replied vaguely, turning to look up at her youthful self sitting above them on the wall. 'Back in 1974 it was worth around two thousand pounds.'

Half an hour later Katya was back at home and the picture was leaning in the hallway, waiting to be taken to the address Maggie had given her. Milo was upstairs in his cot now, and had shown no signs of stirring. She paced the sitting room restlessly, as Gordon had the night before, trying to get her head around the latest twist in the tale. This was serious. The drugs frightened her. She didn't want to go near them, she might get deported, end up in jail. There were so many bags of them. She didn't know what they were, or how much they were worth. But no wonder someone had been after Connor, and whoever they were, they'd now be after whoever had the drugs. It was no surprise that Janice and Shelly had decided to clear out. Poor Connor. The only positive element in all this was that it made Zahir seem clean again. She toyed with her phone, wondered if she should call him. It didn't make sense, his sudden disappearance, his silence. She hadn't deserved that from him. Where had he gone?

She began to scroll through her address book, to get to the bottom, to his name, last in the list, under Z, but at that moment there was a knock at the door and she opened it to find Billy and Melina standing on the threshold. She'd forgotten they were coming round and was immediately struck by the intensely private atmosphere between them. How had it happened, this intimacy? She had known nothing of a relationship between them until yesterday, and it made her feel fragile. When did they first meet? And if it was recently, how could two strangers seem so unified in one another's company, so soon? Considering all that had happened to Melina in the past forty-eight hours, she also seemed very calm.

They came in together and Katya sat on one sofa, the two of them close together on the other. Although they weren't touching, it made no difference, the air between them was fused. Melina was quiet, repeatedly smoothing her long black skirt down over her legs. Katya understood, didn't press her; instead she took the opportunity to tell them about Maggie's first request – the one involving a trip to Cork Street. The latter she kept to herself.

'Come on then,' pronounced Billy, once she'd finished. 'Let's do it. I've paid to have my car in the zone today.'

Katya got the impression Billy wasn't the kind of man who liked to hang around. Fortunately at that moment there was a wail from upstairs.

'Milo's awake,' she said. 'I get him, then we go.'

19

'It's roughly ten per cent of the value,' Billy told Gordon. 'The Fisk bloke said he'd give her the rest once they'd sold the painting at the next Sotheby's sale – minus their twenty per cent commission, of course.'

Billy's hands were shoved in the back pockets of his faded baggy jeans and he rocked back and forth in his Pumas. He was standing in his front room, beneath Warhol's Marilyn who was also smiling broadly, as if in on the joke. Gordon sat on the brown leather sofa. Both of them appraised the three blocks of banknotes on the coffee table, totalling £3,000. Gordon was perched on the arm of the green armchair that had comforted Melina the night before.

'It's money for old rope,' Gordon said. 'Maybe I should become an art dealer. From what Katya says Maggie's got an entire collection in there.'

'Ah, hang on. Before you change career completely, I've got an idea I want to talk to you about,' Billy replied.

Gordon felt flattered. Billy was cool, Billy was out there, a mover and shaker. He had mental agility and a physical energy Gordon knew that he himself lacked.

The combination was compelling. Often Gordon sat completely still for hours. By contrast there was always some part of Billy that was active. At this moment, for example, he was no longer rocking back and forth, but was tapping his fingers against the wall, like a drum beat. Then he turned and took out a cigarette, lit it and inhaled deeply.

'I'm all ears,' Gordon said. Normally he despised smokers, would rather leave the room when someone lit up. But Billy inspired his admiration, cigarette hanging from his mouth or not. 'Tell me what's on your mind.'

Billy started to pace again as he talked it through.

'I want to do something positive with the kids in the street, to catch it, the mood. I want to put them on the map. Make them count. Encourage them to do some filming, to record this difficult time. And to remember Connor. It might lead to something interesting down the line. I'd like to try and hit the BBC or Channel Four with a documentary next year; maybe it could be based on this lot. The local development trust has offered me funding for a social doc' around here before – I'm sure, if I go see them again, there'll be some level of cash on the table. It's the right time for me. It would need to be gritty; sharp, political. But we need to act now. I just wondered whether you'd like to help me get some footage together over the next week, you know, the aftershock, the preparations for the funeral and all that?'

Gordon felt a blush rise upwards from his neck, prickle his temples. It was a great chance for him to pay something back. If Immy agreed he could use some of his paternity leave to work on this. He was pretty sure she'd understand and he'd still be around for her and for Kitty Louise. He might even ask the paper if he could run with it as an assignment. It would go some way towards making amends for ignoring Connor, for not going to help him when the girls were kicking him senseless on the ground, for not stopping him before it was too late.

'OK, I'm in,' he announced spiritedly. 'Maybe we should approach Mark, you know, the vicar at St Matthew's, to help us first.'

Billy moved to sit down next to him, took another drag of his cigarette, then stubbed it out.

'Already did. Meeting him tomorrow morning at ten. He knew Connor better than anyone, even knew his mum, Lorraine. He's helping plan the funeral. Joe's on the floor. It'll be a miracle if he even makes it up the basement steps on Wednesday, let alone into St Bride's. It's going to be Catholic but Mark says he doesn't mind. And now Maggie's got the cash for it, we can make something special happen. Mark can talk to Max and Casey and the others; get them to participate in the service like no one else can.'

Gordon liked Billy more by the minute. 'I'll do what I can,' he told him. 'Immy has to stay in hospital for five more nights. We'll have to get Katya to agree to help with Milo. She's supposed to be taking time off.' He lowered his voice. 'And then of course there's the other issue, the Melina problem.'

Billy looked pensive. 'I think that's going to be a slower burn,' he said finally. 'Melina needs to stabilize first. Although . . .' He hesitated, seemed to think better of it. Silence hung smokily in the air between them.

In the background Gordon could hear the girls whispering together in Billy's kitchen as they fed Milo his tea. Katya had texted Gordon at the hospital earlier and asked him to drop in at Billy's on his way home. She'd insinuated they all had something to talk to him about. He'd assumed it would be with reference to Melina. Yet so far Connor had been the only topic of conversation. Maybe he'd misinterpreted the message, but the way Billy left that last sentence hanging made Gordon wonder if there'd been something else they'd all really wanted to discuss, something to do with Melina, not with Connor, something they'd decided, since Katya sent that text, not to share with him, after all. He had a sense he was being left out and felt a moment's disappointment, then relief. He wasn't sure he wanted in on the Melina affair, whatever they were deciding to do about it. It was a can of worms. He rose. 'I think I'd better get Milo home,' he said. 'I'll try and make it to Mark's tomorrow.'

As if on cue Katya appeared, Milo in her arms, and announced that they were ready. Billy threw on a crumpled linen jacket that was lying on the sofa, then grinned at Melina who was hovering behind Katya in the doorway.

'I'll walk up to Maggie's,' he told her. 'Give her the money.'

'I stay here?'

'Yeah, yeah.' He scooped up the wads of cash and shoved them unceremoniously into a leather 'man bag'.

'Melina gave me key,' Katya told Billy.

Gordon glanced between them, questioningly. Katya had assumed wrongly that he wouldn't hear her. Melina looked at the floor.

'Don't worry, it's going to be fine, Melina, promise,' Billy murmured.

Melina retreated to Billy's room, but Billy and Katya remained where they were. They returned Gordon's gaze, their eyes giving nothing away, their mouths set. Gordon wanted to ask whose key Katya had been talking about – Maggie's or someone else's? Suddenly, passionately, he wanted to be part of it, whatever it was, then a split second later he felt old and foolish, disinclined to become any more involved than he already was. Connor's funeral, the possible documentary, it was enough to be getting on with – and Kitty Louise, too. He felt guilty that she wasn't his first thought. However appalling Melina's story was, he needed to protect his family from its fallout. Immy would lose it if she knew Tim had raped Melina. He wanted his wife to remain calm and focused on the baby, on Milo, and, to be completely honest, on himself too. He needed her to look after them all if he was going to be strong, take a stand, really try to make something that counted. He suddenly believed that Billy was giving him the first opportunity in his life to put his back into something. He went to the front door and undid the latch and they all now headed up Meanwhile Street, Billy and Katya following slowly behind him and Milo.

Gordon thought about Tim. He had never felt at ease in his company and in general he offered the guy no more than a curt nod when they passed in the street. There'd been a few local events involving the kids and the nursery, where their paths had crossed, and they'd always been civil, swapped stories and opinions about their au pairs, their kids. Tim was old school, seemed too confident to Gordon. Gordon was a grammar school boy. He'd earned everything he possessed by his own endeavours. He was modest, whereas Tim had the swagger of someone who had always been told he would succeed. Gordon's newspaper was split by the very social difference he recognized between Tim and himself. It was part of the reason he didn't feel his future was clear. There were the redbrick grafters like Gordon himself, who would never make it to the boardroom, and the noisy, upper-middle-class Oxbridge boys whose eyes were always focused an inch above the skyline. A deep part of him would like to see Tim fail, to watch him fall, to lose his swagger, be forced to recognize he couldn't grab what he wanted without paying harshly. Gordon would like to see him put on display and humiliated. It was an offence to the male sex for a man to violate a woman. He'd like to see Tim strung up for it. Even so, he still believed that they shouldn't force Melina's hand to bring about Tim's downfall.

He turned and waited for Katya and Billy, wondered what they were planning. There was something tacit between them and it made him nervous. He worried that Katya had encouraged Billy to take matters into his own hands. He got the feeling she could be impetuous, that she had a strong, simplistic sense of right and wrong. He could imagine her wanting resolution at any price. Her passion was possibly inspired by her youth, but it could be dangerous.

Right now they were silent as they walked. Milo was snuggled up in Gordon's arms, quiet too. The early evening air felt starchy; the sky was mutating from pale grey to a sickly yellow, like a ripening bruise. The sun must be up there somewhere, Gordon thought, toasting them obliquely through the clouds. He wondered briefly if summer might finally be on its way, or if tomorrow would bring another storm. It was impossible to tell.

Their inner crevice of the city was suddenly extraordinarily quiet. You'd assume there'd be noise at all times here, but there were moments, in the dead of night, or very occasionally at dusk – like now – when a heady silence swung across the street like a fist. It winded you, made you pause to wonder what it was that was suddenly missing. You felt, in moments like this, that anything might happen.

Milo coughed and the moment passed.

'Well, it's sure to be enough for a decent send-off,' Maggie said, looking at the money a touch suspiciously. 'Take it away again, Billy dear, make sure it's put to good use. You know what I want. Don't skimp now, only the best coffin, clothes for the children to wear, a suit for Joe, the flowers, the wake. And I want a proper plot for him in the cemetery, too, not some cheap seat at the back.'

Billy gave her his assurances and stowed the money back in his man bag. It was amazing, this place. Like something out of a time warp. His mind tripped to the opening shot of his planned documentary, aware that Maggie needed to be part of it. She represented so much that was dying, the flicker of light from a past where community included everyone; where she would have been central. Now Shelly and Janice had scarpered, however, and with Connor gone too, there were few people left who would be looking out for Maggie. Those left behind were all too busy looking out for themselves.

'There's a lot more to come, Maggie, that painting of yours is worth at least £30,000,' he informed her.

She didn't look surprised.

'What'll I want with that kind of money?' she said. 'I'm beyond needing things. You'll have to do something with it, for the young ones, Billy.'

'The kids?'

'Someone's got to help them, to stop any more of them from going the way of Connor. Money can always help.' She waved her hands dismissively at the rest of the pictures. 'When you have a moment take them all down to Mr Fisk. He can value the lot. I should think there's a fair few more bob waiting to be collected from my walls.'

'But Maggie, they are your memories,' protested Katya. 'You may need more help one day. Proper care.'

'There'll be no time for that,' Maggie replied. 'And I've got no one of my own to leave it to. I'll not be needing much more in the way of time.'

Katya caught Billy's eye. Understandably Maggie had descended into self-pity, but they both knew that there was more to it than that. She was clearly unwell. She had a troubling cough and her breath was rasping. It seemed likely that she had an infection in her lungs. How serious it was they didn't know. But the way she was talking now was a form of giving in. She seemed to have decided that her time was up. Who knew what would happen to her next? Maybe she would need full-time care. Then the money would make all the difference. But right now, as they were all too aware, there was another even more pressing issue to attend to, lurking like a silent threat under her bed downstairs.

'Maggie, there's the other thing,' Katya began falteringly. 'I asked Billy. We return Connor's things to Joe. And, umm, lose suitcase.'

Maggie looked at her knees for a moment and sighed, before glancing up sheepishly between them.

'You be careful,' she muttered.

'No one's going to get hurt who doesn't deserve to, Maggie,' Billy reassured her intently. 'And once it's gone, the least said about this the better. For us all.'

Maggie retrieved her stick from beside the sofa and led them slowly back down the stairs to her room at the front of the house. Within moments the case had been pulled clear of the bed. From out of his bag, Billy now took a pair of black leather gloves.

'Can't be too careful,' he winked, attempting to lighten the tone of the moment, but neither of the women laughed. 'Now, Katya, the bag, please.'

Katya opened her rucksack and pulled out a folded supermarket bag. Then she put a pair of black gloves on too, and knelt down to open the case. Although he knew what he was about to see, Billy still sucked in air as Katya took one, then the next plastic-wrapped block of gear from the case. He had been so good all week, but this was like showing sweets to a child. He had to remain practical. He sat back on the bed by Maggie and watched as Katya hurriedly pulled out the third block, then tipped the contents of the case on to the lid and retrieved the three other blocks from underneath. With trembling hands she put them all in the supermarket bag, with one of Connor's T-shirts squashed in on top. Finally, she pulled the lid down and clicked the case shut. Then she stood up.

Her face had a sheen across it, from emotional rather than physical strain. She still looked glorious, thought Maggie and Billy simultaneously; glossy like a waxwork model in Madame Tussaud's, of someone very famous and tragically beautiful.

'Let's go,' she urged.

Maggie watched from the doorway as Katya took the bag, Billy the case, and they headed back outside. Earlier Billy had parked the Jag outside Maggie's. Flicking the locks open he slid the bag and case into the boot, placed a thick grey rug over the top of them, then clanked the lid down and locked it again. Then he glanced over at Maggie. 'Do you need a hand back up the stairs?' he called.

'No thank you dear.' She sounded weary. 'I'll take myself direct to bed.'

Maggie closed her door with a gentle click as Billy glanced at his watch: 7.45 p.m. It wouldn't be properly dark for another two hours.

'Katya, I'll text you when I'm back, around ten?'

Katya agreed with a slightly nervous smile that didn't reach her eyes, then crossed the road, opened the gate and scampered up Gordon and Immy's front steps two at a time. She slipped her key in the lock and disappeared inside without looking back.

Billy glanced around him, convinced that no one had noticed their activities, then lit a cigarette and began to wander towards home. A bunch of lanky kids in hoodies appeared from Reeling Road and ambled up the street towards him. They didn't seem in a hurry to get anywhere fast. Before them was a whippet-cross dog on a lead. It cocked its leg and peed against Dren and Ada's railings. He slowed, wondering if he should cross the street to avoid them, then decided not to.

It was only as he drew level that he realized that the kids included Max, Michael and Casey, with three girls he didn't recognize. The boys seemed to have got bigger, even in the past six months. They were gangly, adolescent, and if you didn't know them, en masse like that they might have made you slightly nervous. Max in turn had spotted Billy and smiled bashfully at him. One of his hands held the dog's lead, the other held the hand of one of the girls.

'Wassup bro,' Max mumbled.

Billy bent down and stroked the creature's silky neck. The dog was the colour of pale suede. It had a long fine nose and even paler, pooling eyes.

'Belongs to Solange's cousin,' Max added, nodding towards the girl, whose hand he had now dropped.

Billy grinned and the three girls giggled in unison. They looked like a girl band, with their honey complexions, skinny jeans, crop tops and lip gloss. Each was carrying a small bottle of Evian and they had their arms linked together, like a chain. They were all of mixed origins, their roots unfathomable.

'D'you hear about Con?' asked Casey.

'Sure,' Billy answered. 'Shite, isn't it?'

Max kicked at an imaginary stone on the pavement and his foot slid in the slurry of blossom and leaves which remained after the rain. Billy felt his empathy grow. A genuine sadness pervaded the group. It wasn't fair on them, they were all victims, these kids, trying to get along against the odds, and suddenly he saw that some of them, like Connor, were destined to fail. There was nothing anyone could do about it unless society changed; and there was little chance of that. It was too complex, too complicated. Those inner-city kids who managed to remain afloat should feel proud of themselves.

Sensing Max's discomfort, Solange had moved closer. She linked her arm through his and chewed on her full bottom lip.

'Mark asked if the boys want to do something, for the funeral,' she said. 'With their music.'

Billy looked amongst them and nodded encouragingly. 'I'm going to see him at ten tomorrow morning. D'you want to come along?' In his mind's eye, Billy could see material forming. Footage of this lot could be interesting, and the recordings would keep Connor alive. It would make something good out of something really so fucking bad he still hadn't managed to dislodge the bile it had brought with it, which lingered at the back of his throat. He fished around in his pocket and got out his cigarettes, lit one from the other, tossed the original butt, then leant against the railings and inhaled deeply.

'Know what?' he said, addressing them all. 'I've got the start of a film idea, for Connor. I was going to talk to Mark about it first, but if he agrees, I'm going to need all your help.'

The kids glanced at one another, then back at him. They seemed suddenly to stand straighter. They all knew of Billy, knew what he did, were impressed by him. He was cool, he made movies, was kind of famous – almost a celebrity.

'Do you think it really was an accident?' Casey mumbled awkwardly.

Billy looked between them. Their faces were all fixed on his. Conspiracy theories had been circulating among them all day. It hadn't occurred to him that they wouldn't believe the police account of Connor's leap to oblivion, but now they were asking, he could understand why they might want to question it. The reasons for his certainty were less clear, and Connor's end, he supposed, would always be open to question. But, to his mind, there was something sadly predictable about the way Connor had gone. He hadn't stood a chance, from the start.

Billy suddenly saw the boy again, at nine or ten years' old, whizzing round the corner into Meanwhile Street with that golden mane of hair, those piercing green eyes, that reckless grin. He'd carried the wild energy of the wind. In five more years the city had knocked it out of him. As a child Connor must have believed he could do anything, that one day he would fly. Maybe, deep in his psyche, last Wednesday night, he had still believed that he could. Billy took a quick drag, blew smoke out above their heads.

'There's no way the police pushed him,' he said. It was, he felt, what they all needed: a clear answer. 'There was stuff going on, he was involved. I think he was scared. You saw him, Max, earlier, being kicked around. He'd been cornered. He didn't know what else to do. It's sad, it's miserable, but it was an accident. I'm as certain of that as I can be.'

No one spoke, but Billy noted Max wipe his forearm across his eyes, and despite his height and broadening frame, he suddenly looked like a lost child. Meanwhile Casey looked away, down the street, as if he was waiting for someone – maybe Connor himself – to appear, like a miracle, to make them all feel better. Michael simply stared at the ground. The girls hung back. The atmosphere had taken an abrupt turn.

'Don't s'pose anyone's seen Shelly?' Billy tried, as casually as he could. He'd really appreciate knowing if she was planning to show up. It might affect his plans.

The kids eyed one another furtively, then looked at the pavement, shook their heads. They were probably afraid to know too much about all that.

'Apparently they're staying with Shelly's aunt, want a transfer,' Max mumbled eventually.

So the rumours were true.

'I heard that too,' Billy replied. 'Come to Mark's in the morning if you like. Take it easy now.'

He touched fists with each boy in turn, grinned at the girls, then left them hanging out and shuffled off home. It was fucking terrible for everyone – especially for Connor.

When he got inside Melina was already asleep. He watched her from the door for a moment, felt the urge to move across the room and slide in next to her, to wrap himself around her, nestle his head in her silky hair. She told him she'd been feeling sick all day, that the pills she'd taken had made her retch. She needed sleep to restore her energies. He wasn't going to let her down. His conviction was strong. He felt clear-headed, but very restless, partly due to the lack of narcotics in his system. Billy crept away and got a beer from the fridge, lit another cigarette. He was definitely smoking too much, but he'd address that issue later. At least there was no cocaine in his system – only a stash of it filling the boot of his Jag. He paced around for the next couple of hours, thinking about Melina, then about plans for Connor's funeral, and made some notes in his BlackBerry. He was filling time, waiting for the moment when the last deed of the night could be done.

Finally at five to ten Billy headed back up the street. Now he was wearing a dark brown hoodie and black jeans, had his gloves on again. Katya was loitering outside her gate. She was similarly dressed in dark clothes and gloves. It was dusk now, yet oppressively hot, cloudy but still, with no more rain. Neither spoke as they crossed the road and after a quick glance in each direction, Billy flicked the boot of his Jag open, took out the supermarket bag and closed it again. Together they walked decisively back down the road until they reached number forty-three. Without speaking they strode confidently through the gate and up the steps. Katya turned the key in the lock and the two of them entered the house.

Less than three minutes later they reappeared, Billy holding the plastic bag in one hand, rolled up, empty. In the other he had Connor's T-shirt. Katya moved back down the steps ahead of him, two at a time. Billy pulled the blue door closed behind them and followed her. Again they both glanced up and down Meanwhile Street but saw no one, nothing to make them think they'd been observed. Neither spoke as Katya held up a hand in farewell and entered her house. When Billy got in Melina was waiting in the hallway, in the dark.

'Where have you been?' she asked.

'There's nothing for you to worry about, Melina, nothing at all,' he replied evasively. 'Come on, let's go into the living room. I need a drink.'

20

The teenagers were hanging around outside Max's, waiting for Billy. Michael's aunt, Gladys, was on the pavement opposite with Ada, talking up at Maggie, who seemed to be back on watch. Ada had a green housecoat on, her hair up in a red patterned headscarf and she held a big old broom in her hand. She'd spent the past hour hanging her carpets up along the railings and was now giving them a good beating. Saturday morning: spring-cleaning day. Her kids were running up and down the pavement with the Iraqis, kicking a football about and shrieking. The baby was positioned in its buggy, watching. Every so often the ball bounced into the road and the baby called, 'Ball, ball,' and Max or Michael or Casey ran out to retrieve it for the smaller ones from under parked cars. Everyone appeared happier now that the rain had stopped and they could get back out here, breathe in some air, run off some energy. The teenagers had the dog with them again and he was straining to get off his lead.

As he approached, Billy flicked on his camera, stood filming on zoom for a moment before he was noticed.

Gladys saw him first, came waddling up the road,

wagging a finger his way. 'What you doin' filmin' our kids?' she demanded. 'You got a licence?'

Billy managed to get a shot of her ample frame before lowering the lens. Now he explained his rough plan for a documentary. Gladys listened with an enquiring expression, her thick hands settled on her wide hips. Billy took some papers from his rucksack – consent forms – and handed one to her.

'We're doing it for Connor, and for the rest of the kids; to show people what they have to deal with, every day,' Billy cajoled. 'Come on Gladys, the WCT are going to fund it; it's a social project, good for the kids.' He had a way about him that bought people's trust. Despite herself, Gladys's scowl shifted.

'I'll try to get it back to you later,' she said.

Billy grinned, knew she'd succumb, then picked up his gear. As he began to make his way towards the teenagers Gordon came out of his house with Milo in the buggy. Ada's kids ran up to greet them. Milo kicked his legs in the air hopefully, keen to get out. Clare watched them from her gate.

'Need parents' consent before you start profiling kids on film,' she said.

Billy held up another form. She came down the steps in her dressing gown and took it.

'I promise, Clare, nothing's going to get aired without your prior approval – and Mark's monitoring the entire project,' he told her. 'We're doing it for Connor.'

She raised her eyes skyward. 'We've all got a lot to think about,' she replied, then looked guilty. 'But of course it matters – to think of him.'

Billy threw her an understanding smile and Clare found herself reciprocating. For a brief moment she wished she wasn't standing there in her dressing gown, hair lank, no make-up on. What was it about good-looking men, she wondered. They could flick a switch in you, whether you wanted them to or not. Her mind briefly turned to Mark Scoles, how charming he had been, but the thought felt sacrilegious and she pushed it away.

She had no luck with the male sex. Even Max seemed on the verge of deserting her. Since Wednesday Solange hadn't left his side. Their physical intimacy made her feel sidelined – worse than that, dismissed. Whenever she spoke to Max these days he threw her a withering glance, seemed unconcerned by her point of view – particularly where this Connor business was concerned. Didn't he understand that she had his best interests at heart? His attitude left her nowhere to go. Her control had gone. And what was left? She was washed up and nearly forty, without anyone looking out for her. This Connor thing was getting out of hand, too. She didn't want Max tainted by it. Sure, they'd been at school together, but they were hardly best friends. She told Billy she'd think about his project, then made her way up the steps, shut the door behind her and went back upstairs for a Saturday morning lie-in. First she opened her curtains and glanced out. Max and Solange were ambling off hand in hand with that scrawny dog on its leash, the rest of the gang ahead of them, following Gordon and Billy like lambs to the bloody slaughter.

* * *

Billy felt cheered. It was early to expect kids to be up and about, particularly on a Saturday morning, but here they all were, Michael, Max and Casey in sloppy jeans and T-shirts, the girls, too, make-up already perfected around their expectant eyes, swaggering off as if they were heading to a Hollywood film set. The atmosphere was better between them all this morning, a touch brighter now they had something positive to think about. Soon they were all stationed in a pew, Mark before them, Billy and Gordon next to him, their backs to the altar.

'We want the funeral to be something a bit different, something with a vibe that makes you think of being young, of being alive,' Mark said, trying to sound young and cool himself.

He was simply dressed in dark linen trousers and a pale blue shirt, looking more like a financier on dress-down Friday then an inner-city vicar. There were bags around his eyes. It hadn't been a good week. He'd lost two residents to age and disappointment and then, of course, there'd been Connor, Connor whose death, he feared, as he stood here looking at the teenagers, had all but broken his faith.

Billy held a camera in his right hand, was filming the kids as Mark talked. They seemed more animated than usual. The camera, both Billy and Mark rightly assumed, had something to do with it. That was OK. Billy knew that if he hung out with them for long enough they'd soon forget it was there at all.

'We want you to help everyone remember Connor as a kid who lived and breathed, who was part of all our lives,' Mark added as they all looked on earnestly. 'And Father

Patrick agreed that playing a piece of your music at the funeral could be a great way to do that.'

'Which day is it?' enquired Michael, glancing at the camera with an inadvertent smirk – a frame to hold on to, thought Billy.

'Wednesday,' said Mark. 'Only three days to rehearse.'

Max let out a dramatic sigh.

'Harsh,' said Casey.

The teenagers went off with Gordon and Milo to get their kit together in the back room, while Mark and Billy headed off to see Joe and discuss details for the funeral itself. It was to be held at St Bride's, with a committal at Kensal Rise. The cemetery was two hundred and fifty years old, held a quarter of a million souls; in eternity Connor would not be alone. There'd be some recompense from the benefits office, for Joe was on both incapacity and jobseeker's allowance, but even with that added in with Maggie's cash, they'd be lucky to see any change from four grand. Their hope, at this hour of the day, was that Joe might not be too drink-sodden to answer the door. As they strode up the street the sun made a brief appearance, but the sky was still swamped with blustery clouds that yet again indicated rain. It was sticky, oppressive weather that made you feel dirty and uncomfortable, uncertain what clothes to wear. It was an odd season, unsettled, unclear. Spring? Summer? It felt tropical, the rainy season, something uncommon, something England didn't usually experience.

As they now went down the basement steps they spied Joe still crashed on the sofa, but their repeated knocking eventually got him up. He shuffled to the door and stood blearily to one side to let them in. The stench inside was more unbearable than the last time Billy had been there, only twenty-four hours earlier. He left the front door open behind him, hopeful that some of London's flaccid air might creep into the living room with them and loosen the odour, even a touch. He was disappointed. Joe seemed aware of their distaste, confessed he hadn't shaved or washed since Connor had died. His eyes were bloodshot; tendrils floated around tight pupils. Mark gently encouraged him to try to get himself back on his feet before the funeral. He exhaled stale whisky as he apologized over and again.

'Sorry vicar, yes sorry vicar, but I don't know how to handle me grief.'

Billy couldn't decide whether he despised or pitied the man more. Either way he couldn't stay down here any longer. He wanted to see Melina before getting back to the kids again, too. She felt clean, spirit-lifting. He made his excuses and left them to it.

When he entered his flat it was silent. He peered around his bedroom door. Melina was still sleeping. He crept in and approached the bed as she stirred, looked up and smiled tentatively. Billy was afraid to move closer, to touch her, although he longed to. He explained his plan for the day, to spend it filming the kids. Melina had arranged to see Katya and they agreed to meet later on.

After he left, Melina got up. She felt sluggish and her stomach hurt. Otherwise her body still felt numb. She wondered if it would ever become her own again. She was frightened of going outside too, in case she saw him. She wandered from room to room, marvelling at Billy's kindness. He'd trusted her from the start, left her there alone to do as she wanted, rummage through his things if she so chose, eat his food, sleep in his bed. She was anxious not to let him down. Thoughts spun like washing inside her, jumbled up, a blur. She closed her eyes and tried to find a blank space for her brain to inhabit, just for a moment. It was only when she slept that she felt any release, and even then Tim regularly invaded her dreams, his body forcing itself on to and into hers, his sweaty face and his sour breath all over her again and again.

'There is no one there,' Katya reassured Melina when she arrived an hour later. 'I took the key, had a look. Lulu and the kids gone away. And Tim, he absent, too. Maybe with them. I don't know. I will watch if he come back. But we must go out, you need air to breathe, on your skin. You are so pale and it has stopped raining.'

Melina nodded vaguely.

'Come, we go shopping. I have extra money from Gordon, I take you to Primark. Buy you present!'

Finally, Melina was convinced. The two girls headed out, turned the opposite way to Melina's former residence, and left Meanwhile Street behind them for the day.

'When you look the way you look
then you cease lying,
In the slum you slice through the scene.
No fade into the kids who are dying.'

Billy filmed and Gordon observed as the kids rapped along to their track – clumsy lyrics courtesy of Max and Casey, slightly ripped off from some US band they'd found on MySpace, backed by a bland bit of rap that they could just about play. As he took a break for a cigarette outside the church, Billy mulled it over. Like Connor's death, the words and music lacked either cohesion or drama. Music had become their means of expression, and the language they used to communicate came direct from rap tracks they had learned: they called each other *man* and *bro*, referred to their area as *the hood*, as if they were living out their lives in some LA ghetto. In a dangerous urban environment they were using it as a means to an end; their 'grime' sound was giving them an identity, but the lyrics were harsh, the beat aggressive.

He'd been to see the shrine to Connor again this morning. It had grown over the past three days: now there were T-shirts hanging along the wall with messages to his memory scrawled over them in black marker pen; blown-up photocopies of the photograph that had appeared in the *Evening Standard* – evidently the only picture of him that anyone had had – written over with messages of condolence; poems, lyrics from songs. There was also a line of black and white bandannas tied to the railings, all signed with the names of the other kids in his 'gang'. This was the ultimate irony, for although Connor hung around with the older kids at the end of the block who wore them, he didn't wear one himself, and as far as Billy was aware, he'd never been accepted into their gang as a true member. Even so, in death, he gained iconic status, became a hero from the hood, someone to be mourned as a brother in arms. It was sinister, all fucked up. The kids had written messages on the pavement too, and following Tyra's early example, a bizarre array of all Connor's 'favourite things' had begun to grow: cartons of Ribena, Wotsit crisps, a half-eaten bar of Galaxy chocolate, some Chewit sweets, more chewing gum, a pile of biscuits; kids' snacks, nothing sophisticated or out of the ordinary. It was the stuff they'd all bought from Ali's on the way to school. Its presence rendered Connor's juvenility in death more striking. Billy filmed it all.

After the initial piece in the paper, Connor's death hadn't triggered a media debate; hadn't even made it to the national news reports. Pathology results had shown that there was a slight trace of cannabis in the teenager's system, but nothing stronger, and although the investigation remained open, Billy for one didn't believe they'd ever find out who'd been chasing after him – or that the full truth would ever come out. Of course he understood that Connor had been chased by the dealers Shelly was accountable to and that she must have told them who to go after for the case. If he knew what was inside, by denying all knowledge of its whereabouts, Connor had been protecting the old lady. But the drugs had still been sealed up inside the case when Maggie had got hold of it, so how was Connor to know they were in there? It appeared that he'd kept his mouth shut to save Maggie. Billy now understood from the kids that Janice gave him the case, as he needed one. This in itself suggested that she too had been duped by her daughter; had naively assumed their trip to Cancun to be a genuine holiday.

The problem with having nothing was that you forced yourself to believe things that could make life just a little bit better, whether they were morally sound or not. Janice, Billy imagined, had ignored her suspicions for the chance of a brief adventure, a moment in the sunshine. She hadn't allowed herself to ask questions, had chosen to remain in blissful ignorance. Billy almost felt sorry for her. She was of a different generation, wouldn't necessarily have put two and two together – why should she? When she was growing up there was nothing stronger than weed on the streets of west London. Now the game had got far more dangerous – indeed had changed beyond recognition. Billy reckoned Shelly would have been the only one in the know. She'd used her mother and daughter as mules to bring cocaine in for Marlon. She was pathetic, lower than vermin – like Tim, morally defunct. Maybe she'd learnt her lesson, but even with Marlon and Stevie's arrest and Connor's death, he doubted it. She'd always see herself as the victim, the one who'd been born without a silver spoon, without the celebrity lifestyle she devoured daily in populist magazines, the opportunity to be something more. She would always lay the blame at someone – anyone – else's door, even a vulnerable fifteen-year-old boy's. She wouldn't feel remorse, regret or responsibility.

Billy understood that about girls like Shelly. He thought of Tim. For very different reasons, both Tim and Shelley felt superior to the law. Well, they'd get their comeuppance in different ways. Tim was about to feel the threat of the law, even if, as Billy suspected, he would get off with no more than a caution, and Shelly wouldn't ever be able to forget – she had a scar down her face to remind her of

Connor's death for the rest of her days. But she also had a kid. There was no point roughing it up any further for her, and anyway Billy would be surprised to see her face around here again. She'd had her moment, and if she had any sense she'd stay away from now on. Even the girls at the end of the block appeared to have retreated indoors, which said it all. Connor's death had shot a big hole in their operation's side. It would take a while for things to get back up and running again.

Thinking about drugs turned Billy's attention to his own cravings. He took another drag on his cigarette. His stomach didn't feel so twisted up with the need as long as he kept very busy, all the time. This filming was already firing him up; it was a perfect antidote and it had a value, if he could get it right. He wondered whether what he filmed would prove sufficiently incisive to result in a documentary with enough energy and analysis to reflect this crazy street and the kids who lived in it. It was a place that was calm one moment, volatile the next; a place where nothing, apparently, could happen for months, but where shit could kick off at any moment. He wanted to capture that sense of silence and stillness you got here sometimes, followed by the crescendo of action that came and left when you were least expecting it. He didn't want to miss any of it. Billy finished his cigarette and made his way back into the church. The kids had moved on, were now practising a well-known track by a successful band. It was better, stronger, easier to manage. He would encourage them to go with that for the funeral. Safe.

* * *

The band worked in earnest all day. Milo clambered around happily and Gordon warmed up; seemed to be enjoying himself, building his own quiet rapport, particularly, it seemed, with the girls. Billy felt they were getting somewhere, already; it was a good feeling.

At around four o'clock Melina and Katya appeared with a bunch of plastic bags. Billy had asked Katya to take Melina shopping, given her some cash, asked her to say it was from Gordon for Katya, lest she refuse it. It was a time for spending money on anything other than drugs. Melina's eyes seemed more alive, her manner lighthearted. He dared to kiss her cheek. She smiled happily. Retail therapy had evidently done her good.

'Come on, tea's on me, round the Lebanese,' he called out. 'I think you guys have done enough for one day.'

Gordon and Milo went off to see Immy and the baby, and everybody else headed round to the Cyprus. On the way Max knocked for Clare, who initially said she wouldn't come, but then she spotted Mark and changed her mind. She told them she'd be there 'in a bit'. When she arrived, ten minutes later, she'd changed into her new jeans and put on some make-up. Max noticed it, was surprised, and if he wasn't mistaken, when she sat down next to Mark, the vicar beamed.

They ordered garlic chicken wraps, coffees in tall glasses and freshly squeezed orange juice while Billy continued to film. He was pleased to capture this shift in the atmosphere, which had suddenly become upbeat, almost festive. The boys were excited by their progress and the girls were pleased to have been asked to provide backing vocals. To be honest the sound that had come out of the day was pretty ropey, but Billy wasn't about to say anything – and anyway it wasn't the point. This wasn't supposed to be about quality, but emotion, about giving, about being there and putting something in, about remembering a boy called Connor who was no longer around to shout out for himself.

After they'd eaten, the mood became more subdued again. Solange got tearful, followed quickly by Tyra, then Sammy. Max glanced across at Clare before putting his arm self-consciously around Solange, then Michael and Casey comforted the other girls. It was past seven. Time to call it a day. Billy paid and encouraged them all to go home, agreed to meet for another session at the church in the morning. Max had a quick chat with Clare, said they were all going off 'to chill' at Solange's house. She smiled encouragingly, watched him go. Then she turned to Mark.

'Would you call this time off?' she asked.

Mark hesitated.

'That glass of wine might really be quite nice,' he replied.

'How are you feeling today?' Clare asked him as they sat in the kitchen over a bottle of three-for-two Sauvignon from Safeway. She'd known Mark for ever, felt no formality. She could say anything to him. Even so, since that moment, when he'd come over, on Thursday morning, something had changed and she hadn't been able to shake him from her mind.

'Honestly?'

'Of course.'

She refilled his half-drunk glass. He pretended to put a hand over it, then smiled and shrugged, took a sip instead.

'Well, I suppose I came here with such high hopes, you know, of making a difference. This has knocked me sideways.'

'Go on.'

'You know I arrived here the year Blair got into Number 10. Secretly I suppose we had similar aspirations. He was apparently casual, open-minded, a good listener. We're the same age, you know, me and Tony.'

Clare laughed. 'And now?'

'Well, while he's off solving the Middle East the economy has collapsed, and I'm still here, dealing with the fallout from his policies. I think he underestimated the challenges of multicultural, immigrant-rich Britain, and maybe so have I. The gun culture, the drugs and poverty gap, the failures of the social system, education. It's not all Blair's fault, of course, not all of it, but I feel unsure of the next step. I feel I've failed. I definitely failed Connor.'

Clare was silent for a while, sat drinking her wine and looking at this modest man sitting at her Formica-topped kitchen table. All she could think was that he seemed lonely, that the weight of what he did was too much for one person to bear alone. There was no doubt he was popular with the local community and that his Sunday services were well attended. It wasn't really her thing, but she knew that St Matthew's played its part in instilling a sense of community amongst Mark's congregation. The government's policy of parental choice in education had increased the number of worshippers there. Clare used to take Max, to get him into St Matthew's school. She'd enjoyed it for a while, had felt guilty when her attendance slipped, but life had taken over again and it had ceased to matter. Until Connor died. Then she found that the church was the only place she wanted to be. It was a safe haven. A place to run to. It was very important to her. And Mark had been there.

'Thank you,' she said impulsively.

'For what?' He looked taken aback.

'For everything you've done here, for everyone,' she said. 'And especially for me.' She reached her hand across the table and Mark placed his inside it.

It had started raining again and Billy was pacing quickly up the road.

Maggie was perched up at the window. 'Hello there Billy,' she called down wearily, then threw him the key. He sensed a change in her: she seemed . . . defeated.

He let himself in. All the paintings had been removed from the walls, leaving intense squares of colour on the flock wallpaper where they'd hung. He thought Gerry must have hammered the nails in when they'd first moved here, decades ago, and they hadn't been shifted since. In his mind's eye Billy could see a younger version of Maggie standing there prettily beside her husband; younger, fitter, laughing in a floral housecoat, guiding him to the correct position for each nail in the wall. Now she stood alone, waiting for Billy at the top of the stairs, looking very frail. Her complexion was pallid. She hadn't bothered to comb her hair today, and the pins she used to keep it neatly in place hung precariously from the bedraggled silver threads. Her eyes looked baggier than usual and her navy blue nylon dress was not long enough to cover her stockings. Her knees bulged fleshily above varicose-veined calves. It was a short distance from respectability to destitution, thought Billy. He'd have to get the girls to come round tomorrow to help her tidy herself up.

'I've spent the day on the pictures,' she informed him hoarsely as she turned and led him into her front room. There were dirty cups in the sink and the sticky-looking surfaces needed wiping down. 'They're all ready to be taken away. I've had a word with Mr Fisk, explained I want him to set up a foundation with the proceeds, call it The Meanwhile Street Trust or something, in memory of Connor Ryan. I want you to use it for the children, to provide them with better social care. You'll think of ways. I trust you, Billy, you're a good man.'

She'd sat down heavily in Gerry's armchair and now her breath was rasping. It sounded as if she might have a chest infection. The pictures were stacked by the wall; there must have been twenty of them, at least. How she'd managed to take them off the walls on her own and place them together like this was a mystery to him. He sat down on the sofa and looked at her.

'We would have helped you, Maggie,' he chided. 'You only needed to ask.'

She shook her head. Her eyes kept drifting shut, then opening again. 'I wanted to do it,' she mumbled. 'For Connor. I wanted to do it.' She seemed to be falling asleep.

'Can I get you down to your bed now, Maggie?'

She held out a hand and took Billy's in her own. His was warm, hers felt smooth and cold. 'No, dear, I'll be fine, sleeping here tonight. I don't seem to have the energy to move. It won't hurt me for once, to stay put.'

Billy put a rug over her knees, switched the main lights off and left a corner lamp shining. He felt uneasy leaving Maggie there, but it wasn't his place to question her. She had a right to be how she wanted in her own home – as did they all. He'd ask Katya and Melina to go back in the morning, to check how she was getting along. In the meantime he had to download the footage from today, see how it was looking. There was already so much material and he knew he would need to keep on top if it. He'd have to spend the next few hours at the studio in Soho. Maggie was already snoring as he let himself out of the front door. It wouldn't do her any harm, he told himself, to spend a night in her armchair.

As he opened her gate he clicked the locks to his Jag, still parked outside. A movement to his left caught his eye and he glanced up the road to see Tim entering his house with a small case in his hand. Billy grinned to himself, fished his phone out of his pocket, and as he turned and wandered homeward, he made a call.

Max and Solange lay on his bed listening to his dad's music on Max's iPod through two sets of connecting ear-plugs, necessitating very close proximity. He'd locked the door so his mum couldn't come in, and very gradually he'd managed to manoeuvre one hand up underneath Solange's top. He'd been stroking her back very slowly, up and down her spine for the past hour, and they'd kissed until their mouths were numb. His hand had ventured to the side of her body, but roamed no further. He didn't dare undo her bra, or even touch her breasts through it. Max had never done this before; it felt good but he needed to take his time. Solange had walked into his life at exactly the right moment. He didn't quite know, right now, what he would do without her there.

For her part, Solange had cheered up once they'd got home from the park, had stopped crying when they were on their own together in his room and seemed content now that he was holding her. She was looking dreamy and cute and made little whimpering noises whenever they came up for air. Her mouth tasted warm and slightly sweet, like bubble gum. He could kiss her all night, would like to wake up with her lying beside him. He couldn't really believe his luck. It was now approaching eleven o'clock, however, and Max knew that soon he'd have to let her go. As their tongues turned together once again he closed his eyes and drifted until, at some point, he slowly connected the subdued light flashing blue behind his eyelids with the fact that there must be a police car outside. He pulled his arm out from under Solange's top and sat upright, listening. All he could hear was the television downstairs. There was, however, the regular throb of blue hitting his blinds. Solange opened her eyes, pulled herself up on to her elbow and rearranged her clothes, then watched as Max moved towards the window.

Maybe Zahir was back and they'd decided to nick him after all, he thought as he peered out. Two patrol cars were parked on the other side of the street, and as he watched Tim appeared at his front door with an officer on either side of him. He was wearing a plaid shirt and navy cords, no jacket, and his bony face was impassive and pale. He was led to the back of one of the patrol cars, got in, then it drove away. The other car now turned off its blue lights as a white van drew up and parked in front of it. As Max watched, three men in white forensic boiler suits got out, along with a couple of Alsatians. They all made their way into the house and shut the door behind them.

'Fuck,' said Max. 'Whose turn is it going to be next?'

Just then Clare tapped on the door. Solange bolted upright, pulled her top down, grinning naughtily at Max.

'Isn't it time Solange was going?' Clare called impatiently.

'Just coming, Mum,' he mumbled, turning the lock. 'Did you see what happened?'

Clare stood in the doorway, arms folded across her chest, and nodded dismissively. 'Let's just keep our heads down. Now Solange, how are you going to get home?'

'I'll text my cousin,' she said. 'He'll come and get me with the dog.'

Gordon perched on the edge of Immy's bed with Kitty Louise asleep in his arms. He had something to tell his wife, something he had been avoiding all week. But now it was time. She'd had four days' rest and he felt it was best that she knew about Connor before she came home.

Her response was predictable: she expressed horror, then sadness, and then, once she'd heard the complete story, she said, 'Gordon, we have to move. We can't bring up our children there.'

Gordon was not at all surprised. The irony was, the

more time he was now spending in the street, the more he disagreed with her. These kids were amazing, the life here was real and pulsating and full of energy, creativity and endeavour. He would hate to walk away from it. You had to watch your kids, of course, to ensure they were safe, but there was so much to learn about life here, so much to celebrate. He tried to reassure her, told her about the filming and reminded her that before this week there had been no incidents of this nature in Meanwhile Street. He was careful not to add any further dimensions to the tale – for example, Tim and Melina's drama remained unmentioned. But he did ask if she minded him attending Connor's funeral in the morning, although it clashed with her discharge time from the hospital.

'Don't worry,' she said. 'You go, bring the baby seat and I can get a cab back home. We have the rest of our lives to spend together, the four of us, somewhere quiet and calm.'

Gordon felt relieved. He had promised Billy he would help him and the filming was going well. They were on to something important, a social document that could speak for itself. If the finished product got as far as a television screening, that would be an immense achievement. He held his wife close to him, their sleeping infant cradled beneath them, and thanked his lucky stars.

At home Katya was in the sitting room in the dark. She looked waif-like, standing there, her pale silk pyjamas shimmering in the half-light from the lamp outside.

'Any sign of Zahir?' Gordon asked, coming to stand next to her and glancing out into the damp, quiet street.

As they looked together down at the dark basement well next door she acknowledged Zahir's continuing absence. A couple of police cars crawled past them, blue lights flashing silently, then stopped further up, outside Tim and Lulu's house on the other side of the road. Two officers got out and mounted the steps of number forty-three, then knocked on the door. It opened and they went inside. Soon they reappeared, one each side of Tim, who looked passive as he was walked down to the police car and guided into the back. As the first patrol car took off, three men in white boiler suits got out of a white van that had pulled up in its place, they had two dogs with them. They made their way into the house. Katya looked at Gordon. Triumph flickered in her eyes and a sly smile escaped across her lips.

'What did you guys do?' Gordon murmured. 'What did you say?'

'Someone must have told them something,' Katya replied.

'I hope you haven't got yourself in too deep.'

'If he is caught, is a good thing, no?'

By her tone, Gordon was certain Katya and Billy had set Tim up. He felt slightly sick about it, for being left out – and oddly, for Tim's sake, too. He had a feeling that they'd duped the guy in some way – that they hadn't reported the truth but had gone for some form of justice through a fabrication of facts. He didn't quite trust Melina's innocence act. He wondered whether she had been flirting with Tim, had led him on then changed her mind, fearing the consequences. There was something needy about her, a little-girl-lost look which could get you a long way, as a young, pretty girl in a foreign city. Look at her now, shacked up with Billy Crouch. It was a result. She'd already got him hooked. Gordon had never had a close rapport with Tim, and could admit now to a certain, subtle form of jealousy at his social ease and fine education. Even so, he didn't want an injustice served upon the man, a humiliation where it was not strictly due. Whatever they were up to, it was going to mess up Tim's personal life, his wife and kids. And in the end, for what?

For her part, Katya felt irritated by Gordon's response. Surely he should be as pleased as the rest of them that Tim had been taken in, even if they'd planted the drugs to set him up for an unrelated crime. And, as Billy had reasoned, even if all that came out of it was that Tim was made to feel uncomfortable for a while, then got off with no more than a caution, the process of extricating himself from the white powder littering his house would prove time-consuming and difficult, and would always put his character under suspicion. There was enough cocaine in that house to feed an addict for a lifetime. Billy had tasted it: pure, uncut cocaine, fresh from the producers, ready to be mixed and quadrupled in quantity for the streets. Tim would need a first-class barrister to clear his name – but then no doubt Tim would know one. As long as Billy and Katya didn't become implicated in the process, what they had done would be worth Tim's discomfort, if nothing more.

Billy was also watching the events unfold from his window, with Melina quivering by his side. He hadn't gone to the production studio in Soho after all, deciding that he ought to hang around to ensure his plan came off. He felt a mixture of relief and foreboding; what if his and Katya's role came back to haunt them? He thought they'd been smart enough, but one could never be too certain about these things. Even so, Billy liked a gamble. He was a risk-taker and he knew, on balance, that it was unlikely they'd ever be connected to this crime. One had to remember that the police were essentially stupid, that in general they only followed the leads right in front of their noses, tried to sew things up as fast as they could jot the facts down, that a resolved case was a good statistic. Tim was the kind of guy they detested, loved to see banged up – he was arrogant, but he wasn't smart. Billy just hoped he didn't have too good a defence lawyer to get him out of this corner. Tentatively, he put an arm around Melina, and she didn't shrug him off.

'Well, he's gone – at least for now,' he reassured her as the patrol car passed by their window.

Melina shook her head. 'I don't know what you did, or how to thank you, Billy,' she whispered. 'But I think you saved my life.'

'No, no, Melina, it's not like that,' he told her. 'I think maybe it's you who's saving mine.'

21

Billy set the camera up in front of Gerry's chair and let Maggie tell it her way. She didn't need any encouragement, took to the lens like a professional raconteur and once she'd begun he had no need to interrupt.

'My body aches and my faculties are blurred,' she confessed with a splutter. 'I've seen the doctor, they say I need to go into hospital, that I have to have tests, on my lungs. But you know, dear, I feel it coming, my end. I don't need machines to tell me. Time goes so slow, you know. It's been a shock for me, losing Connor. I don't know how much more I really want to see. I'm not too old to know it's the drugs. They infect our streets, brought here by people with no feeling for those they're destroying in the process.'

'Do you think that's what caused Connor's death?'

Maggie's eyes slipped sideways from the lens.

'I'm sure they played their part, but Connor's problems ran deeper than that. His family failed him, the school failed him – we all failed him. Oh Billy dear, you know I feel blinded by his downfall; he didn't have a choice in this, even though maybe it appears he did.'

'And how does that leave you feeling, Maggie?'

'Ransacked of my own self-understanding or of God's reason, or role in it all.'

They sat quietly for a moment, then Maggie started wheezing again and pulled a hanky from her pocket, held it to her mouth. Maybe it was just the grief that was making her so defeatist, maybe in a week she'd feel differently about it, let Azi take her to the hospital, get her chest checked out. Maybe. But he felt doubtful. She'd lost weight in the past week and her chest infection had worsened. From being elderly, suddenly now she seemed truly old.

'Tell me something about Connor, something for us all to remember him by,' Billy said gently. 'After all, Maggie, you knew him best of all.'

Maggie paused for a moment.

'Connor Ryan was born with the sun shining upon his head,' she said. 'His hair gleamed and he had the greenest eyes you ever saw. He had a quicksilver way with words. He would do anything for me. All my chores. Never had a bad word to say about anyone. But he had a troubled life. You can't grow up like that without losing your strength. Last time I saw Connor he was fragile. And you know, Billy, I think he died to save me. He should've known not to worry. I'll be going that way soon enough. But he always looked out for me, just as I looked out for him. We were supposed to be playing chess . . .'

Maggie faltered. Billy felt guilty, knew what she was talking about and that he couldn't record it. He switched the camera off again. This was more important than the documentary.

'Because he knew what was in the case?'

'Of course. Not when he brought it here, but later. When Shelly cornered him. He never would have led them to my door,' she said sadly. 'Never.'

She began to cough again.

'Shall we stop there, Maggie? Do you want me to help you down to your room? Perhaps you should have a sleep?'

'What use do I have for a bed? I only sleep for a few moments at a time. Far better to be upright and up here, amongst my memories – and you can hardly talk, my dear, you look exhausted.'

Billy grinned sheepishly. He wasn't about to explain that his pallor and weight loss were due, in the main, to his withdrawal.

'It's been a busy time, Maggie,' he tried. 'I'll take a break after this, maybe get some sunshine. But first I want to get this footage together. It's important to me, a tribute to Connor, something to remember him by.'

'Have you seen Joe?'

'This morning, yes. Gordon and I went over to try and clean him up, before tomorrow.'

Billy thought briefly back to the challenge of waking up Joe from his three-day stupor. He and Gordon had finally managed to scrape him up off the living-room floor. They'd manoeuvred him into his grimy bath and filled it with Radox Relax and as he lay semi-comatose within it, they'd given him a rough shave. Afterwards they'd fished him out and dressed him in a pair of checked cotton pyjamas, some wool socks and a fleece bought by Katya for a few quid from Kilburn High Road. While Gordon scoured the flat for booze to pour down the sink, Billy had urged Joe, now on his squalid wreck of a bed, to sleep it off, to be certain to be sober and ready for the morning.

'The service is at eleven sharp,' he'd informed him. 'The cars will arrive at ten thirty, along with Connor,' with that he paused, 'in the hearse.'

Joe had lain back on his bed, eyes blank, staring into space, and he didn't respond. Billy and Gordon exchanged a look of dismay. They had to assume he'd absorbed the information, that he'd rise to the challenge; but neither would have bet on it. They could prepare him, but in the end no one could force Joe to perform. Gordon had hired him a black suit, which now hung forlornly behind the bedroom door in its shiny cellophane wrapper – the only clean object, other than Joe himself, in the entire flat. Then they'd left several bunches of bananas and bottles of ginger ale and sparkling water by the bedside, and taken their leave.

Maggie wheezed and Billy's attention switched back.

'I've got good news for you, Maggie, a commitment from the gallery,' he told her, keen to change the subject. 'They've made an inventory of all the works.' He pulled a rolled sheet out of his pocket and smoothed it out on Maggie's coffee table. 'Just you take a look at that.'

Maggie reached for her spectacles and glanced down the list as Billy awaited a positive reaction. The Cork Street gallery had been and collected the works and each one had now been documented, its value estimated. In all, Maggie's collection was valued at between fifty and seventy thousand pounds. She absorbed the figures but seemed nonplussed.

'You'll have to be doing something with this, for the children in the street. I'll write it all down, what I want for them. Before it's too late.'

Billy didn't try to argue. Maybe after the funeral she would regain her optimism for her own life. Maybe then they could persuade her to visit the hospital for treatment, and then go away somewhere warm to convalesce, perhaps use some of the money to take a cruise. That might suit her, a relaxing trip over the ocean to a warmer climate. He'd try to remember to get some brochures for her to look at. Some warm air might improve her health.

'How are the arrangements?' she asked, evidently wanting to change the subject again.

'Everything's arranged but the hours are scurrying past me,' Billy replied, and at last Maggie smiled, albeit weakly. 'And the weather's been so changeable I don't know if I'm coming or going.'

'It's not weather for certainty of mood or thought,' Maggie agreed, then coughed some more.

It was true. One moment a downpour tumbled from the colourless sky, the next the sun sliced through the gloom, throwing its accusatory light on to the oily pools that blocked the drains. Everyone in Meanwhile Street who was literate had now read the yellow signs stationed at each end of the road and was conscious that an incident had occurred in their domain – for most, in their absence. It made some wonder vaguely about alarm systems, insurance policies, or the possibility of moving on. For the pragmatists it made no odds whether it happened here, in the next street, or a mile away. London had a growing problem with violent crime. Everyone knew it. Nowhere was exempt. For most of them Connor's ensuing death didn't register at all. It wasn't added to the yellow notices and they didn't stray into the places where it was being debated, down the Ship, at St Matthew's, Ali's corner shop, St Bride's, or indeed here, in Maggie's front room. And because they didn't hear about Connor, most people also remained unaware that their lives had been altered by his death.

By contrast, with each day that Billy spent in the company of Maggie, Mark, Joe, or the teenagers, the significance of Connor's fall seemed to increase. He wondered if Gordon felt the same way. Billy sensed he did, but neither yet trusted themselves enough to voice their true horror at Connor's final choice.

'How are the girls, I haven't seen them yet today?' Maggie asked.

Billy was aware of her growing affection for Melina and Katya, who both felt an earnest desire to help her out. But today they were buying gear for the teenagers to wear for their performance at the funeral, would inevitably be occupied for most of the morning. Maggie had offered to pay for the kids to have new clothes to wear, to make them look like a real 'group'.

'They'll be here in the morning, to help with your dress, your hair. You need to feel your best, for the day.'

'I don't know why I didn't trust that Katya to begin with. She's strong, a fighter. She'll survive in this city OK. I feel an affinity with the girl. But with Melina, I'm not so sure.'

Billy felt his defences rise. 'In what way?'

'You feel affection for her, I can see it,' she replied. 'You could do a lot worse. She's very gentle. But she needs caring for. Are you up to the challenge?'

Billy would have liked to capture this on film, Maggie fulfilling her traditional role as the 'village elder', guiding him into making the right decisions, but the context was too personal. He was surprised to find how much, all of a sudden, her opinion mattered. 'I like her, a lot. She's woken something in me that's been lying dormant for years. Since Lucy, my wife, left me five years ago, if I'm honest. I feel with Melina I might be ready to go somewhere new. But she's carrying damage right now. I guess I have to wait and see if she can get past that and trust in me.'

'But Billy dear, it's the human condition, to be damaged; we all share the burden.'

Billy grinned. 'I want her to believe in me enough to share. But I can't – in fact won't – force her. So we'll take one day at a time, see what becomes of us.'

'Everything in its own time,' Maggie soothed. After a moment's pause she asked guardedly, 'And how about the other side of things, you know – our little problem? Are we all clear now?'

'Seems to be sorted,' Billy reassured her. 'You're not to think about it any more.'

Since Tim's arrest Billy had been so preoccupied with the film and the funeral arrangements that he'd hardly given the man's plight much consideration. Melina was keen not to discuss the subject and it seemed Katya preferred not to stray back into the territory, either. Perhaps talking about it made the dangers of their involvement too real for her. Meanwhile, Billy had kept a careful eye on the house. After an initial flurry of police activity it had remained silent. Lulu hadn't returned and there was no sign of Tim. They'd find out what would become of him soon enough.

There was a knock at Maggie's door now. Billy went down and opened it to Azi. They talked in the hall.

'She has an appointment at the hospital on Monday,' Azi told him quietly. 'I'll be taking her. But she's not interested in treatment. We'll have to work gently on her, once the funeral's over.'

Billy packed up his stuff dispiritedly, left Maggie with Azi and headed round to the church through the rain. Gordon was there already, along with the band in their matching outfits. They were running through their funeral track for a final time, a dress rehearsal. Gordon was sitting on a plastic chair nursing a coffee. When he saw Billy approach he threw him a pained smile.

'Thank God it's tomorrow,' he murmured. 'I'm not sure how much more of this I can listen to.'

Billy patted him on the back. 'Going all right?'

'To be honest I'm dreading the funeral.'

Billy's expression shifted to remorse. Joe and Father Patrick had both agreed to them filming the service, but he, too, was beginning to feel uneasy about the impending day. The teenagers were keen their performance was recorded, and he knew the resulting footage would provide impact. Even so, he was sensitive to the sobriety of the occasion and didn't want to detract from the congregation's grieving.

'It'll be OK, mate, we'll all get through it. It's great that the kids have got a role to play. And we're just the support.'

Gordon's confessed dread was real, but to his private shame his feelings since Connor's death were confused by sudden, unanticipated moments of high elation. He tried to persuade himself they were down to the arrival of his daughter, but knew Connor's story was the real cause, that it had jolted him out of his recent malaise. He felt alive in a way he hadn't for years. Getting to know Billy had played a part in that, too. Through their collaboration a friendship was emerging. It was something he'd sorely lacked in recent years – another male perspective. They sat side by side now, sipping coffee and observing the next generation growing into themselves.

New relationships were burgeoning between the teenagers. There was a sharp energy in the air. Since Connor's death the kids had clearly peeled off into pairs: Casey and Tyra, Michael and Sammy, Max and Solange. Meaningful looks, hand-holding, giggling and furtive kisses punctuated the rehearsal time, but as they were all up to the same tricks no one felt excluded. Gordon had watched with growing amusement. He was gaining a rare insight into their young world and felt surprisingly refreshed by their liberal outlook, their caring natures, their ability to show affection so readily towards one another. The girls were more assertive and upfront with their emotions than he recalled his own female friends having been at the same age. The boys, by contrast, were as gauche as his teenage mates had been, expended as much time and, it seemed, energy, joshing with one other as they did flirting with the girls. All that was missing was a security net around them all – or a clear sense of boundaries. It was something he was keen to explore in the film, had talked to Mark about only this morning. Without guidelines, Gordon understood that the kids had no real freedom at all, apart from the freedom to fail. He went on watching them, and thought about living in Meanwhile Street. Immy would take some persuading, but Gordon knew he didn't want to move on, that the 'meanwhile' of being here was maybe growing in value, that maybe the meanwhile was all anyone ever really had and that within it was all the life you could hope for, expect, or should ever even want. You needed to embrace it. Live with it, accept it, find the good. And celebrate it.

The door opened and Melina appeared, smiling prettily at Billy. She was wearing new skinny jeans and a pistachio-green T-shirt, white Converses, pale lipstick, dark eyeshadow and mascara. She looked normal. Happy, even. He excused himself and went out into the church hall to talk to her in private, impulsively leaning forward to kiss her on the cheek. To his surprise she turned and kissed him lightly, but directly, on the lips. She smelt of Calvin Klein's Eternity.

'Look at this: is unbelievable.'

She was shaking the local paper. On the front page was a photograph of Tim, below the headline: LOCAL COMMERCIALS DIRECTOR HUMILIATED IN DRUGS SCANDAL.

The article detailed the drug haul at his house, and described how Tim was in custody, awaiting trial on serious allegations of possession and trafficking, pending bail. Once he'd finished reading it, Billy's attention slid to the second story, a smaller piece without a picture for support. It detailed Marlon and Stevie's first court appearance and suggested they'd be facing at least nine and seven years inside respectively, for their crimes. The paper hadn't taken it upon itself to remark on the coincidence that both stories came from the same location.

'I don't know what you did to make this happen, but I want to thank you,' she said.

'Does that mean you'll stay?' he asked.

Melina hesitated, cocked her head to one side and then she laughed.

'No I mean it, really, I really want you to stay, Melina.' Billy was surprised by the urgency with which he said it, but it mattered, right now, that she committed to something, whatever it was. Everything around them seemed so fragile, but this seemed real, definite and good. He needed good around him. Melina was good.

Melina looked back at him earnestly, and something deep inside her stirred. It was an excited feeling, a delicious feeling. It seemed to be pushing those other, dark feelings to one side, letting her breathe properly again. She grinned at Billy. And once she started she couldn't stop.

'Can I take that as a yes?' he asked, holding her very close and smelling the lemony scent in her hair.

'Guess you can,' she replied, as her arms tightened around him.

22

It wasn't a day for rain. Dawn broke with a cloudless sky punctuated only by chalky aeroplane trails. People who didn't know it was the day of the funeral rose readily from their beds, whistled as they got dressed for work, ate hearty breakfasts then headed out into Meanwhile Street with a renewed spring in their step. In the night the drains had been unblocked and the oily water had flowed away. The street cleaners were about early, and any lingering clots of blossom were being swept and shovelled into their metal wheelie bins. Meanwhile Street scrubbed up well. The railings gleamed after all that rain and for the most part the houses looked neat and well cared for. The blossom which had survived the rain drifted prettily from the trees towards the dry ground, and people felt inspired as they set off into the city for a good day's work. The yellow signs had been removed and last week's incident was all but forgotten. People set aside their half-formulated plans for increased insurance and expensive alarm systems, decided not to get their homes valued and told themselves that Meanwhile Street wasn't such a bad place to live after all.

* * *

'I just can't believe you're not coming, Mum,' Max growled.

'You know I would if I could,' Clare insisted, 'but I can't afford to miss my review; it could mean a promotion. Mark understood, so I don't see why you can't.'

'What's Mark got to do with anything?'

If he wasn't mistaken he saw his mum blush.

'Nothing,' she said waspishly. As she spoke Clare concentrated hard on applying her make-up in the kitchen mirror. Max sat at the kitchen table with Solange, fingers clasped, tapping his foot under the table.

'Oh do stop that, Maxi, it's irritating,' she scolded. 'You've got Solange with you, you'll be fine. Won't he, love?'

'No problem,' Solange purred, patting Max's arm. 'I'll look after him, don't you worry.'

'It's not the bloody point.'

'Don't swear, Max. And as I keep trying to remind you all, you weren't that close to Connor in the end, hadn't hung out with him for years. We can all get too emotionally involved – just think of all that fuss about Princess Diana, all that outpouring of public grief. You have to question where that came from. We all ought to examine our true feelings about Connor before we turn his death into our own personal tragedy. I mean it's very sad and everything, don't get me wrong, but you need to think about yourselves, your futures, remember the value of your own lives, of working hard, of getting on; of not getting involved with those lowlifes and their drugs. I mean, if Connor had just kept out of . . .'

'That's enough, Mum,' Max snarled, pulling himself roughly out of his seat. 'I don't want to hear it, any of it. Come on Solange, let's go.'

Clare watched despairingly as the two kids turned and left the kitchen, then the house. Max was wearing his new clothes: black jeans, white T-shirt, hoodie. It was what they'd all bought for the performance, a kind of sober yet cool uniform, just about appropriate for a friend's funeral.

Maggie had been delighted when the kids had shown up last night to thank her. The only problem was, when she woke up on this momentous day she immediately knew one thing: that she wouldn't, after all, be attending Connor's sending-off. It was a certainty that came from somewhere deep within her, a feeling she couldn't quite explain, with an other-worldliness to it. She would be staying put today, in Gerry's chair. She wanted to remember Connor alive and also . . . no, she wouldn't even put those thoughts into words, they weren't feelings one should voice, even to one's own inner self.

She heard a key turn in her lock and then there was a gentle tapping on her bedroom door. Katya and Melina were standing outside in the hall, as promised, on the dot of nine. They were there to help her prepare for the day. She studied them as they stood there, young and beautiful and wide-eyed and graceful; one dark and shy, the other blonde and radiant, just as she had always been. She found herself beaming. It was the first night she'd slept in her own bed since all this had begun, and she felt surprisingly well rested – and resolute.

'Now I'd be grateful if you could help me up the stairs and into Gerry's chair, fix me a cup of tea and get my medicine, but I won't be needing your assistance with getting dressed for the funeral, because I won't be attending.'

The girls looked at her, then across at one another, clearly confused.

'You not go?' Katya asked. 'But Maggie, after everything you do for Connor, you must be there.'

Maggie shook her head slowly. 'I feel it in my bones, dear. It's not a day for me to be outside. Connor's sending me messages, inside my mind, telling me to stay put. That I've been forgiven.'

'Forgiven?'

Maggie paused for thought; where had that sentiment come from? She was good with words, intuitive with them, rarely selected the wrong one. It felt right to have said it, but what she felt Connor had forgiven her for was harder to explain.

'Given permission to stay put, that's what I meant to say.'

Katya and Melina were also not attending the service. Neither felt close enough to Connor to be there, and anyway, someone was needed to look after Milo. Gordon handed the toddler over to them when they got home from Maggie's and then he went to St Matthew's to meet up with 'the band'. The kids looked slick in their black and white outfits, but the atmosphere between them was tense. They had set up their instruments at St Bride's the night before, and now there was nothing to do but wait. Everyone was lost in their own thoughts and Max, particularly, seemed downcast. He sat alone, head bowed, in one of the pews, barely even acknowledging Gordon's arrival.

'Had a row with his mum,' Solange informed Gordon quietly. 'I'll take care of him.'

Gordon liked Solange. She was kind-hearted and bright. She'd be good for Max if they stuck it out. It was one way for some of these kids to keep on the right path: find a partner who could hold their hand and guide them into the future, particularly if their parents weren't going to be instrumental in doing so. From what Solange was now telling him, Clare had decided to duck out of her responsibilities towards Max, at least for today. Gordon couldn't understand it, but then again, how could he grasp the full picture of any of these people's daily lives? He and Billy could only scratch at their surfaces. Collectively there were shared concerns, individually they had their own back catalogues, each as complex as the next. In Max he recognized a disaffection that the lack of a father figure went at least some way to explain. Gordon sensed his need to break out from under his mother's thumb, too. Paradoxically, for Connor it had always been the other way round.

Billy showed up, dressed in a black suit, white T-shirt, and his Puma trainers. He was carrying the second camera. With his arrival the atmosphere lifted, just a touch. He informed them all that Joe was up, dressed and ready to go.

'So – shall we do it?' he asked.

He was met with a sober nodding of heads.

* * *

Back in Meanwhile Street silence had fallen; the same mid-morning silence that Maggie had noted a whole week before, on that fateful day Connor had appeared below her window, dragging that blue suitcase behind him, just after Stevie had made off with Marlon's jeep. Today, just as then, if you hadn't known better, you would have imagined it was simply another ordinary day. The sun was brighter now; the weather had become clement. A delivery van stopped outside Gordon and Immy's house and a man in a pale blue sweatshirt with *Flora's Bouquets* embroidered across the back hopped out, opened the back and retrieved a large bouquet from inside. The spring flowers were in riotous fresh tones, pinks, yellows and blues. They were celebrating birth. The man strode two at a time up the front steps and banged on the door of number thirty-two. Katya opened up with Milo on her hip, and accepted the bouquet for Immy.

'Lovely day for a homecoming!' the delivery man beamed at her. 'Especially after all that rain.'

Katya signed for them. Then she watched as he got back into his van and drove away.

'Pretty flowers,' said Milo, promptly pulling the head from a pink carnation.

'Yes, for Mummy,' she said. 'Mummy and Kitty Louise come home soon.'

She looked across and up at Maggie, but the old lady's attention had shifted and Katya followed the line of her gaze, left and up the street.

Outside Joe's flat people were now gathering. Katya could see him standing there, leaning against the gatepost in a smart black suit, his hair combed back, his face pallid but stoic, his hands linked behind his back, shoulders stooped. By his side a couple of men stood forlornly, looking less well groomed than Connor's dad, bunched up in their own ill-fitting suits. A couple of small, square women stood with them, in jackets that were too tight across their shoulders.

As Katya watched a group of people appeared from Reeling Road and turned into Meanwhile Street, made its way towards Joe's gate. Soon she recognized Billy and Gordon leading the kids: Casey and Max, Michael, Solange, Tyra and Sammy, all wearing black jeans, white T-shirts, hoodies and shades. They looked cool, like extras from a film set. They slowed as they reached the Ryans' gate. Billy and Gordon moved forward and shook hands with Joe in turn. The teenagers hung back.

Katya became aware of a subdued engine note from the other end of the road and turned to watch as a hearse slowly passed her by. Along its window was a floral banner with the word CONNOR in dyed bright orange, green and white carnations. Lying inside she could make out a small dark wooden coffin, with two bouquets on top: one a circle of roses from Joe, the other a spray of white lilies from Maggie.

The funeral cars pulled up quietly before Joe's flat and the group stood for a moment with their heads bowed. There was no sound but for the soft humming of the engines. Then the first driver got out and opened the back passenger door. Katya and Maggie watched as Billy moved forward, patted Joe on his back and guided him, then his companions inside. Billy gestured to the kids and some of them got into the second car with him. Finally Gordon got into the third car with the rest of them. Katya glanced back up just in time to observe Maggie moving away from her window.

As the cars were about to pull away she heard the sound of running feet and turned to see a fine-boned woman in a simple black dress and shoes come belting down the road, swinging a black patent leather handbag on a gold chain. She was around thirty-five, with gleaming golden hair. The hearse was indicating to pull away but the driver must have noticed the woman in his rear-view mirror, because he flashed his other indicator, and waited. The woman approached and the front passenger door of the first car opened. She slid inside and closed it behind her. The cortège now made its way to the end of the road, turned the corner and disappeared.

For a moment Meanwhile Street seemed to hold its breath; was silent and still. Then Maggie appeared back at her window, looking dishevelled.

'Do you want us to come up for a cup of tea, Maggie?' Katya called up kindly.

'Oh no dear, not now,' she called down raspily. 'But what might you be doing with all those pretty flowers?'

Katya looked down at her hands, had forgotten she was holding the bouquet. Milo was now sitting on the top step playing with his patrol cars. The sun was strong and warm and reassuring.

'They're for Immy,' she called up. 'She and Kitty Louise will be— Oh, here they are now!'

A black cab was stopping outside Immy and Gordon's open gate. Katya laid the flowers down on the top step and quickly carried Milo out on to the pavement. The cabbie had got out, looked up and gave Maggie a wave, then turned and smiled at Katya and Milo. 'Nothing like bringing a new life home from the hospital!' he said as he helped Immy out of the back, and lifted out the carrycot with Kitty inside.

'Thank heaven for small mercies!' cried Maggie as Immy shaded her eyes and looked up at the old woman.

'Oh I've missed you, Maggie!' Immy replied gaily as Milo grabbed her around the knees. She leant down and hugged her child, then looked back up at Maggie. 'Do you want me to bring her straight over for a cuddle?'

'Of course I do. Here, let me throw you a key.'

Immy turned and hugged her son once more, then kissed Katya. A week on and Immy looked radiant again; it was almost impossible to believe the state she'd been in after the birth.

'Be careful, Maggie has bad cold,' Katya murmured.

'Oh, I won't stay long,' Immy replied, picking up the carrycot. 'After the week she's just had, I expect holding Kitty is just the tonic she needs.'

Milo held his mother's hand and together they crossed over the street with the baby. Katya stayed where she was and watched them. A few doors along, a man and woman were getting out of a car and looking up at a house. A red For Sale sign hung outside it. A young man in a shiny grey suit came trotting up the road, a clipboard in his hand. He had a tarnished look about him. Soon he was shaking hands and leading the couple up the steps to the front door. They reminded Katya of Immy and Gordon, minus the kids. Before they crossed the threshold the woman turned and looked up and then down Meanwhile Street.

'What a lovely place,' Katya heard her exclaim before she followed the men inside.

Katya was relieved that Immy was home, that Connor's funeral was finally taking place, that Tim was locked up, at least for now, and that Melina was still here. For a second she wondered about Zahir. She didn't believe in the terrorist stories about him, but still would have liked to know what had happened to him. There had been something good about him, whatever anyone else might say. But she didn't have time for sentimental reflection. She'd just have to find someone else to occupy her thoughts. She bent down to pick up Immy's flowers from the step and turned to go back into the house, and as she did so she felt her phone vibrate in her pocket. She pulled it out. There was a message from him. At last.

Very terrible week. Am at Baghdad Café. Please come. Let me explain everything. I am sorry. Zahir

Katya put the flowers in water and came back out into the sunshine. Melina was inside, making tea for Milo. She'd make an excuse for her, to Immy, and Katya promised that she wouldn't be long. She'd been very committed, all week, had thought of everyone but herself. But now she needed a moment that was hers. A moment with Zahir. In her heart of hearts, she told herself, she'd always known he would come back. The street cleaner was sweeping the pavement outside the gate. She smiled and he responded with a coy nod of his head, then he leaned on his metal wheelie bin, broom in hand, and observed her as she walked away. Katya could feel his eyes on her back and she swung her hips just a touch. It was hard for men not to watch her and even harder for Katya not to respond.

Last week Zahir had promised to take her to the Baghdad Café, but they'd never made it. Now he was there and she fancied a caffè latte. She knew he'd be able to explain it all, why he'd left and what he'd been up to with Connor Ryan, too. He could not have known about the boy's death or he would have been at the funeral, right now. He would not like the sad news. She would have to fill him in, on everything. And then she would have to console him. Katya walked a little faster as she thought about his smooth, glistening skin, his wise eyes, his strong face and his long, fine hands, and she felt sure of him. She had reached the end of Meanwhile Street and turned the corner without looking back.

MASTERPIECE
by Miranda Glover

Art, fashion, fame and sex – artist Esther Glass has it all. That is, until a ghost from her past threatens to destroy her perfect life. Trying to cover her tracks, Esther goes for ultimate sensation, selling herself as a living work of art. She takes the international art scene by storm, performing as the female sitters inside seven great paintings. But underneath the surface the cracks start to show as Esther is forced to reconcile a very private history with a very public life.

Fast-paced, smart and scintillating, *Masterpiece* gives the reader a rare glimpse into a closed world.

'Gorgeous . . . Glover is an art-world insider and she looks behind the glitter with great assurance'
The Times

'Sumptuous, sensuous and thought-provoking'
Margaret Drabble

'This novel is the ultimate comment on our obsession with fame, celebrity and surface beauty . . . A superbly thought-provoking read'
Glamour

9780553817126